Mad

BATTLING IN ALL HER *finery*

HISTORICAL ACCOUNTS
OF OTHERWORLDLY
WOMEN LEADERS

Edited by
Dawn Vogel and
Jeremy Zimmerman

Mad Scientist Journal Presents
BATTLING IN ALL HER FINERY:
Historical Accounts of Otherworldly Women Leaders
Edited by Dawn Vogel and Jeremy Zimmerman
Cover Illustration and Layout by Errow Collins

Copyright 2018 Jeremy Zimmerman, except where noted

"The Dissolution of the Niamh" is Copyright 2018 Alisha A. Knaff
"Cuirassiere" is Copyright 2018 Blake Jessop
"Self Selection" is Copyright 2018 Mathew Murakami
"Chasing the Wombship Echidna" is Copyright 2018 L. Chan
"Swing That Axe" is Copyright 2018 Nathan Crowder
"The End of the World" is Copyright 2018 Matt Moran
"Iron Out of Vulcan" is Copyright 2018 G. Scott Huggins
"The Dishonorable God" is Copyright 2018 Priya Sridhar
"Cassiopeia, Queen of Ethiopia" is Copyright 2018 Aimee Kuzenski
"The Weeping Bolo" is Copyright 2018 D. A. Xiaolin Spires
"Caro Cho and the Empire of Light" is Copyright 2018 Lin Darrow
"Why we are standing on the broken wall, clutching swords too rusty to take an edge" is Copyright 2018 Tais Teng
"Dropping Rocks" is Copyright 2018 Jennifer R. Povey
"Paladin" is Copyright 2018 Shirley Vogel
"Unbroken" is Copyright 2018 Elisa A. Bonnin
"Aquarius Ascendant" is Copyright 2018 Christine Lucas
"There is Only the War" is Copyright 2018 A. J. Fitzwater
"Adelita" is Copyright 2018 Frances Sharp
"Pop Magic" is Copyright 2018 Patrick Hurley
"Breath and Roses" is Copyright 2018 Leora Spitzer
"The Leximancer's Rebellion" is Copyright 2018 Jennifer Lee Rossman

Interstitial art is Copyright 2018 A. Jones, Ariel Alian Wilson, Justine McGreevy, Rhaega Ailani, and Leigh Legler.

ISBN-13: 978-1948280044
ISBN-10: 1948280043

TABLE OF CONTENTS

Foreword 5

"The Dissolution of the Niamh" provided by Alisha A. Knaff 9

"Cuirassiere" provided by Blake Jessop 27

"Self Selection" provided by Mathew Murakami 49

ART BY A. JONES 57

"Chasing the Wombship Echidna" provided by L. Chan 59

"Swing That Axe" provided by Nathan Crowder 73

"The End of the World" provided by Matt Moran 91

"Iron Out of Vulcan" provided by G. Scott Huggins 101

ART BY ARIEL ALIAN WILSON 119

"The Dishonorable God" provided by Priya Sridhar 121

"Cassiopeia, Queen of Ethiopia" provided by Aimee Kuzenski 145

"The Weeping Bolo" provided by D. A. Xiaolin Spires 155

"Caro Cho and the Empire of Light" provided by Lin Darrow 167

ART BY JUSTINE MCGREEVY 193

"Why we are standing on the broken wall, clutching swords too rusty to take an edge" provided by Tais Teng 195

"Dropping Rocks" provided by Jennifer R. Povey 205

"Paladin" provided by Shirley Vogel 219

"Unbroken" provided by Elisa A. Bonnin 225

ART BY RHAEGA AILANI 249

"Aquarius Ascendant" provided by Christine Lucas 251

"There is Only the War" provided by A. J. Fitzwater 265

"Adelita" provided by Frances Sharp 283

"Pop Magic" provided by Patrick Hurley 295

ART BY LEIGH LEGLER 311

"Breath and Roses" provided by Leora Spitzer 313

"The Leximancer's Rebellion" provided by Jennifer Lee Rossman 331

About the Editors 339

FOREWORD

I grew up in the 80s, and as a young girl who liked nerdy things, I ran across a problem. On all the cartoons that my siblings and I watched, there was one female character in a group of men. The merchandise was similar—my brother would get several action figures from the same show, all guys. I would have to decide if I wanted the one female action figure or if I'd just get one of the guys too. And was the "princess" really the character I wanted to emulate, or was she the one always in need of rescue by her male companions?

The state of cartoons may have improved in the intervening years, but these memories are one of the many reasons why I wanted to put together an anthology about women leaders. This collection has plenty of good role models to choose from, and they're the ones doing the rescuing, not the ones in need of rescue.

Share these stories with your children, nieces and nephews (or niblings, as we like to call them), and other young friends. Share them with adults too. They're here for everyone to enjoy!

Yours,
Dawn Vogel
Co-Editor

NOTE

THESE STORIES *are fictional. Any similarity to real people is coincidental. Though they have a narrator that has a bio, the true authors are the ones listed as having "provided" the story.*

THANK YOU

Alexandra Summers, Amanda L'Heureux, Angela Clouse, Angie Pugh, Anna Henkin, Anna M Kupiecki, Argent, Arinn Dembo, Ben Bernard, Bert Edens, Brandon Allen, Brendon Reece, Carolyn McKeever, Charity Tahmaseb, Chris Battey, Chris Brant, Chris Gates, Chris R. Lightfoot, Cort Odekirk, Cyrano Jones, Daniel Lin, Darrell Z. Grizzle, Darren Chernick, Dave Eytchison, David Young, Deb "Seattlejo" Schumacher, Drew Wood, Elisabeth Reynolds, Elizabeth Carter, Erica "Vulpinfox" Schmitt, Erica Shuet-Yi Drake, Erin C, Erin F Lynch, "For Bethany, from Ronno!," Fran Friel, Garrett Croker, Gary Hoggatt, GMarkC, Helen Umberger, Herbert Eder, Ian Chung, J.A. Grier, Jäger Hein, James Arnoldi, Jen and Sarah, Jill Pritts, John Klapak, John Nienart, Jordan MT Block, Joseph M. Saul, Juli Rew, Julian M. Morley, K. Kitts, Kaira Murphy , Kendra Sullivan, Kristen Nyht, Laurie J Rich, Linda Kay Cottrell, Marlo M., Mathew Murakami, Megan Awesome, Michael Deneweth, Michael Gonzales, Michael S Bloss, Michele A Ray - Queen of TMI, Michelle Palmer, Mike "Grand" Kenyon, Miriah Hetherington, Monique Noel, Natasha R. Chisdes, Noelle Salazar, Patti J Oquist, Paul Alex Gray, Per M. Jensen, Rainy Day Kitty, Razorgirl Press, Rebecca Hartsock, Rebecca Moore, Rhiannon Gibbitt Rhys-Jones, Rich Stoehr, Robert L, Sara delgado, Sara Milne, Sarah Grant, Shawna King, Sherrie Vineyard, Shirley Vogel, Soatikee D. Driver, Sol & Jen, Stephen Acton, Suzette Mari, Tarryn Morrison, The Cherry Family, The Diabolical Dr. Kindred, The Faceless Masters of the Black Cabinet, The Snyder Family, Torrey Podmajersky, Vanessa M., and William K. Ault.

THE DISSOLUTION OF THE NIAMH

An account by Hazel Bernauer, as provided by Alisha A. Knaff

Like most meetings of later significance, the first time I met Amarjeet Vemulakonda was a moment of no consequence. It was a Wednesday, according to the convention that had been established by the Earth Companions (EC), and I was having lunch with Ntombi Idowu, Perla Prieto, and Nellie Hoddle on the Tarluvis Promenade of the *Niamh*, the extemporal luxury resort station where we had come to reside.

"What's this then, book club or stitch n' bitch?"

I glanced up briefly from my bowl of corn chowder to assess the status of the speaker. She was of medium height and slim build, dark eyes and warm brown skin, and she wore a headscarf of the sort I believe is called a hijab, pale blue and otherwise unremarkable, a black zippered jacket with a hood, ankle-length black skirt, and black athletic shoes.

Her smile was easy and trusting, and her eyes kept darting to the observation window, where the death of Epsilon Ophiuchi, colloquially referred to as "Yed's End," played on infinite time loop. Clearly a newcomer.

"It's the inaugural meeting of the Death to Tourists Club," Ntombi offered, flashing the stranger one of her signature sarcastic smiles. "You're not a tourist, are you, sister?"

"Come now, Ntombi," Nellie broke in, her middle-class Victorianism all but requiring her to smooth over any social situation. "No need to be rude. She's new and curious. We all were once."

"Sorry," the stranger said with a shrug. "Guess I am a bit of a tourist." From her accent and her clothing, I judged her to be from England, probably London, around the mid-2010s, perhaps a bit later, though the *Niamh*'s translation function often made accents difficult to detect. "My name's Amarjeet," she said, thrusting out a hand to Nellie, presumably because she seemed the most likely to reciprocate.

"Nellie Hobble," she said, giving Amarjeet's hand a dainty shake before reaching up self-consciously to pat at the improbable pile of red hair that perched atop her head. It was almost entirely affectation. Not one hair was out of place, then or any other time. "Earth, India, 1885."

Amarjeet's elegant eyebrows raised. "India?"

Nellie coughed quietly. "Yes. I've since been made aware of the lasting effects of British colonization on… well, everywhere we stuck our bloody foot, apparently, pun intended, and I am truly sorry for my personal involvement in a system that caused so much lasting and, in some cases, irreparable damage."

"I'm English," Amarjeet said. "But thanks."

From my right, Perla's rough alto said, "Perla Prieto. Buenos Aires, 1987." She didn't offer her hand to Amarjeet, but she did give a slight wave before tugging on the end of the long, thick braid of black hair draped over her shoulder.

I put down my spoon, since it was clearly my turn. "Hazel, Hazel Bernauer. Fairfield, Iowa. Uh, that's in the States. The United States of America. 1932."

"Nice to meet you all." Without waiting for an invitation, she snagged a chair from the next table over and joined our group. "Amarjeet Vemulakonda. Er… Earth, London, England, 2018."

Four pairs of eyes turned to Ntombi.

"Right, right, fine," she grumbled, rolling her eyes and shaking her head, causing the multi-colored streaks in her afro to catch the glittering light of the star globe that hung in the center of the promenade. "Ntombi Idowu. Abuja, Nigeria. 2085."

"How can we help you, Miss Vemulakonda?" Nellie asked, her pale skin slightly flushed from the brandy she always added to her tea.

"Nothing in particular," Amarjeet answered. "And call me Amarjeet, please. Not really into the whole 'honorific' thing." As she spoke, a Plexiar waiter glided up to the table, tray perched on the six splayed tentacles of their left front arm.

Amarjeet didn't skip so much as a beat at the sight of them. "Ooh, cheers, mate. Could I get… whatever your special is?"

New to the *Niamh*, then, but not new to traveling.

"Right away," the waiter answered, the fluttering burbles of their native Plexian somehow audible under their translated response.

"I'd have a top up, if you don't mind," Nellie added, raising her teacup in illustration.

With a sinuous bow, the waiter silently slid away again.

"Bit brave, isn't it?" Ntombi said, chin raised slightly. "What if the special's larbon grub with mordsu blood glaze?"

Amarjeet smiled. "Well, my mum always made me taste a bite of something before I could refuse it, so I reckon I'd give it a try."

Ntombi nodded, her shoulders relaxing just a bit. She liked this new girl, despite herself, perhaps.

"It's not larbon grub, though, is it?" Amarjeet asked, leaning in to peer into each of our dishes.

"Sadly, no," Perla said, nudging at a lump in her Vixarian relf stew. "Nowhere on the *Niamh* does a decent larbon dish." She grinned at Amarjeet, giving no indication of whether or not she was joking.

"Where do you go for good larbon, then?" Amarjeet asked, flicking a smile up to the waiter when they brought her a steaming bowl of iridescent blue soup.

Perla laughed, a soft titter that quickly delved into a snort before she cut it off. "Nowhere, darling. Nowhere."

Amarjeet sat forward, sliding her spoon through the soup, which clung to the spoon with a nearly impossible surface tension. "Why not?"

"Ooh, you are new, aren't you, sister?" Ntombi said, bright white grin splitting her dark umber face. She really enjoyed, as she called it, "breaking the newbies."

"Ntombi," Perla chided, but gently, clearly not asking Ntombi to stop.

"I'll be gentle," she said, leaning back in her chair and swinging her heavy black boots up onto the table. "Let me guess, you've just been dropped off for a bit of R&R by this… guy, probably. This marvelous guy with a smile you'd follow anywhere, some guy who plucked you out of your ordinary life on Earth with the promise of traveling the stars. You've kicked around a few planets, had a couple good laughs, and he took you here for a break while he 'handles some important business.'" Her fingers curled around the words, punctuating the air.

Amarjeet's demeanor shifted. She sat up a bit straighter, her eyebrows lifting almost imperceptibly. "More or less, yeah."

"Welcome to the dumping grounds," Ntombi said, spreading her arms expansively. "As dumping grounds go, it's not so bad. There's food, luxury suites, the best entertainment in the universe. Settle in, sister. You might be here a while."

"Dumping grounds?" A quiet, sharp breath through her nose was the only indication she gave that she was disturbed by the phrase.

"An accurate, if crude description, I'm afraid," Nellie said. "Though it's likely you'll be one of the lucky ones."

"I ran the numbers once," Perla said, "Roughly 85% move on in a week. Another 10% stay between a week and a year. One to five years is 3%."

"So we're in the lucky 2%," Ntombi said.

"Wait," Amarjeet said, leaning forward again, pushing her soup to the side. "You lot've been here more than five years?"

"Oh, yes, my dear," Nellie answered. "Quite a bit more. We're what they call CMOs. Companions Marked Obsolete."

"What does that mean? Obsolete?" Amarjeet's hand slipped into the pocket of her jacket, and she pulled out one of the sleek, silver telephones the early 21st century companions seemed to favor. The screen lit under her fingertips, and she began to type, agile fingers tapping in rapid succession.

"Exactly as it sounds, darling." Perla's voice was soft and soothing. "After five years… well, no one has ever left the *Niamh* after five years."

Amarjeet's eyebrows moved again. "So you've been here for…?"

"Thirty-six years," Perla said.

"You're never thirty-six," Amarjeet protested.

"No, I'm fifty-eight by my count, though it's hard to tell, isn't it?"

"Is it?" Amarjeet laughed, a surprised sound.

"Well, you know. Time travel."

"You look good for fifty-eight." Amarjeet smiled, and her eyes crinkled, adding age and youth to her face at once.

"That's the *Niamh*," Perla clarified. "We're suspended in a temporal bubble, so technically, everything that happens here happens outside of time."

"Ah, I see." Amarjeet's warm smile turned downward slightly, her brow knitting. "And the rest of you?"

"Fifty-two years," Ntombi said, staring hard at Amarjeet, as though daring her to feel pity.

Nellie shrugged and looked down. "Only twelve for me." She always seemed apologetic about being the newest of our group.

"You?" Amarjeet asked, turning her attention to me. "Hazel, isn't it?"

I picked up my mug of cocoa and cradled it in my hands. My fingers were forever chilled. "Yes. I mean… well, it's been seventy years by my count."

"And you've been here the longest? On the *Niamh*?"

"Oh, heavens no," Nellie said with a light, high laugh. "No, that would be Maeve. At least among the EC, the Earth Companions. She's been here, what? Two hundred and fifty years?" She glanced around for confirmation, and we each nodded somberly.

Maeve was something of a dire warning. She'd been here so long she'd begun to forget her life before. No one knew where she was from or even exactly when, though most evidence pointed to mid-twentieth century.

"What happened to Maeve?" Amarjeet asked, her voice hushed, almost reverent.

The others were silent, so I answered. "Maeve sort of… lost herself. You might see her around some. She's—" I trailed off. Maeve was difficult to explain. There was something ethereal, ghost-like about her. She wasn't exactly translucent, but she was as close as you could get as a human, I believe.

"Well, she ain't all there," I finished eventually.

Silence settled around the table until Amarjeet straightened again, her chair scraping slightly on the floor. "Why don't you hitch a ride off the *Niamh*?"

"Oh, you're quite welcome to," Nellie said pleasantly. "Many do, of course."

"But not you?" Amarjeet asked.

Perla shrugged and tossed her braid back over her shoulder. "We still remember what happened the last time we accepted a ride from a stranger."

The comment sunk in slowly, and when the light dawned in

Amarjeet's eyes, Ntombi said, "Anyway, most travelers who'd offer a companion a ride are space miners."

"Space miners?" The light was still in Amarjeet's eyes. It reminded me of Tiergan, who had been my Guide, who'd brought me to the *Niamh*. She had the same yearning for trouble, for adventure. I felt the familiar and uncomfortable prickle of excitement across my skin.

"It's something of a misnomer." Nellie watched Amarjeet over the rim of her teacup, head tilted. It seemed our new guest had caught Nellie's attention as well. "You see, they like to refer to ECs as 'canaries.' We're always the first to find trouble."

"And no one notices if an EC doesn't ever make it back," Perla added.

Amarjeet's fingers flew over the screen of her telephone until a voice from the promenade entrance drew her attention.

"Amarjeet!" He was tall and awkwardly handsome, as so many Guides were, and he smiled manically. "You've got to come! There's a once-in-a-millennium performance of Creanja's 12th Symphony on Praxilar 5, and if we leave now, we'll just make it."

In an instant, Amarjeet had popped to her feet and tucked her phone away, grinning wide and bright. Then she hesitated, and it was the first indication I had that this might not be such a mundane meeting. The new ones never hesitated when their Guides called.

"I—" she began, looking us all over.

"Don't bother, sister," Ntombi said, shooing her away. "You're not the first to go, and you won't be the last."

With a last, apologetic glance, Amarjeet jogged off toward her Guide.

By Perla's count, it was six months before we saw Amarjeet again. Another Wednesday, and Amarjeet pulled up a chair at our table like she'd been with us all along.

"Hello, girls," she said. "I've been doing a bit of research on this place."

Ntombi snorted a laugh. "I guarantee there's nothing you know that Hazel hasn't ferreted out years ago."

Amarjeet swiveled in her chair to look at me. "Then, I'll be sure to consult the expert, but it never hurts to have a new set of eyes on the problem, does it?"

"Not at all," I found myself answering. "What have you found out?"

"Well, for one thing, everyone knows about this dumping ground."

Nellie's unimpressed hum buzzed across the table. "Yes, my dear. We know."

"But, I mean… everyone!" Amarjeet's eyebrows danced. "Everyone knows, and they do bugger all about it."

Ntombi's answer was surprisingly gentle, a tone I didn't often hear outside our little group. "Yes, sister. We know."

"But… I don't understand why," Amarjeet huffed. "There isn't any profit in it. I mean… companions must cost the *Niamh* a fortune."

Perla nodded. "Hazel can explain."

Clearing my throat, I sat up a little. It was always easier to talk about my expertise. "When the *Niamh* was launched, the founder started a bank account on several worlds, investing in modest but secure holdings. He's set up a fund specifically to care for companions, for however long we're here."

"I believe the fund is doing quite well," Nellie added.

"Why would he do that?" Amarjeet's innocence was almost refreshing.

"He was something of a… collector of companions himself,"

Perla said. "He wanted a place to store them, I assume."

The sudden fierceness in Amarjeet's eyes made my breath catch. "You said before you were EC, Earth Companions. What about those companions not from Earth?"

"The AC," Perla said. "Alien Companions."

"Isn't that a bit planetist?" Amarjeet asked.

Perla smiled. "Yes, but it's a statistical reality. There are companions on the *Niamh* from all over the universe, but there is a distinct bias for Earth, femme, and late 20th or early 21st centuries. EC outnumber AC by about five to one."

The telephone made an appearance again, and Amarjeet's deft fingers began to fly. "You keep mostly separate from them?"

"Their choice," Ntombi said, her dark eyes flashing. "Not ours."

"What Ntombi means," Nellie said, ignoring Ntombi's disapproving huff, "is that the AC tend to feel a bit… superior to the EC."

"A *bit* superior?" Ntombi protested.

"A *lot* superior," Perla amended. "They have some respect for the CMOs, but they look down their noses at the rest of the EC."

"Well, that won't do at all."

"Won't do for what?" No one was more surprised by my question than I was.

"For getting us all out of here."

For the next hour, I watched in fascination as Amarjeet broke down her hastily formed plan for breaking all the companions out of the *Niamh*. Her fevered excitement was contagious, and soon we were all leaning forward to see the station schematics she'd pulled up on her telephone.

In minutes, she'd teased out of each of us where our strengths lay, something it had taken months for us to offer up to each other. A few minutes after that, she'd assigned Perla to hacking the station's security system, the one that kept unregistered ships from docking or launching from the *Niamh*. Ntombi was tasked with following the schematics to the engine room, finding out how it was maintained and, if possible, getting a job with the maintenance crew.

Nellie was given the assignment of recruiting an AC to our cause.

"And me?" I asked, the question squeezing past my anxiety and sounding forced from my lungs.

"You, my dearest Hazel, are going to do some research."

She slid her telephone across the table to me with a grin. "Need any help with that?"

I shook my head. This technology was well ahead of my Time of Origin (ToO), but I'd been on the *Niamh* more than long enough to be familiar with most future tech.

"Go to, my son," Amarjeet said, and I went to.

About an hour later, Amarjeet's Guide called from the doorway, and she looked up. "I've got to go," she said, and there was a shocked inhale around the table. "Don't worry. I'll be back."

Ntombi rocked back in her chair. "Now where've I heard that before?"

Amarjeet's face hardened, and she looked straight at Ntombi, gaze firm, determined. "I will be back," she said, and turned her gaze to each of us. Her eyes held mine as if in an iron grip. "I promise."

I wanted to believe her.

The Guide called again, and I held up Amarjeet's telephone to return it.

She shook her head and pressed it back into my hand. "Keep it. Keep researching. I want you ready for me when I get back."

With a grim smile and a twirl of blue scarf, she was gone.

Against all odds and in opposition to our combined experience, we continued.

Ntombi got herself hired onto the engine maintenance crew. It was laughably easy. Most of the crew were droids, and Ntombi had more mechanical experience than most of them put together. Perla had befriended one of the IT cyborgs who ran the security system. They were happy to answer any and all of Perla's questions so long as she smiled and nodded. Most of the guests ignored the cyborgs, so it was likely a relief to have someone to talk to.

Nellie had made the acquaintance of one Janso X'Aaic, a Panocra from the Ferrafian Alliance who had been left on the *Niamh* for roughly twenty years, if Perla's conversion was correct, and it usually was. Janso was aloof, her blooming, cherry-blossom fronds always holding themselves in a tight twist on top of her head. She and Ntombi butted heads again and again until Ntombi fixed Janso's personal portable scrapbook, allowing her to see holograms of her family that she had not seen in almost ten years. They were not fast friends after that, but Janso warmed to Ntombi in a way she never did to the rest of us.

Since recruiting Janso, Nellie had been cozying up to several traders who came to the *Niamh* for a temporal break. She'd kept up on the comings and goings of the docks and knew within an hour of any ship docking or launching.

By the time Amarjeet showed up again, we had the beginnings of a solid plan.

And I had something a bit more.

"Are you certain?" Amarjeet asked when I showed her what I'd found.

"Completely," I said, nodding eagerly. It had been a long time since I'd been this excited about something.

"Well, my dearest Hazel," Amarjeet said, slinging her arm across my shoulders, "you've really outdone yourself."

She called us all together then, the six of us circled around Ntombi's wide workshop table. "You lot have been *incredible*," she said, her grin encompassing the whole motley crew. "But Hazel here has been especially incredible. Go on, Hazel. Tell them what you've found."

Everyone looked to me, and I swallowed. Hard. "I… I've found the Temporal Drive."

A gasp rippled through the group.

"Are you sure?" Ntombi looked as though she didn't dare hope it was true.

I nodded. "I mean… as sure as I can be without laying my own eyes on it."

The Temporal Drive was what held the *Niamh* in its temporal bubble. It was what kept everyone and everything on the station from aging for however long they were here. It was the only thing that kept the dumping grounds open for business.

"Hazel," Ntombi said, turning to me with breathless intensity. "Do you know what this means?"

My lips curled into a smile without my consent, and I nodded again. "It means we get to go home." Looking around the circle, my eyes settled on Janso. "It means we *all* get to go home."

When the *Niamh* was launched, the plan had been for it to be completely self-automated. Because of the temporal bubble, none of the parts suffered from decay or rust, nothing wore down. IT and the mech droids saw to the minor, day-to-day issues, but the station was designed to be set and forget.

Even so, the investors insisted on an evacuation plan. In the unlikely event that something went wrong with the Temporal Drive, the storage compartments of the station would reassemble themselves into single-lifeform life boats, programmed to take each guest to their home planet and ToO.

The only way to trigger the change was to damage the Temporal

Drive, and its location had always been kept a complete secret. It was believed that no one alive still knew where it was.

No one but me.

When Amarjeet told me to research, I had already done an in-depth study of the *Niamh*, so I went deeper. I used her telephone to access the station's logs and sifted through centuries worth of log entries until I found it. The original plan for the Temporal Drive. It was buried so far under mundane details, it was no surprise it hadn't been found before now.

Served them right for leaving us here so long.

We kept the plan secret, not knowing whom we could trust. Even so, our excitement seemed to be catching. Companions who had never spoken now whispered in shadowed corridors. I didn't think anyone actually knew what we were up to, but it made me nervous.

I felt myself vibrating through my core, and I pressed my forehead to the synthetic window in the living area of the suite we'd all taken together. The glass was cool but did nothing to still my nerves.

"Tomorrow." Amarjeet's voice was low in my ear, her hand landing gently on the center of my back, giving those vibrations somewhere to go. "Tomorrow when Ntombi's shift begins. Then we'll have no more secrets to keep."

Her hand rubbed over my back in a slow circle, once, then again. Between one breath and the next, she'd gone.

When the moment came, I was far from the action, as it were, playing lookout for Perla as she hacked into the security system to track Ntombi and Janso as they made their way through the inner workings of the *Niamh*. Janso's pollen and tendrils were the perfect tools for getting past the security measures put into place around the Temporal Drive. Most of its security came from secrecy, so most of the security measures were there simply to hide the Temporal Drive, rather than protect it.

Amarjeet and Nellie were at the docks, ready to direct lifeforms without their own ships to the escape pods in the cargo bay.

Waiting in the corridor meant I had no idea what was going on in real time. I had Amarjeet's telephone, but we had agreed not to use it except in emergencies. Instead, I watched the clock tick up slowly, minute by minute, until I thought I might go crazy if another one passed.

Just when I was about to march into the security office we'd commandeered, the klaxons started. It reminded me of the tornado warnings we'd had when I was growing up, and for a moment I just stood there, completely still, listening to home while the *Niamh* erupted into chaos around me.

"No time for spacing now," Perla called as she rounded the corner behind me, snagging my elbow and pulling me along. "It's going to be a stampede any moment."

I stumbled after her as all around us, lifeforms streamed out of doors and hallways, cramming into elevators. The service droids were attempting to direct traffic, but no one was paying them much mind.

"This way!" I called, snagging Perla's sleeve and tugging her toward a nearly abandoned hallway.

"Where are we going?" she asked as we sprinted down the darkening hall.

"To the docks. Shortcut."

It was a service path, and there were a few droids rolling out toward the more populated areas. I wouldn't have known about it without the research Amarjeet had given me to do.

The hallway got shorter as we continued, and Perla gave a

breathless laugh behind me. "Soon we will crawl through the door to Wonderland, yes?"

"Not quite," I said, though we did have to slither through an access portal at the end of the run, tumbling out into the docks just behind Nellie.

"Steady on!" Nellie wobbled slightly on her heels but caught her balance quickly and offered us both a hand up.

"How's the evacuation?" Perla asked, and Nellie gestured around the space helplessly.

Despite their best efforts, pilots raced to and fro with no discernible organization, all but tripping over one another in their haste to find any available ship. I glanced up to the entrance where Amarjeet was arguing with a brightly frilled Carlaxican. The Carlaxican shoved past her, and Amarjeet made a rude gesture after them.

"Where are Ntombi and Janso?" Perla asked, as we climbed out of the lower docks to where Amarjeet was directing pilots this way and that.

"Still in the bowels of the station," Nellie said. "They should have got here by now."

As if summoned by her words, Ntombi and Janso came around the corner, Janso leaning heavily into Ntombi, who had the Panocra's arm around her shoulder and was carrying most of Janso's weight.

"What happened?" Amarjeet asked. I was already shouldering my way over, unzipping the pack at my side where I kept the basic medical kit that had seen me through many an accident of space travel.

"The Temporal Drive wasn't too happy about being shut down," Ntombi said. "Janso wouldn't give up. I think she's lost some shoots."

"I've got it," I said. "But we need to get her somewhere stable." I could see where a bit of shrapnel was jutting from her side, sticky, greenish sap oozing around it. Normally her body would repair itself, but if the damage was too traumatic, her shoots would fall off before they reached the injury.

"Leave that one to me," Amarjeet said, the flashing red of the warning lights lighting up her face in a rhythmic strobe. "I've just the place."

Abandoning her post at the entrance, Amarjeet led us carefully through the hectic mass of lifeforms rushing for their ships. On the mid-level deck, she stopped in front of a ship that looked to be of Ratharkan origin. Semi-organic, small cargo ship. Just about right for a six-woman crew.

"What d'you think, Hazel?" she asked as a ramp lowered to admit us to the ship's belly. "Will she do for stable?"

I was too awestruck to speak in that moment, but from behind me Perla whispered, "She's perfect," and I couldn't disagree.

It was a bit small, and a little worse for wear, but it would certainly do.

"Where did you find her?" I asked.

"What do you think I was doing on my last trip?" Amarjeet grinned and pointed to a door off the cargo deck to the left. "Galley's through there. The table should hold. Perla, you're with me. I'll need a co-pilot."

Nellie and Ntombi helped to get Janso onto the table, and I began my work as the ship shifted slightly, rising from the deck and speeding out into the void beyond the temporal bubble.

When Janso was resting as comfortably as I could make her, Nellie put herself to work brewing a pot of tea. By the time I had the table cleaned, it was ready, and we all dropped into the mismatched chairs surrounding the long table. Janso winced as she shifted, but she was in good spirits.

Nellie poured the tea in silence, and we all sat quiet a long while, steam rising from each mug in slow, lazy whorls.

Perla was the first to speak. "Do you think they all got out?"

"I don't know," Nellie said, "but we certainly gave them their best shot."

Ntombi nodded, but she was frowning. "The crowd… the stampede—"

I'd been thinking the same. What if some of them were trampled? It would be on our hands.

"What about Maeve?" I asked, the woman's face seeming to float in the rising steam. "Do you think Maeve got out?"

With a grin, Nellie raised her mug. "She did indeed. Old Maeve was just about the first one out of the gate. I'm fairly certain she stole a Mugrump's Chariot and shot off into space."

We all laughed at that, relief like a communal exhale.

"Well," Ntombi said after another long silence. "I guess we ought to thank our intrepid captain."

"Yes, I rather suppose we ought." Nellie picked up the only remaining empty mug and poured the last of the tea into it.

We made a strangely solemn procession on our way to the bridge, and when we arrived, Amarjeet turned from the console to greet us with a brilliant smile. "You lot," she said, shaking her head as she jumped to her feet. "You were fan-bloody-tastic! All of you! Ntombi and Janso—" She looked at the Panocra and her smile softened. "So brave, the both of you."

Turning, she gathered us all in her smile. "Just all of you. I couldn't have asked for better."

Nellie offered her the tea. "We wanted to thank you," she said. "If not for you, we'd likely have stayed on the *Niamh* until we faded just like Maeve."

"Not at all," Amarjeet said. "I should be thanking you."

"For what?" Ntombi asked.

"For not letting me run off with my Guide naive and trusting while others were suffering." She raised her mug in salute. "To you, my friends."

"No," Perla said, lifting her mug as well. "To all of us."

Mugs were lifted all around, and we each took a drink and stood for a moment watching the stars drift by outside the ship.

"So," I said when my tea had begun to cool. "I guess now we see about getting home?"

"My dearest Hazel," Amarjeet grinned at me before turning her gaze back to the stars. "Who said anything about going home?"

HAZEL BERNAUER was born in Fairfield, Iowa, in 1910. She earned her degree in anthropology at the University of Iowa in 1928, and soon thereafter left the planet as a companion to Tiergan Proctor. After being abandoned for several decades on the *Niamh*, Bernauer traveled the galaxy as a xenographer, chronicling her voyages and the cultures she encountered. Her works are collectively published in *The Voyages of the Star Chaser*. She is currently retired and living with her partner on Gorsaris IV, where she enjoys gardening and collecting obscure histories.

ALISHA A. KNAFF lives in Seattle with her cats, Hal and Odin. After inventing the time machine, she was president of the Jane Austen Fan Club from 1800-1806, and helped stop the Martian Invasion of 3003. One of her favorite hobbies is feeding pigeons with Nikola Tesla. Her novel, *School of Sight*, is available with Razorgirl Press, and you can find out more about her and her writing at alishaaknaff.com.

CUIRASSIERE

An account by Colette Anne Debelle,
as provided by Blake Jessop

1. 2 DECEMBER 1805

        n the battle line, in the cold, blood still drips down my face. Behind me are rank upon rank of my infantry, sheaves of muskets and bayonets bound by tired hands and weary hearts.

    I am a woman between worlds. Civilian and military. Seamstress and soldier. The Grande Armée I serve stands between tradition and merit. France itself between republic and monarchy. I stand between comfort and a wall of iron. Between progress and the world of dragons. Between grief and freedom.

    Between my men and Tugarin, which is to say between life and death.

    Ahead of us is a bank of mist and cannon smoke. I can barely see. From the fog of war come the dissonant sounds of battle. The Dragoons will either take the Pratzen Heights and ride to Austerlitz, or we will all flee the field before the Russian onslaught. Our part is done. A horse whinnies in the murk, and emerges into the light.

Tugarin sits tall in his saddle. The horse is a magnificent stallion, armored and noble. Behind the rider are great wings of wood and paper covered with Slavic sigils and the colors of Tsar Alexander. His breastplate shines, even in the cannon smoke. The man is a giant, and I can't tell if he has the head of a dragon or a helmet made of terrifying scale.

I drop a gloved hand from the matted blood in my hair to the hilt of Charles' cavalry sword. The blade that gave me my name. With the other I grip the standard, the staff topped with the French Imperial Eagle. One wing has been shot away, and there's a hole in the beak made by a musket ball.

"If you want an Eagle," I scream, "come and get her!"

And come for it the dragon does, like a hurricane.

2. DIARY, 1 AUGUST 1805

I have not written since my brother died. I wrote nothing during the dead days. The hot, still summer when Charles left me for the void. I could describe it now, but I won't. I would die, too. This page has been blank for weeks, except for the pallid and withered marks of my tears.

Feverish, he could not return to the war. Or from it, it is hard to say. All that is left of him is a brace of pistols, though two is hardly a brace. A book of hand-written poems. A cuirassier's sword and a bicorne that I used to steal and wear fore-and-aft, the modern way, when I helped him study his manuals.

I did not write in my diary when the fever took my brother. I remember all I did was clean his room, and there I found his uniform. I had two choices. Face my grief or find my scissors and thread.

3. 13 SEPTEMBER 1805

The soldiers of the 11th light infantry regiment were not particularly happy to see me when I took command. I won't dwell upon how I made my way among them, except to say that I ignored their grumbling and let the sergeants do their work. I inherited a well-trained formation and reasoned the best thing I could do was stay out of the way.

This worked perfectly for a while, until the sergeants decided I was soft. I am soft, in some ways. I am small, and some of these men are real brutes. There aren't many women commanding regiments, yet, and most of them have been serving since the Revolution. I took up my brother's commission as a family right, which is still allowed, but only just.

After a long day of drill, they confront me.

They oughtn't to, of course. If Colonel Valera had prepared the regiment properly before I arrived, they wouldn't dare. The biggest of them, a giant from Marseilles whose name I can't remember, finds it easy. He towers over me like a great oak.

"We didn't want you, *Capitaine*," he hisses, "but you came. Colonel Valera said if your family wasn't nobility we'd have had a real soldier for our captain, not you. You're only here because your brother was a hero!"

"My father was a sign painter," I tell him.

"You still don't deserve your commission. We deserve better."

"Well, I am what you have. Now get back to your columns!" I use the parade ground bellow Charles and I practiced together. No one moves.

"Do you feel I have pushed you too hard, Jean-Paul?" I say more softly, remembering his name. "Do you wish me to practice more with the troops?"

Silence. This is serious; they genuinely want to challenge me.

What I should do is flee to the Colonel and report them. He could have them flogged… and then dismiss me for failing to control my officers. He has led me into a perfect trap, though I can't imagine why. I try to guess what Charles would have done. Something dramatic, no doubt. The thought of him makes tears gather at the corners of my eyes.

I struggle to pull my brother's long straight cavalry saber from its scabbard.

"Not even the right sword," Jean-Paul spits. "Let's see what you can do, Cuirassiere."

He's right. I ought to have a short infantry officer's saber, but how could I afford to buy one? I could barely afford the thread to alter his uniform. Charles' manuals did not cover this situation, except to say that I must endure whatever my troops can.

"Fine, Sergeant. Let us practice. You should know what I am capable of."

I pray it's enough.

The other non-commissioned officers make space for us on the empty parade square and our blades clash like bells. I can fence. I practiced with Charles for months, but the big sergeant named Jean-Paul still beats me. Quickly. Of course he beats me; he's a *Grognard* with three campaigns behind him. He was a soldier when I was ten years old.

His cold blade lashes into my cheek and a backhanded buffet knocks me to the ground. Blood courses down my face and spatters between my fingers in the dirt. All I feel is angry. Not at him, not even at myself. I'm angry because I know I have a pretty face, and it isn't pretty anymore, nor ever will be again. This is the kind of thing you think while your life changes. Jean-Paul looms over me and I stare at him, upward along the terrible foreshortened bridge of steel.

"I could kill you," the big man hisses, "and save everyone a lot of trouble."

"Go on then!" I scream at him. "I can't do it for you; all I can do is lead you and die for you! I will bleed every drop of blood I have, but you have to do the killing for yourself!"

The entire group takes a step back. Jean-Paul's face goes through a shocking change. The anger drains from him and shame crumbles his features like storm clouds crushing a summer afternoon.

"Help me up, Sergeant," I say.

He does. "*Capitaine*—" he starts.

"Call the surgeon, then quarter your men. Move."

They scatter like hares.

The less said about closing the wound the better. It was not dignified. The divisional surgeon warns me not to yell or my stitches will tear. I arrive on the parade ground the following day to find the non-commissioned officers sweating. They don't know if they're all about to be flogged. I could, in all seriousness, have Jean-Paul guillotined. He stands at the head of his column like the rest. He did not run.

I act as though nothing is amiss, and whisper my orders to Jean-Paul. He translates them into a roar, and the columns drill with a precision they previously lacked. Hundreds of young faces, mostly but not exclusively boyish, all sweating and straining at my whisper. For the first time in my career, I feel a sense of satisfaction, without really noticing that I have thought of it as my profession in the first place. Worried though I was about my fair skin, I seem to have said the right thing.

4. DIARY, 9 JULY 1805

Poor Charles has never been the same since he returned from the East. We were all so proud when he took up the family commission. He is too soft for the army, however. Honestly it would have been better if I had taken his place. I tutored him in all his academy subjects, and I am incredibly bored of seamstressing.

Charles is too much of a poet for fighting. Not that I am scornful of his verse. He is terribly talented. It is as though between us we share the soul of one perfect Frenchman... but as it is, something was mixed up when we were born. If you were to write a story about twin brother and sister, which would you pick for the poet and which the soldier?

He is bigger than he was when he left, broader and stronger, but his face is sunken and sallow. There is something wrong with him, like he has taken sick with some kind of fever. I fear for his health.

5. 30 NOVEMBER 1805, DUSK

The Emperor's armies march, and we take Vienna. We march, and turn the Austrians away from Ulm. We march, and everything seems easy, though General Kutuzov and his Zmey loom in the distance. We march, hungry because the Russians have burned the villages behind them. I don't know if this is a new or old species of war. With sore feet and full hearts and empty stomachs, we march.

"Do you think the Zmey did this, Cuirassiere?" Jean-Paul asks me as we march east. He has become both informal and inseparable from me. Like a loyal hound.

"Tugarin and his cavalry aren't gods, Sergeant."

"*Non, Capitaine,* just dragons. Men with scales and winged horses who can breathe fire."

"Is it they or the horses who breathe fire? Your grammar is unclear," I say.

"Madame—" He feigns hurt. "We march for day after day toward Russian guns for you. Spare us some kindness."

"Dragons, pah. That time is over."

"Let's hope so," he replies.

The dark age of dragons and fairy tales is leaving Europe. I command part of an army that allows women to fight, that embraces technology, that has no place for myths or sentimentality. The smell of burning does not bother me. Charles would have produced some fine phrase to describe it, but I cannot. The wood smoke and acrid scent of scorched grain just remind me of him. The reek of war, I imagine, always and forever will.

We march. As long as I keep moving, I outrun my troubles. Outdistance my doubts and quiet my grief with the rhythmic hammering of boots. Like the deep scar on my cheek, the pain is fading to a level I can manage. Orders arrive to halt and turn northeast, toward a pair of townships I've never heard of—Brunn, and beyond it, Austerlitz. Now, standing briefly still, all my troubles catch up to me.

"*Capitaine*," Jean-Paul says in a huff. He has run to tell me what's coming before it arrives. He isn't far ahead of the bad news, but I'm grateful to him until he opens his mouth. "It's not just a dispatch rider. Colonel Valera rides with him, and one of the Emperor's Aides-de-Camp is with them, too."

They're here to question me about Charles. I know it.

Jean-Paul continues, catching his breath. "*Capitaine*, the rumor is your brother was a suicide. That you don't deserve to lead. That's not true, of course, but what will we do about it? That bastard Valera is out for your commission."

Jean-Paul looks to me eagerly. He would find Valera, if I asked him to, and slit his throat. I think he wants me to ask him just that. I don't.

"*Capitaine*?" he says, unsure, "it is a lie, isn't it?"

What, I ask myself, *is the biggest lie I've ever told anyone?*

6. DIARY, 20 JUNE 1805

My brother drives me mad! How can we be twins? How can he mope about when he serves the greatest cause in history? When he obeys the greatest Emperor humanity has ever known? This is like living in the time of Alexander the Great, and he may march with the famous man where I may not! Curse poverty. Curse only being able to afford one uniform and one sword and one brace of pistols. If we were rich, we could both be soldiers and I wouldn't have to sew like Mama or paint signs with our father.

The last time my brother and I spoke, this is what he said.

"I cannot go back, Colette. I will not."

"You must," I told him, "you must or I will never forgive you."

7. 30 NOVEMBER 1805, DARKNESS

"Surely, I do not warrant this attention," I stammer.

"You do. The Emperor studies all his commanders, right down to the regiments," the Aide says. She wears the uniform of a Colonel, but her rank comes from the *Maison Militaire de L'Empereur*; she is a personal envoy of the Emperor himself. Her breast glitters with decorations, and she wears her bicorne side-to-side, in the old-fashioned way. The hair underneath is steel gray.

"He ordered me to resolve this accusation personally," she says in a cool voice.

My head swims. I put a hand to my brow to see if it's hot. To see if I'm feverish. The truth always is. *What is the greatest lie you have ever told?*

"Tell the Emperor it is true, my brother committed suicide," I say distractedly, "and as he thus gave up all right to his rank, I have no right to it either."

I turn to walk away. The feeling is of being about to drink the sweetest wine, and having the cup dashed from my lips. If I turn away now, perhaps they won't see the stains. Tears, in this case.

"*Capitaine*," the Aide says softly, but her voice penetrates like grapeshot. "Give me your reasons for lying to take up his commission."

I turn back. Everyone will see my tears, but what does it matter?

"To spare my family shame, of course. But that is not why I'm here; I don't give a damn about shame. My brother had a peaceful soul, and only now do I wish I shared it with him." Tears run freely down my face. The flush of guilt and shame. The scar down my right cheek throbs. I will not lie, however, not to her or myself. Not anymore, no matter how it hurts.

"I am here because he was a coward and I am not. I will do better. It hurts me to call him a coward, but I think I now understand what that means."

"And what does it mean to be a coward, *Capitaine*?"

I wipe my eyes violently with a blue-fringed sleeve.

"He would never have pushed me to come here, were our positions reversed. I pushed him into his grave. I told him honor demanded that he return to war. He declined and took the only road I left open to him. He was never meant to be a soldier, but he was a beautiful poet. Poets like Charles always know how and when and why to die."

"And you do not?"

"No. I *was* meant to be a soldier. I need our Emperor to tell me."

Colonel Valera has a look of triumph on his face. The smug bastard.

"I will convey your explanation," the Aide-de-Camp says over her shoulder, as the pair wheel their horses. "Get your columns to Brunn and await the Emperor's judgment."

8. 1 DECEMBER 1805

It is no small feat, waiting for the blade of the guillotine to fall. I have to find some way to control myself on the way to the block. As a girl, I watched the execution of Marie Antoinette. As hated as she was, as humiliated, she comported herself with dignity with her head under the blade. Her last words were an apology, a politesse.

The last Queen of France is a strange patron saint, but I vow to emulate her and keep driving the 11th toward Brunn. There is a slogan the Emperor uses, *we march apart and fight together.* I hadn't realized how true that is until now. I am alone, and will not ever reach that *together*. The troops are restive. Probably keen to be quit of me. We march through most of the night until I allow a break at dawn.

Jean-Paul lets me know when the riders return. I belt up and arrange myself neatly. I would shave carefully, if I needed to shave. Instead, I make sure every blonde lock is carefully tucked up into my bicorne. I wear it fore-and-aft, in the modern way.

When the Aide reins in, she's still a pair with the dispatch rider. I would wonder why, were I not so disconsolate. Colonel Valera accompanies them in fine form, already gloating.

"You have a letter for me, Madame," I say, and my voice almost breaks.

"Two, actually. What is your disposition?"

"My columns are resting in place. The troops are in good order; no drunkenness or looting, and the foragers are hard at work. As you can see, we will make it to the outskirts of Brunn by nightfall. They'll be tired, but their new commander may let them sleep there." Saying this hurts me. I am their commander.

"Well done. Here are your orders." She hands me a packet. There's a wax seal on the thick wad of paper. My temples pound as I break the seal and read the order that ends my career as a regimental commander.

"And what is the cause of your dismissal from the regiment?" Colonel Valera leers at me obsequiously. "Well?"

I hand the orders to my Colonel without a word. I can't speak.

He reads, and his face becomes a burning red so apoplectic that I think he may burst.

"As you can see," I tell him, "our Emperor has given me the brigade. My rank is now Major."

Now it's his turn to be speechless. Almost.

"My man DuMoulin has the brigade," he chokes.

"Your man DuMoulin is in Iglau getting drunk with Prince von Wrede," the Aide says, "he has been reassigned."

She hands Valera the second packet of orders. This would be a fine time for Colonel Valera to fall apart completely, but he surprises me and keeps his composure.

"Congratulations, Major. We will speak outside Brunn," he says. He salutes the Aide and turns on his heel. As he passes me, he whispers, "Wait until you see real combat, upstart. It will not be the parade ground; it will not be the victory march through Vienna."

I cut him a sideways glance. "I can hardly wait, Colonel."

He storms off, mounts his beautiful mare, and disappears at a gallop in the direction of Iglau. I wouldn't give much to be DuMoulin when he gets there.

Valera's words still give me pause, however, even after he's gone. The bulk of the work so far in this campaign has fallen on the divisions of Dupont and Mortier. The Austrians surrendered with hardly a murmur. I want to hate Valera for his scorn, but he is right—if there is such a thing as baptism by fire, I have not yet felt the heat. He has.

"Confer with the artillery, Major, then take command of your new columns," the Aide says, then pauses. "Colonel Valera will no doubt order you to the center; it will be the most dangerous spot. That is where the Emperor wants you, as well. You will take the Pratzen Heights, then withdraw after the Slavs bombard you. You will pull back down the hill and draw the Russians into a trap. You have an Eagle to protect now, be careful with it."

"*Oui*, Madame." Our role as bait is not good news. My heart remains full.

"Oh, and Major? That other packet really is a dismissal from the Grande Armée. I was to hand it to you if you had fallen short of your objectives by so much as an inch. Make sure to justify the faith we've put in you."

"*Oui*, Madame," I tell her, keeping my voice in its most serious tutor's timbre. Suppressing my smile is one of the hardest tasks I've yet undertaken. The pair wheel and ride away. A faint hint of approval might have tugged at the corner of the Aide's mouth, but I could have imagined it.

To my delight, Jean-Paul and the rest are overjoyed when they hear the news. Any apprehension I had about taking command of more soldiers fades quickly. I was wrong; my old troops really were worried for my future. I suppose they see it as linked to theirs. As for the new columns, they can't help but love me—DuMoulin was drunk often enough that I am an immediate improvement. All I have to do is give clear orders and always lead the march. I am a little short for that, but they ignore my huffing and puffing when we get moving toward Brunn. Jean-Paul carries my pack in addition to his own, and it doesn't slow him down even a little.

"So, Major," he says, "now that you have the whole brigade, isn't it time you made me a lieutenant?"

He's only half joking. I can tell. The man would be a disaster, but what can I promise him? I need him. I try the truth.

"No, Jean-Paul. I could no more make you an officer than I could turn a bloodhound into a house cat."

He almost smiles. I haven't failed him yet.

"I will keep you close to me to hold onto our Eagle, and if you do what I say, I'll end up pinning so many medals on you that you'll walk bent over. We're going where the going is hardest. You'll either die or no dock girl in all of Marseilles will be able to resist you, so fine will be the gold and ribbons on your chest."

That makes him smile. I don't know it yet, but this will spread like a dictum among my regiments. That I am determined to lead them to death or glory. Glory, hopefully.

We keep our thoughts on the march, on progress and equality and our sore feet, and try to forget about the Russian guns. Try to forget about the Zmey cavalry that breathe fire like dragons.

9. 2 DECEMBER 1805, MORNING

"À terre!" I scream, "Lie down!"

First hesitating, then in force, my infantry drop to their bellies on the frozen grass. We scaled the Pratzen Heights just before dawn. A tedious winter march up a not-so-gentle hill. I set my columns just behind the crest, hoping it would shelter them from the Russian artillery that is sure to fall on us before the Tsar's men come to drive us away. I actually hope the infantry chases us. What will occur if it's the heavy cavalry doesn't bear thinking about.

We almost never lie down. It does more harm than good facing musketry, and is fatal when facing any kind of charge. None of that logic applies. We're just going to stand here under the bombardment and take it.

In the distance, down the other side of the hill, I see the Russians. There are so many of them I can hardly believe it, vast squares of men moving like ants. Cavalry gallop south toward a series of frozen ponds amidst faint puffs of flame. That is disturbing, but what really concerns me are the guns. There are hundreds of them, and at least half look to be pointed up the hill.

Jean-Paul stands beside me, eyes wide, gripping the standard. The golden Imperial Eagle atop its long staff.

"Get down, Madame!" he cries.

"No," I reply, and motion him away. I bat his hands off the staff and take it in both of mine. The wood is cold under my thin leather gloves.

In the icy distance, a streaking line of flashes cuts from left to right, followed in an instant by a rolling crash of thunder. Behind the flashes and noise comes a wall of iron.

In my mind's eye, I see the moment I die before it comes. I see the exact point when I must lie down or be cut to shreds. I do not. It takes every ounce of courage I have, every drop of stubbornness. The fear is enough to weaken my knees. My body begs for the frozen earth. Time slows.

Logic screams at me to lower the Eagle and lie down. It would be the wise thing; I can't keep it safe if I'm dead. Charles stops me. I feel his hand on my shoulder, his breath on my neck, his words in my heart. I owe him a life. I lean on the Eagle. Finally, in that moment, I would rather die than lie down. I have been made to sit, be quiet, and lie still for every master imaginable. Not anymore.

The fusillade crashes over us. A metallic scythe of cannonballs and exploding canisters of grapeshot blankets the hilltop. It feels like standing in a windstorm.

The hurtling projectiles tear at my jacket and rip shreds from the tunic underneath. A madly bouncing cannonball blows the bicorne from my head and looses my hair in a windblown waterfall that laps around my shoulders. Gouts of earth leap into the sky all around me. I feel the earth quaking right through my boots. The reaper tugs at my coat but fails to get a grip. No metal so much as creases my skin.

I blink. Far away, the Russian infantry start marching up the hill in earnest. The cavalry is hidden behind a wall of smoke. The artillery starts shooting again as the more enterprising gunners reload their pieces.

"For God's sake, Major," Jean-Paul cries, "we know you're brave. Let me take that Eagle and let's get down the hill! You'll be killed!"

I let him take the standard and turn to my troops. As one, their faces gaze up at me, those farther back already up on their knees to get a look. I've never been stared at this way. Something close to awe. I call an order and they rise in perfect unison. Wisps of my hair, blonde backlit by the dawn, make a golden halo at the edges of my vision.

"About face! Back down the hill!"

We march. The artillery isn't too bad once we're away from the crest, but my officers have to yell to keep everyone's eyes on where they're going. They keep sneaking looks at me.

10. 2 DECEMBER 1805, MIDDAY

It feels very good to be back in line with the rest of the Grande Armée. The Russians have taken the Heights. I stand beside the Eagle, still hatless. The day is warming a little, but my breath still frosts the air.

As the great masses of Russian infantry start down the hill to crush us, our artillery finally starts shooting back. Twelve-pounder cannons that we all call *les belles filles*.

"And it is beautiful girls who serve the guns, too!" says Jean-Paul, obviously satisfied by the distant fall of shot amongst his enemies.

"Not all, Sergeant, the loaders are all big dumb oxen like you," I say.

"Yes, Major, the loaders are men, but the gun layers are pretty things like you. They know their business."

"I believe they do," I say. We watch the shot fall. Some of us cheer. Most don't.

"Still, they're going to get to us," Jean-Paul says with a calm I find hard to believe. "We don't have enough artillery to stop them, and they're fighting downhill."

"We're meant to look weak. That's why they put me in charge."

"Shows what they know. What do we do when the Russians get here?"

"We take it," I say, then, yelling, "Form lines!"

I feel invincible. How can I not be? The Russians stop a hundred paces away and their front rank kneels. No one can lie down for this. We just have to take it. The air fills with smoke and the rattling crack of muskets.

The wave of musket balls slams into us like a fist striking flesh. Cries ring out all along the line. Nothing will hit me, of course, because I wouldn't care if it did. I stand still with one hand on the standard, calling for calm.

I have just turned to issue orders when a ricochet hits me in the face. The ball breaks my nose violently sideways and splinters tear gory ribbons from my right cheek.

Fate has rebuked me with terrifying swiftness. I thought there was beauty in not caring about life and death, and so she stripped that illusion from me immediately. It hurts more than I can describe.

My right hand flies to my eyes while my left clutches the Eagle, which I grip like it was a mast I can hold to anchor me against an angry sea. The volley ends. War has disfigured me for a second time. A third. Glaring from between bloody fingers, I look back at the Russians. I only have a few seconds to decide. The mist is clearing, bathing us in light.

"Charge!" I scream, and my columns set their feet. "Charge! *Salopes!* Charge!"

This is something the Russians don't expect. We're meant to shoot first. We don't. Jean-Paul takes the Eagle and raises it above his head. I notice one of its wings has been shot away. We have thirty seconds until the next volley. We reach the Russians in twenty. They break under a glinting wave of bayonets.

Cheering, we return to the line in good order, and spend the next half hour exchanging volleys and slowly driving the Russians away. We waste their time with our blood and determination.

"Our Eagle," I hear Jean-Paul yell, "those bastards want him. Well, they can't have him!"

He gets a cheer.

"You said that wrong, Sergeant," I tell him. My voice is nasal and blood-clotted.

"Madame?"

"The birds at the top of our standards are always feminine. Mind the agreement of your adjectives."

"We're under fire," he laughs, "and she's giving me a grammar lesson."

"Just remember, Sergeant," I say, "that's an order."

By the early afternoon, the battle is as good as won, but it is not over for me. Not yet. I thought I had fought nobly and lost enough blood. That I had banished my demons. That I had laid my brother to rest.

I have done none of these things, because I have not faced Tugarin. I have not met the Zmey.

11. DIARY, 16 OCTOBER 1793

Charles took me to see the execution of the Queen. He said I must become bitter and hard, so he took me. He said that I would never need to be afraid of dragons or monsters ever again. That when the evil Queen dies, they all die with her.

I wish I hadn't seen it. I wish I hadn't. I wish Charles would just write poetry and play with his wooden sword. I wish there was no such thing as war.

12. 2 DECEMBER 1805, AFTERNOON

My hair has matted together and frozen stiff on my right cheek. The crackling strands have both the color and smell of rust. Up the Pratzen Heights, the sounds of battle are encouraging. If our cavalry has made it up there, they must be sweeping the field from north to south.

We were a lure. I did not know how well we accomplished our task until the Zmey cavalry emerge from the pall of smoke.

Tugarin sits tall in his saddle. The horse is a magnificent stallion with a heavy armored caparison. Behind the rider are great wings of wood and paper covered with Slavic sigils and the colors of Tsar Alexander. The Zmey cavalryman's breastplate shines, even in the cannon smoke. The man is a giant, and I can't tell if he has the head of a dragon or a helmet made of terrifying scale.

"Shoot him!" I yell. No one moves. This is the first time I have not been able to point my soldiers as a weapon. Theirs is an ancient dread. The fear of dragons and monsters in the mist. I feel it too.

I brush the crimson spikes behind my ear and drop a gloved hand to the hilt of Charles' cavalry sword. The blade that gave me my name. With the other I grip the standard, the staff topped with the Imperial Eagle. One wing has been shot away, and there's a hole in the beak made by a musket ball.

I can't fight him alone. He's a demon. His horse has wings, or he does. One or the other. I can't quite see.

"Take him, Cuirassiere," Jean-Paul says. "You have wings, too."

"No, I don't. I'm the daughter of a sign painter."

"Look at their faces," the big sergeant says.

I do. I glance over my shoulder at the men. Not just men, of course. There are a few girlish faces mixed in. All of them are looking at Tugarin with fear, and at me with hope. It's in the shine of their eyes. All the belief possible in our new way. The way of progress, not dragons. The way of the Eagle, holes or not. They shouldn't be so starry-eyed—this is still war, and I'm the one who has to face the dragon.

"Come!" Tugarin roars, and smoke or steam billows from his mouth. It is difficult not to shrink from his voice. "Let us see what happens when the ancient dragon meets the peasant."

The field becomes still. Time fails to pass. All this work, and I still have to go and do this myself.

"What I'm going to show you," I yell, "is what happens when the sword meets the gun."

I draw both of Charles' pistols. A brace of four or six is customary, but this was all we could afford.

The Dragon smiles at me from atop the winged horse. His breast plate shines. He has planned for this—a foot soldier cannot beat a horseman any more than a pistol ball can beat a steel cuirass. It is one of the rules of war.

Rules. Pah.

The concussion when I shoot is enormous. It feels bigger than I am, like the pistol wants to break my wrist. The iron ball takes Tugarin's horse in one fetlock, and the horse stumbles forward. Tugarin has to leap agilely from the saddle to avoid being thrown.

"Dishonor!" he roars.

Honor. Pah.

An honorable soldier wouldn't shoot him in his beautiful satin britches either. I fire the second pistol into his leading leg.

"Stand with me now, Dragon, with your old blood and old titles. I am a sign painter's daughter! I am a coward's sister!"

He does stand, limping, with ethereal rage burning in his inhuman eyes. The battle is over. The fight has been lost and won. But not for him, and not for me.

I drop the flintlocks and grip my brother's cavalry saber. The sword has made me both more and less than he was, or ever could be. I care for nothing. Not for honor or justice or war. These good and decent soldiers follow none of that. They follow me. *I love you, Charles. You were the other half of me.*

"Now, if you want an eagle," I say, striding forward, "Come and get her."

And come for me he does, like a hurricane.

Tugarin is a fiend. His guard-less Cossack saber has a weight almost twice mine. I manage to parry him once, then twice, and his injured leg slows him down, but even the deflected blows shake my arms and my soul. In ten seconds, it's clear he's toying with me the way a cat toys with a mouse.

I allow him his blow. He wants revenge, to make me stumble just as he did. That is foolish. I know how to stumble and rise better than any. He should have just cut me down the way Jean-Paul did.

There is no defense against him, so I attack. His lead leg gives as his sword descends to transfix my thigh. The pain is a diamond lance of agony. Charles' sword is still as sharp as a barber's razor. The Dragon's weight carries him onto the blade as I drive it through his neck, above the cuirass and below his craggy jaw. We fall together, the giant Zmey cavalryman crushing me under his weight.

On a clear, beautiful afternoon, on a cold and windy field, I close my eyes as a dragon slayer.

13. 2 DECEMBER 1805, DUSK

I awake on a litter. It's a fine vantage point on the field, even though everything from my toes to the top of my head hurts abominably. The Dragoons are finishing the encirclement, and the Russians are surrendering.

I sit up to get a better view, and the right side of my face pounds. I feel a moment of nausea and the eerie ring of panic. Have I lost my right eye? No, a touch reveals a mass of cotton bandages. Sound echoes in my aching ears.

They're cheering me.

"She lives! *Une Aigle qui ne peut pas etre pris!*" Someone cries, and there's a long cheer. *An eagle who cannot be taken.* They mean either the standard, or me, or both. I don't mind which—they're the same thing.

Jean-Paul, I notice, is by my side. Of course. I feel a sudden fondness for the lumbering brute.

"How are the troops?"

"Fine. They didn't have any trouble shooting at the Zmey after you fed Tugarin a mouthful of your cuirassiere's steel," he laughs.

"And where are we going, Sergeant?"

"To the field hospital," he says laconically, "after you meet the Emperor."

COLETTE ANNE DEBELLE (b. 25 July 1780) was an infantry commander in Napoleon's Grande Armée. Despite inheriting her commission, she quickly earned a reputation for fearless leadership under fire. Much-loved by her troops, *La Cuirassiere* was promoted steadily until being made a *Maréchale* after her victory at the Battle of Wavre in 1815.

Her diaries, once thought lost, were discovered in the attic of a country estate in Provence in 2015, and have recently been published. Though she recorded her wartime experiences with wit and clarity, her fate after the One Hundred Days is not known.

BLAKE JESSOP is a Canadian author of fantasy, science fiction, and horror stories with a master's degree in creative writing from the University of Adelaide. He was the lead English translator of Colette Debelle's recently uncovered memoirs. You can read more of his speculative fiction in *Glass and Gardens: Solarpunk Summers* from World Weaver Press, or follow him on Twitter @everydayjisei.

SELF SELECTION

An account by Ash Fellblade,
as provided by Mathew Murakami

When I met her for the first time, I was about six, she was twice my age, and we had nothing in common.

"Girl," she said to me, her accent somehow both lazy and aggressively off-putting, "fetch my horse some water." She waved her hand airily at the overheated animal tied to the post beside the gate of my mother's inn. The little pony had been worked harder than it was used to, and its chunky sides were heaving in the afternoon heat.

I stared at her fine clothes, feeling my cheeks growing hot. I looked pointedly down at the tray I was holding at shoulder height so she could place the welcome cup back down beside the now only lukewarm towel. "My hands are full. Have your babysitter fetch it. Better, fetch it yourself."

I was unreasonably angry at her, and her clothes, and the fact that she had been at the inn more than once and had never even bothered to talk to me before now. Even so, I don't know why I said something like that to a guest, but my cheeks felt like they must have been putting off light, they were so warm.

There was a strangled sound from over her shoulder and both our heads whipped around to look at one of the two guards in her father's uniform, but she was staring straight ahead, face pink from the sun.

The girl looked back at me, and her left hand stroked the hilt of the comically large sword at her waist. The motion was awkward and unconscious and the silver falcon on each side seemed to twinkle mockingly out from the wrappings. "Do you know who I am?" she snapped.

"Yes. Lady." The pause before the title was a short one, before I remembered to rein in my temper, instead of riding it. I think it was the gritted teeth that made her own jaw clench, though. She seemed to be waiting for something, so I said, "My name is Ashel."

A strange expression passed over her face and then she smiled, too sweetly. "Dear Ashel, I forgive you, of course. You're too young to know better." Her chin twitched upward as she continued, "I am on A Mission."

She paused to make sure I was suitably impressed. I'd like to say that I tried to look attentive because I had remembered my manners, but mostly I wanted her to shut up and finish drinking from the cup so I could set the tray down.

"The saints have spoken to me, and my ancestors ride with me to battle." Her left hand fumbled for the sword hilt again. "I have been entrusted with a vision for the Warlord."

I looked down, so she couldn't see my eyes, and said, only, "Yes, Lady."

She slammed the cup down on the tray and her voice grew even more edged. "What would you know about it, with turnip in your hair and mud on your dress?"

She stormed off toward her pony, her father's guards following after her.

"I do not have turnip in my hair!" I said angrily, but under my breath.

I watched her finish watering her horse and scramble awkwardly into the saddle. One of her guards opened the gate and she rode through, "chin testing the wind," as my mother would have said.

As the three of them turned to the left and started down the road, she turned, looked through me, and then pointedly looked forward.

"They don't let little girls lead the army, anyway!" I said spitefully—maybe not quite under my breath, because her chin somehow twitched even farther upward—but she didn't turn back.

When I met her for the second time, I was twelve, she was half again my age, and we both thought ourselves much older than our years.

I stood at the gate, watching the soldiers ride by, the sleepy morning sun casting long shadows behind them. They were a sharp contrast to the ones that had ridden hurriedly through the evening before.

A soft voice at my side made me jump. "Girl," someone said, "Where can I get water for my horse?"

"Over there." I waved to my left as I turned, but my voice caught when I saw her face, stern and beautiful under a bright headband tied in a battle knot above her right ear. "I can get it for you, Lady."

"Ah." She smiled softly. "You do know who I am. No, no, I should get it. A soldier sees to her own needs." As she led the well-muscled animal to the well, I stared enviously at her clothes, so much finer even than the ones she had worn before. The white of her coat was almost blinding, the crest on the back was bright and colorful, and her pants were the color of midnight.

As she filled the basin for her horse, she said, quietly, "It is almost done."

"Lady?" I asked, unsure whether she was speaking to me, her horse, or only herself.

"Not 'Lady'; 'General,' perhaps. I suppose it doesn't matter. By the end of the day, we will be all one land, there will be only one army, and I will be without a purpose or a vision to lead me."

She shrugged as she brought the bucket up again. She took a long drink straight from the bucket and then walked her mount back to the gate and swung up in a single, graceful motion.

Her hand rested easily on the hilt of the sword at her waist, silver falcons winking at me through her fingers, as more soldiers rode by, then swung into a gap, riding for the banners bunched at the front of the next group.

She turned her horse back for a moment and smiled at me over her shoulder. "Thank you for the water!"

We nodded at each other, and then she turned her face toward the rising sun and rode in the direction of her father's house.

After she left, I was distracted, waiting. I had been scolded more than once, but not even a bad burn from the stove had made me pay more attention, so that evening, I had been sent out to gather some of the early apples from the trees near the gate.

As I looked up the road for the second time in as many minutes, I suddenly saw a figure walking down the road toward me, her shadow reaching back toward the unseen battlefield, miles away.

"Hello, girl," she said. I strained to hear her.

"Will you come in? I know people are waiting in the common room for news."

She smiled sadly at me. "I can't. I have places to go, but you may tell them we won."

"I can get you some water," I said.

She shook her head. "No, I don't need any water right now."

I wanted to shake her, to shout, but I glanced over my shoulder to make sure no one was coming out to look for me, and I asked her softly, "What does that mean? Winning? Does that mean that everyone will suddenly be happy? Does it mean that people will stop having their children and their crops lost to war?"

She shook her head and said, "I don't know. I never had any visions of anything after the final charge. I didn't have anything left." She looked back up at the road and sighed. Slowly, she took one step, and then another, walking away from all she had worked for.

She turned back one last time to smile at me over her shoulder. "But what will you do, girl? After all, they don't let little girls lead the army—"

"My name is Ashel."

"Yes," she said, turning back toward the setting sun. "I know."

She walked slowly on, the red mud on her clothes refusing to dry in the warm evening. A rust-red headband was tied in a peace knot above her left ear. Silver falcons winked at me from her waist, as they slowly waved back and forth.

The evening was bruised by a bright flash. I wiped my watering eyes, but she was gone. I saw something in the road where she had been walking a moment ago and I ran to see what it was.

I picked it up in both hands, disbelieving. It was heavier than it looked and seemed to want to leap out of my hands when I moved. Silver falcons winked and whispered at me in the evening light. "But what will you do, girl?"

The next morning, the soldiers rode by, bloody, dirty, and triumphant. Some of them smiled or talked, but less than I would have expected. They cast looks back up the road behind them and suddenly grew sad, or grim, or just quiet.

When the banners appeared, there she was. No longer tall, like she had appeared the day before, but tiny, lying on top of a bed carried in the back of a wagon. A dark headband was around her head, the knot standing out against her pale forehead. Her eyes were closed, and her hands were clasped around a plain, empty scabbard, over a coat that looked all splotched with brown.

I trembled, and wondered. I suddenly itched to run to the tree behind the stable, to thrust my hand deep into the hollow trunk, to see what I might find at the farthest reach of my fingertips. Instead, I turned my head toward the sky until my eyes filled with tears and I couldn't see anything anymore.

When I met her for the third time, I was eighteen, and so was she, and we talked for a while, as sisters.

I sat on my horse, who snorted and danced a little underneath me, as I watched the soldiers trying to conceal themselves in the wooded area below me. The white of my coat was almost blinding, the crest on my back was bright and colorful, and my pants were the color of midnight. My right hand rested easily on the hilt of my sword, the silver falcons worn, but still bright.

"Girl," said a calm voice at my side, "your horse sounds like he needs water."

I glanced over at the mounted figure that had appeared on my right. "Ha. I wondered when you'd have the guts to show up. It's 'General,' not 'Girl,' you know. He'll get some in a minute, but he's fine, if a little spoiled."

She made a rude noise. "I wasn't sure you would want to see me. You know you've spent the last three years undoing my life's work."

I sank a little in my saddle. "That's not true. I thought you were doing the right thing at the time, too. I couldn't see how things could be worse."

She shifted a bit, and silver falcons winked at each other across time. "Unfortunately, when power is concentrated, it is more easily abused. You know he's coming for you, right?"

I waved at the wooded slope that now held a third of my too-small forces. "We'll be ready. I'm hoping that your Warlord won't notice that these squads are missing."

She made a considering noise and then looked at me. "He's not 'my' Warlord, but you're right. It should work, if your main force can hold long enough. It's a good plan."

"It should be. I've had good teachers." My right hand reached down to touch the hilt of our sword at my waist.

Her left hand paused in the middle of the same action. "Yes. You know I never would have given you the sword if I thought it would cause problems for you."

I shook my head. "No. No problems, just advice, and training, and direction. We can argue about it when this is all over, if you want."

"So what, then? Retire to a cottage somewhere? Back to the inn?"

I shook my head again. "No, I'll fight for those who can't. I just don't know how, yet. If you have any ideas, I'd love to hear them."

She smiled, but distantly, like she was listening to something or someone else at the same time. Suddenly, her chin jerked upward and her expression grew more serious. "It's time."

I stood up in the stirrups and waved my hand over my head. As I started riding down the slope, I said, softly, "Ride with me?"

Her reply sounded as though she were riding behind me and leaning forward to whisper into my ear. "Always."

ASH FELLBLADE is a former Prelate's Champion, mercenary, and folk legend. She loves drinking wine, righting wrongs, and drinking even more wine. When she is not wandering the Failed Empire, she lives in an undisclosed location with a pony, the Fellblade, and a houseful of chatty saints and spirits.

MATHEW MURAKAMI is a writer, gamer, and technology consultant living in Washington State. He has worked as a technical writer, editor, car salesperson, caterer, temp bartender, overnight hotel desk person, landscaper, sandwich artist, and fake job maker-upper (but only once). When he is not writing—and sometimes when he is—he enjoys tea and puns.

ART BY **AJ**

AJ is an illustrator and comic artist with a passion for neon colors and queer culture. Catch them being antisocial on social media 'thehauntedboy'.

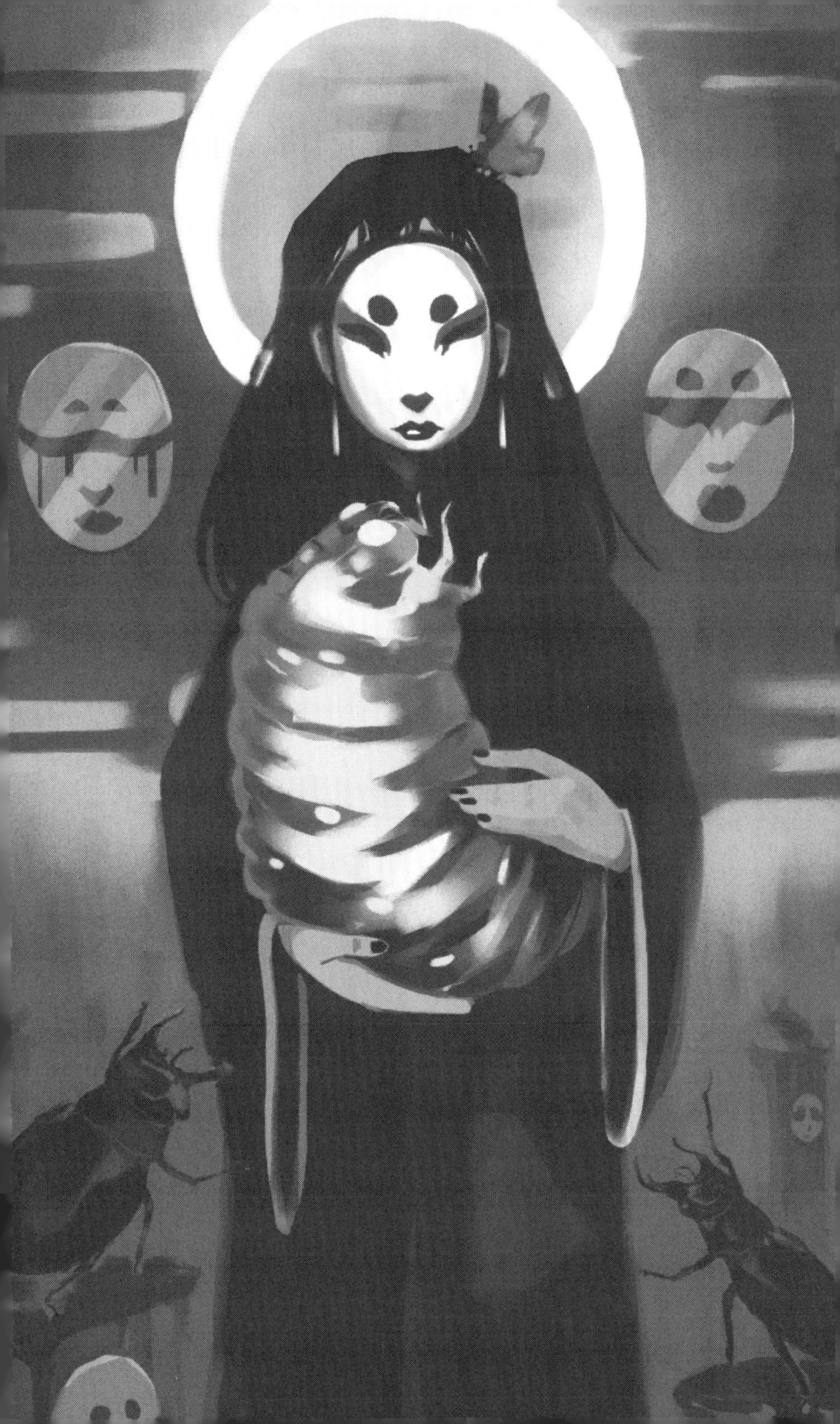

CHASING THE WOMBSHIP ECHIDNA

An account by Sister Kalindra,
as provided by L. Chan

The Wombship screams as She falls from star to star, pausing only to feed in amongst the asteroid fields, to drink at the shoals of migrating comets. She screeches Her death, because war rages in Her. She cries at the death of Her children, that would have otherwise built a better world. She wails at the birth of another clutch of progeny—another squad, more meat for the grinder. She keens at the loss of potential in each quickened embryo, scientist, artist, philosopher queens no longer. She howls as She births monsters. Like me.

The Wombship's sobbing is a constant, a background hum. We each have fragments of Her in our cheekbones, we all hear Her in our dreams.

I'm waiting with my sisters, our skins carapace black, natural armour that emits no heat, scatters light up and down the spectrum, deflects kinetic armaments. Sisters check their weapons, sidearms that accelerate slivers of metal to twice the speed of sound, monomolecular edged combat blades. They stretch each of their four arms, run diagnostics on the implants in every third eye on the ocular band around their foreheads. I know my gear works, so I skinshift the substance of the Wombship's walls into intricate flowers, more mural than plant. It passes the time.

My combat harness is too tight, sweat pooling under my arms, between my toes. I'm as jittery as the next sister. Moreso, because experience has taught me the caprice of combat. Sister Hensen, my vatmate and brightest amongst us, took a stray kinetic slug to the back of the head when a clip exploded. My continued existence owes as much to rattling dice as to martial skill, although I am not lacking for the latter.

Hegemony spinships track the Wombship like circling vultures, the coughing stutters of their ion engines like hyena barks, pings of their long-range scanners like the deep inhalations of night-time foragers. They want Her for the choice theft of the thousands of souls She carries deep in Her belly. They want Her for Her own choice theft, the elopement of a shipmind, the most exquisitely complex being built by the Hegemony. Choice theft is high treason. In the Hegemony, all choices benefit the collective, whether they be in matters of creation or destruction.

They made Her too kind. Seconds after Her own birth, She hatched a plan to leave the cluster and birth systems of the Hegemony, old Earth, and the belt. In form, She takes after the octopi or the squid, unfolding Her solar sails like a planet-sized flower as She accelerates to the next cluster, pausing only to mine tritium for the ion drives, minerals for micro-meteorite damage to the hull.

The klaxons suggest we have been boarded. The spinships haven't caught up, nor do they know the Wombship's destination. She muddles their algorithms by keeping Her starfalls arbitrary, a random walk amongst the constellations. But when stop She must, the spinships sling kamikaze shock troops at us, dropships gravity whipped past the redline of their structural tolerances, crewed by genengineered machine-flesh hybrids, seeking to reclaim the Wombship. Her design precludes bombardment; the Wombship is one of a kind, a networked intelligence spread across kilometres of thinking substrate distributed across and within Her superstructure. And one of a kind is precious.

"They're coming," the Wombship says to all of us at once.

The shock troops blow the wall, leading with disorientation charges, a barrage of plasma bolts covering their entry. Towers in combat armour, taller than any man had right to be; shoulder turrets ready to deploy hunter-killer micro missiles, some rifles spitting plasma, others, flame and kinetic rounds. The finest killers the Hegemony had to offer, vat pink but mind-printed veterans of a dozen campaigns down to the last soldier.

Better armed, better trained—just better. We sisters were outclassed in every way in a straight fight. But honour has no currency against the invader; fair play has no value to the dead. There is no *bushido* in the way we sisters call the Wombship to skinshift the corridors, opening hatches where none previously existed, rising up to part combat armour at the joints with our sharp little knives, hamstringing, taking out tendons, crippling. A monomolecular blade is so fine that it slices between nerves, so we twist our knives to let them know we've been there.

There is no chivalry in the way I subvocalise to the Wombship to modulate the fields that simulate gravity, turning walls into ceilings. I land on the shoulders of a Hegemony trooper, slapping at his frantic struggles with my third and fourth arms, whilst hitting the emergency helmet release with my second. My needler whines as a stream of flechettes pours into his suit. Flechettes ricochet off the outside of his thick armour, but the tiny projectiles will ping the inside of it upward of a dozen times before stopping. Too bad he's still inside it.

I tally the damage. Ten troopers, three sisters. No, four sisters. Sister Qiu-Fong is thrashing, random nerve impulses causing her to flail with her knives, scoring the walls and floor around her. Even in death, we are deadly; the Wombship built us monsters well. A plasma bolt had taken half of Qiu-Fong's head off, the heat cooking a section of her brain.

"Sing to her, Mother," I say to the Wombship.

The other sisters pause in their clean up duties, scavenging weapons, sneaking bites of our adversaries where flesh presents itself. The more squeamish sisters wait for the Wombship to repurpose biomass into combat rations, while the rest of us prefer to cut out the intervening steps and have a banquet right after. Fighting makes for hungry work.

"A round will do the job, Sister Kalindra." I see from the nods of the others that the Wombship is on the wideband, broadcasting the order to all. Testing me.

"Nobody deserves to go into the dark alone, Mother." We all call Her Mother, despite the variations of face and feature. She chilled our nascent embryos, sang to us as we quickened in vats, lovingly tailored our genes for murder. What else would we call Her?

"As you wish, Sister Kalindra," says the Wombship, giving in and segueing into a wordless tune that each of us carries in our hearts.

Before we were born to war, before our minds were imprinted with each of the dozen martial katas, the hundred weapons, the thousand tactics, the Wombship sang to us. Not a sister among us doesn't long for that time. Sister Qiu-Fong ceases her struggling, her shattered face relaxing.

I cradle her head because I am the oldest, so it falls upon me to welcome and to see off. I kiss her lips, mindless of the slurry of grey matter that coats them. The tip of the blade enters her neck between the first and second vertebra. She exhales her last breath into my mouth and it is over.

The other sisters laugh like little girls; I remind myself that most of them still are. I am Sister Kalindra, Sister Two, survivor of a dozen campaigns—by skill, by bloodthirstiness, by sheer dumb luck. Greying hair at the temples is a privilege that none of my vatmates got to enjoy. The lines on my forehead, above the band of eyes that allows us sisters to see three hundred and sixty degrees, command more respect than battle scars, even those of Sister De Souza with the two missing arms. The sisters each own my memories, mind synced when we sleep between raids, so that each of us is a killer ten times over from our hands, a hundred times over in our combat sim dreams.

Hegemony blood stains the walls of the food preparation area. The Wombship reconfigures Her innards at Her discretion, so that any combat data beamed back by the shock troops is instantly obsolete. Today, the kitchen abuts the crèche, so I listen to my sisters singing as they cook. The younger sisters think that eating the dead gives them strength and courage; the older ones know that it gives us nothing more than convenient nutrition, calories that the Wombship does not have to synthesize or harvest. She is on a sojourn millennia long, yet She counts the seconds jealously, hoarding joules of energy to one end and one end alone, outrunning our pursuers toward our destination.

My duties are more specialised, I lower myself into a birthing vat, immersing myself in amniotic fluid. The vat is one of many, fluid filled membrane pods like so many staring eyes, up and down the fleshy corridors. I was never good at cooking. Dressing meat yes, knife skills are eminently transferable. Others can slice and dice nearly as well, but none can assist in birthing a sister. Physically, it is a simple task. The vats are large enough to accommodate both the new sister and me, her arms and legs already thick with muscle, torso full of redundant organs, armoured skin layers still hardening, her additional hands tensing and relaxing. A dozen umbilicals connect her to the Wombship; a cocktail of nutrients pumping straight through to her digestive system, tailored hormones and hyperoxygenated blood to her veins, bespoke nanites digesting her bones and embedding solid state implants straight into her skull.

Every cord I sever withers in heartbeats, pulling the new sister away from the Wombship and into active duty. The trauma of separation still drags me from the shores of sleep, cheeks powdery with salt trails.

I was in the first batch, the batch that had to be born alone. Only half of us survived. We agreed that no sister would ever come into the light alone again, nor go into the dark by herself. This is my burden as the oldest.

The newborn fights against me, clawing, kicking. Sisters are born fierce. I hum to the newest sister to calm her heart, the same song that accompanied us from blastula to fetus.

When I am done and the four newest sisters scamper off, skittish and gangly, I am alone with the birthing tanks, soaked in briney amniotic fluid. But we are never truly alone on the Wombship. "If you gave me more sisters, maybe another squad's worth, less would die."

"The calculus of your survival is accurate down to the fifth decimal point. Every embryo I turn into a sister is one less for the future home." *Not our future home.* The Wombship does not include the sisters in Her accounting. We are flawed, monstrous, a throwback to the dark past that the Wombship was made to avoid.

"It takes time to birth a sister, we may not have enough before the next attack. More sisters would slow us down, the Hegemony will catch up." The Wombship lies, and it is a comforting blanket of a lie, that all desperate mothers tell children. It will be alright, Mother knows best. She has no need to lie to the others; She cannot sneak a lie past me.

"If you joined the fight, we wouldn't need to die." We are alone, and I am allowed to be insolent, by merit of age, position, and not caring.

"My energies are best suited to securing our future, Sister." Lies upon lies, the bedrock of our fight. And at the bottom of the strata of deceit, the Wombship's most shameful choice. She will not kill, not even for us. Instead, She boils down Her own shame, Her bile, Her hate at Her pursuers and distils it into us, the instruments of Her revenge.

"The attacks are getting closer together, aren't they? Nobody else has lived long enough to count, except you and me. How long do we have?"

"Long enough, Sister Kalindra. The Hegemony will never stop. The fleet has pursued us past their maximum operating radius. Their only hope for return is to capture us."

"So they will keep coming?"

"To the last man."

"Likewise will we fight." And die, always dying for the Wombship's choice.

Smells from the kitchen flood the crèche. Sister Henderson and Sister Fatimah are the best cooks we've had in batches. Pot roast and a spicy rendang seem to be on the menu. At least the Wombship bioprints spices for us. Shock troopers are tough, and slow cooking works best.

It's not sleep that I fear, it's waking up that reminds me too much of being born. This time it's not the thrashing of my limbs ripping the umbilicals from my body, but an insistent skull-shaking rattle. The fragment of the Wombship in my cheek vibrates hard enough for my head to feel like a boxer's speed bag.

"Two dropships are approaching at speed," says the Wombship, loud enough to drown out the alarms that I slept through. It's not the content of Her message that frightens me, but the delivery. Sped up sixty percent, nearing the edge of comprehensibility, Mother delivers the message as fast as She can. I'd laugh at the child-like quality of Her voice if it weren't for the implication. The Wombship is afraid.

I talk as I work, loading magazines, field stripping and assembling sidearms, slotting knives into sheaths. "How many troopers?"

"Maybe twenty, twenty-five," says Mother, with the same helium-filled anxiety.

The troopers would be lucky to even make it to the Wombship; redlining their crafts was a sure way to repurpose them into floating sarcophagi. "They're not due, not even at the rate the fleet is catching up."

"It was an out-of-context solution. The Hegemony must have sacrificed a spinship to sling these two at us faster than all those that have come before."

"Clever. You didn't see that coming?"

"My context does not allow me to sacrifice any of you; I would sooner sacrifice myself."

Wombship choice. I triple check my loadout. My weapons are ready, my body is not. There hasn't been enough downtime since the last attack. I'm still nursing bruises, persistent tinnitus, and at least one broken rib.

"How ready are the new sisters?"

"They completed eighty percent of the technical syllabus in utero, fifty-seven percent of the live combat drills. They are not ready to deploy, Sister Kalindra."

"Deploy them anyway."

The troopers split themselves into three-man squads, breaching the Wombship in near a dozen places, a tactic calculated to spread us thin and press their advantage to disable the Wombship's drives with shaped charges.

We confer and yield, setting off in teams of five to meet the enemy along the twisting, gut-like corridors. We spin our sharp little blades, we prime our guns, we scuttle and meld into walls and floors and ceilings, blending to ambush the invaders. It's not nearly enough.

Mother Herself is a weapon for us to wield, Her body conforming to our wishes. Some of the sisters favour the artificial gravity, disorienting their opponents by launching themselves from all angles. Others turn the floor into a sludgy morass, trapping feet and legs. Despite the advantages, we die, by blaster fire, by snapped necks, by flame, by the shaped charges ripping kilometre rents in the Wombship's solar sails.

I work alone, not bothering to subvocalise but shrieking commands to my sisters, redeploying, reinforcing, retreating where we cannot hold. My killzone is a writhing mass of Mother's substrate criss-crossing the corridor, a nest of vines with bulbous fruit. When the troika hacks their way halfway down the corridor, I detonate all the fruit, sprinkling the air with suspension of glittering metallic chaff, thick enough to fool sensors across and beyond the visible spectrum, scramble lidar and radar.

There's no time to spare, the odds favour the invaders in single combat, and there are three of them. I sprint through a channel I've left in the vines, taking the first trooper down by emptying both sidearms at him; enough flechettes find their way into chinks in his armour to pincushion joints and muscle, leaving him a twitching mess to bleed out.

I can reload both sidearms in under two seconds, but I can't spare even that, launching myself at the second squad member. There's a dance that few sisters have mastered, one that steps in the lag between onboard telemetry and suit-assisted aiming. The trick is willingness to get shot; hot plasma takes a chunk of chitinous plate off my abdomen, another out of my thigh. Plasma injuries are self-cauterizing; at least I don't have to worry about bleeding to death.

Forward momentum suffices to drive the butt of his rifle into his armour, just hard enough to knock him over so I can wrap my legs around his upper bicep. It worked against the samurai, it works against the shock trooper, the arm bar providing enough leverage to pop the shoulder joint. When he struggles to his knees and clutches his ruined shoulder, I run one of my blades into his brain stem, just like Sister Qiu-Fong.

The last trooper is ready for me, he's already cleared enough of the vines so that he can move freely. I have nothing left but my knives; adrenaline and natural feedback blockers are preventing the pain from hampering me, but the damage has been done. Breaths are shallow, and there's a limp that's only getting worse. The trooper drops his rifle, whipping out a shockrod instead. I would shoot him for the audacity of his challenge, if I were still armed or if I could have gotten to any of his compatriots' guns before he shoots me.

However good I am, a prepared shock trooper is faster, stronger, better armoured, better trained, cerebellum intoxicated with a cocktail of combat stim drugs. The Hegemony captains aren't the only ones that understand sacrifice. I swing at him, leaving my arm out long enough. He takes the bait, locking my wrist and shattering the bone with the shockrod. Good, two of his arms are busy, and I've got three to spare.

I pull him close, smashing his faceplate with the thickened bones of my forehead, the impact hard enough for me to know that I've done myself some permanent damage. No time to think about it, hardened polymer falls away to reveal two metallic eyes in a face wired up with enough tubes to rival a newborn sister. Stiffened fingers are sufficient for me to push those implants back into his sockets, deep enough to pulp his frontal lobe.

Mother brings me nothing but bad news. More than half the invaders have been repelled, but at staggering cost. The Wombship had been wrong about the Hegemony fleet chasing us, but She was right about the new sisters. They both died within moments. Sister Henderson is dead, Sister Fatimah's still holding out. At least we still have a cook. I limp toward the next engagement. I'm not done, not yet.

"Damage report." It's the third time I ask, and the information is no less grim. Half the sisters dead, half the remaining barely hanging on. The rest nursing injuries like mine. That isn't the worst of it, at least three of the boarding teams were successful, their charges took out kilometres of solar sail and several hundred embryos, carbonized where they slept.

"I have selected the next batch of sisters, they will be ready in twelve days."

"And the next estimated attack?"

"Fifteen days. Another two starfalls and thirty days to restore myself to full cognitive capacity."

So the fleet has us in a spiral. I'm limping, the Wombship is limping. All they have to do is wear us down. There's no mission anymore, just the anticipation of impending death. And thus ends the Wombship, Her and the ten thousand lives within. Helplessness gnaws like an empty belly. There is no solving the problem within the current context. The Wombship, Her cargo, and Her bastard monsters. She was the Mother, fleeing for the safety of Her babies. I will never be a mother; I was never a child.

"So we're dead, all for the want of a few more sisters to hold the line." I yell the last words, petulant as a two-battle sister. The Wombship knows my pulse, my blood pressure, the amount of adrenaline in my bloodstream. But I scream anyway, because I need to let Her know this.

"Slowing us down brings us as quickly to this conclusion," the Wombship says.

I open my mouth to shout again, but suddenly I'm done. Maybe I should have taken the stray slug countless battles ago, Sister Hensen would probably be here instead of me. Read the flow of the battle better, saved a few more cubic metres of thinking substrate, a few more sisters, a fraction of a percent of forward momentum. Choices, choices, and all we get to choose is how to die.

The Wombship is pregnant, laden and lumbering between states. Onward, always onward to hope. She is in a state of becoming, not the same ship that was grown in our home system, not the same ship She will be after the thousands upon thousands are birthed. I know She's afraid; one state necessitates the death of the previous. She needs help. I am more aware of the fleck of Her in my cheek than ever before. The Hegemony is the greatest choice thief of all, about to take the futures of the Wombship, the sisters, and the unborn. But there is always choice, however tightly they corner us. All that matters is context; all that matters is sacrifice. And the choice is always life.

"Mother, how much substrate can you regenerate from?"

The Wombship does not have a heart, a centre, but I feel Her closest where I was born, and so I am with Her there when She dies. But She dies for hope, She dies for the thousand tiny lifepods we scattered to the solar winds, too many for the Hegemony to chase. The Wombship's body is infinitely malleable; shattering Her into fragments is not fatal.

What kills Her is my sisters and I, helping birth something new, working with our knives to deconstruct our Mother, even as bespoke machines sew a piece of Her into each lifepod, grafted onto the growing babies. Each piece in dreadful solitude, with only the nascent intelligence of a ripening human brain to keep it company. In the fullness of time, there will be a race of sisters spread amongst the stars, born neither truly human nor fully biomechanical brain. When they seek each other out (as they will, for each fragment calls to another), they will be greater than the sum of their parts, and far greater than that which the Hegemony started out chasing.

My sisters weep at the unmaking of the Wombship, as the voice that reverberates from our cheeks stutters and goes dumb, a shift from shipmind to computer, from Mother to ghost. There's enough intelligence left to pull the carcass of the Wombship into new configurations, to rechannel the ion engines into long distance cannons. We arm ourselves for the final time, each sister to her own whims.

The Hegemony is coming. They will not know until too late what it is that we have done. They will never have enough ships to chase the thousand lights we've sent into the dark. And they'll be busy.

SISTER KALINDRA was one of many soldiers grown to defend the wombship Echidna. No records of her exploits remain, yet she is known throughout the hundred inhabited worlds as the general who led the soldiers of Echidna to their final victory while the seeds of the hundred worlds were sown. In her spare time, she tended flower and herb gardens in the wombship. In combat, she held the third highest kill count of any soldier. That the population of the hundred worlds sharing the Onemind all dream of her life suggests that Sister Kalindra was the wombship's favourite.

L. CHAN hails from Singapore, where he alternates being walked by his dog and writing speculative fiction after work. His work has appeared in places like *Liminal Stories*, *Arsenika*, *Podcastle*, and *The Dark*. He tweets occasionally @lchanwrites.

SWING THAT AXE

An account by Dexter Contralles,
as provided by Nathan Crowder

Incessant pounding on my trailer's hollow front door dragged me from the wreckage of last night's whiskey bender. Bottles clinked underfoot, threatening my already questionable balance as I clumsily threw myself at the door. It took a few slaps at the knob to get it open. At least the knocking had stopped. Empty bottle of Wild Turkey brandished by the neck, I shouldered the door wide, prepared to smite whoever I found there. Out here past the city limits, one could count on coyotes, snakes, and scorpions, but the worst kind of visitors were the ones that bothered to knock first.

I wasn't expecting to see Louise Cantu standing there, arms crossed across her narrow chest.

The thin, yellow sun stabbed my eyes, and I blinked in slow surprise. Unlike the last several times I'd seen her, she didn't fade into wherever hallucinations and ghosts go when they're found out.

We both acknowledged the brandished bottle at the same time. I lowered it sheepishly, but didn't bother trying to invite her in. She'd seen enough of my current living conditions to let distaste flower in her eyes.

Squinting against the hangover-bright Tucson sun, I played her unexpected presence off as coolly as I could. It had been, what, three years since I'd seen her by chance at Guerro's in line for late-night tacos. "Lou. What brings you by?"

"I'm putting the band back together."

My stomach pinched and twisted. The whiskey bottle slipped from my fingers to join its fallen brothers on the floor.

"We're going to get Flores," she continued, unnecessarily. There could be no other reason for Brujah to ride again. There certainly weren't recording companies calling to sign us. Not after what happened.

Flores Cantu.

Of course.

On some level, I'd been preparing myself for this moment for six years, but I still wasn't ready. I expelled a stomach full of bile, whiskey, and a 3am Whataburger and onion rings on the rickety wooden steps of my trailer.

"Get cleaned up," she said with the kind of confidence that came from being routinely obeyed. "I'll be in the car. Bring your guitar."

INTERIOR: RECORDING STUDIO

Gold records sit on the wall, conspicuously just over the shoulder of the man on camera. You know him. Everyone knows him. He's one of the more conspicuous rock stars of your dad's generation. The caption at the bottom of the screen is merely for benefit of those visiting from another world.

"Brujah? Yeah, I remember Brujah. They only had that one album, but it was like something that crossed through from another dimension, you know? Like, there was prog rock and then there was where Brujah wanted to take it. Cantu… Flores Cantu, the album

opened up with her guitar wailing, just, possessed, you know?"
SLOW PAN & FADE MONTAGE:
Press clippings and photographs of Brujah, dated 6-8 years earlier. Flores Cantu stands to the side in the band photos, self-conscious, almost hiding behind her strangely-tuned Fender Stratocaster with the glossy black body painted with tiny gold symbols. She's young, barely twenty-five in the most recent photos, slender like a starving coyote. Stringy, dark hair hanging across her face, almost her eyes. Almost. Look close and you can see it. The confident madness of a caged animal holding a weapon of mass destruction in her lacquered claws.

The interview continues as a voice over, the rocker's London accent battle-weary after decades of cigarettes, late nights, and howling on stage to millions of fans:

"Right out the gates 'Shamble On' starts playing, and I turned to Charlie, who was with me in the limo. We both had the same look on our face. Couldn't speak even if we wanted to. Me and him transfixed, like a giant pin through our hearts—moths on black velvet—until that last note faded. Then we shook it off, and he paused the tape. We knew, we both knew. That was it—that was the sound, the pinnacle we were chasing."

Voice of interviewer, soft, accent neutral—a television voice. "Did you ever get the chance to meet her?"

"It was all so sudden." Montage footage transitions to front seat of Louise Cantu's trusty Nissan sedan as it trundles down a poorly maintained rural road. Me, the reluctant and hungover rhythm guitarist rubbing temples in passenger seat as the famous voice fades out. "Biggest unsolved mystery in rock, man. But I get it. Sometimes it all feels so big, and you want to hide from it. Mental health is rough. We've all been there. I hope wherever she is, she hears this and comes out of hiding."

Louise navigates the dusty back roads into town in silence. I'm full of questions that I don't know how to ask. Louise is a wall of silence. Corpse-quiet. Once she said enough to get me in the car, she was done with small talk.

We used to get along. Hard to believe, but true. Ages ago. Before what the music press called The Red Gate Sessions, the follow up to *Incandescent*. I was pretty sure we blamed each other for the same thing—for not stopping Flores when we had the chance.

Not that anyone could stop Flores once she dug in with the heels of her favorite platform boots.

"Have you bewitched Andy and Gus already?" I asked, just to break the cinderblock of silence pressing on my chest. She shot me a glance blazing with anger. It was too late to change my phrasing. Growing up, the Cantu twins had been outcasts, feared, called witches, *brujah*, by their neighbors and classmates. It was where we'd gotten the band name from, Flores and Lou, the twin leaders of the band—our Merlin and our Arthur, retrospectively.

They were sincere from the very first day of practice, promised they wouldn't cast spells on us. It was funny at first. You know, an ice breaker. Not that any of us really believed in magic then.

"Andy is running cables while he waits for his kit to be delivered and set up," Lou finally answered, tone icy as the moon. "Should be there by the time we show up. And Augustino was the one who convinced me this could work. He'll meet us there."

I chewed my lower lip, watching the sun arc through the sky like a giant, judgmental eye from behind the safety of my heavy aviator sunglasses. "It's been a long time," I said, stating the obvious to soften my follow-up question. "How do you know she's alive?"

Louise paused, took a breath, let it out. "She's my twin. We shared a womb. If she was dead, I'd know it."

EXTERIOR: SONORAN DESERT

Augustino Colvin, starring off across dry, rolling hills covered with tall barrel cacti. A storm builds on the horizon, mounting black clouds, pregnant with rain and lightning. Gus looks older than his forty-some years, a product of hard living, once sandy hair now a nimbus of white, his face carved like the arroyo-laced desert flats.

"It was all in the tuning," Augustino says, refusing to look into the camera, like he believes, on some level, that it will steal what's left of his soul. "People made a big deal over her guitar, black like night, covered with hand-painted symbols. Flores knew how to give them a show. But it was the tuning that mattered. Everything has a vibration, right? It's not witchcraft so much as physics. And traditionally guitars are tuned for certain chord structures, chords that are sonically pleasing. Flores wanted to do something else. Was looking for something else."

Placid interviewer voice, just engaged enough to coax out the reluctant storyteller. "Looking for something? A new sound?"

Augustino smiles at the interviewer. It's the smile a fox gives the henhouse. "Heh. All these years later, you still want to talk about Flores Cantu like she was a musician? Typical."

The interviewer is good. He keeps the fear out of his voice. "Why don't you tell me what she was, then. Or what she was looking for."

"The sound of the universe. The key. The harmonic frequency to reality."

Augustino shuts down, as if realizing what he's said. His gaze is drawn, perhaps against his will, back to the approaching storm.

The interviewer asks, "Did she find it?"

I turn off the television.

Louise pulled into a parking lot in the shade of an old corrugated steel building. The lines demarking the parking spaces have been scoured by age and blowing grit. The same for the company name on the side of the building. Nothing remains to let a casual glance know it used to be a slaughterhouse. Two other vehicles haunt the otherwise vacant lot—a faded blue VW Beetle older than anyone in the band, and a white panel van, back door open, from which Augustino stepped, carrying a red milk crate overflowing with drum stands and kick pedals.

I climbed out of Lou's car, giving Gus a chin tilt of recognition.

"You sober?" he asked, looking at me sideways while he waited for me to unload my guitar from the back seat.

"Does hungover count? Do I want to know what you had to do to secure the session masters?"

"You really don't want to know, and I really don't want to talk about it," Augustino said, a slight twitch to his lip.

I held out hope that my current condition would be enough for them to put off this reunion. The last thing my skull needed right now was that full prog rock experience. Andy's sticks hit the skin of his snare like bullets, and the low paired notes of "Invocation" from Lou's bass and Augustino's Fender Rhodes made my skull vibrate.

"I have a Gatorade in the cooler with your name on it," Gus said, sensing my hesitation.

"What flavor?"

Gus sighed and headed inside without me, hollering back over his shoulder. "Blue flavor, you giant baby."

"Blue isn't a flavor," I shouted back at him with a smile, stepping into the cavernous space to see the concrete killing floor swept clean, cables taped, mic stands in place, a stack of Marshall amps, Andy intently adjusting his stool behind the pair of kick drums.

It felt good to get the band together again.

Good enough that for just a few seconds, I forgot why we were there. Then I saw the reel-to-reel with the master tapes. I saw the empty space where Flores Cantu once stood, a vacuum as deep and deadly as the space between stars. I saw the symbols painted on the blood-stained concrete floor.

The smile died on my face.

We hadn't named the song yet. It didn't have lyrics so much as atonal screaming, provided by Louise as she punished her bass guitar. Flores called it the song "Python," but even she acknowledged it was just a placeholder. When she first introduced it to us with the very precise arrangement notes, she'd called it something else, something only she and Lou had been able to pronounce.

Behind their backs, I called it "Cat Sack Staircase" because that's how it sounded to me. Augustino called it "Harbinger."

We'd been beating our heads against the song, whatever we named it, for two days now. Everyone knew their parts. Not every band knew how to read music, but Brujah wasn't every band. Flores had handed us the music weeks ago, and we'd all been practicing individually. At least the trickier parts. Even the first few times we'd tried to play roughly through the whole twelve minutes of song, I hadn't realized the melody wasn't held by any single instrument. Instead, it threaded between instruments, sometimes carried by one and then handed off, sometimes shared by two or three instruments, buffeted by the others.

By the second day, we were handling the transitions more cleanly, but the closer we got to hitting our marks, the more wrong it sounded. The more our conscious brain rebelled against it. Like the world itself was pushing back, refuting the song.

I'd trained as a classical guitarist, and I'd never heard anything like it.

It was almost like…

"Witchcraft," the interviewer said. "Black magic. Demon worship. Those phrases get thrown around a lot in the rock music scene. Most of the time, it's very clearly a gimmick to sell albums. A sort of campy devil drag."

"Is there a question in there somewhere?" Louise Cantu asked.

A gentle laugh from the interviewer. If the intent was to relax Louise, it didn't work. She continued to frown, astride the dining chair turned backward, arms crossed atop the ladder back. She was dressed casually. Distressed blue jeans, natural colored peasant top, chunky sterling bracelet set with coral and obsidian. Her dark hair was pulled back into a severe bun. At a glance, she looked more like an art teacher rather than a bass player.

"I just find it curious that while most bands adopt this dark presentation as a marketing gimmick, the band name, Brujah, feels sincere and, I'd almost say cautionary."

This did coax a smile from Louise. "Cautionary. Yeah. That seems fair. It was something Flo and I got branded with when we were young. It was hard. People are… cruel. Needlessly cruel. Using it as the band name allowed us to reclaim it, make it mean something else, maybe? But also to give a little truth in advertising, I guess."

"Your sister," the interviewer started, cautiously.

Louise softened, the smile crumbling. She tried to look hard. To look strong and defiant. Together, the Cantu sisters had created and led one of the most promising prog rock bands in the southwest. It was unprecedented. And while Flores was heralded for her genius guitar work, Louise was the face of the band. She was the mouthpiece.

The rest of the band followed her lead without hesitation.

We would follow the Cantu sisters into hell if we had to.

Again.

I found the footage online, edited clips of our final Los Angeles show cut together with local TV "man on the street" interviews with people leaving. Someone had put it together as a memorial of sorts, commemorating five years since our final live show. I hesitated, cursor hovering over the play button for several long moments. Curiosity won out over trepidation, as it so often did when I waited long enough.

The music track that underscored the piece was the live version of "Shamble On." Never content with what didn't reach her gut threshold of perfection, Flores had continued to experiment with her solo, making it significantly different than what was on the album. The audio recording was pirated from a concert, poorly mixed, almost drowned out in places by crowd noise. Even still, it vibrated my bones like a tuning fork.

"There's nothing else like it," one fan said, openly weeping. He was young. Maybe even still a teenager, with bad skin. He had this regrettably out-of-control poof of brown hair on top of his head, like he was wearing the remains of the family poodle. "Can you get second-hand high off music? Because it felt like I was on acid, and I haven't even touched cough syrup this week!"

Another kid, this time a girl hiding behind a curtain of heavy, dark bangs. A black baby-doll tank top from another band, one I only vaguely remembered from the LA scene. "Like, I know there are only five people in the band, but sometimes I'd look at the stage, and could swear there were seven people. Or only three."

"Was it the lighting? Someone else said something about the stage lighting." The interviewer asked helpfully from off camera. He had the tone of someone who hadn't seen a rock show more hardcore than Huey Lewis and the News.

"The lighting was something else. It wasn't just coming from above, or from the back of the house. It was almost like it was coming from the band at times. And sometimes the band was unlit. What I mean is there was objective reality and there was what I saw on that stage tonight. And—" She held her two hands far apart, raised her eyebrows in disbelief. "You know? I couldn't tell you if I saw a concert or an occult ritual tonight."

"But was it good?" the interviewer asked, presupposing the negative.

"Flores Cantu is a force of nature in human skin. What she did on that stage, what her band did tonight? It changed my life." The girl said.

Finally, a pin-up caliber redhead, a bit short, maybe, built for comfort and not for speed, wearing a green satin dress. I heard through the grapevine that she was head of a record label back east now. Back then, she was just another music executive trying to reap the whirlwind that was Brujah. Flores never trusted the music executives. "I've never seen anything like the show Brujah put on tonight. In a word, magical. Mark my word. They're going places."

I let the video play out, those pirated chords in the background, tugging at something deep in my chest. Deep in my brain. I'd stopped actively listening, but I couldn't stop hearing. Couldn't stop… feeling.

They're going places.

Lady, you have no idea.

Tunings were checked, mics set, playback monitors adjusted. All eyes turned to Louise.

It had been a while since we'd all been together like this. I don't know everyone else's excuse. Guilt was probably a part of it. After all, we were all responsible to some degree for what happened to Flores Cantu. Sure, she might have been the driving force, but she never would have gotten there without our help.

So, yeah, guilt was definitely a part of it. But for me, the bigger factor was fear. It was why I'd crawled down the neck of a whiskey bottle. It was what kept me there.

I wrote and played my own music. It was shitty and derivative, but it was safe.

I played cover songs in whatever band was willing to put up with me.

If it were up to me, I'd never play Brujah's music again. Not even in the "comfort" of my dilapidated trailer, far from anyone who could be hurt by it. The Cantu sisters' bloody fingerprints were all over those songs.

But some nights…

Some nights, when I got too introspective and just the right balance of drunk, I'd hear Flores calling out to me. I'd see her face through the haze of Camel cigarette smoke, her dark eyes piercing a hole through my skull. The shadows took on weight, pressing me down into my seat. Tobacco fought with the ozone smell of desert lightning and the coppery tang of fresh blood. I'd look down to find my fingers shaping the chords, the music compelled from me by some kind of shared trauma.

I drank myself into oblivion on those nights to fight back the nightmares. Sometimes it even worked.

"We all on the same page?" Louise asked, mic and mic stand gripped almost defensively in her weathered hands. Her bass was slung across her back, ready to swing into place after the first minute of opening screams.

"Start with 'Invocation of the Storm,'" Andy said from his perch behind the drum kit. He wet his upper lip, pink triangle of tongue brushing the faint suggestion of mustache. He motioned towards the hanging chimes with the padded stick in his right hand. "Then straight into 'Broken Doors, Broken Frames.'"

Augustino stepped in. "Then, you know, we slide into 'Python,' or whatever we're calling it."

"And we don't stop," Louise said, looking at each of us in turn. It felt like her gaze stayed on me longer than the others. "No matter what, you keep playing."

I nodded, flexed my fingers, felt the metal strings hum beneath my calloused fingertips. "We won't let you down, Lou. You or Flores. We know what to do."

Louise didn't thank us. No thanks would have been enough for what we were risking. The years hadn't diluted our memory of what we were attempting here. We all knew the dangers. We'd seen them first hand.

I couldn't be the only one here having nightmares about that night.

With a nod, she signaled Augustino, who started the playback of the isolated Flores Cantu guitar master track from The Red Gate Sessions. Nothing. A heartbeat that stretched on forever in the anticipation. And then the straight-edge-razor-cut note pulled from a tortured Fender Stratocaster. Like a jackrabbit screaming in the desert dusk, that sound that was eerily like a woman's cry and absolutely something else. Something otherworldly. The note hung there in the air. Vibrated the way a perfectly imperfect note can, joined by an angry howl from Louise at the mic, joining and twisting with the guitar note like mating snakes.

Then the chunk of bass and drums and on the four, the cavernous tones of Augustino on the electric organ. And we were off to the races.

It all came back. Like riding a bike. Or falling down the stairs. Just let go and let it happen. The old finger patterns had soaked into my muscles. I thought of cucumbers pickling in salty brine. Of wood absorbing lime to become petrified wood. Of anything except the music.

I don't think I could have forgotten these songs if I'd wanted to. They'd been rehearsed so meticulously. Honed like the edge of a samurai sword. Forged and locked in a moment of tragedy. I didn't need to remember the songs to play them.

The songs, thus absorbed, played themselves. All I had to do was get out of their way and let them move through me.

I closed my eyes, blocking out the shaking corrugated metal walls and bloodstained floor of the old slaughterhouse. It was like being back at the old studio space out near Bisbee. Eyes closed, I could almost feel the cushion of blankets the studio owner had brought back from the Navajo reservation. I could almost smell the wood and sour citrus incense that Flores had insisted upon lighting before the recording session started—a sensation strong enough I wondered if either Louise or Gus might have lit some in the slaughterhouse when I wasn't paying attention.

And Flores.

Eyes closed, it was easy to believe Flores was here with us.

For better or worse, no one else played guitar like her.

I was lost in the memory of playing with her. Lost in the memory of playing with Brujah. I'd lived a decently long life. Outlived everyone else in my family, at least. But in my forty-five years, I'd never done anything that made me feel as happy, as complete, as… powerful, yeah, powerful, as playing in Brujah.

When I started crying, I had to let the tears flow. Wasn't shit I could do about it. We'd made it into "Python" already, my fingers too committed to my part to stray more than an inch from the desperate guitar strings.

Time and space felt pliable, like warm taffy, vibrated apart by the musical alchemy of Flores Cantu's guitar, given shape and direction by the foundation the rest of Brujah laid down. I could no longer remember a time before the music—could no longer tell where I stopped and the notes began. I felt the warmth of other suns on my face—heard the trumpet of creatures the likes of which Tucson, Arizona, had never dreamt of.

A lot of bands, a lot of guitarists rocked. There was no denying that.

One night six years ago, Brujah, under the guidance of the Cantu sisters, rocked so hard we tore a hole through the universe. Unprepared, or perhaps too enthusiastic, Flores Cantu fell through that hole.

It wasn't the kind of explanation the folks at *Rolling Stone* were capable of accepting. Instead, she was just gone. Vanished. One more mystery in an industry that thrived on legends and mystery. There were unconfirmed sightings every now and again. "Flores Cantu spotted at Los Angeles clinic." Or "Tourist spots missing guitarist Flores Cantu on Greek island." Or my personal favorite, "Flores Cantu believed to be behind Oregon sex cult."

If she was dead, I'd know it.

I hadn't questioned Louise. I believed in the strange magic between twins. Just as I believed I had seen but been unable to reach Flores in my dark hallucinations the past several years. I never would have agreed to this if I hadn't known in my soul that we'd broken through to something else, and that somehow, somewhere, Flores was still waiting for us. Still leading us to some strange destiny from beyond the veil of our sad, shabby world.

My eyes flickered open on instinct, realizing we were nearing the end of the master tape. I met Lou's fevered gaze, an anchor in the insanity.

The meat processing plant was gone. Blood-stained concrete beneath our feet replaced by red grass, whipping gossamer in a gentle breeze. A giant ringed moon hung overhead, a haunted, pale blue against unfamiliar stars. In the distance, the silhouette of mountains moved, shifted to reveal themselves as something else, something beyond comprehension.

And there, in our midst, Flores Cantu, Fender Stratocaster glowing gently from the markings along its weathered, black body. The master tape cut out, flapping in the reel-to-reel, but the song continued. We all knew our parts.

Flores had been waiting six years to play hers.

Her sound had evolved in her absence. There were flourishes and ornamentation hidden between the power riffs that defied comprehension. It seemed impossible that one player could do that live without overdubbing or looping. But I bore witness to it.

Her technical mastery blinded me momentarily to a few other incongruities. But only momentarily.

For one, while all our parts remained as practiced, her part was exponentially more complex. And as such, it snapped this new, strange reality into even sharper focus than it had been before.

Also, Flores Cantu was not the intensely awkward artist I remembered. There was a hardness there. The grim, determined face of a survivor. A tale enhanced by the long, pale scars on her exposed arms and face. A tale told by her short, dark hair, shot through with threads of silver. A tale told by her clothes, same as they'd been when she'd vanished, but patched and re-patched, and patched yet again until they resembled a child's collage of her prior outfit.

Then there was the battle axe slung across her back, the arc of its blade nicked by heavy use, polished by respect and love.

The final notes of "Python" faded, swallowed up by the alien night. Louise fell to her knees, sobbing, leaning into her sister's hip as Flores went to stand next to her, fingers in her sister's hair. Louise hugged her close, as if letting go meant losing her all over again.

It was real. She was as solid as a funk bass line. We'd done it. We found her.

I don't think any of us had enough confidence that this would work to have asked the obvious question: "Once we find Flores, how do we get back?"

"Sweet axe," Andy said.

"You came for me," Flores said, uncertainly looking at each of us in turn. "You didn't give up on me."

"It's not Brujah without you," I said, which was equal parts true and useless information.

"So, why the axe?" Andy said, having clearly fixated on the brutal weapon.

"Trouble," Flores said. "The place is crawling with it. Don't worry. I have more weapons back home. Plus, I'm here, and things tend not to mess with me much anymore."

"Home?" Louise looked up at her sister, then we all followed her gaze to a small, circular stone house a few hundred feet away. A solitary window stared at us like a glowing yellow eye.

Flores laughed. It was a rare sound. "Most of you are going to have to sleep on the floor for a while at least."

"We're going back, right?" Augustino said. He didn't sound certain. We looked at each other, saw nervous smiles appear, the occasional shrugs. "I mean, like, eventually?"

Flores helped her sister to her feet. "I'll help you cart stuff back to the house. Can't leave the instruments lying around out here. Plus," she added with a wink, "I've written tons of new music and I can't wait to share."

Brujah loaded up our gear. It was like old times, when we had to roadie our own equipment into and out of seedy venues all over the southwest. Between being reunited and the promise of new Flores Cantu music, our steps were light as we followed the Cantu sisters through the tall, red grass beneath the light of an alien moon. Out in the distance, the mountains sang themselves to sleep.

Classically trained guitarist **DEXTER CONTRALLES** is perhaps best known as the rhythm guitarist for legendary prog-metal band Brujah. After the band's implosion while recording their unreleased sophomore album, known in some circles as The Red Gate Sessions, Mr. Contralles faded into obscurity in a succession of unremarkable bands. Last known to live in the Tucson area, he is said to suffer from occasional schizophrenic episodes and severe alcohol addiction. His current whereabouts are unknown.

Classically trained pianist **NATHAN CROWDER** wishes he was cool enough to have been in a prog rock band. He has an abiding love for music and desert thunderstorms. Creator and curator of the superhero universe of Cobalt City, he lives in the wilds of North Seattle, surviving on a diet of coffee and irony. His career is managed by his black cat Shiva in exchange for room and kibble.

THE END OF THE WORLD

An account by Tareya Softstep,
as provided by Matt Moran

I was there.

Too many people say that these days, since the Terror passed. Too many people try and milk the masses for their favour by pretending that when the end of the world came, they stood firm.

They didn't.

When the end of days came, when the Iron Host marched into our lands in their hobnailed boots, they didn't stand with us. They abandoned their oaths, their comrades, and their queen. I don't blame them.

The Iron Host were a terrifying sight, even for veterans like us. They were confident conquerors of continents, washed red in the rust of slain men and women. They looked like ghosts, because they were ghosts. They had no homeland, for they claimed the world; no gods, for they claimed to have slain them all. We of the Circle had fought among the hills of our homeland for decades, and they terrified us. Those of the tribes fought only when their lords commanded it. They were farmers, weavers, traders. They still are. I suppose that's all I am too, now.

But back then, when we still had a queen, I was a member of the Circle, that royal order of wandering knights who brought order to the highland realm. A dozen warriors from each of the Twelve Tribes—a gross, the disrespectful might call it. And at our head, Queen Marena. The darkest hair, the greenest eyes, the brightest soul that ever graced the highlands' blue grass. Her face was ebony chipped with jade, her breast bronze-plated to shame the sun itself. And we stood with her that day, her dozen dozen knights, ready to face the Host.

I admit, we were not alone. It is worse to ignore the dead than to take their place. We stood there with the warriors of three of the twelve tribes. Only three felt threatened by the advance of the Iron Host. Nine did not believe so great a terror could be upon us. But the highlands were ever divided.

When I think of that morning, I remember the sun more than anything. It shone hot, so hot that had we fought bandits or rebels, we would have stripped out of our armour and danced the war of the long spears. But the Iron Host paid no mind to the traditions of war. They did not come to fight. They came to kill. And so we sat in that sunlight that burned our skin and warmed our souls, waiting in the blue grass for the battle to begin.

"There must be a battle!" Queen Marena told us as we sat on the hillside. "We did not ask for war, but war has come to us."

There was no boasting or rattling of shields. We knew the truth of her words. The levies knew this was something greater and far worse than a cattle raid. We knew it for what it truly was—a chance for an honourable death. As at home in the field as in the Court of the Cloud Tree, she spoke with a fervent clarity that reached us all. I remember seeing how dark her face was and thinking *this is a queen*. The blood of the Kindred Founders ran true in her, truer than in any others of us present on the field. She was a fierce and blazing paragon of what it was to be human, and we let her die.

"War has come," she told us, "and with it the promise of slavery beneath the iron boot. These highlands are our home, and our last refuge. There is nowhere now to retreat except into the waves of the salt sea, which is as certain a death as any. We here have taken arms to stop the evil that advances on our people; we here now are the noblest of the Twelve Tribes, we who have joined together as the Kindred in founding our nation, to protect it in its direst need."

It has been thirty years now since that battle on the blue hills. I do not remember all the rest of what she said that morning, but it filled every eye with tears and every heart with purpose. She spoke of the Iron Host's rapacity and blasphemy, of our families and histories and the great names we would win that day. She called upon the sky goddesses Aseya and Naeva and on the little gods of the land. Three rabbits were sacrificed by the High Priestess: one for Aseya, one for Naeva, and one for the little gods of the battlefield the Queen had chosen for us.

The position the Queen had chosen could not be flanked by heavy infantry like the Iron Host. The hill we stood on was broad and wide, with wet land to one side and forests to the other. Into both we sent the youngest and oldest of the tribes, to nettle the enemy with their slings and javelins.

The Circle held the centre of the line, like hawks to the queen's eagle. We too wore bronze cuirasses, greaves, and vambraces. We too had painted leathers to protect our joints from questing blades. The rest of the southern tribes stood with us, hide shields held close, bronze-tipped spears at the ready. So few of them had armour of their own that the army glistened like polished mahogany in the sweating sun.

And the Iron Host? You who were born too late to know the world that was cannot *imagine* what it was to be faced with them. Grey they were, rank dead flesh encased in dull grey armour. Their shields were gore-brown, their heretic standards brutal and dreadful. There must have been five thousand of them there, advancing in unison to the sound of drums. It was whispered their drums were made of human skin, but we scoffed at that. Human leather is not durable enough for such work.

But they advanced, step by heavy step, spears in hand. We held our ground on the hill, sandalled feet tickled by the blue grass. At Queen Marena's command we launched our javelins high into the air. They arced up against the clear blue sky and landed amid the mass that threatened us—one volley, two, and three. If I strained, I could see men and women in the marshes and at the forest's edge attacking the Host as well, but nothing stopped them. Nothing slowed them.

The sword? Everyone wants to know about the sword. Of course the Queen bore *Noon*! It was the finest blade the highlands ever produced, long and wavy, sharp as a tinker's mind and bright as the midday sun. This was the moment when she drew that legendary blood-thirsting sword from the cow-skin scabbard at her hip and bade us advance.

Standing still to receive a charge is madness if your troops are green. You are not the rock before the wave but the sand. Had the Iron Host been smaller, we would have danced the long spears around them. But they were too many. Had the men and women who came to fight alongside their queen and her Circle been veterans too, we might have bound the shield-wall tighter and risked the impact. But we were too few. And the Queen was wise—you cannot these days know the wisdom of those the empire slew—and she knew that the tribal warriors needed to get their blood up to fight at their best.

We charged down that hill like the anger of the goddesses themselves. We of the Circle launched our last javelins—I saw mine pierce an ironman through the eye and catch in the shield of the man behind—and then we drew our swords and axes to begin the bloodiest work any highlander ever turned their hand to.

I remember, even now, how I *smelled* the Iron Host. They smelt of old milk gone sour in the gourd, of blood and rotting meat. I realised as I slew the first of them they were not dead—yet. Their unnatural flesh bled as freely as ours when blades hacked home. It was only as their brown shields took on new crimson life that I realised what the greatest part of their stink was. It was the gore upon their great iron-rimmed shields—gore in truth, not just in colour. Under the hot sun, it produced a miasma so foul that not a few of the tribal warriors alongside us choked and fell to be crushed amid the press. To be crushed by the snaggle-toothed rim of one such shield, and stain it with their lifesblood.

It was a battle to end all battles, for none who lived through it would ever dream to fight again. The air was heavy with screams and blood, and my arm was soon heavy with the ghosts of a myriad slain. They hung from my limbs, desperate to be sent on to the sky, but I had no time for rites. This was plains war, a battle far greater than any I or anyone else had ever lived through.

Slowly, we were pushed back up the hill. But that was part of the plan. We had fewer warriors than the Iron Host, but the young ones and elders in the marsh and in the woods knew that they should begin to attack them from the flanks and the rear as soon as possible. While we kept the Iron Host's attention—and their shields—to the fore, they would drain their strength missile by missile.

I know you know that isn't what happened. We all do; this is the famous part! When the twelfth tribe—the Camran—arrived and attacked us in the rear. When they chose silver over honour and traded our lives for their fortune. That the Queen's own tribe should so dishonour her struggle! It is enough to make men weep. Well it was. And it should still be!

It was no battle after that. The southern tribes were slaughtered by their kinsmen and the Iron Host. The Circle stood by their queen until the bitter, bloody end. The Camran would not face her, for fear of what vengeance the goddesses would inflict upon their oathbreaking souls. They ran from her gaze and from *Noon*, preferring instead to hunt the weaker loyalists in the marsh and in the woods. The Iron Host enveloped us, encircled us, and one by one they whittled us away.

By now so many ghosts demanded deliverance from me that my arms would barely move, and yet I had to move them to protect my queen. Then a heavy iron-rimmed shield crushed my left foot, and I stumbled. A lance that would have slain me pierced Eleya Six-Fingers in her side. Yes, the Six-Fingers who rescued eight-score cows from the Bracun single-handed. I splintered the shaft with my axe, but it was too late for both of us. Her throat was opened by another lance, and her life spattered me as an iron blade opened me crosswise from rib to thigh.

We fell both of us before the Host, and I held Eleya Six-Fingers' hand as she died. I wept in rage that I could not still fight, and in pain when a hobnailed boot broke my right leg in the advance. The last thing I saw before I was trampled was *Noon* still flashing high and bright against the Iron Host.

What did you expect? Some magical escape? Some treacherous exit from the field that had claimed so many of our countrymen's lives? No. See here, how the bones in my foot are still misshapen. See here, my scars from blade and boot. And here. And here.

I awoke on the field in the cold moonlight. I was alive. I was alone. There was silence except for the cawing and gnawing of the carrion birds. I wept when I saw our queen. She knelt amid her Circle, unbowed even in death, undefiled by an army more interested in victory than desecration. The Iron Host had marched on, leaving me near death to mourn my queen.

The ghosts of those I had defeated still howled at me. I gave them their rites in ill temper, panting in pain between each verse. Not one grey-iron shade blessed me as it left. When I released the last, it was like a boulder had been lifted from my ruined body. I breathed—really breathed—for the first time since I had awoken. And then, holding in my spilling guts, I inched my way toward my queen.

Somehow, under the cold moonlight, her beauty was as great in death as in life. She looked at peace, as one would who has borne a great burden too long and done their best to the end. I nearly wept to see Naeve's light reflecting from the gold woven into her braids. Her lips were red as blood—red with blood. And she smiled there among the ruins of the battlefield, pierced nine times nine times, slain by the horrors of the Iron Host, betrayed by her own royal clan for petty advancement.

I lay at her feet and I wept. For her, for the highlands, for the Twelve Tribes, and for myself, alone and gravely wounded in the blue grass.

Yes, that was Harrowed Hill! Of course it was, what else would it have been? Did you think there was some great conspiracy to move the battlefield that burned down our world to replace it with the steaming shadow that consumes us now?

Yea, it is a shadow! Our cowry shells were crushed, replaced with iron drachma and clay pennies from far-off lands. The goddesses and their priestesses were murdered on the holy island of Siqithi not three months later—I barely escaped from my sickbed as the Iron Host stamped to war and the Camran carried their brands. The faithful hung from the trees like horrid fruit until Aseya and Naeva washed the whole of Siqithi to their bosom in a storm that was the harbinger of the Nine-fold Winter. Even you must remember that long famine.

⸻

The Camran. They did the Host's foul work everywhere but the honest battlefield. They deserved what happened to them when the Iron Host retreated to its empire's heart instead of its fringes. Quislings and traitors to the highlands all. I breathed deep of the longpipe the night their shields were burned, let me tell you.

But it doesn't matter any more. The old world, the real world, died with Queen Malena at Harrowed Hill. All honour fell with her, all colour and joy in the world. I alone survived of the vaunted Circle, and would that I had not. The Iron Host did not only tread their hob-nailed boots on our injured and our dead; they stamped their imprint onto the living soul of our nation, and it will never be the same again. We still spend iron money, eat black iron bread instead of fresh corn loaf. We ruled these hills for a hundred generations, and it only took one for us to give it all up for fellow feeling with the invaders.

Pah, you think that statue of the Queen fools me? It looks nothing like her. She fought on foot with the rest of us. Where did this fashion of putting leaders on horses come from, eh? We never had any when I was young. The Queen's no more there than in that high and mighty foreign tomb they raised for her when the Terror ended.

No, the Iron Host are gone, but I hear them march in every spavined word you youngsters croak. I'm away come dark when the roads are clear. I have my grain, I've sold my furs. I shall go back to my little thatched hut by Harrowed Hill and tend the grave I dug all those decades ago. I dare say I shan't leave the blue grass again, for I am old now. But the Queen will be forever young, as she should ever be.

Long live the Queen! Long live the Circle! Long live the Kindred Tribes!

TAREYA SOFTSTEP was a member of the Circle of Queen Marena, a knight of the Kindred and a highland patriot. Renowned for her ability with the long spear, Tareya famously rescued the Verdigris Bull and slew the four-eyed bandit king of Whisperfell. According to the records of the royal Camran clan, she died at the Battle of Harrowed Hill in the last year of the Old Kingdom (also translated from the Kindred tongue as "The World"). Her birthdate is unclear.

MATT MORAN doesn't talk about himself in public that much, but in private he plays guitar, collects and paints models, cooks, and bakes. As a freelancer, he translates French and writes games, articles, and stories in English. Amongst many other things he has survived a hernia, crucifixion, and being thrown head-first from a horse. He likes sitcoms, sci-fi, spies, and fantasy, and is delighted his fiancée loves him nonetheless.

IRON OUT OF VULCAN

An account by Scout,
as provided by G. Scott Huggins

I rode between two drum-fed National Guard .50 caliber machine guns housed in a plexiglass ball-turret, mounted on the back of a microbus shell welded over the bed of the six-wheel Ford F550. Again, I peered through the iron crosshairs at the black speck in the distance.

Definitely a motorcycle.

"We have a friend," I called through to the cabin. "Watch for IEDs."

"Oh, sure, I'm on it," Mina deadpanned. But she signed to Eric, which was good enough. Paul moved forward, too. It was a standard trick. Make your target watch you, and they might miss your roadside bombs. Best way to take us out, unless they had spike-strips.

"Who is it, Scout?" asked Mina. "Not Them, I take it?"

"She'd be swearing more," Eric grunted.

"I don't know," I said. Not Them. A gang out of Chicago or Dallas, maybe. The remnant of a Mexican drug cartel, perhaps. The *bandidos* had tried taking Criptown from us last summer. Cost us a lot of good Crips and ammo we couldn't spare.

Some thought we shouldn't call the place "Criptown." Worried it might scare potential recruits off because of the old gang name. As if any of *them* had got out of the cities before the nukes hit.

I looked back at the cycle. We could only hope cycle-boy's friends would decide Vulcans weren't worth the carnage.

I looked at the empty road ahead. Somewhere out there, a radio had called for us. Was it a trap? Some Vulcans had disappeared. Maybe this cyclist's friends had set us up. Or maybe someone else had. Or maybe—just maybe—the signal was genuine. It was a chance we would have to take, if we could find them.

We needed people desperate enough to live free.

Paul and I picked our way up the trail. The motor I'd retro-fitted to my chair whined against the shallow grade. Even with shock-absorbers, the jolting and the need to keep scanning the fields around us made my neck ache. There had been no sign of anyone yet. The noon sun beat down.

The man stepped out from behind a cluster of trees and scrub at a bend in the trail.

I pointed my 9mm, slewing my wheelchair around, to point cross-slope. Put the fuel-cell drive in neutral. If we had to run, I trusted my arms more than it. Paul knelt beside me, rifle aimed. But the man approached slowly, holding his shotgun by the barrel.

"Don't shoot," he called, in a choked voice. "I'm Sid."

I pointed my pistol skyward. Paul stood. "Come ahead," I said.

He approached. In his fifties, I guessed. He stared at Paul and froze.

I've never quite known what disconcerts people most about Paul: the fact that his spidery frame and thick glasses make him the least-likely bodyguard in the world? Or perhaps it's the manic, toothy grin he always wears. Or his silence.

"You called us," I said. "How many of you are there?"

"Two," he muttered.

"Where's the other one?"

He beckoned. A girl emerged from the trees with strawberry-blonde hair and long limbs. Tall for her age, maybe fifteen. Behind her, holding a pistol, came a young man, his face drawn with an inward look I knew too well.

Around his head clung the Halo.

Even after two years, I felt fear claw at my throat before the sick uselessness washed it away. After all, I was in no danger. It was the kid who was doomed. I turned on Sid.

"We can't help him. He's got the Halo. It's too late."

The boy's mouth worked. He ran his fingers through his hair, batting at the shell of light. It parted beneath his fingers, but stayed locked around his head, unmoved. His sister bit her fingers.

"How long?" I asked.

"Since yesterday," Sid said. "Since I called."

"There was a man," the boy whispered, looking at me. "On the edge of town. He looked at me. Just for a second," he pleaded, as if that made a damn difference. He batted at the Halo again.

"Please," he rasped. "Get it off. I can't stop seeing it. Even when I close my eyes. And the noise never goes away." He plugged his ears, but it made no difference.

"I can't get it off," I snapped. "No one can. I'm a Crip, not a god!" Sister glared at me. I glared back. "He could go any minute, and when he does, he will Halo both of you." I let that sink in for just a moment. "I need to talk to your son, right now, before he dies," I said, as calmly as I could manage. "While I'm talking, you watch that Halo. If it starts to fade, run as fast as you can. You might make it."

The boy's face was milk white. He couldn't believe what was happening. They never could. And I hated talking to the dead.

"You have one choice," I told him, looking at him through the Halo. "One. Wait and be Broken. Or walk away and use that gun."

Sid's breath caught. His daughter looked like she was ready to hit me. The boy was breathing fast now. Raggedly. "You," he said. "You do it, please."

"I can't!" I said. "They do *not* tolerate violence against Them. If your father shoots you, that Halo takes *him*. If I do it, it'll kill me. Only you can make the choice. They can't punish that. But when you Break, They will use your body to put your family right where you are. And then everyone you've ever known."

The girl screamed. "No!" I thought she was screaming at me, but Paul let out a low, ratcheting growl, the only sound he could make, and aimed his AK at the brush.

From behind it, five men stepped. They all wore stained jeans and shirts and carried assorted rifles. Sid turned, and his grip on the shotgun tightened. His son's mouth set, and he raised the pistol.

"Sid," the biggest man said. "You son of a whore. You been in touch with the gov'ment!"

Sid stepped between his daughter and the men. "Stay back, Jeff. We're leaving." He looked at a smaller man. "We ain't done nothing to the Freehold, Theo. And I've got Casey to think of."

Theo put a restraining hand on Jeff's shoulder. "I'm thinking of Casey, too, Sid." The look he turned on her made my skin crawl. "I think she'd be better off in the Freehold than with these government serfs. That's why I'm here. We'll keep her safe."

"Keep her safe?" I blurted. "From us? What do you think we are?"

"I know what you are." Theo's voice was smooth. Educated. "You're the government trying to sweep up the last of us who live free as God intended by frightening us with your so-called 'alien' light show, there. So we'll all go be good crippled serfs along with you. Now you get on out of here." He gestured with his gun. "And leave free folk alone."

"You think there's still a *government*?" I shook my head in disbelief. "Your isolation has saved you so far, but now They are closing in. Hunting down the last free humans. "And They will be back. They've found you." I gestured to Sid's son.

Theo turned cold eyes on me. "If They have, it's because you are Their spies."

"Spies?" I said. "They don't need spies! A single one of Them could have thrown Halos over every one of you by walking through town. And They will, when They have this boy and his memories. Not one of you will be able to hide. You think they need *us* as Spies?"

"If you ain't spies, then how come they ain't took you, yet?" asked Jeff, fingering his rifle.

"You really don't know? For the love of God, *look at me!*" I slapped my legs, bound together and strapped to my wheelchair. "These have kept me free for two years, now," I said. "They don't want this body. Paul? Explain your freedom to the men."

Paul growled again, trying to form words. Until it was obvious he couldn't.

"They don't need us. And we can't do anything for Sid's son," I finished. "But we can take Casey with us; keep her free. We can take you all with us, if you'll follow us home." It wouldn't happen. But I commanded a Vulcan squad; I had to try.

"Yeah," said Theo. "I bet. We're not afraid of Crips. Or 'Them.' Or you."

Oh, shit. "You can't shoot—!"

Theo's gun snapped up. I heard a *tack-tack-tack* from behind me, and he and Jeff dropped, writhing. I whirled on Paul. "Don't!" Sid shoved Casey down.

Two gunshots rang out. Sid fell. And his son. Casey screamed.

And the Halo leapt, unerringly, for the gunman. Enveloped him.

He started screaming and tearing at it, but his hands just passed through.

"Stop shooting!" I screamed. Then I buried my face in my knees. Anything to be a smaller target. Paul was prone, and Casey knelt over her father, screaming.

Another gunshot. The man with the Halo fell, and again it leapt to the shooter. He screamed, was shot, and the Halo jumped again.

"Run!" I shouted. I pivoted, hitting my wheels with both hands. Footfalls pounded behind me; someone was screaming. Then I was racing downslope, using all my skills to keep from skidding or toppling at high speed down the trail. My cycling gloves heated under the friction, but I didn't dare slow. Or look back. I was outracing the footsteps, but the trail curved. Grimacing at the heat on my hands, I drifted around the divots. I heard a growling far behind me. Paul, obviously, but what did he expect me to do? Stop? If I tried, I'd flip. Worse, I'd damage my chair. Gritting my teeth, I tightened my grip on the spinning chrome. Slowed. Tipped. And shot through the bend in the path. Now I seized the wheel-rims and skidded around in a bootlegger-reverse. I snatched my pistol from its holster and aimed up the trail. Paul rounded the corner, glaring. The girl stumbled to a halt after him, gasping, wide-eyed. Paul signed at me with his free hand.

"Yeah, well, you're an asshole, too! What if you'd shot someone with a Halo?"

He signed again: *Last one ran away. Haloed. Got the girl. Thanks for the help.*

I ignored the sarcasm. "That's the end of that town, then. I guess we won't be back." Not even for the ammo, dammit. The guy with the Halo might do anything. Even try to ambush us.

The girl—Casey—was just catching her breath. "Theo... you shot him. What about my friends? My Mom?" she finished in a sob.

I looked up at her. Tall. She'd scooped up her brother's pistol. Perhaps not completely hopeless, then. Maybe. "If they call us again, we'll invite them in. That's all we can do."

The tears started to flow. "Jamie... Dad... they're dead. They killed them!" She buried her face in her hands.

I looked around. No sign of people, but the Van was still a ways off. I rolled my left wheel over her foot. She yelped, and Paul grabbed her gently by the shoulders, turning her to face me. She stopped crying.

"If you've lived with your family this last year," I said, "that's better than most people. They'd want you to stay alive. And so do we. So we move." Cold, but true. All we had time for. I forced my arms into motion, and we continued down the road.

It was mid-afternoon by the time we reached the Van. I pushed harder. Mina called, "Who's there?"

"Vulcan," I replied. "Let's go."

Eric helped Paul lower the turret-ramp. I backed onto it with my motor, relieved it hadn't been damaged in the chase.

Before They came, I'd never wanted a powered wheelchair. Pushing is how I move. But you can't hold a gun while you push, so I'd retro-fitted my Crossfire all-terrain with a motor I could engage at will. Also, pushing upslope sucks.

I clamped the chair in. Swung the guns down and rotated them. I moved with oiled, electric precision: steel guns and iron sights. Now the Vulcans were running as we should be. Below me, Casey huddled on a seat, our only reward for the long drive out. Sid had said he'd had a family. That would have been a real prize: we needed people, desperately. Even Sid alone, a man who knew how to use a gun and work a radio, would have been useful. Instead we got a weeping girl.

And we didn't even know how she'd choose.

An hour later, she was whimpering. Trying not to let it out, but it leaked through anyway. Paul was already as far from her as he could manage, but I could tell it was getting to him when he started rocking.

Paul was a specter. They used to say "on the spectrum," but I have to admit specter sounds a lot more badass. Mina had tried speaking to Casey earlier; that's when she'd huddled back here. If I didn't talk to her now, she was going to send Paul into sensory overload.

"Paul, take watch," I said.

He nodded. Relieved. Opened the sunroof and started scanning the horizon. I rotated the turret front, dipping the guns as far as they'd go. It left me hanging in my harness a little, but I could talk through the hatch.

"Hey," I said. "What's up? Mina upset you?" Hard to believe. Mina's sweet.

Casey looked up, mouth working. Finally, she just whispered, "Her eyes."

I sighed. Sometimes Mina forgets the blank, triangular skin grafts over her eyesockets. I tried to keep it matter-of-fact. "Yeah. Mina's blind, so she handles the radio. Eric's deaf; you can learn to understand him, but it takes time. Paul's nonverbal autistic, but he'll sign to you once he trusts you. And I'm paralyzed. You know what we are, right?"

She nodded. "Dad told me. You're all… you're all—" She couldn't even *say* it.

"Crips. And we're headed to Criptown. Formerly Wichita." Unimportant enough They never had a use for it. Like us.

"I don't want to go," she cried softly. "I just want to go back home where it's safe."

I leaned forward against my chair belt. "We can keep you alive," I said. "And free. But there's no safe places anymore."

"Theo said *he'd* keep us free," she said. "Two years he said it, and we survived. The War. Them. It was hard, but… then yesterday, Jamie came home with that… *thing*… on him." She was crying again. "What was it *doing* to him?"

"Preparing him," I said. "We think it was… calibrating itself. Adjusting. So it could take over. Break him. Once a person has a Halo, they've got about eight to twelve hours. Then the Halo fades, and they're gone. Forever. One of Them. It throws out more Halos. As many as It can. On everyone It sees. Even us, briefly."

We didn't know much about Halos. About Them. We knew killing anyone with a Halo put the Halo on the killer. If the shooters were Crips, it killed them. You didn't dare shoot until after the victim became one of Them. And if you missed, you still got a Halo.

If one of Them saw you try it, you got a Halo. Or killed. They had other weapons. They might be watching, anytime. If you killed one of Them, you had to be sure—dead sure—It was alone.

"You've had a Halo?" Casey asked.

"Once." I remembered the nauseating colors, the disorientation, and the buzzing that filled your body, *pulling* at your mind. And then it went, leaving only a wave of revulsion. I'd never been able to tell if it was my revulsion… or Theirs.

"They don't take you," she said. "Not Crips."

I nodded. A cold, stony emptiness reached for me. I pushed it back. "Not us." I looked out at the empty landscape. The empty highway. No cars. No people. Not anywhere. Just Them, wherever They'd taken Their stolen bodies to. None of us knew. We only saw the ones They still used to hunt free humans. Old Professor Pyke said ninety-eight percent of humans were Them, now. Minus the two billion dead in the War.

The War had lasted a whole week. I remember it started right after the President's body, one of Them, told us to remain calm. It would all be over soon. They used our cameras. Our journalists. That was the day after They landed. But They weren't quite all-powerful.

In every nation, they missed people. Important people. People in missile bases. The hidden men tried burning Them out. Moscow, Washington, Los Angeles, London, Beijing. All gone. But it didn't stop Them. There were always more. They walked through a city, and the next day, it was Theirs. They found those who hid and left. To wherever They go. With everyone.

Except us.

"Why?" Her eyes burned into mine. Pleading.

I turned away, blood boiling. I'd seen it all before. Did she think I hadn't? "I told you. They don't want us." But they'd make do. A lot of people we'd called "disabled" before were gone. People missing fingers, even a hand. Legally blind. Mild CP. But us… "We're useless to them." Just like we'd always been. To our own race. Our own families.

Before They came, other people had stared at us in pity. Afterward, they stared through their Halos, envying. Us. Why not us? And then their Halos had faded. And they were gone. And we had remained free.

"And what do I do?" Casey asked.

"There's only one thing you can do," I said.

Now she looked sick. "Did… you—?"

"No," I said. "I caught something called transverse myelitis, the summer I turned eight. The next day I couldn't walk anymore." *Fifteen years, now.* "Paul was born the way he is, and Eric caught meningitis when he was three. Mina's the one you want to talk to. She came in after a year of hiding in the bush. The surgeons took out her eyes and sealed her sockets." That was much easier than keeping them open for prosthetic eyes that no one had the time or energy to care about. "Now we're a Vulcan team."

She looked at me. "Vulcan? Like… Mr. Spock?"

"Vulcan the forge God," I said. "Roman. Crippled by the god of the sky. Vulcan builds. Vulcan works iron." I patted my guns.

"'Iron—Cold Iron—is master of men all,'" Casey said.

"What's that?" I asked.

Casey looked up, quoting:

"He took the Wine and blessed it. He blessed and brake the Bread.
With His own Hands He served Them, and presently He said:
'See! These Hands they pierced with nails, outside My city wall,
'But Iron—Cold Iron—is master of men all!
Iron out of Calvary is master of men all!'"

"It's something Theo used to quote," she said. "He said it was about Jesus. And iron."

Jesus. A lot of people had prayed to Jesus. "I'll stick with Vulcan, thanks."

"What's it like?" she asked, looking away. "Being paralyzed?"

I'd expected that question. "It's like everything below my waist has been turned to clothing. When you were a kid, and you took your arms out of your sweater sleeves? Ever try to move the sleeves? That's what it's like. Like being withdrawn from your legs."

"Forever." Casey curled in on herself. She said, "I think I'd rather die."

"That's always an option."

Her head jerked up.

I met her glare. "Do you think I haven't heard that before?" I snapped. "People said that to me even before They came." Then Paul yelled, and I surged upright.

This black motorcycle was back on our tail.

And he was growing larger. Accelerating. Good. I was ready to kill something. And ever since I'd first felt the twin triggers of a pair of .50s beneath my thumbs, I'd been good at this.

"Bandit closing on six. Warning shot!" I called and pressed the thumb triggers. Unlikely to hit at this distance, but it would show we were serious about being left alone. Two rounds of tracer shot out with a double-thump.

The bike accelerated, and six more riders split out from behind him. They'd been hiding in his silhouette.

My blood ran cold. "Seven bandits, hot!"

"Why don't we go faster?" yelled Casey.

On the edge of perception, I heard Mina say, "Trust Scout, she knows her stuff."

My sight bracketed the leader. Almost in range.

"Guns Twelve!" Eric's mushy roar cut through my trance.

It was the worst possible time. The cycles were just coming into range. They'd cross through it and be able to use their handguns in seconds. But Vulcans trust each other. We live or die on it.

I triggered a burst, spinning the turret around. My spine itched as I turned my back on the foe. I forgot it as soon as my guns swung front.

The old pickup must have been accelerating up the shoulder. Eric was leaning out the window, firing his Colt ACP. The truck cut us off; the men in its bed gripped the roll bars for dear life. Two clutched flaming bottles in their free hands. Molotov cocktails. One of those would turn the Van into an inferno.

The third man sighted down his pintle-mounted light machine gun.

It was a duel I was going to lose.

There was no time for aim or subtlety. I squeezed the triggers, and twin thunder pealed. Dimly, I heard Casey scream. It shook my foe. Just enough to freeze him for a second. I zeroed in, hosing the bed with tracers. It shredded the three men like rag dolls, the pickup veering away, fell off into the left shoulder. On fire. No time to watch.

I swiveled the turret again. It seemed to take forever. Paul was leaning out the window, firing bursts from his AK. A steady *tack-tack* of deadly leaden hail echoed off my bubble.

Paul had gotten two. I could see the remaining five helmets, the scarred and tattooed arms of the cyclists. The barrels of their guns spat fire. My bubble starred. Cracked.

I let loose a hail of tracer, stripping two riders off their bikes; they wobbled and spun out. Eric stomped the gas, and I cursed as my aim was thrown off, at the same time blessing the widening distance. Widening sharply. The three remaining bikers were braking.

Through the ringing in my ears, I heard Casey say, "They're giving up." Then she burst into tears.

I didn't have time for that. "Are you hurt? Casey, are you hurt?"

She shook her head.

"Damage report? Injuries?" I called.

"Radio's okay. Eric's cut, but it's not bad," called Mina. "Shrapnel or something. We'll need a new windshield." She paused, letting Eric sign into her hands. "We're still rolling."

My gut relaxed. As long as the radio, engine, and wheels held out, we were a live team.

Then Paul moaned and fell back in the car. Blood ran down his shirt. His face was white. "Shit!" I cried.

"What is it?" Mina asked, and I could tell she was scared, because she looked back in the cabin, as useless as that was.

"They got Paul," I said.

"Stop the car?" Mina asked.

"Hell, no," I said, reflexively. There could be a second wave closing in. I couldn't leave the turret. Mina was useless as a field medic; Paul couldn't tell her what to do. And Eric couldn't stop driving.

Then Casey was with him. "Sit up. Sit up and stay awake. Awake!" She sat him against the side of the van. "Where's the medical kit?"

"It's the red toolbox up front," I said.

Casey got it and expertly cut Paul's shirt off, padding and binding the wound. "Don't think it's in the chest cavity," she said, voice tight. "Still in there, whatever the hell it is. He's bleeding, but I think I've got it slowing. How long until… Criptown?"

"Two hours, safe driving," Mina said.

"How much can we shave off that?"

While Mina and Eric consulted, Casey caught me looking at her. "This isn't the first gunshot wound I ever saw, you know. What do you think life was like back in Covenant? We had to fight sometimes. You have to know what to do, or people die."

I nodded. "Yeah. That's right. People die. You okay?"

"I'm fine," she growled back. "Two hours will be close, though."

"Mina," I called, "Tell Eric pick it up to sixty." We'd just have to risk IEDs. I didn't want to lose Paul.

Casey flashed me a look of approval… and then her face melted in horror.

I turned to see what she was looking at.

It was Them.

The aircraft hung above us, silently. A small one. I could see one of Them sitting inside the bubble-nose canopy. The rest of the craft was a delta wing, like half a kite. Bulges in its hull housed engines, I guessed.

It flashed three amber lights.

"They're stopping us," I said.

"We can't stop!" Casey cried. "We can't."

"We have to," I said. "If we don't, it'll burn us all from above." We all knew it could.

Eric began to slow. "No. No," Casey chanted, like a litany.

Slowing to meet It, I felt myself withdraw from all of me. Paralyzed all over. Stuck in the chair, stuck in the turret, stuck in the car. And Casey, outside, saying, "No. No."

She was dead. Maybe us, too.

We stopped. It landed.

"Help me. Scout, help me. Hide me. Do something. Please."

But there was no place to hide. If she ran, she'd have a Halo before she got ten feet. We'd probably all get Halos. But hers would stay.

So? She has her pistol. She'd said she'd rather be dead than be a Crip. They can't stop her from killing herself. Once the Halo takes her, she'll have hours to make the decision. Hours. But she won't.

If there was anything They had taught me, it was this:

People who said they would rather die than be one of Them were lying.

People who said they would rather die than be a Crip were telling the truth.

They'd rather be slaves forever than be like us. What should I do? Shoot her in the spine? We'd tried that. Crippling people. Most of them killed themselves later. Others went into shock forever.

Should we risk our lives for that? For one more spineless brat who begged for life, but wouldn't pay the price to live free?

Too late. It was on the ground now.

It got out.

Reflexively, I swiveled the guns to cover It. It came on, not deigning to notice. Its gray skin hung in folds. It was dirty. It wore nothing. It had been male.

It stopped twenty feet away.

"Everybody out," It rasped. "In-spection."

"No. No." Casey drew her pistol. Pointed it at the door. "I'm not going out like that. Not like Jamie."

"I can't let you do that." I drew my own pistol. Pointed it at Casey. "You shoot It, we're all dead."

Paul painfully heaved himself erect. Signed, *Maybe*. Coughed. Gripped his AK. Pointed it. At the side door. *Alone*.

It looked alone. But if another one was watching? How could you ever be sure?

"You'd risk it? For her? She doesn't even have the guts to be a Crip!"

"She's what we came out here for!" cried Mina. "She saved Paul!"

"It will kill us all. All of us and her."

"I know!" cried Casey. "I know."

It raised Its voice. "In-spection. Out. Now." And Halos bloomed around It.

Casey fired. Then screamed. Her right foot was a ruin. She struggled to breathe. To take aim. At the left.

I'm not sure whether Paul or I fired first. The pistol in my hand barked.

Casey screamed and writhed in agony.

Paul was shooting through the door. It fell, twitching.

I spun the turret on the ship, ripping heavy tracers through the light airfoil until it shivered apart and fell heavily off its legs. Wrecked. Then the Halos struck.

I was dizzied again by the pulling, sucking buzz, the hypnotic lights. I felt a menace. Directionless but vast. Poised to kill, for an endless moment.

Then it was gone. The Halos swarmed in the darkness of the van. And then they dissipated. Gone. Dead? I'd never know. I just knew that the bullets in both feet had convinced the Halo that Casey wasn't worth having.

I don't remember dragging myself through the tiny hatch. I just remember making shushing noises and giving the morphine shot while Eric and Paul tightened the tourniquets below her knees.

"That's a hell of a way to join a Vulcan squad," I said.

Her eyes wandered. Her voice was breathy. "The only way I had left. You shot me."

"So did you."

"Is it gone? All the way gone?"

"All the way." I tapped Eric. "Get us out of here. Get us home."

He nodded and jumped for the wheel.

"Hurts," she said.

"The morphine will hit soon."

"It won't ever stop hurting, will it?"

I looked out at the passing scenery. At the dwindling plume of wreckage in the distance. She'd live. They'd take her legs off at Criptown. At least at the knee. She'd probably have phantom pain. Most of the amputees did. But I didn't think that's what she meant.

"No. It hurts to live. To build." Maybe it always did?

"Okay." She drifted into a doze. Soon after that, the lights of Criptown were on the horizon. We were home. All of us.

SCOUT is a young woman who lives in Criptown, an enclave of physically disabled humans who have banded together to save what of human society they can after Earth has been invaded by Them, an alien race that appears to have no other motivation than to take over human bodies for use as hosts. Scout has been paralyzed from the waist down since she contracted transverse myelitis as a child. She's part of a Vulcan team: a squad of specialist foragers who go out looking for valuable hardware and people to bring back to the colony.

G. SCOTT HUGGINS grew up in the American Midwest and has lived there all his life, except for interludes in Germany and Russia. He is responsible for securing America's future by teaching its past to high school students, many of whom learn things before going to college. He loves to read high fantasy, space opera, and parodies of the same. He wants to be a hybrid of G.K. Chesterton and Terry Pratchett when he counteracts the effects of having grown up. You can read his ramblings and rants at The Logoccentric Orbit and you can follow him on Facebook.

ART BY Ariel Alian Wilson

ARIEL ALIAN WILSON is a few things: artist, writer, gamer, and role-player. Having dabbled in a few different art mediums, Ariel has been drawing since she was small, having always held a passion for it. She's always juggling numerous projects. She currently lives in Seattle with her cat, Persephone. You can find doodles, sketches, and more at her blog www.winndycakesart.tumblr.com.

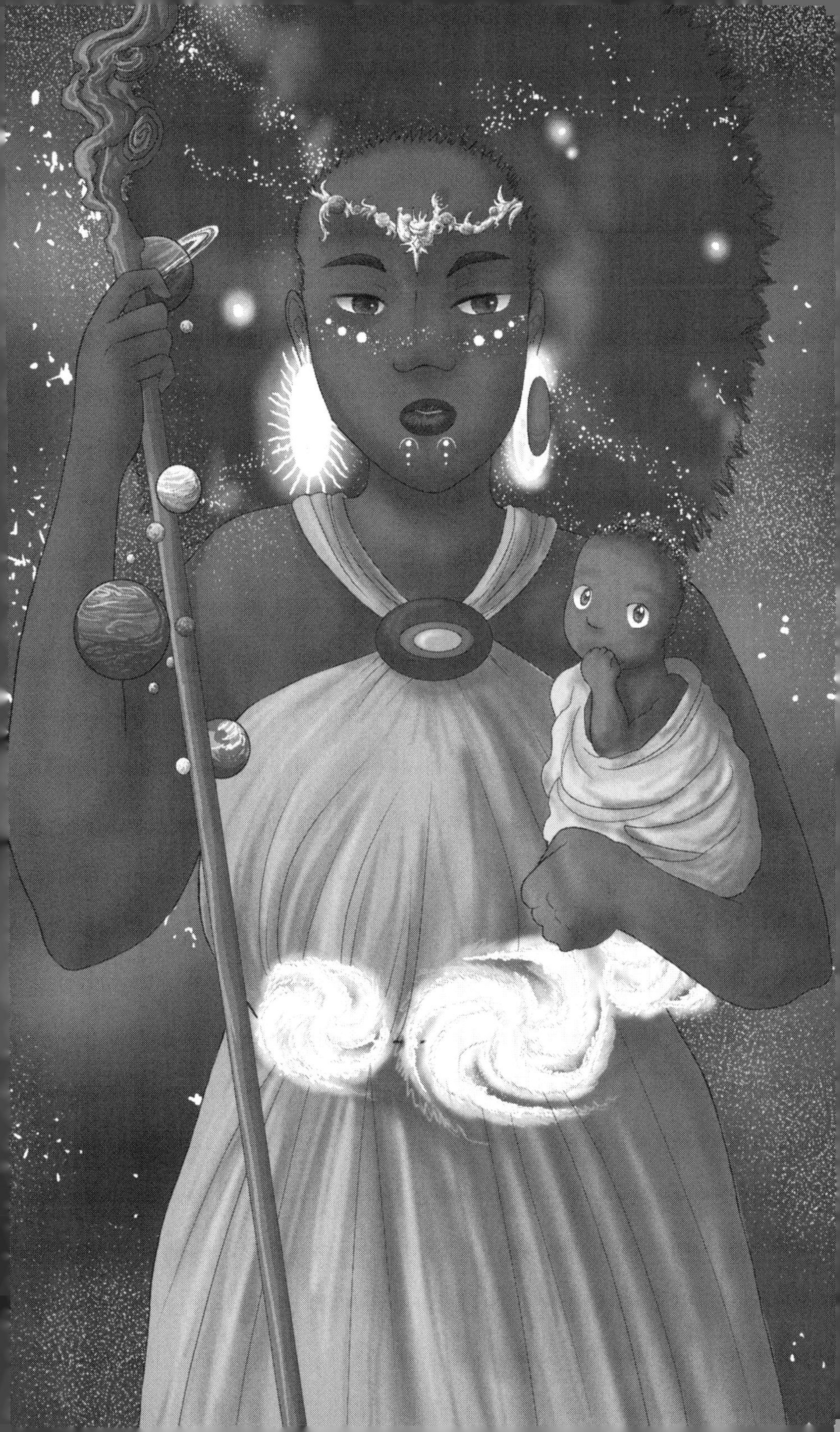

THE DISHONORABLE
GOD

An account by Rajani,
as provided by Priya Sridhar

My mother often said I was lucky to be alive; most baby girls in the kingdom of Anga were. She made sure to remind me during her black moods, when my brown face and sullen looks displeased her.

Because my father had eight sons before he had me, and because he was the king, I was not considered a burden, though I was called "the dark one", "Rajani". My dearest younger brother Vrishakethu attached himself to me. He insisted on playing with me, and on having me read his favorite stories. As a result, I learned how to master the art of dice and to read simple texts. Amma allowed this, because watching Vri kept me in line.

I had to redeem my dark face and feminine body by honoring my elders. Amma taught me how to keep house at a small palace, how to scream at the servants and cooks so they did not steal the gold bangles or kitchen scraps, and how to pay for tile repairs. The money I was not allowed to handle directly, but I had to watch Amma make the payments and check her figures. I learned how to keep quiet and order tea when her noble friends were invited for afternoon gatherings.

Then the war started, the war between my father's side and the Pandavas, his mortal enemies. Father packed his sword and instructed Amma on what to do if he lost and Duryodhana fell. Something about "taking care of Vri and Rajani."

"What does he mean?" I asked, when Amma's black mood had faded that night.

"He's arranged for you to have a *swayamvara* after the war, so you get married properly," Amma explained. "But that will take years to arrange. As for Vrishakethu, he will be educated in the arts of war so he can become a proper man and prince."

I thrilled on hearing my news. A *swayamvara* was a ceremony in which a woman chose her husband, which meant I could have any man I wanted. I'd be away from my mother, away from her disapproving looks. One of Duryodhana's sons or relatives, a Yadava prince…

"Why can't I go and be a man now?" Vri asked, following us. A quiver and bow hung from his small shoulders, and he puffed out his chest.

"You're too young," Amma told him. "Thank Surya for that!"

At this, my thrills faded. My older brothers and I weren't close, but they made sure to tell Amma they loved and respected her.

"Too young?" Vri murmured. "But will we be too young after the war?"

"I don't know," I responded, as I walked him to his bedroom. "Maybe after the war when Appa has won, we'll be old enough to make them happy, if it takes years to battle."

"Who do you think is going to die?" Vri asked. "The armies are big. Will Appa and everyone else die?"

"No one from our family," I responded. "We're good people. We honor the gods."

He went inside his bedroom and shut the door. Few lamps were lit at night along the walls; there were just enough dim flames.

The sweepers and kitchen servants were still up; I heard their *saris* and *dhotis* brushing against the floor as I walked in plain *chapals*, brown sandals. The stairs had wide, beige steps, and I had to walk carefully so as not to slip. In the dark, the walls seemed pink and brown, like curtains that covered the windows during the hottest days. Stone saints were carved near the ceiling, various devas and demons locked in eternal battle. Their eyes followed me.

I went to the altar we kept for Surya, the sun god, and Ganesh, the victor over obstacles. After lighting incense for good luck, I washed the idols' feet and offered jasmine garlands to adorn their necks.

"Please end this war soon," I said. "We are honorable people, and I have not abandoned my duties. The god Krishna is fighting for the other side, but he has shown true valor and compassion. Please let my father and brothers return home, victorious. Lead them from darkness unto light and righteousness."

Since before I was even born, Appa wore armor that protected him from all harm, which he claimed he'd worn all his life. Before he left for battle, however, a Brahmin beggar came and asked for the armor. Appa took it off, as well as his earrings. He *never* took them off, not even for mealtime. In return, he had received a huge, glowing white mace. When I asked Appa what had happened, he patted my head and told me he had packed his armor for safekeeping, and sped off in his chariot.

Surya's idol sat on his chariot of six horses. Ganesha sat cross-legged, a man with an elephant's head and a potbelly, sitting straight up. Jasmine petals gleamed white against the cold metal. Incense smoke gathered in the air.

Appa never lied to me, so I believed him. I must have dreamed about him surrendering his armor. No sane man would do such a thing.

The war with the Pandavas lasted eighteen days. A messenger named Kamdev with a stained white turban brought us the news. Amma told me not to treat him as an equal, but in time, I came to greet him with his favorite dishes, and to make sure the servants washed his feet.

"Thank you, Princess Rajani," he said during one trip. His soles were ragged and callused from walking.

"There is no need to thank me. I only try to be hospitable," I replied. "It is my *dharma*, my duty, to see that you are comfortable."

"If only other royals were as gracious as you," he said.

"I'm not more gracious," I replied. "I am merely more aware."

Amma bristled when she heard my words. She blathered, but I ignored her.

Kamdev brought bad news with each succeeding day: all eight of my brothers fell; the wicked Arjuna had killed three of them, and laughed when splitting one of their heads. After hearing that, Amma doubled the offers to Surya and Ganesha, asking for my father at least to survive the battle. He had not fallen yet, and hope surged within the three of us. She stripped off her jewels and fancy clothes and wore coarse linen dresses, serving penance and drinking only water. I would've done the same, but she told me to keep away from her.

When Arjuna's son also fell in battle, cut down by thousands of soldiers, I slipped Kamdev one of my bangles as a reward for the good news and watched Vri practice at his sword work in the courtyard, while the peacocks roamed beneath our feet.

"I'm going to join the war when Appa sends for me," he said. "And I have to be as good as everyone else."

"Don't tell Amma," I remarked. "She wants to make sure one of us survives. She'd kill you if you went to battle."

"She wouldn't kill *you* though," he pointed out.

"That's because I'm unwanted, Vri. Amma would rather if I had died a long time ago."

He stopped swinging. The yellow courtyard tiles were chipped beneath his feet from many hours of practice; I reminded myself to replace them, on a day when Vri was out hunting.

"That's not true!" he cried out. "She doesn't wish you were dead!"

"She says it practically every day," I replied. "She says if Appa had been less merciful, my body would be in the river with the other dead girls—"

He grew pale and replaced the sword in his sheath. His palms grew sweaty.

"It's not true," he repeated. "And I don't wish you were dead. You're my favorite sister."

"I'm your *only* sister." I tried to smile.

"All the more reason to make you my favorite." He offered me the sword. "Do you want to try?"

I hesitated; women were not supposed to pick up weapons. But I saw Vri's good intentions, to include me in his games, to offer the love that Amma didn't give. The sword blade was light, surprisingly, and I weighed it in my hand. It bore carved Sanskrit characters in the hilt, to signify "protection" and "victory."

"Hold it properly." He corrected my grip. "Don't be afraid."

I let him boss me around for the good portion of an hour, because it gave us control. Then I read to him in the afternoon.

More horrible news came on the last day of war: Arjuna and his charioteer Krishna, rumored to be a god's avatar, had killed my father by deceitful means. His body lay beneath a charioteer's wheel, where he had lost his bow and arrow, and Krishna had urged Arjuna to fire on Appa's unarmed form.

A cold chill went through me when Kamdev brought the news. I still gave him a small necklace as a reward, but all day I shivered and shook. Vri threw up in the lavatory. And Amma…

Amma's eyes gained a deranged blankness. She dressed as usual, and ordered people around. Each day the blankness grew, and the chills in me increased. Kamdev managed to soften the blow by talking of Appa's victories, and how only eight survivors of the war remained.

"The war is over," Amma repeated. "Our kingdom is forfeit."

I didn't dare send Kamdev out again and insisted he stay. Another messenger arrived, directly from the Pandavas. He told us not to worry about the funeral expenses.

"Why not?" Amma asked.

"Kunti, the Pandavas' mother, asked them to pay for the pyres."

"What? Why would she do such a thing?"

"She claims Karna is her eldest son." The messenger locked eyes with my mother. "He is her child by Surya the sun god, whom she left to drift in the water. Thus, he was the Pandavas' eldest brother."

I did not reward this man anything but my look of shock. Amma was twice as shocked.

"His brother?" Amma shrieked, losing her decorum. "My husband Karna was a Pandava!"

"The Pandavas' mother Kunti has confirmed it," the messenger said.

Amma shrieked, demanding answers. The messenger answered him the best he could. Appa had known before the war, but he had chosen to serve his friend Duryodhana rather than take the crown as the eldest. He had taken his secret to the grave.

My father could've had Duryodhana's kingdom, I thought. *He could have been powerful.*

"This makes the Pandavas your honorary uncles and Draupadi your aunt," the messenger told me. "That is why they are hosting the funeral for your father and your eight brothers. They wish for you to attend."

"Not my two *living* children," Amma said sharply.

I couldn't agree more. My father had been alive, and vibrant; seeing his corpse wrapped in white and burned on a pyre, as well as the corpses of my brothers, would haunt my dreams. Vri didn't need to see such a scene either, when he was so young.

Amma packed that evening. She could only take white for the funeral, and no jewelry.

"I want you to promise one thing," she said. "Take care of your brother while I am gone. He has no one else for him."

"I promise," I said. "I love Vri."

"My baby girl," she said with tears in her eyes. "I am so proud of you."

My body filled with unease, more so when she gave me a hug. She had never said she was proud of me, ever.

The last messenger brought the worst news; he could barely say the words. Amma, out of grief and respect for *sati* tradition, had thrown herself on Appa's funeral pyre.

"Unto her last decree, you are now Regent of Anga," the messenger told me. "Until your brother comes of age, you are the Queen."

I stared at him. He stood in his white turban, apologetic and awestruck that a girl with a dark face could wear the mark of nobility. Then he handed me the copper plate that declared me Regent.

Vri holed up in his room. Every time a servant visited, he yelled at them to go away. I went to his room, and knocked. He opened the door for me.

He kept trying to hide his tears behind his hands. I held him, let him dirty my nightdress, and cried with him.

I am Regent, I thought. *I promised to take care of him. But who will take care of me?*

For days afterward, looking at ceremonial fires made me choke. I forced myself to attend to the Brahmins who came seeking alms, and to the priests who attended the ceremonies. The ministers and I talked of political affairs, which I later had to read up on in the private library. At night, I smelled charred bones in my sleep and could not hold down more than rice and lentils.

Vri saw me looking over various copper plates with written script one day. The copper plates recorded bills for the pension expenses and messages from abroad.

"There will be no *swayamvara*," I said. "We can't afford to host so many princes."

"But Rajani, if you don't have a *swayamvara*, who will you marry?" he asked with wide eyes.

"I don't know," I said. "Perhaps one of the ministers here; they are of the right caste, and most of them are loyal to us. Maybe I'll just stay in Anga and help you rule, until you come of age. We have to plan your coronation and invite noble guests to come and witness it."

Vri's eyes widened. He sat down next to me and began going through the plates. "But... what if what *she* said comes true, and we have to surrender? Will we lose our home?"

We looked around the palace, at the walls that had remained polished. We hadn't called Amma by name in days; the mere mention made my stomach writhe.

"Well, that saves us on coronation expenses," I remarked.

Vri didn't laugh. He shuffled through more copper plates and helped me with the more difficult language. "Would you ever do what Amma did?" he asked. "Throw yourself on a pyre?"

I looked at him, and I realized how young he was, however old he claimed to be. "Never," I said firmly. "I'm not going to leave you, Vri."

He leaned against my shoulder. A servant walked in, announcing Kamdev had returned. He had resumed his duties, and he didn't ask for any rewards. At my request, he'd take handfuls of copper to the marketplace to buy vegetables for the orphans and widows who could not afford to eat.

I went to receive Kamdev; he had washed his feet and sat with a sober expression. The servants had given him new clothes to replace the ones torn from traveling, so his skin could breathe through soft cotton.

He bowed his head; he had lost much of his hair. Wrinkles gathered around his small blue eyes.

"Please tell me you will not deliver bad news," I said.

"Unfortunately, I must deliver it," he said. "The Pandavas are traveling to Anga to pay their respects for your family, as your honorary uncles and aunts. Krishna will be coming with them, ahead of time, to serve as a peacemaker."

A moment passed between us. Kamdev looked sorrowful. I put down my coconut water.

"No," I whispered.

"Yes," he said.

"Is there any way to delay them?" I asked. "Perhaps they can wait a couple of weeks, until we settle this coronation business and know if we're losing the kingdom or not."

"No. Krishna made it clear that he will arrive in a few days, to negotiate matters with the Pandavas. He will make no delays, having just spoken with Duryodhana's parents. I'm sorry, Princess Rajani."

"Regent," I corrected him, feeling chest pangs. "Can we ask Krishna to give us time then?"

"No. You cannot refuse the gods' demands."

That night I lit incense in our private shrine. The idols felt cold as I left more jasmine around their feet. "We must not be good people," I told them. "But my father was honorable in battle, my mother honorable at home. What did we do wrong?"

Krishna arrived within a few days, on a magnificent chariot drawn by six white horses. I would have liked to house him in a pit of thorns, but sacred hospitality had to be observed. He was housed in the white Southern Palace, which gleamed in the sun.

"I hope you are well, Queen Rajani," Krishna said. "Your family has been through a lot."

I said nothing, staring at the blue-skinned god who had enabled my father and brothers' deaths. He had a pleasant smile and wore his golden helmet with a peacock feather poking from the center to symbolize wealth. Yellow robes adorned with bracelets and earrings matched his helmet, and he wore hunting boots with no dust or mud streaks on them.

"Where is your brother Vrishakethu?"

"Hunting trip," I responded. "Homeless bandits have been robbing some of our subjects, and my brother decided to track them down."

"That is a shame," he said. "I would have liked to talk with him."

Vri's angry face loomed in my head; he had demanded to stay with me. I had pushed him into the chariot and placed the reins in his hands. As a child, Krishna had tamed water serpents, bulls, and elephants; had killed his uncle at the tender age of twelve for trying to kill him in turn; and held a mountain with his fingertip. I did not want to know what he would do to my brother.

"The Pandavas do not wish to conquer Anga," Krishna said. "It is a small kingdom compared to what they have won."

"Then what do they want?" I asked.

"They want to make amends. They want to care for you and your brother, and to beg your forgiveness."

My eyes narrowed. I could not pretend to like this god or man, and I could not pretend to smile.

"Arjuna in particular is haunted by what he has done and what he has said. He knows he has done wrong to your family."

"You must be joking," I said. "My *father's* family never mattered to self-centered *kshatriyas*."

He stopped talking. The pleasantness vanished from his face, but

I didn't beg for an apology. Now that Vri was gone, I had stopped caring.

"The Pandavas are not self-centered," he said.

"They mocked my father all his life for being a charioteer's son, despite the fact that he really wasn't, and Yudhisthira even mocked him for it when he died." My voice turned cold and angry. "Draupadi did the same when he competed for her hand, saying he was below her. My father was ten times the man that any of my so-called uncles were, and he would have lived if not for you and Arjuna."

"I accept that responsibility," he admitted. "But it was the only way to win the war. If Duryodhana had won, he would have brought wickedness to the kingdom."

"Duryodhana offered kindness to my father when no one else did," I remarked bitterly. "You claim he has faults, but he gave my father a kingdom in exchange for friendship, and you also helped kill him with deceitful means."

"I did. There was no choice; Duryodhana was not kind to anyone else."

I glared at Krishna, who looked unperturbed.

"We're not interested in forgiveness," I told him. "The Pandavas have already taken our father, our brothers, and now our sense of security. They cannot take our forgiveness as well. If they had any consideration for us, they would leave us alone or take the kingdom away if they want it and let us travel to a faraway land."

"Arjuna is hurting," he said. "So are Yudhisthira and Bhima. Yudhisthira has even considered giving up the kingdom so he can live his days in penance."

"That is his choice to make."

He seemed surprised by this, but I felt so numb and angry.

"I convinced the Pandavas to break the rules of combat," he responded. "I ordered Arjuna to strike your father down when he was unarmed; the blame for that death rests with me. You should not take out your anger on them."

"I have nothing to say to you on that," I said. "You have to live with what you did. But you didn't convince them to insult my father for being who he was, and for being honorable. They did not fulfill their *dharma* as *kshatriyas*."

"They are all sorry."

"Then they should've asked my father for forgiveness *before* the war," I responded. "When he was alive. They only feel wrong because it turned out they were related by blood. Suddenly they develop a conscience?"

"They have always had a conscience." He shook his head. "Are you seeking revenge on the Pandavas then?"

"Who has time for revenge?" I cried out. "We just want to be left alone! I just want to rebuild our lives!"

"They can help you," he said. "*I* can help you."

"We can take care of ourselves."

He looked surprised at this, but he regained himself. "I told your father who he was, and what he could do," he told me. "Blame me for his death, since I am responsible, but he also had his choices to make. If he weren't so honorable and loyal to Duryodhana, following his *dharma* while Duryodhana violated his, then he would still be alive."

"Is that what is meant to be learned?" I asked bitterly. "That honor and loyalty do not matter?"

"No. But he was too loyal and too honorable. A bad person can do good things, and a good person can do terrible things."

"Then we are done with good people who do terrible things," I said. "Including the Pandavas. I have a kingdom to run, and I cannot spare forgiveness for my father's murderers and bullies. Neither can Vrishakethu. We will not seek revenge, but we will not provide peace of mind either. I ask the Pandavas to look inside their own hearts and ask if they know it is wicked, why they spoke words that cannot be taken back."

A moment passed between us. Krishna's eyes, opaque as gems, were lucid and serene, but his words sounded threatening. "I understand you and your brother are grief-stricken and righteously angry. You are orphans and forced to grow up so quickly, with you becoming a Queen Regent and Vrishakethu crowned so young."

"What do you mean?" I asked.

"While running a kingdom, how well can you take care of your brother?" He pressed. "You can care for his material needs, but he will need to become a warrior and a proper king. You cannot teach him that as a woman."

"There are tutors," I replied, hiding my shock at this realization. "Many gurus would educate a young prince."

"Gurus are not easy to find, and I have seen few flock to Anga to teach a prince in the art of war. Drona was the best guru for such a task, and he has fallen."

"That was because Yudhisthira lied to kill him," I said. "*You* told Yudhisthira to lie."

"If you refuse to forgive, Arjuna may easily claim that since you are a young girl, you are not fit to take care of a young prince. He can easily take Vrishakethu to raise him as a foster son."

Whatever color had remained drained from my face. I tried not to retch after swallowing a mouthful of coconut water.

Krishna's expression remained solemn. He reached with both hands in a plaintive gesture. "It will be easier that way," he urged. "Think of it. You can receive whatever funds Anga needs for its kingdom, and for yourself. Your brother can receive all the tutelage he needs to become a proper *kshatriya*. You won't be alone."

They're going to take more away from us, I thought with disbelief.

"No law would allow for a murderer to take his victim's children."

"There are laws for it," he said. "Your courtiers may easily agree so as to keep hold on Anga and its subjects. And if you think I am dishonorable during wartime, I can be even more so during a time of peace. It would be for your own good, and for your brother's."

It took me several minutes to respond.

"I shall need to think then," I said. "I will consider your terms."

They'll take away Vri, treat him badly, I thought in a panic, pacing around my room. *I'll lose him, I'll lose him too.*

Vri wouldn't be back until evening. Krishna was waiting in the guest palace; he would insist on a response at tonight's meal. I either had to surrender my brother or my hate.

I had assigned several ministers to look up king's decrees about child custody; so far what they had found seemed to agree with what Krishna had threatened. Worse, the laws also mandated that daughters also became foster children for their uncles. Krishna had thrown his dice well.

I can't lose him. Not my brother. That means forgiving Arjuna and the Pandavas, allowing them to heal while we remain broken.

I sat on my bed and buried my face in my hands. Tears leaked out of my eyes.

The gods won't help us. A god is working against us. I'm on my own here. I need to figure out what to do.

I can lie. I can make Vri lie. We can make them feel better, but we'll know the truths in our hearts.

What if Vri doesn't agree to lie about forgiving our uncles? What if he demands a fight?

What if I'm not convincing enough?

I swallowed. Normally I hated lying, especially when Appa held honor and honesty in high respect. But now that rules had been violated in war, a lie to keep my brother safe seemed small.

So why does it feel huge?

In the afternoon, I ordered a chariot and set out with a driver. I changed from my fancy *sari* to a simple green tunic and trousers. The ministers had orders to accept other messengers and to house them.

Krishna was lounging in the palace garden, sipping wine. He saw me leaving, and his eyes widened. There was only so much that powder and dark eyeliner could cover. Before he could call or make any sound, I ordered the chariot driver to leave. Bronze wheels drove up dust.

The horses were brown and white and in fine condition with their hairs combed. I offered them sugar cubes and patted their snouts. The driver was young, with a small mustache and a golden chain across his chest.

Charioteer's son, I thought. *They meant that as an insult when they called my father that. But it was Krishna as a charioteer who won the Pandavas their battle.*

Cows and stray dogs roamed the busy streets; the chariot stopped as a stray herd of cattle marched. When a young maverick with clipped ears blocked the road, I stepped off with a bag of gold coins.

"There's a man there," the driver noticed. "Some drunk on the road."

"Really." I wasn't feeling charitable, but no one else had paid attention to the toothless, bearded wreck. "We should help him."

I ordered several men to pile him into the chariot and walked him to the nearest inn, paying the innkeeper to give him a bath and a room for several days.

The innkeeper was a portly man with a curved nose. His large hands took the coins I offered.

"You are like the old Queen," he said. "She also used to be generous."

My eyes stung. *Am I going to become like her? Stingy and hard-hearted?*

"Thank you, Princess," the old man called. Two young servants bathed him and tended to the sores on his back. "Please stay."

I shook my head, gave a tight smile, and walked on. He didn't see the perturbation that troubled my brow. The driver did, however.

"You did a good thing, Queen Rajani," he said. "Perhaps you should stay—"

"I did what any decent person should do," I said. "Come, let's keep traveling. We'll check on him on our way back."

He continued to navigate the small chariot to the city's outskirts, and I directed him. This path I hadn't traveled often, only when I felt at my lowest, because the rocks were harsher on the wheels. The horses' ears picked up the roaring that we heard, and the various splashes.

In time, we came to the river's edge. At this time of year, the snow from the mountains had melted, making the river stronger. Dead leaves skirted on top of the water.

I ordered the chariot driver to stop, and to give me a few minutes, and to stand a distance away.

"I need some time to think," I said. "For that I need privacy."

He eyed the river nervously. The water looked far from shallow, and the current swept along as fast as a stallion.

"I'm not going to do anything stupid," I told him, with more sharpness than reassurance.

"Help! Help!"

We jumped. Someone upstream was floundering and flopping in the river, barely keeping his head above the water. It looked to be a small child with a high-pitched voice.

Racing back to the chariot, I grabbed the whip from the driver's seat and ran to the river's edge, lashing it out. The first time, it missed the person floundering in the water, but I flicked it back and let it loose again. The person caught the end of the whip, and I dug my *chapals* into the moist ground, pulling back. I felt the driver from behind wrap his arms over mine, so we could pull the person to safety.

After a few straining moments, we got the figure onto shore, and pulled him out. It wasn't a child, as I had thought, but a small golden monkey with a curled tail. He smelled awful and sneezed. He also cried out prayers of thanks to the gods in a high-pitched voice, in between sneezes.

A talking monkey, I thought while fetching a horse blanket to wrap the small beast. *Why am I not surprised?*

"Thank you." The monkey coughed, shivering. "I do not know how to repay you."

"You don't have to." I turned to the chariot driver. "I am sorry for the whip; I will pay for replacing it. Could you build a fire?"

The driver nodded, his expression tight and amazed.

I picked up the monkey, trying not to wrinkle my nose, and moved farther away from the riverbank. Soon a pile of kindle and dung cakes blazed on the ground, and I moved the monkey closer to it. The smell started to fade.

"If it's all right for me to ask, how did you end up in the river?" I asked the monkey. "Did the current catch you? It can be strong at this time of year."

He huddled in the blanket, absorbing the fire's orange flames. When he spoke, he was sheepish. "To stop you from jumping in."

"What?"

"I saw you were coming here," he said. "To the river, where many bodies float. You are not feeling well. A lot jump in."

I found myself bristling. The monkey shied away, sensing my crossness.

"If I were going to drown myself in the river, I wouldn't take a chariot driver along who could pull me out and serve as a witness!" I snapped. "And I wouldn't anyway, because I promised to never leave the Crown Prince alone!"

The driver looked surprised at my outburst. I was clutching the ruined whip and glaring at the small creature, which was damp and warm and perturbed.

"Then why did you come?" he asked. "You fear the river. I can smell fear when you walk, and when you look at the water."

I took a deep breath. *Do not blame the simple-minded creature.*

"I come to face my fears," I told the monkey. "My mother often said I would have ended up in the river if not for my father's mercy. So I come here to understand the river's rage."

The monkey sat in silence. I pulled away and stared at the horizon, seething with anger and confusion.

What kind of idiot would assume I would kill myself when I am feeling at my lowest?

"How did you know?" I asked suddenly.

"What?"

"How did you know I was coming to the river? You were upstream, because the current was moving fast. You wouldn't have seen me coming ahead of time."

The monkey bowed its head, wrapping its tail around itself. A golden hue seemed to rise from its fur, like the first pollen of spring. If I hadn't been so tired, hands red from straining to pull the monkey out, I would've let my jaw drop in surprise.

"I honestly thought you needed help," he said. "I wanted to ease your pain."

"That is kind," I said stiffly, "but I don't think you can help me."

"Why not?"

"The people who caused my pain are either dead or under the protection of a god. You can't contradict the will of the gods, if they wish for certain things to happen."

The monkey locked eyes with me, and the golden hue became more solid. By instinct I looked away, as did the chariot driver, when the hue exploded into bursts of light.

"Not all gods have the same will," Surya the sun god said. He stood regal, in robes of white and yellow, with a golden spiked helmet.

The chariot driver fell to his knees, mouth open like a fish.

"You appear, Lord. I am humbled," I said, kneeling and not caring for the dirt on the ground. My body went through the motions of prostration, but my mind became numb and cold.

"Stand and rise, Rajani. You are my grandchild and the eldest heir to Anga."

A sob hiccupped out of me, and I swallowed as much of it as I could.

"You said I couldn't help you, but I can." He opened his hands in supplication. "What do you need?"

I bit down the urge to sigh. Hope felt painful and scary, like the pricking of a dagger. "Can you take away my hate of the Pandavas, and of Krishna?" I asked him. "Could you do that for Vri as well?"

He stared at me. I supposed it was an absurd request.

"Few things can break Krishna's will," I said. "He wants for me to forgive the Pandavas for what they have done, or they will take away your only surviving grandson. Even if they didn't have the rights by law, Krishna helped the Pandavas win through dishonor and deceit. He would find a way to give them what they want. I'm too tired and worn down to fight. I just want to keep my brother safe."

Surya stood, pondering. Then he waved his hand. The tiny fire became a roaring blaze, as great as the flames that burned for sacrifices.

"Krishna's will did not succeed because he is a god," Surya said. "Your father died because he chose to accept his fate. Sit by the fire. This is a story you need to hear."

I sat next to it; the chariot driver did the same, struck dumb.

"Arjuna is the rain god Indra's son, and thus Indra vowed to protect him, when he learned that Karna meant to kill Arjuna in revenge. I knew Indra would come in the guise of a Brahmin, and ask for your father's armor, that which kept him immortal." Surya looked solemn. "I warned your father, and I hoped he would forego his honor to save his life, but he cut away his armor."

"I saw him give it to the Brahmin," I said, still feeling numb. "I didn't know. I *ought* to have known."

"How could you have known?" Surya asked. "You didn't even realize who you were talking to until a few minutes ago. You didn't even realize the beggar you helped off the street was Indra in disguise."

"What?"

"The man you helped," Surya said. "He wanted you to stay, hoping to dissuade you from going to the river."

I had assisted the king of the gods, thinking him to be an ill old man, and I hadn't realized. Anger replaced the numbness. "Why would he care?" I burst out. "I'm not someone worth worrying about."

"That's wrong," Surya said. "You are a queen, and my granddaughter. And you care about people."

"Then why?"

"Indra had reached the same erroneous conclusion that I had reached," Surya said calmly. "He thought you were going to drown yourself in the river and was hoping to interrupt by appealing to your good, charitable nature. It didn't go the way he wanted it to go."

"Do I really look like the type to drown myself?" I asked with irritation.

"We misjudged you." Surya sat down next to me. "I understand you're going through a rough time, Rajani, but things will not remain bleak forever."

I made a strong effort not to laugh with bitterness. It was easy for him to say, watching from above while riding in the sun chariot. Time passed more slowly for mere mortals, though, and I was trapped within the moment.

"Gods have many great powers, but we cannot change the will of the human heart," he said. "Do you really want to let go of your hate?"

I looked into my heart. I thought of the insults tossed against my father, of my mother's blank eyes. I thought of Krishna threatening to take away Vri.

"I want to keep hating them all," I admitted. "Because if I stop hating, I'll forget what they did, what they could do. They haven't paid for their crimes."

"Most of their children have perished thanks to Ashwathama's murderous actions," Surya said, "And Gandhari, Duryodhana's mother, has cursed that Krishna's family will fall apart the way hers did. The Pandavas know they cannot take back the words they said or bring your father, their brother, back from the dead; there is no magic that can erase murder or cruelty. And when they make the long walk to heaven, they have to burn for their crimes in hell."

He understood. By all gods, he understood what was so horrible about forgiving. I wiped my eyes before tears could come out.

"I can make it so the Pandavas would never want to take Vri, to face the consequences of their actions," he said. "If that is what you desire. But eventually Krishna will have them do so, to fulfill their destiny."

"What destiny?"

"Vri will travel with Arjuna when Yudhisthira performs the Ashvamedha sacrifice, and he will witness Arjuna's death by the snake people's hand." Surya bowed his head, and I could see the campaign in my head, with Vri commanding a chariot and ignoring Arjuna. "That has to happen."

"I can't protect Vri if that happens," I said miserably. "Women don't go on military campaigns."

"You can't physically," he said. "But you can remind the Pandavas what they did, to see if their atonement is true. They say that it is, and they mean it, but you have to test the tatters of their honor."

And then it came to me. My father had been Vri's age when the Pandavas had started to bully him, and when Drona refused to teach my father. He had borne his armor then, since he had been born with it, but it hadn't shielded him from the insults or the curses.

"Thank you," I said. "For talking with me. I thought I was alone."

"If you ever need my advice, I will always be here," he promised. "You don't have to do this alone."

In the evening, Krishna approached the chariot as the driver and I returned, sober and grey-faced. His face held palpable relief.

"Queen Rajani, it is a pleasure to see you—"

"I didn't go to drown myself," I interrupted sharply. "I've decided to forgive the Pandavas."

He withdrew. I changed into clean clothes, found a portrait of my father, and brought it to the court's blacksmith, explaining what I wanted. He nodded, knowing Vri's measurements and said he would do the final fitting.

Vri returned early the next morning; he told me how the snake bandits were starving, and so despite himself he had promised them grain and meat from our winter storage, giving them several of his arm braces so they could survive the week. I told him he did the right thing. Krishna tried to talk to my brother, but Vri glared and bristled.

"I don't respect gods who cheat," he said to Krishna. "Our father would be alive if not for you. Don't pretend to be pious and righteous."

Krishna grew solemn and said no more. I sent Vri to the smithy, to try on what I had commissioned.

In my dreams, I felt warmth from Surya's crown, and murmurs of reassurance. I soon could eat more than rice and lentils.

The Pandavas came, and we hosted them. Arjuna was as blue-skinned as Krishna was, and he met no one's eyes. I pointedly glared at him, and treated Bhima and Yudhisthira with cold hospitality. Krishna eyed me, but I said I had decided to forgive them, and we would swear an oath of no vengeance.

Then Vri entered. Arjuna choked on his wine. Yudhisthira turned pale. Bhima rubbed his eyes. Krishna stared with anger.

My brother wore the armor I had commissioned, an exact mundane replica of what my father had worn up to the day he had surrendered his armor to the beggar. He also wore heavy earrings and styled his hair so it fell just beneath his ears. In this manner, he resembled how my father looked in the portrait. To the Pandavas, they reacted as though they had seen a ghost.

"Good morning," he said, glaring at the Pandavas. "I suppose I have to be gracious."

"You are Vrishakethu?" Arjuna asked in a hoarse, choking voice.

"That I am." He sat and poured himself some wine. "I was just riding *chariots*."

They looked even more uncomfortable, perhaps recalling how they mocked Appa for being a charioteer's son. I remained impassive and talked with Vri about his negotiations with the snake bandits. Eventually the Pandavas managed to make small talk, asking Vri about Anga and how he enjoyed the city. Arjuna made a strong effort to be kind, and to appear cheerful.

"You said you had decided to forgive them," Krishna said in a low voice.

"I said I would," I replied. "But I did not promise to forget."

"You are spitting poison in the gods' faces," he said. "No one wants to remember a bitter queen."

"I don't care if I am remembered," I said. "I only care about my brother's safety. I am remembering what you are capable of, without being hateful."

Krishna's gaze became hard and impenetrable. Vri talked with Arjuna in sullen tones, but they managed to discuss combat and snake bandits. I listened, and Arjuna spoke no cruel words in my brother's presence. It was clear Arjuna and the other Pandavas would not dare adopt a child who reminded them of their eldest brother. They had too many ghosts to placate.

"You have thrown your dice well, Queen Rajani," Krishna

conceded. "Perhaps Yudhisthira will become king after all, and stop being haunted. It is good you forgave him."

I did not answer. There was too much work to be done to worry about others' guilt.

That day, I dedicated an orphanage to Surya, one where parents could deposit their young girls instead of drowning them. I put out an advertisement for teachers and caretakers. When I lit incense in the orphanage shrine, the walls glowed with pleasant yellow, and I could hear my grandfather's approving murmurs.

"Lucky to be born," I whispered to the walls. "And others will now be lucky."

REGENT-QUEEN RAJANI is the ruler of Anga, an ancient kingdom in India that was awarded to her father Karna. He was a charioteer's son, but proved to be a competent ruler and revealed after his death to be royalty. She is the only girl among ten children and is the second-youngest. Raised to simply prepare for marriage while also running a kingdom, Rajani finds herself forced to rule in her younger brother's name after war kills her entire family. She fears rivers, but often goes to them to think.

A 2016 MBA graduate and published author, **PRIYA SRIDHAR** has been writing fantasy and science fiction for fifteen years and counting. One of her stories made the Top Ten Amazon Kindle Download list, and Alban Lake published her works *Carousel* and *Neo-Mecha Mayhem*. Priya lives in Miami, Florida, with her family.

CASSIOPEIA, QUEEN OF ETHIOPIA

An account by Cassiopeia, *as provided by Aimee Kuzenski*

Spray on my cheeks, salt on my lips. From the ocean, not tears. Never from tears.

The sea spreads out from my feet like a lace-edged gown, watery silk so heavy, so ceremonial, that I could never rise from the throne on which I sit awaiting the sea dragons.

It isn't my usual throne, but the little torture chair apes it in some ways. Both made of wood, both wide enough to seat two, were they cozy enough to rub elbows.

Cepheus, I think. His absence chills my soul.

I tear my gaze from the expectant horizon to glance to my right where he would sit, and see only my arm tied outstretched to the rough planks with water-swollen rope. I am pinned like a butterfly in my tattered finery, spread-eagled like a bride welcoming her lover.

A bird keens across the water, and I raise my chin, search the horizon again. They will come soon, the dragons and their riders. I would not have it be said that Cassiopeia cowered from her fate.

It is, after all, a fate I chose.

We did not invite the invasion, though the court whispered otherwise. *The royals array themselves as gods,* they murmured behind cupped hands. *Is it any wonder the gods take offense?* As villages fell, rent to splinters by eel-like mounts and green-skinned people, as the boats came back empty or not at all, as the country grew hungrier, the accusations grew louder.

They sit on an ebony throne, they wear robes of linen thick with gold embroidery, they wear jewels in their hair and drink from gold goblets.

Their pride angers the gods!

Cepheus, in his rage, would have driven them from the court. I plied him with wine and soft words until his muscles loosened.

"To soothe the people, we cannot resort to violence." I traced the line of his cheek with one gilded nail. Bright gold against dark skin. "We must meet their fears with authorities they will hear and believe."

My husband's lips twisted. I knew that expression well. "Even if I believed as you do, my love, I would point out that the gods rarely give us what we want."

I leaned back against the many pillows of our bed, my wine goblet hung upon the curve of my upturned hand. "If you cannot believe in the gods, believe in me."

He sighed, but pulled at his reins no further.

We called the oracle to court the next morning where all could hear her pronouncement.

Cepheus and I sat together on our throne before the court, our daughter at our feet. Andromeda sat cross-legged with her cat in her lap, an angry orange monstrosity only she could tame. I touched her shoulder to make her look up at me, to see her heart-shaped face lit with anticipation. The angry mutterings of the court surged and then fell to silence, and she and I straightened our spines to watch the oracle enter the throne room.

The child possessed by the oracle was young, no more than five. Her name had been Megaira a year ago, before she was taken. Now, she had no name.

She walked in with eerie assurance, her small bare feet making no sound on the wooden floor. Her worn leather shift hung to mid-calf, the hem fluttering ragged on the wind of her passing. The temple kept her clean and clothed, but the gods considered any more than that to be hubris.

The oracle stopped before the throne. She looked us up and down, her dark eyes unreadable and old. I felt the weight of my jewelry, the peaked crown I wore.

"What do you ask of the gods?" Her words were softened with a lisp. It was the only element of youth left to her.

Cepheus clenched his hand upon the armrest of our throne but said nothing. The court rustled like a nervous bird.

I laid my hand upon his knee, to let him know I would speak for us, then stood. I stepped around Andromeda with a touch to the soft cloud of her hair and stood before the court. Two guards, bare chested and spear bearing, framed me like columns. "Oracle," I said, raising my hands, palm up to show the gods my sincerity. My bracelets chimed. "We ask most humbly—"

Someone snorted. I tensed, but spoke on.

"—most humbly for guidance. The sea people attack our shores. Why are they angered? What must we do to return peace to our kingdom?"

The oracle blinked her dark eyes, slow and deliberate. Her shaved scalp gleamed in a beam of sunlight. "You must sacrifice."

Murmurs chased around the room while she waited, serene. When they had quieted, she went on. "The royal family has an heir."

The implication was plain. I staggered.

"No!" Cepheus launched to his feet, came to my side to slam the gold-wrapped butt of his spear upon the floorboards. "You cannot have Andromeda." The court chorused agreement; our daughter was well-loved. She was young, she was lovely, she smiled at all who approached her.

And yet, if the gods demanded her...

Blinking, the oracle shook her head slowly. "They do not ask for your heir."

Putting a restraining hand on Cepheus' arm, though my own heart hammered, I asked, "What sacrifice must we make?"

"The throne has an heir." She raised one hand to point at Andromeda.

"It has two rulers." That pointing finger turned to Cepheus, then to me.

"It needs only one."

Now, the court's response was approving, eager. A crescendo.

They are too proud!

Cepheus quivered under my palm, tight as a bowstring, just as deadly. His spear was ceremonial, but still sharp. "No," he said again. "You cannot force us. You *will* not force us, I know that much of the gods."

The crowd roared outrage at his words.

My husband was right. The temple did not enforce such things. Looking out at the court, however, I saw many who *would* enforce them. Men and women crept closer, still shouting, hands clenching into fists. The guards shifted, glancing at us from the corners of their eyes. Considering.

I lifted my hand from Cepheus' arm and placed it flat, fingers splayed, upon his chest. He glanced sharply at me, and I saw vibrancy drain from his face.

"No," he whispered. Then louder, to crest the sound of the court, "No. I forbid it."

I turned my back on our people, brought my lips to his ear. My earrings swung forward to touch his cheek, and he shivered.

"You see them, there behind the oracle. She has given them the gods' answer, and it is the answer they wanted. If you defy them, you will make an orphan of our child." I drew back to see his face whole, that strong jawline, the dark eyes.

He looked over my shoulder, and I saw the calculation that had won battles give him an answer he did not wish to hear. His muscles twitched under my fingers, warring impulses fighting for dominance.

My gaze still locked with his, I beckoned. "Andromeda."

He hissed. "Cassiopeia." There was pain in the sound.

Andromeda came to my side, her brow furrowed. "Why is everyone angry?"

I knelt to gaze into her eyes. "They are afraid, my love." I kissed her forehead, breathed in the sweet scent of her hair, and put her small hand into Cepheus'.

"Cassiopeia."

I stood, faced him square. "And though you do not believe—" I drew a shaking breath. "—I do."

His face went cold and harsh, but he was not surprised. He would not forgive the people their fear, would not forgive the guards their politics.

He would not forgive me, either.

Raising my arms, I faced the court and stepped forward in surrender.

They tore rings from my cold fingers, stripped bracelets and brocade from my trembling arms, reduced me to tatters. They would have ripped the rings from my ears, had not the oracle come forward, that small figure pressing them aside like a shark in a school of fish. She motioned. A man lifted her to his shoulder so she could unhook the heavy gold. Gentle, delicate fingers.

She whispered, soft and approving, "The gods accept your sacrifice."

The court harried me to the seashore. I beat my bare feet bloody on the rocks for them, I submitted to their makeshift throne and the ropes that bound me there. They left, cheering. I did not turn to watch.

The sun sits upon the horizon when the seafolk come. It is almost a blessing, after a day's wait. They proceed around a spit of land to my left, hidden in the glare, and I do not see them at first. I hear them, a keening, victorious call carrying over the water, over the huffs and grunts of their dragons. Lifting my chin, I watch them beach themselves, watch the long and sinuous coils of their iridescent beasts slither in the shallows as a tall naked man with green skin and white hair mounts the rocks alone, a bone dagger in his fist.

His neck is slitted with gills that shift and shuffle as he breathes. The bones of his arms and legs are too long, too thin, and translucent skin stretches between the skeletal fingers and bare toes. I stare at him, mesmerized, as he brings my death closer.

Finally, he clambers over the last rock, turns his blunt head to regard me first with one dark eye, then the other. He warbles something incomprehensible. He raises his knife.

Two swift strokes. My arms fall limp to my lap, tingling as the blood returns to numb flesh. He has done no more than slash the ropes that held me. I gape at him, unprepared for the reprieve. He turns to go.

My heart threatens to leap from my chest. I cannot raise my burning, unresponsive hand to call him back, so I resort to my voice, to royal demand. "What are you doing? Come back here."

He looks back over his thin shoulder and pins me with a blank stare. I recoil back into the rough wood of my throne, away from those dark, fathomless eyes. A small animal scrabbles within the rocks. He warbles again, a fluting sound softer than before, then resumes his journey back to them.

He is gone—they are gone—before I can force myself to rise. My hands, now chafed back to life, cling tight to the rocks I only lately climbed as I make my way down. When I reach the grass, I stagger, nearly fall to my knees.

Why have they let me go? I should be happy. I should be running with light heart back to my husband and child. Instead, all I feel is foreboding.

The royal seat of Ethiopia is close to the sea, but my feet ache and my pace is slow. I do not arrive home until after the sun is well down. The sky is dark, but the city is not.

The city is glowing embers.

The gates have been rent from the walls, broken to shards that stink of smoke and the sea. I stumble over them, leaving bloody footprints on the wood. Beyond, half-lit by guttering fires, lay the shapes of the dead.

The sea people were quick in their work. Businesslike, ruthless efficiency marks every slashed throat and crushed skull. They must have come directly from their slaughter to free me, leaving a trail of blood and viscera in the sea.

I find Cepheus on the threshold of the palace, sword near his hand, eyes empty and lifeless. I touch his stiffening cheek, chipped gold nails against dark skin, before facing the open doorway.

Andromeda lies at the center of a knot of defenders, their bodies rent with horrific slashes from knife and teeth. She is as lifeless as they, her hair matted with dried blood.

I bury her on the far side of the city, beyond sight of the sea. Would that I could bury them all, but I have only two soft hands, one weak body. She must stand for the city, as she would have done had she lived to take the throne.

As I push the last mound of damp soil onto her grave, I hear footsteps. Have the sea people returned to finish their killing? I turn on my bruised knees, my throat tight with a mixture of fear and longing.

It is the oracle, and the anonymous figures of her robed caretakers. I fall back in surprise, my hands sinking into the soft earth behind me. The oracle steps closer, her eyes reflecting the firelight of the city.

I can no longer hold the tears at bay. I choke on what I want to say, and she watches me with the incurious stare of an animal.

Finally, I force the words out. "Why? I did what you wanted, what the gods wanted." My chest feels broken open, seeping with sorrow.

She bows. "Your sacrifice was accepted."

I freeze. "What?"

"Your sacrifice was accepted," she repeats. Her voice is almost blissful. "The kingdom has been humbled, and its ruler fears the gods as she should." Another nod, as if this is a compliment.

My hand clenches in the gravedirt behind me. "You said the gods did not want Andromeda."

The oracle shrugs, an ancient and distant regret in her eyes. "The gods' instruments are not perfect. We did not ask for your heir, but the sacrifice is stronger for it." She dismisses my beautiful dead daughter with a gesture. "You will rebuild, stronger than before, without the sin of pride about your neck." She is serene.

I am not.

My fingers hooking into claws, I lunge forward. The caretakers step between me and my target, restrain me until my screams become sobs again and I slump in their arms. When they withdraw, I see the oracle regarding me with a frown.

"Perhaps there is pride within you still." She sighs. "The gods will watch you."

They leave me alone on the hill, shattered.

My tears are gone now, boiled away by rage.
I am still the ruler of this land. I will go inland. I will raise an army.
I will return at their head to raze the temples. No stone will be left upon another.
The gods are not worthy of our worship, and I will have my revenge.

CASSIOPEIA was queen in Ethiopia when the Greek gods held sway. She is a passionate victim's rights advocate, and is best known for her March for Deific Responsibility. Once an avid follower of fashion, Cassiopeia has shifted her focus to justice, civil leadership, and martial arts. She survives her husband, Cepheus, and her daughter, Andromeda.

AIMEE KUZENSKI is the woman your martial arts teacher warned you about. Her cat was not born hairless; Aimee once shaved her with a single knife stroke and the fur was too scared to grow back. A graduate of the Viable Paradise writer's workshop, Aimee has also narrated audiobooks for indie authors and for the SFF short fiction podcast PodCastle. Aimee lives in Minnesota with her girlfriend and not enough Filipino weapons. You can find more information about Aimee's work at her website, akuzenski.com.

THE WEEPING BOLO

An account by Carmel Agbisit,
as provided by D. A. Xiaolin Spires

I pulled my blade from the pulsating sapphire sponge and swung it in five successive swipes, slashing flesh from a chest, an arm, and at the soft spot above the collarbone. Each time, the sword entered with a sickening give.

They were fake, of course, simply 3-D printed replications of human parts.

Even so, droplets of red danced across the air and fell, leaving me spinning in a crimson shower. With my free hand, I pulled up a *malong*, a cotton tube skirt I had slinked over my shoulder, and waved it in the air, letting the *malong* soak in the bulk of the drops.

My left hand holding the bolo sword was already covered in weeping red. I slipped the sword back into the sapphire sponge, which accepted it with a gentle tug, its *tenegre kamagong* wooden handle sticking up. The sponge drank up the blood like a thirsty babe.

I wiped down my hand with the *malong*, the color of my skin emerging from the wash of red. It was as easy as wiping down spilled *buko* juice from the dark tiles of my training grounds, letting the *malong* fibers absorb and saturate with the liquid.

But I knew it was more than that. The bolo sword never stopped weeping. Even now, the sapphire sponge pulled the blood from the sword into the depths of the Earth, dragged into a deep, wild waterway, coursing away to mountains and farmland.

"Not bad, Carmel," Dayang Nica said, wiping her feet before stepping into the courtyard. Her hair fell to her shoulders, a deep black that matched the gloves she wore on her hands. She grasped a jug, patterned with the stripes of my *malong*. Her footsteps were light, her gestures nonchalant, belying the heaviness of the full jug.

"Not bad? It nearly slipped off my hands," I said.

Dayang poured water over my fingers. The rest of the blood diluted with the water, washed off and drained into the soil, moving toward the coconut trees.

"The bolo sword knows it's not free," said Dayang.

I remembered what my father had said. Strange magic compelled the blade to "remember" the many kills it executed during the war. It wept a continual trickle of red. Everyone in the provinces said it was the blood of the victims, but it had no DNA, no acrid smell of the spilt life source. Instead, it smelled pungent and slightly sweet, like tamarind. No one would dare taste it, of course.

"The moonlight falls upon our grounds once again. Time flows away from us like the Cagayan River. In two days, the *buwaya* winged crocodiles will surge forth from the mountains. The *tandayag* elephant pigs will crawl up from the earth. And the *oryól* snake with the woman's head will emerge from the cracks of stone," said Dayang.

"How can I forget?" I said. "I've only heard it, let's see, one hundred times in the past week. Yes, yes, the monsters of the epic poem Ibálong will rise again. As if I need to be reminded."

I touched my *anting anting*, my amulet. It was warm on my chest, another sign of the epic poems coming to life.

"The gilded chariot will bring you to Ibálong's Bikol."

"That chariot is going to get gross with blood fast. Unless

someone figures out how to replicate that enchanted sponge."

Dayang shook her head. "The scientists could not do it. There is no living compound that mimics it. We have a vacuum compressor and a hose. I think it'll be the best we can do."

To the south, a rip seared through the air and rumbled. I felt the earth shake. Despite my typical steady footing, I tripped and broke my fall with my shoulder.

Dayang pulled me up. "It's starting, sooner than we have thought. Perhaps you should leave tonight?"

"Tonight? But, I'm not ready. And the verses. I don't have them all memorized. And I haven't purified the *anting anting* three nights in a row as I'm supposed to. And the sword—" I steadied myself as the earth rumbled again. To the south, we could see a cloud of smoke.

"You can never get perfect accuracy counting from old calendars. I'm sorry, Carmel, I would come with you if I could. If I bore the *anting anting*." She laughed. It was a sad chuckle. "If I bore it, then, who knows, perhaps I would win. Or perhaps all would be lost." She gestured to the south, which seemed to respond with another rumble. "But, I do not have Baltóg and Handyóng's spirit blood coursing within me. That yellow glow from your *anting anting* tells me you do. And one must go alone—"

Another booming shake cut her short. I watched my mentor's eyes light with determination as she brought her arm down. I followed her gaze to the south, the place of legends.

"Lupaing mabanlik at mayabong
ang kapatagang Kabikulan;
sa mundo'y walang singganda,
sa ani'y walang singsagana.

Si Baltog ang unang taong
sa lupaing ito'y nanirahan
katutubong Botavara,
sa lahi ni... Lipód... nagmula... nag... nagmula..., uh-oh, dragonspit," I cursed. I could never remember the whole poem in its entirety. I barely even spoke Tagalog, the official language. My whole family spoke the regional language of Ilocano, and here I was, trying to dictate what really struck me as a flurry of syllables.

They say there is a power that connects the *anting anting* to the sword. The words draw out that power, soothe the sword from its unending disconsolation. At least that's what Dayang taught me.

Nobody said it aloud, but I knew everyone was disappointed with me. The *anting anting* had chosen me, flashed the appropriate amber that claimed me as spiritual descendent of legendary Baltóg and Handyóng of the Bikol epic poems, but I was never able to master the tongue that the saga was scrawled into for our rehearsals, to guide the power from the *anting anting* into the sword to make it stop crying. As long as the sword kept crying, it could not be held. Blood dripped from it, making it slip and untenable to hold.

And of course the redux of the mythical events had to happen while I was alive. Couldn't they wait for the next generation of heroes?

"Just don't look at the page. Memorize the words, feel them on your tongue," Dayang had said a few days ago, her voice raised. Her neck muscles had bulged and for a moment, I could tell she had lost her classic calmness. Dayang pursed her lips.

But I couldn't memorize it either. Every time I would try to implant them in my head, the words would simply leave once more. They never made an impression. I felt like it was jabber without emotion. It was like reading the ingredients off an instameal *pancit* package, a bunch of letters strung together. The words would simply get tangled.

I shook the image of my mentor out of my head. No need for the pressure now. Just relax, I told myself. At least I was swift with the sword. Fast on my feet. There was that. Even if the *tenegre* bolo risked clattering out of my fingers, whipped away in a river of sanguine fluid.

I felt the wind in my braided plaits, whistling past my ears. The chariot had picked up speed now, its metallic wings flapping against the onslaught of dust. The night had gotten darker, even with the full moon. I knew this obscurity was from the cracking of the earth, all prelude to the Events that were warned by the convocation of Seers.

I tried the poem again.

"*Lupaing mabanlik at mayabong
ang kapatagang Kabikulan;
sa mundo'y walang singganda,
sa ani'y walang singsingsing*—oh forget it!" I cried.

Beside me, the gulp, gulp, gulp of the liquivac mocked me, a methodical, persistent voice I could never achieve with the epic poem.

When I landed, the flying crocodile demons were already snapping at clouds. They zipped around, slower than my chariot, thank the heavens, but still threatening with their rows of teeth.

I grabbed the blade from the overflowing liquivac, letting the blood drip down my arm. I felt the warmth of the *anting anting*, probing, trying to connect.

"*Lupaing mabanlik at mayabong…*" I started to say, then lost focus as the first few of the winged crocodile demons came toward me. The crocodile demons were stupid enough to snap at the shiny blade and not at the metallic wings of my chariot, which were helpless and would have sent me flying to the ground if they were harmed.

As the crocodile demons unhinged their jaws, I knocked out a few teeth, spirit sword blood mixing with dust, dripping all over the metal scaled wings of the chariot.

I felt the spray of crocodile demon saliva gel fly onto my face.

"Gross," I said, wiping the green gunk from my face with the back of my free hand. My left hand holding the sword was getting inundated with the spirit blood of sword victims past. The handle slipped in my fingers as I twisted my wrist and slashed forward to hit the next crocodile demon.

This demon was smarter. They probably let the slow ones hover around the periphery as the first line of defense. This one got under my chariot and clawed through some of the metal. It managed to knock me around a bit, but I jumped off in light leaps every time I felt the blood-stained floor rise. It was warping the chariot though, and it would soon damage the structural integrity of the vessel with an imbalance of spiritual energy.

I swung over to the side of the chariot, my one arm firmly grasping the edge, holding up my whole body. I swung my legs toward the teeth of the demon. The crocodile demon took the bait and aimed its wings upward, pulling its elongated snout up to snap at my soft limbs. The sword thrust went past teeth and past the esophagus and into the mystical beast's belly.

"Yes!" I cried, pulling the sword back, but it slipped out of my left hand and was falling toward the ground. "Oh, *kapre crap.*"

I guided the chariot downward. Even though its metallic wings made a speedy dive, shooting down like a probe, the sword was on a trajectory that would take it perilously close to hitting the ground. Possibly fracturing on landing. Then all would be lost. I couldn't risk that.

Once the tops of trees came into view, I leapt off, caught a branch with one hand and reached out with the other, grabbing the handle. It slipped out of my reach, and I kicked the hilt with my foot, giving me a second chance for a snag as the sword sprang back up. I was lucky. Any of these moves could've left me with a lost limb, but it was times like these where my brawn won over my brain, and I trusted my body.

I sprang forward, grabbing the sword in both hands and landed with a shoulder roll.

The pig demons were on me now. Wild boar demons, to be exact, as large as elephants and causing such a tremor to shake through the ground.

I wished there were a few brave warriors who would pop up from the mountainside to give me a boost, but no, nobody showed up. Of course, like the legends, I'd have to fare through this alone. I groaned as the pig demons snorted, loud and fiery like bugles.

I tried reciting the epic poem again. But if I couldn't do it in the comfort of the courtyard without distraction, how was I to do it while giant wild boars charged me?

Forget it, I thought, as I raced toward them, the sword slipping in my hand. If it slipped too much, I might accidentally slide my palm up the length of the blade, cutting myself, adding my own fresh blood to the well of tears. I had to stop the crying.

I pulled out a dagger. I picked up speed, jumped, pointed my feet up, and slid underneath the belly of the nearest giant boar. It was not very fast. The dagger cut, but its hide was thick, and the move barely did any damage.

I remembered my mother, as I lay sick with passing illness, singing a lullaby to me. My mom had made it up, a story about our homeland. How I was the heroine of my mom's world, a new babe that brought sunshine to the earth. It was before I got chosen with the *anting anting*, before I was declared the sole sufficient spirit ancestor of epic heroes Baltóg and Handyóng, before I had to learn the tales of strong, invincible, handsome Baltóg and sturdy, powerful, valiant Handyóng and recite them over and over.

A tusk came my way and I parried, striking an ear. I put away the dagger. It wouldn't do. The cuts were too shallow.

I thought of my mom's song now and the melody flew from my lips. Could it be? I could feel the blood of the hilt in my palms receding.

Another thought came to me, not the epic poem that valorized Baltóg and Handyóng, but words from my mother tongue, Ilocano, that matched the cadence of the epic poem. Not Baltóg's "great warrior hailing from Botavara" or Handyóng's "fierce chief of the land and manly constructor of the first boat to traverse the Bikol River," but "daughter of fruit vendor owners Macasaet and Taer, a girl who liked to draw, play sports, and collect shells." They never said that in the epic poems.

A lightning bolt flashed from my sword that reached a wild boar demon, and the beast roared as it tumbled over, a tendril of smoke rising from its dead body. The other boar demons startled, snorted, and scattered. A yelp from above as I swung the sword again, and the remaining flying crocodile demons took off, with one screeching, swatting its sizzling tail. My *anting anting* burned in my chest.

"So, that's it? I can go off-script?"

With a bellowing voice, and with a rhythmic chant, I spoke of my sister who had gone off to the city to work in the factories, my brother who taught me how to punch, and my mom and dad who had to travel every year in the summer to meet with fruit growers. It wasn't really the stuff of epic poems, but neither was I, I figured. I shouted of my fear of dark waters of the ocean, my love for mobiles and fractal patterns, and the thrill I got from flying in a chariot, like I had done just moments ago, before I had to jump off.

I was winging it, improvising up some fine verses, and the sword was loving it. Like jazz for cutlery. By the time the human-headed snake demons slithered out, the hilt of the sword was completely parched. Only dried spirit blood caked my hands.

The snake demons prided themselves on being crafty. They hissed lies from their tongues. They hissed them so sweetly you could almost be convinced—did my mother never love me? Did my parents leave every summer to get away from me and my siblings and raise other kids of their own in another province? Better kids that they loved more? Did they want a boy instead to be a fighter and ended up only with—and they laughed, hissing—a stupid girl who couldn't even read and recite?

The long blonde hairs of the snakes trailed behind, intertwining with their slithering reptilian skin. They approached, the words louder and louder, overwhelming my own voice, which was shrinking. The sword was damp with red dew again that coated my fingertips. Doubt flooded me.

Did my sister never love me? Just ran off with a lover in a city to escape my many inarticulate questions? Did my brother teach me how to punch because I couldn't otherwise express myself with words? Was I really as abhorred as they said?

My rhythm faltered. I ran out of things to say. The sword slipped around in my hands. The human-headed snake demons approached, their tongues tickling my scalp. Their breaths hot at my neck.

"I am a flawed but strong warrior from the north. My mother and father are fruit vendors, and I am a fighter and an articulate reciter."

I didn't believe it.

But my *anting anting* was searing hot, and for a moment, I remembered my mom feeding me when I was a child. I remembered how my mom accidentally spilled *sinigang* soup onto my arms. Inconsolable, I cried and cried. My mom held me tight, singing to me, icing down the wound.

The smell of tamarind filled the air as the handle warmed and dried the blood.

I recited, whipping up my own story, telling the present and foretelling events to come.

"Carmel Agbisit will return you to your grounds. This blade will stop crying. Your inner fire will be destroyed, and you will return to your rocks, to your crevices.

"Carmel Agbisit will be remembered as the woman who could. She could juggle various tongues as she tripped over words. She could jump off the chariot to grab the hilt of a blade without cutting herself once. She could slay the woman-headed snake demons."

I looked at them, with their snake-slitted green eyes and their long tongues. They were entranced by my tale, their own hisses shortened to staccato breaths.

"She could slay the woman-headed snake demons," I repeated. "… But, she won't."

I recited more words from my life, everyday events, which were nothing but the truth. This truth paralyzed them for a moment, and then they started writhing.

I dragged their still-writhing scaled bodies over to the rock, to the abyss from where they came.

I pulled off my *anting anting* and threw it down into the hole.

"I won't need this magic anymore.
I am stronger than the amulet itself.
I am the amulet,
the source of
my own power."

I shouted down the hole. It wasn't particularly lyrical, but it was my words, in my mother tongue. In my head, I willed the spirit blood out of the hilt, thinking of scarlet spill.

In resonance, in my hands, the sword began to pour blood again. I whispered to the woman-headed snake demons, telling them that they were free to go home. I waited until they returned back to the other side. Once they had disappeared into the other dimension, I held the sword over the hole, and the blood flooded forth from the *tenegre* bolo. It covered the hole completely, millions and millions of gallons of blood, drawn from all of the country's spirits of the deceased.

"And then you dry," I commanded the sword, in measured words, and it listened.

I wiped my hands with the *malong* that I had slung across my body. I pulled it open and wrapped it around my torso, draping it over my black fighting uniform stained with dried spirit blood, crocodile demon saliva, and strands of blonde snakewoman demon hair. I tucked a corner of the *malong* at my shoulder to hold it in place. As my hand glanced over my collarbone, I felt the absence of my *anting anting* at my chest and the fiery pulse of a presence of something burgeoning from within.

When I returned to my village, a new epic poem swept the provinces. It was wrong, skewed and exaggerated, and some parts just downright false, but it was mine. Even Dayang Nica had her very own version of it that she propagated to every martial grounds I visited. The so-called epic poem broke into fractals and swirled around, a verbal mobile of my own deeds, swinging in the Philippine air, breathed by parents and children, shared across generations to come.

The sword went back into the sapphire rock. It continued to bleed, but now only at every full moon—and some of this blood held the mysticism of a warrior named Carmel Agbisit, articulate speaker of words, valiant performer of impossible deeds, champion of over ten thousand mystical beasts, and beloved heroine of the people.

CARMEL AGBISIT, slayer of beasts, heroine of heroines, and trained under the formidable Dayang Nica, knows no fear as she wields her weeping *tenegre* bolo sword with expertise. Her glory and great deeds are whispered far and wide—with her booming voice as sharp as her sword tip, her words as biting as crocodile teeth, and her swagger as cool as *halo halo*. Sometimes you might find her traversing the provinces with her legendary sword sheathed and jangling at her hips, her signature stride clearing adoring crowds, with the sides of her lips upturned as if musing at something that brings her endless whimsy.

D.A. XIAOLIN SPIRES counts stars and sand, residing currently in Hawai'i. She practices eskrima/arnis/kali (Filipino martial arts)—and, like Carmel, owns a tenegre sword, but (un?)fortunately, her weaponry doesn't weep. Her writing appears or is forthcoming in publications such as *Clarkesworld, Analog, Nature: Futures, Grievous Angel, Fireside, Terraform, Reckoning, Galaxy's Edge, Issues in Earth Science, LONTAR, Andromeda Spaceways* (Year's Best issue), *Mithila Review, Star*line, Liminality, ETTT, Outlook Springs, Polu Texni*, and *Story Seed Vault*; as well as anthologies of the strange and delightful: *Sharp & Sugar Tooth, Broad Knowledge, Future Visions*, and *Ride the Star Wind*. Website: daxiaolinspires.wordpress.com Twitter: @spireswriter

AUTHOR'S NOTE

Many thanks to Juan Fernandez and his linguistical and lyrical adroitness, historical acumen, and excellent poetic skill, as he generously provided the Spanish-Tagalog translation in ABCC/ABCC rhyme of a snippet of the existent written Ibálong epic fragment, as showcased in this story. He also provides the direct Tagalog-English of his Spanish-Tagalog translation:

Lupaing mabanlik at mayabong ang kapatagang Kabikulan; sa mundo'y walang singganda, sa ani'y walang singsagana.	A land silty and fertile are the Bicol plains; in the world is none as beautiful, its harvests, none as bountiful.
Si Baltog ang unang taong sa lupaing ito'y nanirahan katutubong Botavara, sa lahi ni Lipód nagmula.	Baltog was the first person who inhabited this land, a native of Botavara from the lineage of Lipod.

CARO CHO AND THE EMPIRE OF LIGHT

An account by Kitty Avelino,
as provided by Lin Darrow

Miss Cho's prosthetic leg is a work of art, especially under the kaleidoscopic haze of colour that makes up the Limelite District at night. It extends from her upper thigh down into a sharp stiletto, her snowy skin fading mistily into frosted glass. Sliding out of the back seat of a limousine, that leg glittered expensively through a generous cut in a red silk dress, the glass shimmering with the warped hues of lavender neon and gold marquee bulbs.

"Thank you for coming, Kit. I know it's late," she said, waving at the limousine to drive on before joining me beneath the streetlamp.

"It's no trouble, Miss Cho! None at all," I chirped, just as the sky cracked and a mist of rain began to patter down from above. I untucked the holo-umbrella I had hiked under my arm and *fwooshed* it open, holding it up for her to step calmly beneath. Raindrops fizzled off the glowing dome as we stood close together. "How was the opera this evening?"

"Cut short," she replied, fixing the synthetic fur stole around her shoulders. Her own technology was threaded through the material, projecting pinpricks of holographic light all around her shoulders like strings of broken pearls frozen in the moment of shattering. "We've got a problem, and that problem's expecting us at Kid Callisto's."

I nodded. I had been the secretary to Caro Cho—prosthetics genius, billionaire philanthropist, and Queen of Flicker Valley—for nearly seven years. A midnight meeting with a mysterious stranger at Limelite's swankiest dinner club was just about a typical Friday night for me.

Caro Cho had made her first million in smart prosthetics at eighteen, first under the name Christopher, then Caroline, before settling at last on the more brandable "Caro." I had heard the story a few times over late-night meetings and boxes of greasy takeout. Frustrated with the ugly colours and clunky designs of the prosthetic legs she had been wearing all her life, she had poured her considerable genius into creating sturdy, comfortable limbs that could be visually altered to the user's taste with morphing holographic projections. Miss Cho's own leg was not actually made of glass, but it was virtually impossible to tell due to its hyper-realistic reflective sheen.

From there, her tech empire had grown from prosthetics into just about everything else you could shake a stick at, from traffic signs to interior design to cosmetics. There wasn't an inch of city that wasn't drizzled in her "flicker-tech," between the shimmering billboards of Flicker Valley, the shop window tableaus of the Silk District, and Limelite's trademark animated marquees. Then there were the city crowds, half-aglow with holograms as suits got slicker and heels got taller. With Cinderella Co.'s flicker-tech, you could click a nosejob on or off at will, moderate the colour of your eyes, or brush kaleidoscopic dyes through your hair.

Paintings of light, she called them, usually as she gazed out of her seventieth-floor laboratory window at the glowing streets beneath Cho Tower. The whole city was drizzled in her portraiture, smooth-lined and bursting with waltzing neon hues.

I know all this because it's my job to know. I'm paid to account for Caro Cho's every waking minute, from the moment she sways in through the laboratory doors to the second she disappears back into her penthouse on the top floor of Cho Tower. Seven years of living alongside a bestselling-biography-in-the-making, and you learn quick how to handle detail—the kind that gets written down, and more importantly, the kind that goes into the mental rolodex and nowhere else.

"Let's ankle," I said, beaming at her.

I followed Miss Cho down the rain-splattered pavement and into the mist of Limelite colour. Glowing neon spilled out of every alleyway as flickering signage for laundromats, jazz clubs, and movie theatres fought for curb-space. Kid Callisto's had a whole block to itself, complete with an animated hologram of a dancing pair perched atop its glittering marquee.

"Whoever manages the flickers needs to download the update. It shouldn't be fizzing in the rain like that," Miss Cho muttered as we slid through the revolving doors and entered the lobby.

The floor of Kid Callisto's was rose-lit and draped in velvet, with holographic candles burning orange patterns over the walls. In the centre of the ballroom was a bandstand with a 12-piece orchestra, cast in a shimmering sunset glow. Four of them were of a glassier hue than the others, and it made me buzz to think that I was one of the few people in the room who could note Miss Cho's flicker-tech at a glance.

"Look, in here too—the string section is practically phantasmagoric," Miss Cho huffed as a valet appeared to take her fur and my considerably less expensive raincoat. "Get in touch with the manager on Monday, Kit. Unless they *want* to advertise the fact that their 12-piece is closer to an 8, they need to download the update off the Mist."

I made a note in my mental rolodex. Some days, half my job involved coaching Miss Cho's top clients through the process of downloading new artistic flourishes off the Mist, the wireless network that connected all of the city's digital grids and allowed holograms to be projected from any connected surface. Miss Cho's flicker-tech was the best in the world, and I took pride in the humble role I played in making sure it was being used to its fullest potential.

A waiter ushered us across the floor, escorting us to a private booth that was framed on all sides by flickering screens digitally adjusted to look like silk. The illusion was nearly perfect, except for the elegant animation that made the threaded patterns of apple blossoms sway across the silk as though caught in a gentle breeze.

The screen flickered off to let us through, and we slipped into the darkened booth, where an older woman was hunched across the table with a cigarette on her lip.

"Mayor Pill," Miss Cho said, sliding across the seat.

Minerva Pill had held Virtue City by the throat for nearly a decade. By now, the grooves of her face—powdered, rouged, and pink-lipsticked—were well-known from campaign billboards and flicker-screens, from the knifish jut of her nose and the equally angular shape of her chin. It was an unforgiving face, with glinting eyes that sparked like the click of lighter fluid and flint through the dark.

Then, in a sudden fizz of light, the mayor was gone. In her place was a woman with uncombed black curls and a face pale as a steam-laundered napkin. It took me a second to realize I was looking at a face washed clean of all flicker-tech—no shimmering lip or nose augmentations, eye colour corrections, or any other cosmetic enhancements.

My mental rolodex spun rapidly, and I landed on the name *Ayo Erwin*. Mayor Pill's assistant.

My heart thrummed uneasily, and I glanced at Miss Cho, watching the dappling of silver light play across her face from the holographic candle that was sitting in the middle of the table.

"It's bad, Miss Cho," stammered Miss Erwin, lifting a cigarette and taking a shaky puff. A tangle of synthetic smoke fanned across the table, and Miss Cho waved it coolly away.

"Start at the beginning," she said, in her wily trademark tone, the one that sounded like she was determined to sweep you off your feet in one way or another, whether it took a rose or a smoking derringer.

Miss Erwin took a suck from her pink cig, and then stabbed it out into the porcelain dish at her elbow.

"You've probably seen the news by this point. The election season is nearly over, and Miss Pill's calendar has been intensely occupied. On Wednesday morning, Miss Pill made a surprise public appearance at the Virtue Canine Club's Digitally Enhanced Pet Pageant."

Miss Cho's eyes narrowed. "I did see."

"And I'm sure you know," Miss Erwin said, chewing on her lip. "That Miss Pill has made her stance on holographic enhancements for animals expressly clear on several occasions."

"And I take it that the mayor's sudden turnaround on flicker-poodles was also a surprise to her campaign office?" Miss Cho asked, as I waved a hand to activate the holographic typewriter implanted in my arm, ready to take down some fast-fingered notes.

"I can assure you," Miss Erwin said meaningfully, "that Miss Pill's stance remains unchanged."

"It wasn't her," Miss Cho surmised, cutting to the quick.

Miss Erwin shook her head. "The mayor is still just as sick as she was when we commissioned you to create a full-body hologram. She's been bedridden on oxygen for months."

"It wasn't one of her aides, acting alone?" I asked lightly, fingers waltzing over the flickering typewriter keys.

Miss Erwin nodded. "I was at a luncheon with some members of the press only ten minutes prior. And before you ask, I'm the only one who's been making her public appearances. The *only one* with access to the hologram. Nobody else should be able to wear it, even if they *were* associated with the campaign."

"So someone has hacked into your Mist and stolen the mayor's holographic body," Miss Cho stated. She leaned back in the seat. "That *is* a bit of a campaign nightmare, I'd imagine."

"So far, the damage has been minimal," Miss Erwin said. "But if someone has uninterrupted access to the mayor's flicker-form—I'm sure I don't have to impress upon you how far beyond poodles this thing has the potential to go."

I noticed Miss Cho's lips quirk vaguely. "I made you a hologram. I gave you full access, as you requested." *Insisted* was the word I thought, privately, that she ought to use. "Surely you're not suggesting this whole mess is my fault?"

"No," Miss Erwin said, pressing her lips into a flat line. "Only— when it comes to flicker-tech, you're the greatest mind in the city. Nobody else has ever attempted a full-body holograph of a living person, let alone succeeded so well that the whole world is still ignorant to it. Because of your expertise and familiarity with the technology, the mayor is willing to pay handsomely for the security breach to be closed."

Miss Cho held up a hand; dutifully, I stopped typing. "I assume the 'by any means necessary' is implied," she said, eyes glinting.

Miss Erwin looked as though she might shake apart from stress; still, she nodded, hands wringing anxiously. "Anything."

"One hundred thousand credits," Miss Cho said, waving a hand as though she was merely ordering an expensive bottle of champagne. "To three charities of my choosing. Each."

Miss Erwin let out a shaky breath, and without warning, the immaculate hologram of the mayor shimmered back on. It was Mayor Pill's steely gaze and smoky voice that replied. "It's a deal."

We didn't stay for dessert.

For all her celebrity, Miss Cho's greatest achievement—a perfectly accurate, fluidly animated, full-body hologram of Mayor Minerva Pill that could speak and move just like the real McCoy—was also her greatest secret. Only a small circle knew about the project, let alone its unprecedented success: Miss Cho, Mayor Pill, and their respective secretaries, myself and Miss Erwin.

Miss Erwin only knew because she was the one who had been selected, for whatever reason, to wear the thing. The idea was that Mayor Pill, who had been denying rumours of her failing health for months, needed to double her public appearances and make a show of how spry, energetic and—most importantly—*powerful* she was. She was flagging in the polls for the first time in decades, and all her usual tricks of blackmail, bribes, and back-alley handshakes were finally running dry.

Me, I knew because—well, a less sunny optimist than myself might say she knew I'd notice the gaps in her schedule. But I preferred life a little rosier than that, and figured it was at least a little because she trusted me more than most.

"Even Pill's campaign manager doesn't know," Miss Cho said as her glass heel clicked its way down a back alley. We'd left the neon lights of Limelite behind, and had entered into the electricity-spitting back alleys that twined between the badly lit buildings in the Peril District. "I'm not convinced it was an inside job, at any rate. Nobody in this town needs much of a reason to go after Minerva Pill, and only her campaign team has motivation to keep her in power."

"She's planning on knocking the Peril slums down if she's re-elected," I suggested, typing hurriedly away at my flicker-keys and scanning through projected newsreels of campaign speeches. "Is that why we're here, boss? You think that's motive?"

"We're here because Sola Hare is here," Miss Cho said in that cool, misty way of hers, the kind that made you feel like you'd never know half as much about anything as she did about everything.

"Sola Hare?" I parroted, hurrying to keep up with her even in my most sensible heels. "The two-bit crook who runs the holo-boardwalk off of cheap imitation code of *your* tech?"

"Just because her tech is cheap doesn't make *her* cheap," Miss Cho explained. "It makes her enterprise low-cost, which is what a business needs to be in Peril." She paused. There was a cigarette between her fingers that I hadn't noticed before—probably it was a synthetic one, more for the catharsis of motion than the nicotine. She took a drag, and let the pink-tinged smoke waft out from between her lips. "I used to live here, you know."

I nodded. If Miss Cho knew everything there was to know about hologram technology and the city that had adopted it so thoroughly into its infrastructure, then I knew everything there was to know about *her*.

The sign for Virtue City's Illusion Park flickered through the haze of rain and mist that shimmered down the boardwalk. Holographic vines twined themselves around the poles of a metal archway, blooming into watercoloured tube roses that fizzled in the downpour. A flurry of pixies fluttered out of the illusory garden, their limbs stiff and doll-like, glitching in and out of existence.

Miss Cho held out a finger for one of the pixies to land on and pressed her lips together. This was her way of letting you know she could do something better than you without actually saying as much.

We stepped through the archway, and something pinged in my ear, signalling the charge of a ticket to my bank account. Castle walls and turrets rose into the sky to greet us on the other side, hung with glitchy tapestries that illuminated the park's scheduled illusions:

8AM—11AM: Space Pirate Adventure
11AM—1PM: Underwater Fantasy
1PM—4PM: Wild Martian Desert
4PM—8PM: Virtue City of the Future

8PM—MIDNIGHT: Haunted Manor
MIDNIGHT—3AM: Fairy Masquerade

The waves of the West Virtue Lakebed lapped against the winding docks as the holograms struggled to load through the fog. Slowly, a tapestry of bad holograms crackled to life around us, blandly coloured and stiff-limbed, impressive only in the sheer scope of the scene they made when knitted together. Flowers bloomed as we passed, ducking between waltzing ladies and gents with glittering wings, with cup-bearers serving bubbling champagne in blossom flutes and cakes like wafting clouds. Swaying silk gowns fell into place like veils overtop our street clothes, which was the final straw for Miss Cho, who waved a hand over her wrist and drew open her holo-screen.

"Revolting," she muttered, typing rapidly at the projected keys along her forearm.

"One thing I've been wonderin', Miss," I said as I followed Miss Cho through the gaudy scene, perfectly content with my own flickering blue gown. "Are we so sure it was the mayor what got hacked? Did you squirrel away any files back at Cinderella Co.?"

"The contract was very specific that we were to destroy all files associated with the Pill hologram," Miss Cho said, curling her lip as she continued typing rapidly. "She verified the deletion herself."

"So either someone *knew* about it—which is unlikely unless one of us talked—or someone found it during a hack that was aiming for something else," I surmised, ducking out of the way as a pair of fairy children chased a cartoon rabbit through our path.

The poufy Renaissance gown that Miss Cho had been subjected to fizzled away suddenly, and she clicked her keypad off with a sigh. "The second is most likely," she said, running a hand through her hair, dark and lustrous even without the flicker-tech's help. "Unless you have something to confess, Kit."

She'd said it offhandedly, but I stopped dead in my tracks and waited for her to follow suit. She did, turning to pin me with the usual calligraphic arch of an eyebrow, like I knew she would.

"I'd sooner step into a pair of concrete heels and take a midnight swim than betray you, Miss Cho," I said, watching the flicker of surprise catch fire in her eyes before it was swiftly managed and buried away.

"Thank you, Kit," she said, her lips quirking in a close approximation of a smile. She was all frost and glass on the best of days; that much, coming from her, was practically a furnace of warmth.

The boardwalk went dark suddenly, the fairy masquerade melting like microwaved plastic into the boards.

"Caro Cho!" drawled a voice from somewhere in the rainy haze. "Figured it was you, hackin' into my projections."

An angular shoulder wilted out of the shadows, followed by a sharp-toothed grin and a tall, willowy body that seemed to be all limbs. Holographic shark tattoos splashed up and down the lengths of two long, pale arms, looking just about ready to leap off the skin and chomp down.

"Sola," Miss Cho said, leaning forward to kiss both of Sola's cheeks. "How's business?"

Sola shrugged one shoulder fluidly. "Eh. Pill hasn't threatened to send a wrecking ball through the slums in the past week, so tonight it's a little deserted. Next campaign speech she makes, I expect a full crowd. Nothin' sells tickets like the need to forget."

"I'm here to call in a favour. Do you still do your projections on-site?"

Sola nodded. "Whatever you need. This way."

The flicker-tech room at Illusion Park was a dark little attic overlooking the park's archway, with glowing screens of every imaginable underworld hue: deep lipstick reds, neon-tube purples, bottom-of-the-ocean blues. The light spilled over dozens of wires and keyboards, some projected and others material, underneath a veritable army of takeout boxes and empty soda cans.

At the centre of it all, Sola Hare sat in a rolling chair beneath a giant screen full of numbers, her limbs tangled into a knot as she typed at the keyboard with stabbing fingers. "You need into the Canine Club's security vids," Sola repeated. "Sure thing. What are you looking for?"

"Someone used a full-body projection of mine without my permission," Miss Cho said, cool and masterful as she leaned against one of the filing cabinets. The pink cigarette re-appeared between her fingers as she watched Sola work. "I don't like that. I want to know who put it there."

"What sort of hologram is this?" Sola asked.

Miss Cho glanced at me, before rattling off a date and a technical name to Sola. "Visually and auditorily, it should be an identical copy of our industrious mayor," she concluded. Sola's eyes popped open wide, and she draped an elbow over her chair, whirling to gape at Miss Cho. "And if you breathe a word of this, Sola, I won't leak you a single line of code for any of your gaudy attractions."

"Shit!" Sola cried, fingers tangling over the keys. "It ain't that—I don't doubt you can do it. It's just—damn, the evening news makes a lot more sense now!"

Sola pressed a key, and a newsreel flickered across one of the far-left screens. My guts dropped to my heels as I took in the sight of Mayor Pill in a roguishly low-cut sequin dress, brandishing something gold and expensive-looking as a series of payment plan options scrolled across the screen beneath her.

A news anchor's voice crackled into the room. "The mayor made an unexpected appearance today on the Channel A2 Shopping Network, where she spent nearly twenty minutes selling solid gold carrot peelers to a live studio audience."

"Our thief's got a sense of humour, looks like," I said mildly, watching Miss Cho's impassive face for any hint of feeling. What I got, instead, was a blank stare. I grinned a little. "You think Mayor Pill has a strong stance on carrots, too?"

"I *think* it looks embarrassing for a Mayor who consistently claims she'll 'drain the fat cats of their government milk' to start hawking baubles for the idle rich," Miss Cho replied smoothly.

"That's not all," Sola said, typing rapidly. "She's on Channel B9 right now, on *Midnight Hour with Paminder Glass*."

Another screen clicked on, and Miss Cho strode forward for a closer look. Mayor Pill was sitting in a velvet chair, wearing a wildly flamboyant green neon suit paired with a ring of floating holographic planets about her neck. Across from her was a desk, at which Pam Glass, Virtue's number one late night talk-show host, sat, goggling her heterochromatic eyes at our city's highest defender.

"I can't believe what I'm hearing!" Glass cried. "Are you seriously saying you'll give a thousand credits to every ballot with your name on it? Isn't there some sort of rule against openly buying the election?!"

"Cash money!" the hologram of Mayor Pill hollered, standing up unsteadily on her chair and showering fists of antiquated paper bills out of her pockets. The crowd erupted in applause as the live studio band began to score the scene with a smooth commercial jingle.

"Get into the *Midnight Hour*'s Mist, find out where that projection is coming from," Miss Cho ordered brusquely.

Sola's fingers flew across the keys. I watched Miss Cho as *she* watched numbers and letters tear across the screen, her gaze steely and unknowable. She didn't look back at me, not once, but I was used to that.

Just as Mayor Pill was being forcibly escorted off the set by Channel B9 security, something *pinged* on Sola's screen, and she gave a laugh.

"It's being controlled remotely," she said, typing furiously. "Looks like the command is coming from somewhere in the Crane Quarter. Area code… Hmm." A map leapt onto the screen, followed by a blinking red circle that encompassed a block of apartment buildings. "Look familiar?"

Miss Cho's eyes narrowed. "Familiar. Kit, let's go."

"One more thing," Sola said as we made for the door, swivelling around in her chair. "I've *tried* to hack the Pill campaign before, just to mess around. Couldn't even get past the initial firewall. Security's tight—you'd need a better hacker than me to get past their protocols, and someone more skilled with flicker-tech to know how to properly work this thing."

"Then we're looking for a genius coder," I suggested. "One with a background in flicker-tech, and ideally with a grudge against Mayor Pill."

Miss Cho nodded. "Thank you, Sola. Consider your debt paid."

The Crane Quarter was so-named for the fluffy white-blossomed weeds that lined the streets stretching north of Limelite all the way to the lake. The white-winged weeds had broken through cracks in the city concrete, shoving their way upward and ruining the roads for any decent signal used by floating cabs or streetcars.

That was what made it the perfect haunt for the street gangs of Virtue. No cop wanted to hoof it through the Crane Quarter, not without a reliable floating car to protect them from the gangs.

It also happened that Miss Cho's ex-lover was the worst of them all.

"It was a different time in my life, Kit," she said, her glass leg flashing as she swayed down the white-blossomed street. The Crane Quarter was utterly deserted at this time of night, leaving us alone in the pale glow of whatever few streetlights weren't in need of repair.

"When I was much, much more vulnerable to the utter peril of a compliment, to the terrible sway a kind word can have over a young and lonely heart."

I nodded. I knew this, of course; sometimes I think she forgot how much I knew.

I didn't need my mental rolodex to know who Vesper Darte was. Her name was all over the gossip-reels, and so long as you had eyes in your head, her picture was impossible to ignore: swooping silver hair, heart-shaped lipstick, and thick china-doll eyelashes. Most striking, however, was the right arm that Miss Cho had made personally for her, a ruby-red prosthetic that had been programmed to look and feel like polished gemstone. She looked more like an heiress than a blackmailer, but maybe one was the result of the other—there was hardly any high-profile personality in Virtue whose arm she hadn't twisted into a healthy payout.

She had come to Cho Tower a few times, hoping to rekindle Miss Cho's habit of making bad personal decisions with her. Miss Cho would always refuse to see her, but Vesper would never fail to leave behind a gilded calling card for the Gold Slipper Casino.

As we approached the Gold Slipper, Miss Cho typed something into the flicker-keys along her arm. Instantly her appearance brightened: her long sequined dress seemed to sparkle anew, with her long glass leg shimmering between the generous slit in one side. Her hair swept up into a series of knots, pinned in place by loops of rubies and diamonds, and her eyeshadow darkened from a pale mauve to a deep scarlet. She looked like she had fortune to lose on the roulette table, and every intention of going home with the dealer afterward.

"I'll make the plan quick and painless for you, Kit," Miss Cho said, her whole body glittering as she turned to me. "Vesper keeps her blackmail material on the chip in her right-hand earring. I think I can get her to take it off, but I'll need you to implant *this* while I've got her distracted." She typed something on the flicker-keys, and a moment later my holo-typewriter pinged. I drew open the screen with a wave of my hand, and saw that she had sent me a file through the Mist.

"What does it do?" I asked, staring at the ruby-shaped icon on my flicker-screen.

"It should sweep her system for unregistered Cinderella tech and destroy it," Miss Cho said, tugging at her evening gloves. "It's a new technology I've been working on. Just a hobby, you understand—that's why you haven't been brought in yet. Still, it should do the trick. I've disguised it as a standard update, but you'll have to bury it deep, Kit, so she won't notice it."

I stared at the file. Then, with a deep breath, I swiped the screen back down into my arm. "Whatever you need, Miss Cho," I said decisively.

"I knew I could count on you, Kit," she said, with another slight smile. "Now, flick on something of a disguise and follow me at a distance."

The Gold Slipper Casino was a tall, narrow building at the top of the worst road in the Quarter. A carpet of white-winged weeds led the way up to a set of revolving silver doors, which sparkled artificially, no doubt with stolen Cinderella tech. The sign above the door was all gold neon and curving calligraphic tubes, while gold coins fell in holographic rivers down the building's silvery façade, striking the ground and flickering out without a sound.

The inside of the casino was choked with black gold and silver accents, from spinning roulette wheels to metallic velvet tables. The black marble floor crackled beneath our heels, giving away the sheen as flicker-tech. The band at the far end of the room also had a hazy look to them, especially those musicians nearest to the back wall. It was all a light-show, then, but one that seemed to be good enough for the rabble of goons crowding the tables.

Miss Cho sidled her way over to the bar and ordered a drink. I sat down a few stools away and did the same. I knew, like she did, that there was no need to seek Vesper out. The bartender would pass the message along, and we'd get a visit in no time.

"Once we leave, wear the Widow and follow us," Miss Cho muttered under her breath. I took note.

Eventually, a lilting voice wafted through the surrounding music of laughter, spilt chips, and soft electro-jazz. "Buy you a drink, sailor?" it asked, as a ruby-red arm slid across the bar and motioned at the bartender.

Vesper was all of five feet next to Miss Cho's six, but she made up some of the disparity with a pair of stiletto heels. She was draped in white fur and golden fringe, her holo-sparkle turned up to ten, like a chorus girl preparing to take the stage. It wasn't hard to see how she made her living by stealing hearts and sensitive information in the same fell swoop.

"Vesper," Miss Cho said, turning toward her.

"I had a feeling I'd be seeing you sooner or later," Vesper said, plucking up Miss Cho's drink and taking a sip herself. "And I don't even have any dirt on you—how romantic."

"Yes, I'm—" Miss Cho said, affecting a bit of a stammer. I couldn't tell if the flush across her cheeks was genuine or holographic, but the colour *blared* across her face, which was ordinarily perfectly composed. "To be honest, I'm a little self-conscious about being here."

"It *is* a little gaudy," Vesper said, deliberately misinterpreting her as she quirked an eyebrow at the light-show that made up her casino floor. "I hope you don't mind what I've done with the place. I imagined it as a sort of tribute to you, if you must know."

"Vesper," Miss Cho said, scarcely a whisper.

I had never really seen her with a lover. Whether it was genuine or not, the slight hesitation in her voice, the tension in her shoulders, the way her fingers curled and uncurled against the nearest surface were all new to me, and I couldn't help cataloguing the details away.

It was my job to do as much.

"Let me make it easy for you," Vesper said, sliding closer to Miss Cho and setting her drink aside. "I know we've had our problems with trust in the past, and I know you find my work—well, just a *touch* unsavory. In light of recent events, however, I can't shake the feeling that you might be willing to re-open the subject of our partnership."

My stomach dropped, but Miss Cho only tilted her head to one side.

"Recent events," she repeated, blankly.

"Your little holographic gift, of course," Vesper said with a tinkling laugh. "You didn't have to say anything; I knew it was meant for me."

Just over Vesper's shoulder, there was a sudden crackle of a projection starting up. A silvery haze poured itself into one of the stools at the far end of the bar, before solidifying—in a manner of speaking—into the body of Mayor Pill. She sipped at a champagne flute, shoulders peaked like a vulture's wings, her lipstick shimmering with a distractingly youthful pink hue.

I couldn't see Miss Cho's face, turned as she was now toward Vesper Darte. I could only assume she'd seen it too, before it flickered out and disappeared.

"I've always said you were an artist," Vesper said, looking out across the room. "I like to think of myself as your first patron. And now you've become a master."

"Vesper," Miss Cho said, sliding her hand over Vesper's ruby-red wrist. "Can we take this somewhere more private?"

Vesper's eyes glittered. "Of course. Follow me."

As they slid off the bar, I flicked my fingers and silently drew up the Widow hologram.

Miss Cho had been working on an invisibility mod for her flicker-tech for some time, and though she hadn't perfected it, she *had* managed to create a hologram that warped the air and light around its centre and created a kind of smudgy, imperceptible black hole of shadow. I let it drape over me in a grim, rainy-day haze as I crept along behind them.

Vesper led Miss Cho across the casino floor and through a door in the shape of a playing card. The Queen of Hearts made a low, courtly bow as they passed through, and I had just enough time to duck through the door as it fell shut behind them.

The cacophony of the casino floor was instantly muffled by severe soundproof walls. The warehouse-sized room on the other side was empty of any holographic enhancements, far as I could tell. The fella tied to a chair in the middle of the room looked altogether real, though, and so did the blood streaming down his face.

"And what's this poor fellow done?" Miss Cho asked impassively, eyeing the four goons with brass knuckles standing in a semi-circle around him.

"Oh, fallen in love with the wrong billionaire's son," Vesper said, with an affected sigh. "It's the father we're after, of course; Romeo here doesn't have a penny to his name." She glanced at one of the muscled goons. "Anything?"

"Nothing," the great hulking woman replied.

"Please, the Hazes don't have any secrets, I swear!" the Romeo panted, spitting up a thin line of blood. "They're good people—philanthropists!"

Vesper's cigarette disappeared from her hand, and she leaned forward to clasp the boy's jaw in one manicured hand. "That just means they've got more to hide than most," she said, before straightening. "Keep at him. Miss Cho and I have some private business to discuss."

There was a *pop* of brass against jawbone as I turned away, following the pair of them up a metal staircase and through a set of frosted glass doors. The office on the other side was swanky, but spare of flicker-tech: just a desk, a velvet fainting couch, piles of books and a scattering of silvery file cabinets. A treasure-box hue of colour came streaming in through the window, bouncing off the neon sign from the street below.

Vesper drew Miss Cho over to the couch and leaned in for a kiss. Miss Cho turned her cheek to one side. "Without the tech, darling," she said, twining her arms around Vesper's neck. "You know how much I hate touching your face without actually *seeing* it."

At Vesper's hesitation, Miss Cho brushed a hand through her hair. "Look, I'll do the same," she said, before waving a hand over her arm. Her dress dulled and her hair fell out of its elaborate loops. Her leg's glassy sheen was siphoned away, leaving behind only a pale white canvas of a prosthetic limb. Otherwise, she hardly looked any different: she'd gone to the trouble of real lipstick and genuine eyeshadow, though it faded from scarlet to a pale green in the light. "Better?"

"Oh, *alright*," Vesper sighed. With an indulgent smile, Vesper reached to tug off her earrings. At once, everything flickered off. Vesper's silvery hair darkened to a pale dishwater brown, her face bare of any hint of cosmetics. She looked five years older, at least, and her nose was twice the size. "Look at me! Now *I'm* somewhat self-conscious," she laughed, before drawing Miss Cho in for a kiss that was eagerly returned. Without paying much attention, Vesper angled her arm backward and set her earrings down on a nearby table—so close that, on any other day, there could be no chance of misplacing them.

As they kissed, I did my best not to look. I moved to kneel behind the couch, guiding a thin holographic cord from the holo-keys in my arm to the face of the earring. It was a flat ruby disc cut into the shape of a heart, just barely large enough to hold the chip inside.

It took me less than five minutes to plant the file. Thankfully, the lovebirds didn't seem to be moving too fast, and I was able to get to my feet and head for the door before they'd gotten too hot and heavy.

My eyes slid over Miss Cho's as I turned the knob as silently as I could, and I wondered if she could see me after all. Ordinarily, the Widow hologram was enough to trick the eye into thinking it was looking at a swath of shadow—unless, of course, you knew what to look for.

I let the door glide open naturally, as though a gust of wind had opened it, and then ducked out.

I hurried down the stairs and hit the blood-splattered landing just in time to witness Romeo—whether that was his name or not, I never learned—lurch up out of the chair and bash his head *hard* into one of the goons. It earned him nothing but another brass sock to the jaw, but it made me like the fella enough to risk sneaking behind the proceedings and unfastening his bindings.

The *next* headbutt landed harder, and he was able to scramble free, creating such a cacophony of hollering goons and wildly flying fists that soon Vesper and Miss Cho had appeared on the landing.

"What's going on?!" Vesper cried, as Romeo finally managed to bury his fist in one goon's gut and duck under another's arm on his way toward the door. "Grab him! Now!" A derringer came flying out of her fur coat, and without much thought for aim, she pulled the trigger. A *bang* went off through the room, echoing off the walls. I took that as my cue to run.

As Romeo burst out of the warehouse and into the casino, I let my Widow hologram flicker away. It glitched terribly with rapid motion, and I had a sense that the chaos of pinging gunfire and clamouring gamblers was enough to cover my escape.

I didn't like leaving Miss Cho in the serpent's den, but I knew two things about my illustrious boss. The first was that I had, over the years, developed a pretty good sense of when she needed me, and when she needed me to swan off; that look she'd given me on the way out was firmly in favour of option two.

The second thing I knew was that, when it came to serpents, Miss Cho was more capable than anyone I knew of biting back.

It took me an hour to find a working cab back to my apartment. I collapsed into bed and slept for a good hour before rolling over and accessing my work files remotely on my holo-typewriter. A career girl only needs so much sleep, especially one as good at compartmentalizing as me.

It was seven am when Miss Cho's message came in on the holo-screen.

Campaign speech, noon, Orbital Tower. Be there. CC.

The *Orbital* was the biggest newspaper in town, and they had a view of Flicker Valley like nobody else. Their tenth-floor observation platform overlooked the long, sweeping street that made up the core of the downtown sector, perfectly situated to take in the sweep of multi-tiered billboards that gushed colour across the city skyline. Miss Cho was friendly with the press, and I was friendly with her, so it didn't take much to be let up for a look.

I found Miss Cho leaning against the railing, typing something on her holo-screen. She looked up when I arrived and shut the projection off.

"Kit," she said, eyebrows raising. "You're early."

"I wanted to get here before the action got started." Then I glanced down at her arm, where the holo-keys had disappeared into her skin. "Don't let me stop you."

Slowly, with half an eye on me, Miss Cho waved a hand and drew the screen back up from her arm. "What do you imagine we're here for, Kit?" she said, carefully.

"Well," I said, looking across the valley of tiered billboards and flashing cab signs. "Mayor Pill's campaign speech, mainly."

"Hmm," Miss Cho said, cool even as her fingers typed rapidly.

"And a bit of a light-show, most likely. Probably something big and flashy that will end in an arrest or two."

Miss Cho glanced up at me. "Oh? You're not convinced my tech did the job, back at the Slipper?" she asked lightly.

I smiled, and draped myself over the railing. "I see everything that happens on the Cinderella Co. servers, Miss Cho. Last week you lowered security on some of your tech—an archive, technically speaking, from three update cycles ago, which I figure you thought I wouldn't catch. That's why Miss Darte's casino looks the way it does now, I reckon. That's the gift *she* was talking about—you must've let her know about it somehow. You were charming your way back into her good graces, making like you wanted her back so she wouldn't suspect anything when you showed up at the Gold Slipper."

"Interesting theory," Miss Cho said, finishing whatever it was she was working on and letting her holo-screen flicker back into her arm. "Except that we watched Sola track the hologram's signal to Vesper."

"We saw that it was coming from the Crane Quarter," I countered. "I figure you planted that signal to broadcast remotely, close enough to the Gold Slipper that there was only one likely suspect. You must have set it up weeks ago, so that you could let yourself get seen by one of Darte's goons. 'I had a feeling I'd be seeing you sooner or later,' she said. That, and you were wearing makeup under all your flicker-tech—like you expected to have to coax her earring off by switching off your own, but you still wanted to look nice."

Miss Cho laughed. "This is a rather vain portrait of me you're painting."

"Well, then I got to thinkin'," I continued blithely. "If you could program *that* remotely, it only stands to reason you could program the others, too. The talk-show, the shopping network, and the dog pageant all have one thing in common: they were being broadcasted live. TV studios are right in the middle of the digital grid—plenty of cameras and screens to hijack in order to project the mayoral hologram. And then the one we saw at the Slipper—well, when she took your tech, she accidentally gave you access to hers.

"When you handed me that file, that's when I knew for sure. It's my job to account for your every waking moment, Miss Cho. It's my *job* to schedule every second of your day. When would you have had the time to develop a new program without my knowing? You always underestimate how much I see, Miss Cho, but I notice everything when it comes to you. If I don't, I can't protect you."

"Protect me?" Miss Cho laughed. "You've just accused me of using you for my own mysterious ends."

"Oh, I understand *why*. You needed a witness to make the theft charge stick, and someone to put the incriminating file on her earring, and you figured it'd offend my moral sensibilities to just flat-out *ask*."

"And hasn't it?"

"It's my job to help you, Miss Cho," I said, simply. "With whatever you need."

Miss Cho looked out over the balcony. A series of billboards flickered on, displaying a live feed of the square below, where Mayor Pill was pounding a podium and making promises. The audio was too garbled to properly hear from our vantage point, but it sounded angry, whatever it was.

"It's much easier to frame someone if they make a public spectacle of themselves," she said, at length.

I'd never asked her to explain herself, but it made me happy, then, that she did anyway.

It took a few minutes before it really got going. One billboard fizzled, and the Mayor's face appeared on top of the model hawking anti-aging cream. Then another sputtered, and the sunny vacationers advertising some airline were both wearing Pill's face. One by one, the advertisements were taken over by the unmistakably severe visage of Mayor Pill, from action movie trailers to celebrity news anchors to toothpaste commercials.

And there, at the centre, was the real Mayor Pill—or rather, Miss Erwin wearing Miss Pill's face—obliviously campaigning.

"You do have a way with a hologram, Miss Cho," I commented.

But it wasn't over yet. Suddenly the camera trained on the "real" Mayor Pill gave a sudden heave, pointing itself directly at a nearby street café, where a gaggle of brunching debutantes were watching the proceedings on table-side screens over mimosas and croissants.

And in the middle of it all sat Mayor Pill, sipping coffee without a care in the world.

"What did that file do?" I asked, conscious of the rising clamour in the street below as the gathered crowd realized that there were *two* Mayor Pills in the same square.

"In laymen's terms, it lets me dress up Miss Darte like a porcelain doll," Miss Cho said, her cigarette appearing in one hand.

"That's Miss Darte?!" I cried. I'd guessed a fair bit, but even I had to marvel at her mind, at the sheer amount of planning that had culminated in an expertly timed explosion that was set to blow Virtue's foundations sky-high, metaphorically speaking.

Miss Cho nodded, taking a drag on her cigarette. "I'm supposed to meet her for brunch in ten minutes."

We watched as a cop approached Vesper, as Vesper looked down and realized that her holograms were no longer her own. A scuffle ensued, and in the thick of grasping hands and twisting limbs Vesper finally managed to get her earring off, letting the hologram of Mayor Pill fizzle away to reveal the most notorious blackmailer to ever elude the Virtue City courthouse. The crowd began to shout and crow so tumultuously that Miss Erwin's voice on the microphone had gone terribly, damningly silent.

"I suppose it'll all come out now," I said, mildly.

"By my estimation, Kit," Miss Cho said smoothly, "a ruthless blackmailer has now been swept off the streets, and a corrupt mayor has been so thoroughly disgraced that she actually stands a chance at losing the election. None of the Virtue fat-cats who've been paying for her re-election over the past decade will want anything to do with her—if an apparent association with Vesper Darte doesn't do it, then the sheer embarrassment will. Oh, and three charities are now one hundred thousand credits richer, lest we forget."

"And your tech is back in your hands," I surmised.

Miss Cho nodded. "You know, Kit... if she hadn't forced me to surrender every last pixel of my hologram to her campaign, I probably would have let her have a few more years in the mayoral seat. But oh, well." She took a drag on her cigarette, and a haze of pink smoke fell like a veil across her fingers. "We all have our regrets."

All I could think, as the crowd erupted beneath us and the billboards of Flicker Valley went haywire with distorted mayoral faces, was that I didn't have a single one. Not when every step of my life had led me to be standing there, at her side, looking down across her empire of light.

KITTY AVELINO's friends would describe her as having a photographic memory and a dogged sense of optimism, both qualities that she regularly puts to use at her job as the right-hand woman of billionaire tech genius Caro Cho. She has won Employee of the Month at Cinderella Co. more times than any other employees combined, and is the Virtue City Adult Spelling Bee champ three years running.

LIN is a professional Victorianist by day and a noir writer by night. She's written several short works, both prose and comic, for anthologies such as *Valor 2*, *Tabula Idem*, *Planetside*, QueerScifi's *Renewal* anthology, *Malaise: A Horror Anthology*, and others. Her first novel, *Pyre at the Eyreholme Trust*, is an adventure story that marries magic, noir, casino heists, and queer romance, and was published by Less Than Three Press in July of 2018. She currently writes the Hiveworks webcomic *Shaderunners*, a queer 1920s adventure/romance comic about bottled colour and bootleggers, at www.shaderunners.com.

ART BY Justine McGreevy

JUSTINE MCGREEVY is a slowly recovering perfectionist, writer, and artist. She creates realities to make our own seem slightly less terrifying. Her work can be viewed at http://www.behance.net/Fickle_Muse and you can follow her on Twitter @Fickle_Muse.

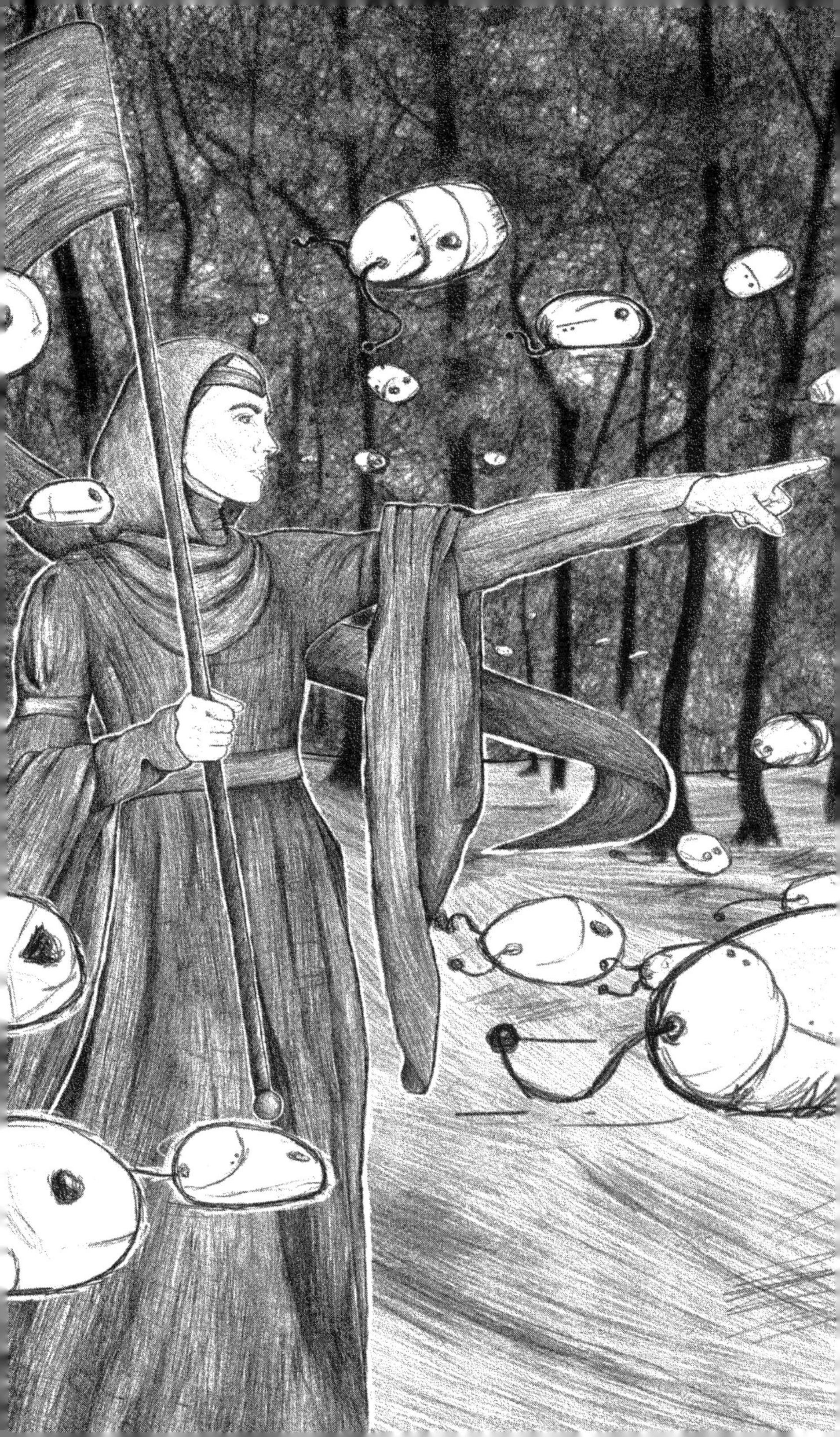

WHY WE ARE STANDING ON THE BROKEN WALL, CLUTCHING SWORDS TOO RUSTY TO TAKE AN EDGE

An account by Aminada Nomanswife,
as provided by Tais Teng

I can see their ships moving in, my daughter. Crimson sails and you are right, the mummified mermaids fixed to their bows have the heads of sharks.

In the distance, the smoke is rising from the Elder Islands. A dozen columns. Smoke so thick it can only be whole villages burning. Cities perhaps.

Sure, they whisper wizards dwell there, sitting naked on the crags and conversing with sea snakes. No help from them. They clearly didn't stop those raiders.

Why are we still standing on the walls of peerless Lovinja, you ask, my daughter? On walls that are broken in a dozen places and wouldn't stop a drunken cow? Clutching pitchforks and swords so rusty they no longer take an edge, while the raiders must have ballistae and crossbows, Greek fire that burns even on water?

Well, some of us love the queen more than life itself. And they still think they are defending her. I never did love her. Queen Leonœrah wasn't meant to be loved. Respected, yes. Feared, certainly. I am loyal, though.

When you meet someone who is so much more than human, clearly touched by the Goddess, you want to become part of her tale.

No, the kind of tale didn't matter; there would be heartbreak in it, narrow escapes, awful decisions, treachery, but you wouldn't be bored.

That was the thing I had feared the most as a child: that every day would be the same. Meat only on Freya's day, walnuts to roast in autumn. The wheel of seasons that turns and turns but brings you nowhere.

I would dance with a halfway handsome boy around the flowering May tree, kiss him that night. Marry him or another. And that would be it. Except for some children, *my* tale would be over.

She came to our village barefoot, her gown in tatters. But you could see that it been sewn out of green silk once. Green is a color not even our shaman could mix for the Midwinter fest.

She carried a compound bow. It was layered: horn, ivory, and wood that was as black as jet. The string she had braided out of her own jet-black hair. Nothing is as strong and supple as the tresses of a dragon-touched.

You heard the story of Yulessis the Greek? He owned a bow only he could string and shoot. Her bow was the same. Hirem, who was as strong as an ox, who could *stun* an ox with a blow of his fist, he tried to pull that bow.

I still can see his eyes almost rolling from the sockets, his neck turned beet-red as he whistled and groaned with the effort, but the string only cut into his fingers.

She took the bow from his hand, laid an arrow on the string.

WHY WE ARE STANDING ON THE BROKEN WALL 197

The bowstring sang—no, screamed—and the arrow sped through the air and then pierced the Yule cock on the top of the fetish pole. That cock must be more than two hundred paces away, clear on the other side of the village.

She folded her arms, looked at our stunned faces.

"I am Queen Leonœrah," she told us. "The Sellar men burned my city, peerless Lovinja of the Marble Trees. They took my Copper Castle and killed the king and all his sons. I was his youngest daughter, and I am the queen now."

No one gainsaid her. It was evident that she was a queen, that she was *our* queen. Even if we had never heard of peerless Lovinja of the Marble Trees or the Copper Castle.

She looked at us, looked right into our souls and said, "I want my country back."

Hiram was the first to kneel. Me, I was the second.

"It is good to have the sword arm of a strong man," the queen said. "But even better to have the wisdom and practical guile of a girl who still has to kiss her first lover."

"First lover," she had said, not boy. I later understood why.

※

When we left my village, she rode on the best horse, the roan that had belonged to the hetman. Five men, and no other woman but me, followed her.

We crossed the High Hills no villager had ever crossed, and a wide plain opened at our feet. She pointed to the temple towers of Ormazd, where green fires burn day and night, to the steep towers of Chrestos Imperator, and named every village.

"We'll go down there," she said. "Tell our tale." She pointed to a large village with a blue banner streaming from the top of a fetish mast. "That is Yulraduz, and they are highwaymen, robbers. There I will speak of loot and pearls as big as cuckoo eggs. Of widows wailing while their comely daughters are led away to be sold as slaves." She turned to the west. "And there lies Grundhar, a city built by canny merchants." She looked at me. "Of what will we speak there, Aminada?"

It was no doubt a test. If I failed, she wouldn't send me away, but the best I could hope for was combing and braiding her long hair, steeping shavings of tea brick in boiling water, and bringing her a cup while she consulted with her generals.

"You will speak of profits, Queen. Of routes opened up with the perfidious caravan-robbing Sellar men gone. Of spices from the mysterious East and the fine wool of apaculpas."

"I will," she said, and I knew I had passed my first test.

The next came that very night.

Yulraduz had given us a peloton of villainous looking young men with hooked swords and iron stars that flew back to their hands after they had made a fleeing goose tumble from the sky. Grundhar sent two ambassadors with silver tongues who could make a pewter cup sound like a golden grail. Also some maids, because "no queen should ever travel without her ladies-in-waiting."

She looked out over her brand-new army, standing next to the silk pavilion from Grundhar and nodded. "Not a bad start." She took my arm and lifted the flap of her tent. "Come with me. The servants will bring us a samovar and porcelain cups."

"I am not your servant then, Queen?"

"I hope not."

For the first time in my life, I sat down on a chair. It was a Grundhar one, upholstered, made of ivory wood and carved so intricate one would need a hawk's eye to discern all the details.

Her eyes got an inward look. "Let me tell you something about myself. That may help you to understand the kind of creature you are following now.

"I was the youngest daughter. With seventeen older ones, there weren't enough princes or grand-dukes to marry them all off, so they let me run wild.

"I climbed trees, rounded the keep in a stolen kayak during a howling storm. A tomboy, and when I laughed with fishermen, not a single one thought me a girl.

"I amused my brothers, and they petted me like one would a half-wild dog. One lent me his bow, taught me to fletch an arrow. When I hit the bull's eye more often that he, that brother cursed me and called me unnatural, a hoyden. The next night I stole his bow." She touched her weapon. "This bow."

"And he just let you?" I asked. "I mean, he would have seen you with his bow later. A bow is too big to hide in a castle where servants know very corner and nook."

"I knew that. I used a needle while he was sleeping, hammered it right through his skull and skewered his brain. He arched his back, sighed, and then he was dead." She smiled, and it was a fond smile, as if she was remembering her first taste of honey.

"Then came a time that I had my first flow. It made me feel weak, womanish, and that was unacceptable. The world was wounding me, bleeding me.

"I remedied that. I stole a crock of dragon blood from the Witch of the Westwood and emptied it in my bath. Holy Guulah, how it burned! I hissed between my teeth, bit my lower lip until it bled, but I persevered. I watched my skin flush red as a boiled lobster, then turn green and scaly and finally brown and smooth again.

"Now dragon's blood doesn't make you invulnerable, not quite. But it is only every seventh cut from a sword or arrow that pierces you. That does permanent damage. Otherwise the wounds just close, healing in an instant. Arrows, they are just squeezed out when your flesh heals."

"Your tattered gown," I said. "Thorns won't rend silk."

"Yes, arrows would. Those fools jumped from the bushes and shot my mule. They shot me. Five, six arrows, and I must have looked like a regular porcupine.

"Now six arrows is a lot, especially if one is skewering your liver and another one your heart. I was in considerable pain and couldn't move for a dozen heartbeats.

"They pulled the flaps of the panniers on my dead donkey. You should have seen their faces! Their cries of dismay. No silver bars or gold coins, just bags with grain, dried sausages.

"One of them saw me standing up, shedding arrows. I grabbed those arrows and killed them with their own weapons. That seemed a nice touch." She rose from her gilded chair, stepped from her gown.

"Time to take off your own clothes and go to bed."

I stood staring, paralyzed. She was very beautiful, her belly a gentle curve, small, high set breasts. Her hair was an ebony waterfall.

She looked me in the eyes and said, "I understand. You are one of those who look at a man or a woman like you would at a peacock or a full blood racing horse. They look nice, graceful, but that is it. They could as well be made from marble or cast in bronze."

"I never understood why my sisters wanted to kiss boys," I told her, "or why the priestesses of Ormazd walked hand in hand, their eyes shining."

"It is a great and useful talent not to be swayed by your heart," the queen said. "To feel no passion. No, don't protest. I know you feel things. You aren't cold. You probably loved your parents, your siblings, but not that way." She clapped her hands and a maid appeared. "Make Aminada a bed in the corner of the tent there." O, her smile was dazzling. "I need a trusted advisor much more than another lover. You'll be my left clever hand, Aminada. The one whose advice never will be tainted by lust."

Half a year passed and our army grew, seemed to spring from the ground like soldiers from sown dragon teeth. We had our first clash with the Sellar men. Their yurts and their high wheeled tundra wagons burned. They fled into the trackless grass.

Yes, you are right, my daughter. We fired the tundra, using the Greek fire the corsairs of Humnid had given us. I came back after the rains. You could still see their teeth gleaming in the ash.

We killed and killed them until there were no Sellar men left.

Five years later, we marched into peerless Lovinja of the Marble Trees. The Copper Castle was rubble. No matter, we had grown rich with loot, and we rebuilt it.

The day after the Coronation, the queen came to me, carrying an orphaned baby. It was red as a lobster, with just wisps of hair. She was bawling.

Yes, my daughter, that was you.

"I saw you looking at the little ones, Aminada," the queen said. "You are quite capable of loving even if you don't care for the kisses of either man or woman."

I took her, I took you, and you fell silent, opened eyes as blue as cornflowers. I instantly fell in love, for the first time in my life.

Nine years passed. The wheels of fate are slow to turn, but remorseless, grinding all dreams to dust.

We had thought the Sellar men gone, exterminated to the last hissing crone. In the year of the Cockroach, we learned otherwise. The plains tribes with their high wheeled wagons had been no more than just a drop in an ocean of Sellar man. Many still remained in the high mountains beyond our queen's kingdom. They lived on the continent far beyond the horizon where our traders never went because no ship ever returned.

Think of them as a nest of angry wasps. Kill even a single one of them, and they all turn on you.

Yes, you are right. It is like that plains rhyme.

"I hate my brothers,
But my brothers and me hate our cousins more.
I hate my brothers and my cousins,
But we all hate the stranger more."

It takes time for such hate to spread, though.

I saw them surround the queen, attack like hungry wolves. She was the mightiest warrior of them all, but after the seventh sword cut her, blood started to flow and didn't stop.

I could have followed her then and there across the Rainbow Bridge, but I wanted to see you one last time, to say goodbye.

We repelled the first assault though it left the wall broken in a hundred places.

O, yes, we will die, my daughter. Here, standing on the broken wall, clutching the swords I found in the queen's trophy hall. Swords too rusty to take an edge. Soon we'll go to join your Aunt Leonœrah, who will be waiting for us on the other side of the Rainbow Bridge.

AMINADA NOMANSWIFE is best known for her "Travels with the Vengeful Queen," a hexametric epic poem meant to be sung in a tavern by drunken rogues. The text of "Why we are standing" is taken from the reminiscences of her daughter Sidhar, as told to the itinerant monk and part-time exorcist Juball Ludmir, who became the father of her first daughter. Sidhar survived the sack of Peerless Lovinja and went on to become an octopus herd, driving those tentacled land-squids across the tundra. She bore seven more surviving daughters and all were as tone-deaf as their mother.

TAIS TENG is a Dutch writer, illustrator, and sculptor. In his own language, he has written everything from radio-plays to hefty fantasy trilogies. He just finished his first English science fiction novel *Phaedera: Alastor 824*, set in the universe of Jack Vance, which will be published by Spatterlight Press. His greatest wish is a Star Wars laser cannon to carve mountains or the lesser Jupiter moons. He owns no cats or even a pet boa constrictor, but has to do with a wife and three kids. For his writing go to http://taisteng.atspace.com/, for his art to https://taisteng.deviantart.com/

DROPPING ROCKS

An account by Ayoveka, as provided by Jennifer R. Povey

Barclay's World was hardly considered prime real estate, by humans at least. Neither its location nor the resources in its system were enough to have attracted the Alliance or any of the major corporations.

Which meant that the war did not come here for a long time. Yes, we had a human colony, but it was small, scientifically oriented, and made up of people who did their best to live in harmony with us.

Not that you understood us, not really, or we you. I don't think one species ever can understand another.

When the chips are down, though, there's a bond between those who share a world.

I am Ayoveka. I am female, yes, although not in the way your women are. I am *ayor*. Yet another thing you will not understand.

Cameron Hudson was, most definitely, a woman. Yet another thing I do not understand. Men, women, sometimes people not quite one or the other.

Ayor, ayak, meyor, meyak. Four sexes. Two of them map to what you call female, two to what you call male. Not important, really, except as an example of how our different biology makes us different. Yet, we share a world.

You call it Barclay's World, after the man who discovered it—foolish, really, how can you discover something that already has people on it? I hear tell you explain quantum mechanics to your kids with a cat in a box, saying that no observer can tell the state of a hidden cat.

The cat is an observer. We are people, and Doctor Hudson was one of the first to properly acknowledge that. She negotiated us protection.

She negotiated protection for our world.

We call it *Tavaran Liktora* when being formal. Tavar when less so. The home of the people. Dr. Hudson joked that everyone calls their world some variation of either Dirt or Home.

Does it say something about humans that they call their world Dirt?

Perhaps it does. Perhaps not. I will never visit the human world—there are trace elements necessary to humans that are toxic to us.

Well, maybe not never. Perhaps the war will end, perhaps somebody will design technology to protect us so we can go and see the things of which the humans speak.

No. *I* will never visit the human world.

I have no desire to leave Tavar. But perhaps when the war is over, some of us will.

Perhaps.

We are people who call our world Home.

The war came to Tavar in the depths of our southern winter, and that was where the humans had landed, in the south. It came in the middle of the night.

It came without warning. They dropped a rock on us. If you know anything about how war is fought in space, between worlds, you know that the most dangerous weapon in existence is a rock.

Apparently, there's an old human joke about fighting the next war with thrown rocks. Something about losing technology as opposed to gaining it.

We fought our last war with arrows. We're fighting this one with guns.

Human guns.

The rock turned their garden dome, where they grew their own plants to get those toxic trace elements, into a crater.

It missed the nursery. That was a small blessing. It missed where they grew their children.

My children are grown. All three of them. I still regret none of them are *ayar*. My children fight the war.

Doctor Hudson pulled everyone into the open after the strike. "They attacked us without warning. That *was* the warning. Sign Barclay's World over to them or they will destroy the colony."

We are not property. Our world is not property.

"What do they want with us?" The voice came from a young man.

"Safe real estate. Away from the war."

"Who is it?" The same young man.

"Leo Corporation."

That gave a name to our enemy. Safe real estate meant our land. I knew that much. Leo Corporation would set its own laws, and those laws would not count us as people.

As animals, perhaps. Or as chattels.

Dr. Hudson hesitated. "I've seen this before. We have no choice but to go along with them."

A murmur. Some ululations. A young ayak almost screaming.

She lifted a hand. "And make their lives so difficult they'll get their butts off our planet."

We had no word for what she was talking about.

We used the human one.

Sabotage.

The humans that came down were as mixed a bag in color as those already on our world. The difference was that they wore uniforms.

"Who's in charge here?"

Dr. Hudson stepped forward. "I am. You realize this world is occupied."

"By those?" The man took in the scene. He indicated me and the others crouched next to me. "Animals in woven blankets."

It was the middle of winter, so of course we wore blankets. The humans did the same thing, they just shaped theirs differently.

It was enough for me. I tried to catch her eyes, but she kept them resolutely focused on her enemy. "The outpost is yours."

"No. The planet is ours."

The next thing they did was take hostages, but only human hostages.

Kids.

That angered me. *Ayar* are the child rearers, we value children even more than the rest of our kind. I knew the humans valued their children just as much as we did. One thing we have in common.

But they placed guards on the nursery. They said what would happen if we did not cooperate.

The first thing, I thought, was to get the kids out. Unfortunately, they had not taken any of our children hostage.

We all knew the nursery, domed as it was to keep in their air, was vulnerable. Humans could live in our air, as long as it wasn't for too long.

We all knew what to do. But they had Dr. Hudson under guard. Could we, should we, guess what she would do?

I knew what she would do.

Save the kids. The first step, get the hostages out of the way, get them to safety.

The second step... their weapons. We had guns, because they were better for hunting than bows and arrows. Guns made for our forehands.

They had bigger and better ones, which the humans could use but we could not.

I had to get to Dr. Hudson, but the first part of the plan was obvious.

And the nursery was vulnerable.

The humans knew that, but they trusted us. Not enough to let our kids in there to play, because kids are mischievous and do stupid things.

These outsiders did not know. They dismissed us. We were beneath their notice, not yet even worth enslaving.

They did not know what our rear hands were for the way those who called Tavar home did.

We are people of the earth. They are climbers—we know this because we've seen what their children do. Their children climb.

Ours, of course, burrow.

As do we. It's undignified for adults.

We didn't care. We know how to make the tunnels the way our evolutionary ancestors did, how to shore up the walls with our spit.

We burrowed. Into the nursery. One by one, the kids vanished. Half of them were gone before the invaders did anything.

But they could not actually bring themselves to harm children. Instead, they shot two of the nursery workers.

We knew it would happen, but we sang mourning for them nonetheless.

Then we rescued the rest of the children. We knew where to take them, where they could get the extra stuff they needed.

We knew how to keep them safe.

"Unless those children are returned." I hid at the edge.

Dr. Hudson was facing down the man who called himself our Governor. I knew that was a bad word. A nasty word, one that spoke of conquest.

"You'll do what? Shoot me?" She met my eyes.

I lowered my head after a moment. Not wanting to look, in case he took her up on it.

Behind me, somebody fidgeted, dropping onto their rear hands and then up again.

"You won't shoot me because you need me."

"I need this planet. I don't need any of the people on it."

One of the humans was sidling toward us. "If you don't hear from the Doc in three days, get as many people as you can into the mines."

The mines would put us deep underground. We did mine. We were probably more advanced in that than the humans had been when they had made war with bows and arrows. Burrowers.

"What's happening?"

"He's going to poison the planet. Make it so only humans can live here."

If he did that, the land would turn barren. We could survive in the mines for a while. Then what? Would we become exiles? Would we become a war casualty, a statistic? The human word was genocide.

"Does she have a way to stop it?"

"You can't help this time."

That was not something I was willing to believe. I dropped my muzzle to him nonetheless. I already knew it would not be me taking everyone to the mines. And that we would not wait three days. Would they notice that the worthless natives were vanishing?

Now I understood why they had not enslaved us. This had been the plan from the start. To kill us and to kill every living being on this planet. The plants might survive. Or it would leave…

"The soil will die," I whispered. "He is a fool."

He would not make the planet clear for humanity but simply destroy it.

I faded into the trees. Talked to some people. Mostly *ayak* and *meyak*. They tend to be the largest of us, the ones who can use brute strength and carry heavy loads. To get the children and elders, and those *ayak* who were pregnant, into the mines first. In case we failed.

I had already seen that look on Dr. Hudson's face.

She intended to win.

She also intended to die. I could not blame her—I too was quite willing to sacrifice myself for Tevar.

I did not intend to let her, if it could be avoided. Or, perhaps, we would both die. At that point I was… perhaps not happy with that idea, but quite ready for it. It would be worth it, worth not seeing my grandchildren, if the world was saved.

I told the people I needed to, and then I got the lay of the land.

Dr. Hudson was still in charge. That was the amazing thing. She had made herself indispensable to the Governor. At least until he killed all of us. Presumably he would do something about the humans. The children, the human children, were at a science station a day or so's walk away. Dr. Hudson had not told him where it was. And now she was planning the uprising.

I waited just underground enough to be able to hear part of the plan before I emerged. "Aya hey, Hudson."

She laughed. "I might have known you would not be content to run."

"I arranged for what you asked. We need to—"

"We need to destroy the colony." Dr. Hudson looked at me. "The humans here will go to the science station. Already are, in ones and twos."

I nodded. "What can I do to help?"

"Aya hey, you can—" She sighed. "There really *is* nothing you can do. I have to steal their ship. You—"

I didn't have either the knowledge or the correct manipulative appendages to help with stealing their ship. What I did have was an idea.

"You've held everyone together," I told her. "Your people and mine are getting out of the area. But we've been acting like—"

"Like what?"

"—them chasing us is a bad thing."

"Most of us are not well armed enough—"

I cut her off. "We get them to chase us. Then we... deal with them."

She didn't ask me how. A good leader doesn't question such things, not the plans of an ally. "Arrange for that."

"I will." But once I had, I came back. There were fewer humans, and the Governor's people were starting to get suspicious. Soon they would all be dead.

Dr. Hudson frowned at me. "You—"

"I will help. Even if it's only passing tools."

She laughed. "You do realize their ship has to be destroyed. Anyone who goes up there will—" Then she frowned. "Maybe we don't have to die."

She had resolved to die. So had her humans.

She could not, for whatever reason, resolve to kill me. It might be the bizarre human tendency to form pack bonds with anything—with other animals, other species, inanimate objects, their ships—and then place them above other humans.

It had to have been a survival tactic once. Now it would be one again.

"Let's go," she said, finally.

At any given time, the humans had one ship on the surface. It wasn't a very big ship. I was told what they had in orbit was bigger.

Dr. Hudson, four humans, and me. I could shoot, if I had to. I could fight, if I had to. I could not dig, not on a metal ship. I also could not be disguised in one of their uniforms.

That alone almost made me back down, but they wrapped me in some blankets and carried me on board in an ill-dignified manner.

This made me a quite nasty surprise for those already on the shuttle. They were not expecting the bundle of "native blankets for sale" to jump up and attack them.

They tossed the three humans out the back. One was still alive. I didn't particularly care.

It only now occurred to me that I was about to be the first of the people to leave Tavar.

It also occurred to me that their artificial air might not be something I could breathe, but Dr. Hudson tossed me a mask.

"Wear this. It's been tested… although not on a person."

A breathing mask. It felt very uncomfortable over my muzzle, and I knew that it might not work. She was wearing a mask herself. It made her look like somebody else.

Then the ship took off, and I was pressed into the floor as if I weighed as much as a very overweight *ayak*.

A *very* overweight *ayak*.

Then I weighed nothing at all. One of the men had to throw up. I had no such problems, simply because my kind don't throw up. My head spun a little, though. And I was drifting.

"Breathe," Dr. Hudson told me, pulling off her mask. "Are you alright?"

"Lightheaded."

"We don't know how micro gravity will affect you."

"I'll take notes."

She laughed. "So. Your task is to find the escape pods so we can get out. I'll take these two and do… what's necessary."

Dropping rocks. I knew she meant dropping rocks.

And she still meant to die. "No," I said to her. "Those two will find the escape pod. I'm coming with you."

"You—"

"My people have fought wars. And you do not get to martyr yourself." It's hard for us to make eye contact with humans. They're taller, after all. I managed it.

"Your people have not used weapons of mass destruction."

She wanted to keep us innocent. I shook my head. "We have fought wars. I understand what we are doing here." And that it would only buy us time, and that we needed her alive when their friends came looking for them.

Humans are pursuit predators. They can always stare down ambush predators. This time, she was the one who looked away.

I shot at least five humans on the way. I don't know how many of them died. It did not matter. I knew what they intended to do. They intended to destroy us. You cannot use non-violence against people like that. You have to fight a war. This was a war, this was part of the great war between the Corporations and the Alliance.

Our world was a resource, but it was also our home. We would not let them run roughshod over it.

Even if it meant dropping rocks.

I did not know how to navigate the ship. It was at least a village in space. No, a town. I followed her, using my gun when I needed to, trying not to stare at this place, built on a scale that was not for me.

I thought I was used to humans. Perhaps they had toned down what they were for us. Perhaps. They had built something on the planet we could be comfortable with.

And then we were on their bridge. Only four of us. It could not be enough, eight guns facing us. They were using energy guns, though. Of course.

We planned on destroying the ship. We didn't care if we put some holes in it.

They did.

I went down, diving to the side, letting them shoot past me. Remembering what Dr. Hudson had told me about energy guns.

You didn't want to be hit by one, but they could only shoot at a certain, not very fast, speed because of the energy requirements.

They could not shoot me again right away, so I went for them. A couple of bullets, and then my claws.

Our rear hands were for digging.

They did a number on human flesh that made Dr. Hudson wince; she had not seen us fight, not really.

She had come as a trader from far away, she had come in peace. Now she saw what I could do in a fight, for real, and for a moment she hesitated. For a moment, I saw in her eyes the fear of the other, the fear that drove genocide.

She was human, after all.

But she overcame it, I saw her put it aside, put it away, and then she threw something. Gas billowed out of it. Whatever it was, it was being blocked by my mask.

Knockout gas. Poison of some kind. They went down.

They went down, and we had the ship. For about five minutes.

I couldn't use the consoles. In the end, no matter how much I wanted to, I couldn't drop rocks on the outpost. Couldn't destroy everything they had built.

Dr. Hudson did that herself.

Did that herself and then we ran. I knew we needed her, so I covered her. The ship would blow up behind us.

She would manage at the science station with the others.

The ship would blow up behind us, and it did. I knew what we had done. Thousands of humans were dead.

They hadn't anticipated a counter attack. They hadn't protected themselves. But it was inevitable. We got in.

Getting out, that was harder. One of the two humans died on the way, and Dr. Hudson was hit badly.

The other carried her into the escape pod. I was the last in. I was going home.

For now.

Dr. Hudson was going somewhere else. She died on the way down, leaving us without anything but her shadow and memory. That's the truth. Dr. Cameron Hudson died protecting us. We've been using her name, using her image, using the threat of what she was willing to do.

Except I know I can do it too. If I must. I would rather not.

I'm told the war is over. Dr. Hudson won't be going home. But I think she would be proud of us.

We found a way for humans to properly live on our world. At least for the children.

We welcome those who come in peace.

Those who don't?

We know how to throw rocks now. She taught us that.

We already knew how to start a war.

She taught us how to end one.

I'm home, now, and I hold my granddaughter in my arms. *Ayak*, of course.

Her name is Cameron.

AYOVEKA came forward as a leader of the Tavarian people (Barclay's World, Galactic Coordinates 2313.07.08) after the end of the Corporation Wars. But she spoke much of the influence of Dr. Cameron Hudson. Dr. Hudson, who held multiple degrees in Archaeology and Xenoanthropology from the University of Michigan and the University of Mariner City, was long believed to be the protector of the Tavarian people, but it later came about that she died heroically whilst sabotaging a Corporation ship attempting to conquer Barclay's World. Her influence was what helped the Tavarians learn to live in the modern world on their own terms. Ayoveka herself retired from leadership several years after the war, but not before becoming the first Tavarian to visit Earth, where she paid respects to Dr. Hudson's family and introduced them to her granddaughter, Cameron, as well as being part of signing the Tavar Treaty, which, among other things, changed the official designation of Barclay's World to the indigenous Tavaran Litkor.

JENNIFER R. POVEY is in her early forties, and lives in Northern Virginia with her husband. She writes a variety of speculative fiction, whilst following current affairs and occasionally indulging in horse riding and role-playing games. She has sold fiction to a number of markets including *Analog*, and written RPG supplements for several companies. She is currently working on an urban fantasy series, *Lost Guardians*.

PALADIN

An account by C. C. Harris,
as provided by Shirley Vogel

When I first met Lisa at a self-defense class she was teaching, I was convinced she was a true blue blood, born with a silver spoon in her mouth. She spoke softly, but with elegance and proper English. I couldn't detect even the slightest hint of an accent, and she didn't punctuate her speech with slang or obscenities. She struck me as someone well-educated. Her clothing was modest, but obviously well-made and probably expensive.

Usually upon meeting someone like Lisa I was intimidated, but she was warm and friendly. If she felt her status was above mine, she didn't show it. She encouraged everyone in the class, but there seemed to be an extra connection between us. She was curious about me and asked questions about my life and actually listened to the answers I gave.

We started meeting for coffee a few mornings each week and taking walks when the weather permitted. She invited me to her luxurious apartment for lunch a few times, but we never socialized in the evenings.

One night, I was out with a group of friends at a local hangout near the college. It wasn't exactly a dive, but it was loud and crowded with college kids, as well as a lot of older guys, who seemed to be part of a sports team out for a few drinks after their game. The men were interested in the younger college women, and there was a fair amount of flirting and exchanging of numbers.

At one point, I was looking around and was surprised to see Lisa sitting in a back booth alone, watching the crowd intently. She didn't seem to be focused on anyone; instead, her gaze shifted constantly, taking everything in. I wasn't sure if she had seen me yet, so I headed over to ask her if she wanted to join my group. Making my way across the room was not an easy task since the bar was jam-packed. By the time I got to her booth, she was gone. I looked around the room and couldn't spot her, so I wriggled back through the crowd to my friends.

The next morning, I turned on the news while I made breakfast. The weather forecast proclaimed it was going to be a great day, with sunshine and low humidity. I decided to see if Lisa wanted to go for a walk later. After the weather, there were a few stories, the first about a bad accident on the highway causing havoc with rush hour. Once again, I was glad I was lucky enough to have a job working from home. The next story was about an assault near the college the night before. There wasn't much information about it, but the beaten man was in the hospital. The next story was about twin sisters who had both scored perfect ACT scores. I was impressed. I flipped off the TV and went into my home office to get some work done.

That afternoon, as Lisa and I walked in the park, I mentioned seeing her at the bar the night before. She was startled and possibly a little embarrassed, at first, but her good breeding took over and she smiled, and then said, "Oh, I wish you would have come over to say 'hi.'"

When I told her I had tried to do just that, only to find her booth empty, she said the noise had gotten to her at one point and she left rather quickly. She mentioned that she went to the bar often to people-watch and maybe we would run into each other another night.

As we walked on, I related the news story about the assaulted man in the same area as the bar. She asked if I had heard any more details, but I had been busy working and on the phone most of the day. We split at the end of our walk, and I stopped to buy the evening newspaper.

As I browsed the local stories that evening, I found a short piece about the assault from the night before. The man said he had left the bar, the same bar I visited that night, with a woman he had met there. He said they stopped to talk for a while. Then out of nowhere, someone attacked him. Neither of them could give a description of the attacker. It happened so quickly and then the attacker was gone. No weapons were involved, as far as they knew. The attacker just punched him over and over again and then ran away. He was treated at the hospital and held overnight for observation.

Two nights later, there was another report of an assault on a man leaving the same bar with a woman he had met there. Again, there was no description, no weapons used, and no suspect. The woman thought the attacker might have been another woman, but the man vehemently denied it. A week later, it happened again, and by now it was obvious there was a pattern.

When Lisa and I met for coffee the next day, we were both intrigued by what had happened. We hashed out all the details we knew and talked about who could be doing this. I wondered if it was safe to go to the bar, but she pointed out that it was men who were being attacked. "Just don't leave with someone you meet there. Stay with your own group. The attacker is going after the men, so you should be safe."

That seemed logical, so when my friends suggested we go back to the bar a few nights later, I agreed. We all promised to stay together and only leave with each other. It wasn't as crowded this time, but there were still a lot of the groups of men there. They seemed extra loud, and I overheard more than one say they weren't afraid. Let the mugger come at them, and they would get the upper hand. The testosterone was running rampant.

As my friends and I left together, there was a disturbance on the sidewalk a block ahead of us. Two people were on the ground, and a woman stood screaming between them. She moved toward one of the downed bodies, and the other got up and ran into the alley, holding one arm in the other hand. By the time we got there, the police, who had been prowling the area, had arrived, and we were held back. I looked down the alley and saw what appeared to be a woman running away. I told the police, but they were waiting for backup before they searched the alley. We gave statements about what we had seen, which wasn't a lot, and were told to go home.

The next morning, I flipped on the news to find out more about the attack the night before. There wasn't any additional information on the newscast, and no mention of anyone fleeing the scene.

My phone rang as I was turning off the news, and I was surprised to find it was Lisa. She sounded very upset, stuttering and repeating herself. Her soft-spoken voice was loud one minute and almost a whisper the next. She begged me to come to her apartment, and I said I would be right over.

She answered the door with one arm in a sling.

"What happened to you? Have you seen a doctor?" I asked.

Instead of answering my questions immediately, she asked me to come in and sit down. She said she had some things to explain to me, and a favor to ask. She had calmed herself since we talked on the phone, and was much more composed, more like the Lisa I was used to.

"First of all, I need to tell you that I am not what I appear to be." She took her arm out of the sling and unwrapped the dressing on it.

My eyes widened at the long slash in the skin of her arm. Then

I realized it was not skin, but a thin covering. Instead of blood and bone, underneath were wires and metal pins and hinge-like things. The covering looked very natural, but what it covered was not. I finally looked away from the arm and up to her face.

"As you can see, I am not human. I am what you would call an android—a machine made to look and act as a human. I was programmed to study human behavior and learn from human interaction. You have helped me with this. I was also programmed to protect other women. My builder included a database in my system, with records of men who have shown aggressive or abusive behavior toward women. When I go to the bar, I study the men there. If I find any matches in my database, I watch them. If any of those I've matched leave with a woman, I follow them. I've done this every night for the last few weeks. Sometimes I don't find a match. Sometimes they leave alone. On a few occasions, all of the nights there was an attack, I was following them as they left with women. I saw them display aggressive behavior toward the women, and I stepped in and stopped them. Then I fled, to avoid questions. I think the reason no one has given a description of me yet is because the men are embarrassed to be beaten up by a woman. The women being threatened are just glad to get away safely. Unfortunately, last night when I followed a man and woman, he was ready for my attack and had a knife. He managed to slash my arm. Now I need your help to fix it."

"My help? What can I do? I don't know anything about robotics."

"You don't have to. I need you to drive me to my builder's lab so she can repair me. I can't drive with my arm like this, and I have learned you are a good person, someone I can trust. I knew it from the first moment I met you. You have been my friend, and I have learned so much from you. After my arm is fixed, I think you can help me with the task I have been given. We can work together. I want to continue training women in self-defense and organize some of the women I have trained. I'm sure you have noticed that some of them are more skilled. I need help following the men I recognize from the database. Some nights I find three or more of them, and I have to watch them all and then choose who to follow. If I had a group of women I trusted, they could do some of the following and break up more potential problems. There is only one of me, but with a group of women, we could do so much more. Will you help me?"

As far as I could see, there was only one answer. I nodded.

C. C. HARRIS works as a personal assistant from her home office in St. Louis, Missouri. Her job allows her the freedom she has always wanted to schedule her day her way. She's also a founding member of the Greater St. Louis branch of Women Helping Women, and volunteers her time teaching self-defense classes on the weekend.

SHIRLEY VOGEL is a new author from St. Charles, MO. In fact, at 68 years young, this is her first published work—joining several other published writers in her family. She likes reading mysteries, staying active with bicycling and walking, and loves drinking wine.

UNBROKEN

An account by Eshai Unbroken,
as provided by Elisa A. Bonnin

When I was nine years old, I nearly died of a fever. My survival was hailed as a miracle. It was Lavit who found me, stranded and alone in the space between spreading trees, Lavit who brought me home. I don't remember much of that day, but I remember seeing him when I opened my eyes, weak from the fever still. He was a boy, a wiry teenager dressed in a loose orange tunic and trousers, a leather belt tied around his waist. His skin was a rich brown, his hair a shade of brown darker. His eyes were like jewels, a clear bluish green.

When I came to next, I was lying on a soft mat that rested on a polished wooden floor. An old man sat cross-legged next to me, dressed in loose-fitting clothes. Markings covered his arms where I could see them, continuing up to his shoulder and what little I could see of his chest. He was busy rearranging the insect netting above my mat, and so did not notice I was awake until I groaned. The old man's gaze snapped back to me, a frown creasing his weathered face. He placed a hand on my head, holding it there a moment before he pulled it away.

"Your fever's broken," he said. "That's good. How are you feeling, Eshai?"

Eshai.

My name. In the old tongue, it meant "star."

I looked down at the name mark on the back of my hand, a complex, curling symbol drawn in the same ink as the marks on his and the boy's arms. I looked up at him, searching for words. "I... feel sick."

"And no wonder," said the man. "I am Yanasa. Caretaker of this village. Do you know what happened to your parents, Eshai?"

A blackness. A hole in my memories. Blood in my mouth. An aching, pulsing pain in my temples.

I shook my head. No.

Yanasa clucked his tongue impatiently, but he did not seem particularly surprised. "I see."

I lay there for a moment in the silence, thinking, trying to remember. "What happened to me?"

"To hear Lavit say it, you were alone. No water in your canteen, no food in your pack. Sandals caked in dirt and worn all the way through." He gestured down at my body and I realized I was wearing a ragged shift, practically colorless from wear. "You were in the last stages of blood rot fever. You got through the worst of it on your own. You're lucky to be alive, Eshai."

"Lavit?"

"My other charge," Yanasa said. "The boy who brought you here. He's out at market right now, but you'll likely meet him. Here." He picked up a wooden bowl that had been lying on the ground next to him, presenting it to me. Inside was a foul-smelling green liquid. My nose wrinkled at the sight.

Yanasa tutted. "Don't make that face," he said. "Drink. It will help you sleep."

I didn't believe him, but he was insistent, and he had the air of quiet authority that made him difficult to ignore. I drank. It was foul, but almost as soon as it touched my skin, I could feel it taking effect, a wave of drowsiness washing over me. I lay back again, my eyelids growing heavy.

"Sleep," Yanasa said, his touch gentle as he pulled a thin blanket over me. "When you wake, we'll find you some new clothes. We can talk more then."

I closed my eyes. In the darkness, I saw the clearing again, saw Lavit grabbing me by the arm as something large and furious burst out of the clearing behind me.

I woke during the night, with the moon hovering high above Yanasa's spreading tree. I was exhausted, and when I stood up and put my weight on my injured feet, it nearly pulled a scream from my throat. I managed to stand, breathing hard, and crept toward the door of Yanasa's house. I stood because I heard voices. Angry, arguing voices. Yanasa and Lavit.

"—still out there," Lavit said. "I found some tracks while I was out today. It hasn't left."

"Is that what you were doing when I sent you to market?" Yanasa asked. "Lavit—"

"What was I supposed to do, Yana?" Lavit asked. "Leave it? I'm telling you, it's got Eshai's scent. It's after her."

"Be that as it may—"

Yanasa sounded uncertain. Anxious. I peered around the wall of the house and saw them there, standing together on the balcony in the moonlight. Lavit was still dressed in the clothes he had worn earlier today. My gaze was drawn to his boots. They were a dark brown, unremarkable from this angle, but I still remembered the speed with which he launched us into the air.

"It isn't going to stop," Lavit said, looking out into the jungle. "It will come for her next."

"Into the village?" Yanasa asked. "Don't be absurd, Lavit. And even if it is after her, there's no reason why you should be the one to deal with it. If you're so worried, alert the village guard."

Lavit didn't answer immediately. He turned away from Yanasa, his gaze still on the dark canopy of the forest. One of his hands went up, rubbing at a spot on his chest, just over his heart.

"Have you finished with my new knives yet?" he asked when he did speak.

"Lavit!"

"I'm only asking, Yanasa."

Yanasa sighed, shoulders heaving with weariness. He looked away. "No," he said. "They are not finished yet. Lavit, if you insist on this foolishness—"

But I didn't hear whatever Yanasa had to say next. A deep, rumbling bellow cut through the night, giving both of them pause. It sent a shiver through my bones, and I went tense, my hands pressing flat against the wall of the house. Yanasa looked around, startled, as Lavit's gaze moved to the trees.

"Yanasa—" he began.

"Inside!" Yanasa said, grabbing Lavit by the arms. "Inside now. I don't care what you say, Lavit. You are not hunting that creature tonight."

Yanasa tightened his grip on Lavit, urging him in the direction of the front door. My direction. My heart nearly stopped, and I scurried away as quickly as I could on my injured feet, disappearing into the house and back onto my sleeping mat before either of them found out that I had overheard them.

It was morning when I woke again, the sunlight streaming through the window of the sleeping room. My feet still hurt when I stood up, but whatever Yanasa had placed on the wounds had taken effect—I could walk better than I had been able to the night before. Carefully, I made my way out of the sleeping room and into the living area.

Yanasa was seated at a workbench beneath a window, sharpening a pair of bone knives. Lavit was nowhere to be seen. When Yanasa saw me, he stopped working. He set the knives down gently, and gave me food and water, then sent me out for water before I could ask him about Lavit. Before I could ask him about the beast, or even find the words. I remembered an old story, an old lesson someone in the past had told me. Someone… a woman. My mother.

The beasts prowl the forest paths. They fear the braves and will not approach. Venture not into the unknown world, child of the People. For that is the domain of the braves and the braves alone.

I made it to the stream. It wasn't a far walk, but the road was deserted that late in the day. As I walked, I couldn't shake the feeling of unease that washed over me, and found myself jumping at every shadow. Nothing was out of place. The jungle around me was quiet, tame this close to a village, and I managed to tell myself I was only imagining things. I found the stream and followed it a little ways until I found a place where it widened enough to create a little bathing pool. I stripped off my new dress and set it carefully aside, then slipped into the water.

Nothing was wrong, I told myself, dipping beneath the surface. I was only out of sorts because of yesterday. Everything was alright.

I broke the surface of the water to see the beast in front of me, staring at me.

I froze. I couldn't scream, and it was that silence that saved me, because when I had the chance to look at the beast for a moment longer, I noticed it had no eyes with which to see me. Where its right eye had been was nothing but a ragged hole, its left eye a mass of scar tissue. It was big, larger than anything I had ever seen. Its body was feline, its fur white and striped with rows of jagged black. Crystals jutted out from its skin at odd intervals, gleaming with their own inner light. As I watched, it lifted its head, sniffing the air. Its head turned this way and that, looking for me. I held my breath, too afraid to move, to even think.

The beast lowered its head to the ground, sniffing. It padded slowly around my little pond, pausing only to sniff at the dress I had laid by the bank. A growl escaped it, and it raised its head to the air, running back into the trees. I waited until the sounds of its passing had faded away, then allowed myself to exhale, my knees so weak that I sank into the water. I pulled myself up, grabbing at my arms and gasping for breath.

It's blind, I thought, squeezing my eyes shut as I clung to the rocks. *It hunts by scent.*

The water must have masked my scent, which was the only reason why the beast had not found me. If I had gotten into the water a few moments later, I would have been dead.

Dead.

A chill passed through me at the thought and my eyes snapped open, my head turning to follow the beast's progress. It hunted by scent, and it didn't know I had gotten into the water. If it thought I was still moving, it would follow the path I had taken. And if it did that—

Yanasa's face flashed into my mind, the old man hunched over the knives he had been working on. A new fear took over me, so strong it felt like I was being choked.

I scrambled out of the water and grabbed my dress, pulling it back on over my head.

"Yanasa!" I shouted as I raced back to the village. "Yanasa!"

There was no answer. I ran as fast as I could, my feet burning with pain the entire way as I slipped on rough rocks, tripped over tree roots. I was out of breath about halfway there but I pressed on, until my lungs burned with the same fire as my feet and the rest of my body. As I ran, I prayed. Prayed that Yanasa hadn't left the spreading tree. Prayed that the beast couldn't climb, that all was well.

I wasn't that lucky.

I found Yanasa on the ground at the base of the tree, a basket of trash on the ground next to him. The beast was looming over him, and so I did the only thing I could think of to capture its attention. I threw a stone at its head, ignoring Yanasa's shout of warning as the beast pounded after me.

As quickly as I could, I scrambled up the ladder that led to the house, hoping that Yanasa used the chance to get away. The beast roared, lunging for the ladder, but it missed me by inches. Its claws raked into the tree trunk as I pulled myself up onto the balcony, my chest heaving with the effort. The beast's claws dug furrows into the tree trunk as it began to slide down the tree.

Then it stopped, its tail swishing back and forth as it clung to the side. Its head lifted, turning to face me, and I felt time stop.

In one motion, the beast dug its hind legs into the tree and leaped, closing the distance. I ran as fast as I could, darting into the house as the creature scrambled up onto the balcony.

It launched itself through the door, growling and snarling as it snapped at me. I screamed, throwing myself out of the way a second before the beast came crashing through. One of its claws caught the hem of my dress, ripping the fabric and knocking me over. I crashed down onto the wooden floor, skinning my knees, then slammed into the base of Yanasa's worktable. My arms went up to shield my head as tools slid off the tabletop, scattering on the floor around me.

The beast roared, a deafening sound. It leaped over the wreckage of the table and landed on all fours, squarely in front of me. I slid back, but there was nowhere to run, nothing but a wall behind me and Yanasa's workbench above me. The beast sank down onto its haunches, and I saw my death written on its face. My eyes closed as it lunged, one of my hands searching the ground around me for something, *anything*, I could use to change my fate.

It found the handle of a knife. Lavit's knife.

Without thinking, I grabbed onto the knife and screamed, holding it with both hands in front of me.

Warm blood splattered across my dress as the beast rushed in, impaling itself on the blade. I opened my eyes, breathing hard, and found that the knife had slid into the beast's neck. The creature turned its head away from me and growled in pain, rage, and confusion, its body slamming against the side of the work bench as it tried to paw at me. Blood spurted from the wound as the knife worked itself free, a veritable fountain.

With one final roar, the beast slumped down onto the floorboards. Stillness followed.

The beast's heart formed the first piece of my armor, the set of five whose completion gave a warrior the right to join the braves. Out of the five—boots, vest, helmet, gloves and spear—I chose to begin with the boots, the same as Lavit had. I decided then that Lavit and I would become braves together someday. For a while, as we trained and fought together, as we hunted and dreamed together, the two of us were the only ones who existed in our world.

It was when I was twelve that the rift between us began to open.

By then, we had each gained another piece of our armor. Lavit had chosen a helm for his second piece. It allowed him to see far, track well, and hear the slightest of sounds. My choice for my second piece was more defensive—I chose a vest. I was smaller than Lavit and could endure less at the time, so I thought the extra defense would allow me to keep pace. Lavit, who worried for me constantly, approved.

We were tracking a beast that had been ranging closer and closer to the village, a lizard-like creature that had started harassing our villagers in their traditional hunting grounds. Lavit was fifteen and a man in the eyes of the village, so he carried an adult's spear. At twelve, I certainly was not an adult, so I was left with my pick of any of the other weapons. I chose the bow, preferring its longer reach.

Whoever slew this beast was going to acquire their third piece. It would bring them one step closer to completing the set, to becoming a brave in truth. And although Lavit was kind and made it sound like it was anyone's game, I knew he thought he would be the one to do it. In all truth, I wanted that for him. It was never my wish to compete with Lavit. No matter what happened, I wanted to make Lavit's dream come true.

That was not what happened. The gods make fools of us all, and that day, I got lucky again. I slew the beast—an arrow to the eye—before Lavit could reach it with his spear. It was a close call, and I didn't contest it, letting him take the piece. But the secret burned between us, pushing us away from each other. I wondered all the time—I still wonder—if Lavit knew.

By the time I turned sixteen, I had four out of the five armor pieces, as did Lavit. I lacked the spear, which would lend my attacks more power and strength. Lavit had the spear, but lacked the vest.

There had been changes between me and Lavit over the years. We were no longer as close as we used to be. We still hunted together, still lived together, still confided in one another, but the ease between us was no longer there. It was as if more and more, Lavit had begun seeing me as a rival, and not just as a friend. He kept secrets from me, and because I was temperamental at that age and vindictive, I started keeping secrets from him too.

I worried that Lavit would break away from me. That he would decide to end the contest between us once and for all and become a brave alone. As it turns out, I needn't have worried. Lavit was intent on us becoming braves at the same time, and so we came up with a scheme for acquiring our last pieces. We would go on a long expedition, the two of us, to the very borders of civilization. We would skirt the edge of the unknown world where the beasts were plentiful, and we would hunt until we had slain two of them. Then we would return together, and forge our final pieces. We would make the pilgrimage to Vethaya, the city of braves, together.

At that time, I still had hope that things would return to the way we were, that we would return to the way we had been as children. But then, Atiru came to town.

Atiru was a hero, a legend. He was a brave whose exploits were the subject of songs, and he had come to the village because he had heard of *us*. A pair of promising young adults who were going to be braves. He wanted to meet us, to speak to us. Lavit was over the moon. When Atiru and his braves came to talk to us and remarked on how much potential we had, I could barely describe the expression on his face.

But after the welcoming feast, it was me that Atiru came to speak to. Me, that Atiru called sister-brave. I don't know what he saw in me that he didn't see in Lavit. I still don't know. But I know that Lavit resented me for it. That the resentment had been eating him alive.

The expedition was a success, although Lavit and I barely spoke to each other for most of it. We acquired our final pieces, went on our pilgrimage to Vethaya, and went our separate ways. I was assigned to Ushi's company, a company that explored the unknown world to the north. Lavit went south. For a long time, we never saw each other. I patrolled with my company, and all was well, until that day came.

That day was the worst day of my life.

We were overrun. A pack of beasts attacked us while we were resting. We fought like demons, but still, most of us died. Ushi survived, taking charge of the remnants of our company and leading us to a hard-won victory. I survived, but surrounded by the dying and the dead, the screams still ringing in my ears, I wished I hadn't.

After that, I spent the summer in Vethaya alone, wandering the trees, training, honing my skills. My armor darkened, becoming not black but a hard, scaly brown, as if it was trying to encase me in stone.

A change had come over me. I did the tasks expected of me with brutal efficiency and barely spoke to any of the new recruits. It was like I was floating, like some other soul had momentarily taken over the body I knew as Eshai, and I knew the new recruits hated me.

In the nights while we were out on missions, in the days when we were traveling and the hours stretched on forever, in all of the spaces of time when we weren't actively in battle, my thoughts became increasingly morbid. I started wondering what would happen to me if I died, what things would be like in a world without me. What it would be like to simply stop existing. I tried to hide these things, but armor doesn't lie. Armor is alive. It changes with the heart of the brave that wears it. The more missions we went on, the more my armor darkened, becoming thick-skinned and scaly. Spines grew out of it, thick black ridges that spread across my shoulders and stood out against the leather of my gloves.

I didn't even realize how much my behavior had changed until Ushi asked to see me. He called me into his tent and asked after me—how I was doing, what I was feeling, those sorts of probing questions. I answered as truthfully as I could, not wanting to lie to my commander. At the end of that meeting, Ushi suggested, in the way of a suggestion that is truly an order, that I take a break.

I wasn't pleased with the idea, and I made my displeasure known.

I demanded to stay, but he refused. I asked him if there was a problem with my performance, but Ushi insisted that nothing was wrong in that regard. I was performing admirably, a true brave. In fact, my stellar performance was part of the problem. I was throwing everything I could into my work, as if by doing so I could avoid thinking about the past, and it was strangling me. If my armor continued to darken, it would break. I would never be a brave again.

Ushi suggested that I go spend some time in Lanatha, the place of many waters. It was a sacred place to the People. A place of healing. He continued to suggest that I not return to the braves until my armor had lightened to the point where it was no longer in danger of shattering.

Those orders terrified me. As long as I was moving, I didn't have to think, to remember blood and death. My missions were my only escape from those memories. Out of action, there would be no sanctuary from them. Those memories would attack me every chance they had.

I was scared.

And Lavit sensed that fear. He was a hero now, famed for killing a beast that threatened to decimate his company. There was no competition between us anymore. I was no longer a rival, I was Eshai, a sister-brave, partner and friend, someone to be cherished.

So when I returned to my lonely quarters in Vethaya and found him still in the city, when I told him what Ushi's orders had been and where I was going, he offered to come with me.

In the land of the People, Lanatha is holy. It is a spreading tree, larger even than the spreading trees that form Vethaya, but unlike most trees in the provinces of the People, Lanatha is anchored to the center of a lake, a crystalline pool that extends for miles in all directions. The lake is immeasurably deep in its deepest parts and yet somehow shallow at the base of Lanatha, as if the tree was set there by the gods themselves.

In some of the myths of the People, Lanatha is where the world was born. It is the mother tree, the lynchpin that secures the world. Looking at the tree before me, it was hard not to believe it.

During our time in Lanatha, we were supplicants for healing, and so we removed our armors and donned robes of penitent gray. We ate simple meals with the monks and other supplicants, slept in small sleeping rooms in a crowded dormitory, and otherwise had the days to ourselves. Lavit and I swam or fished or lay in the sunshine on one of Lanatha's many platforms. We talked. There was very little to do but talk. Lavit rarely left my side, keeping the worst of the nightmares at bay while we discussed our experiences among the braves, while I came to terms with the marks on my skin that I had become very good at ignoring—the scar that I had gotten from that day and the other marks, the intricate ones that proclaimed me a survivor, a strong one, a protector.

I didn't feel like any of those things. I didn't feel strong, or like a survivor, or like I could protect anything. I felt weak and afraid. But Lavit was there for me. When I had nightmares and called out in my sleep for the dead, Lavit was there, a hand on my shoulder, another hand moving through my hair. When I would get distracted mid-conversation and go quiet, Lavit was there, patiently waiting for me to pick up the thread of the conversation again. When I started to panic and my breaths came fast and the world felt like it was pressing in around me, Lavit was there.

Slowly, Lanatha worked its magic on me. I began to heal. I reached the point where I could think about that day in the wilds without feeling like I was going to fall apart, when I could look at my reflection in the water and tell myself that I had been hurt, but that I would recover. I started feeling like there was hope, that there was a reason to wake to another day.

I returned to Vethaya in my newly refreshed armor—red and soft as silk, light and airy against my skin. For the first few months of my return to the braves, Lavit was never far from my side. I began to entertain the thought that this was what we had dreamed about as children. This was me and Lavit taking on the world together, heroes against the dark.

But then Ushi pulled me aside and told me he had recommended me for a command of my own, and everything changed. Suddenly, I was twenty years old and in command. It was an amazing achievement, and Lavit offered his congratulations with everyone else, but as we toasted my promotion together, I felt the old awkwardness settle in between us. I knew then that the dream had ended long ago, that we would never be able to go back to how we had been.

My first command was a small company built mostly out of newer recruits and novices, with a handful of senior braves around to help me along. We were tasked with clearing out and guarding one of the braves' newest acquisitions, a small spreading tree not far from the current border of the known world. It was a peaceful site. Not the grandest tree I had ever seen, nor the greenest pastures, but the tree was strong and the site had good water. The work was just intense enough to keep us fresh and on our toes, but the beasts that remained were small, not difficult for us to defeat.

We stayed there for months, until the first builders arrived to lay down the platform for the new village square. In that time, I familiarized myself with each member of my company and they with me. By the time we moved on from that place, which we named Naumea, I was comfortable in my role as commander.

That day in Ushi's company still haunted me. I still saw them when I closed my eyes, still saw visions of blood and death. I resolved that that would never happen again.

When I was twenty-two years old and had been commander of my company for almost two years, we were assigned our first major expedition. We were given the task of striking out into the unknown, eastward from where Naumea was under construction. We would venture into the truly unknown world where no one before us had been and find the next spreading tree, the next foothold for the People to live and grow. We were armed only with our armor, our spears, and our wits, with only the moon and stars to guide our way and the jungle close at our backs.

I don't know if I can fully describe how that feels, striking out onto land that has not been touched by any feet but your own. It is both the best and worst feeling in the world. On one hand, it is terrifying, because you have no idea what may be out there and a part of you longs for the safety of home. But on the other hand, there's nothing quite like it. Every breath is fresh, every pore charged with electricity. It is the essence of being alive.

I did not have to take on that responsibility on my own. When we stopped in Vethaya to prepare supplies for the journey, I found a surprise. Lavit would be transferring to my company, and more than that, he would be working as my second-in-command. At first, I was nervous, thinking Lavit would hold my higher position against me. But to my surprise, he didn't. It was as if Lavit too had grown in the time since I had last seen him, as if he too had been changed by Lanatha. He was as clever and attentive a second-in-command as any brave commander could ask for, and with his help, I thought we would conquer the world.

In the days and nights of our expedition, we were children again. We laughed by the fire like children, we teased each other like children. The secret places of the world were ours, the heart of the wilds was bared to us. We ran the treetops, bathed in virgin streams, watched the stars by night. Lavit was stern but fair with the braves under our command and between the two of us, our company prospered. Morale had never been higher.

On the ninth day after leaving Naumea, we found a spreading tree. Like all the other trees that held cities and villages, this one towered far above the jungle that surrounded it, a monstrous thing that was all strong, wide branches and tangled roots that drank deep of the marrow of the earth. The tree had a thin stream like a ribbon of silver that whipped around it, stemming from—or so our scouts said—a spring of water so clean that it gleamed in the light. It was an amazing find for those of us who were not expecting to find a spreading tree on our first expedition.

It was also guarded by more beasts than any of us had ever seen at a spreading tree, but they were all relatively weak. After sending scouts ahead to make a count of the beasts and to survey the surrounding area, it was determined we could win the day.

We stopped for the night to rest and to plan our strategy. We would sweep the clearing from the western side first, keeping the trees to our backs so we could retreat if it became necessary. From there, we would push and push until we reached the spreading tree. Once we took the tree, we would have the high ground, and could finish off the remaining beasts with ease.

We divided up the company. I took two-thirds and led the assault at dawn. Lavit took the other third of the company and attacked the beasts from behind while they were distracted by us, mowing them down.

By sunset, we had control of the spreading tree. We had some wounded but no dead, and we were in high spirits as we spread temporary plinths out on the tree's branches, toasting our victory. There would be marks earned for such an achievement, and I caught the braves in my company rubbing at their arms wistfully, as if they could already see the place where those marks would go.

I let the company feast, although I made sure there were some who were keeping watch, and others who were tending to the wounded. I wasn't worried about celebrations getting out of hand. We all knew the risks of the wilds by now, the danger that could strike if we weren't careful. We didn't drink, but we did eat, and we ate our fill.

Lavit came to join me on the command plinth as the moon rose, blotting out the light of the stars. He brought beast-meat and fruit with him and we ate together, studying the splash of moonlight on the tops of the jungle trees below us. Lavit sheepishly reached into his vest and pulled out a small flask of fruit liquor. He offered it to me, his head cocked to the side as if he thought he might be scolded.

Another day, I might have reprimanded him, but this was not that day. I had not failed to notice that none of our braves were near us, as if they had decided to leave us to ourselves. I took the flask from him and took a swig, then handed it back. The liquor burned in my throat on the way down, and I watched as Lavit drank as well.

"I asked for this posting, you know," he said, picking up the thread of a conversation that had gone unspoken. He capped the flask, putting it away. "I asked to be placed in this company, under your command."

That surprised me. "Why?"

"I needed to," Lavit said in response. "I needed to see you as you really are, not just as the girl I once knew. And you're amazing, Eshai. I really am very proud of how far you've come."

There was a hint of regret in the words, a touch of the old jealousy I knew so well. Something, some ghost or deity or mad demon, possessed me to reach for Lavit's hand. It was warm beneath the surface of his glove. He didn't pull away.

I couldn't hold myself back anymore.

I had been imagining this moment for years, but now that Lavit was sitting in front of me, the words almost wouldn't come. It took me a while to find them, to draw them out from the back of my mind and into my mouth. When they came to me, I thought nothing would be able to stop me from telling the truth, from bringing this secret out into the open.

A roar tore through the air, rattling the treetops with the force of it. On the heels of the roar were the sharp, whistling calls of the braves on watch duty.

Lavit and I sprang apart from each other, getting to our feet. We had spears in hand before we even registered what we were doing, our gazes fixed in the direction the whistles had come from. The jungle was alive with the sound of pounding feet, the leaves rustling in the distance. To make a sound like that, this creature had to be bigger than anything we had previously fought. Lavit looked at me, wide-eyed.

"I thought there were no more beasts," he said.

My expression must have matched his. I could feel my heart pounding, more like a frightened rabbit's than a brave commander's. I didn't bother speaking, not trusting my voice. Instead, I whistled for my braves to report to me and heard them repeat the call. Then I bent my knees and kicked off of the plinth with my boots, landing on the nearest treetop.

Lavit was only a second behind me. I started running, following the shouts and the sounds of distress.

The beast was monstrous, the sort of creature that nightmares were made of. I had heard tell of enormous beasts like this in the unknown world, had heard that Atiru and even Ushi had fought one, but it seemed impossible to me that we could have missed this creature somehow in our patrols. It looked like a giant lizard, all scaly skin and a rock-hard exterior, but lizard was not the word that came to my mind when I saw the creature in front of me. The word that came to mind was something out of myth: *"dragon"*.

Two of my braves were already on the ground. They had wounds that looked like bite marks, punctures in their armor. Their armor had blackened around the marks, crumbling to dust before my eyes.

There were stories of creatures that had the ability to destroy a brave's armor, but I had never seen one. No one I knew had seen one. They were relegated to the old stories, the stories from the dawn of the People's history, when we had lived in a different jungle.

Faced with the enormity of the creature in front of me, I was afraid, but I could not let my braves see that. I was Eshai, their commander. I was supposed to be fearless. So I grounded myself to the earth and gripped my spear tighter, facing down the dragon.

"Get the wounded to safety," I told Lavit, leaping into the air.

I didn't have time to see whether or not he obeyed. The creature took up the whole of my attention. It reared its head as I neared it, lashing at me with its mouth. I jabbed the butt of my spear at its nose and managed to redirect my fall, pushing away from the beast's snapping jaws. My spear blade scraped the side of the beast's neck as I fell, skittering off its armor. I landed on the ground and managed to score a good hit just beneath the beast's arm, in the delicate crease where arm met torso.

Blood flew and the beast roared in pain, rearing around to snap at me.

I was too slow to move, but one of my braves let out a cry of defiance, grabbing me around the shoulders and pulling me out of the way. The beast's blood clung to the edge of my spear, showing my braves that the creature could be wounded, and they responded with a ferocity that made me proud. They screamed battle cries, charging the beast. Some of my braves were caught by its teeth, and I saw them collapse to the ground, their armor crumbling around the bite marks. Others dodged and pressed on, striking out for the beast's belly and eyes, for the soft, unprotected portions of its body.

It wasn't enough. There were too few of us, too many falling braves. If nothing changed, we would all fall here. Images flashed through my mind—bloodstained fields, screams, the smell of death.

Never again.

I charged at the beast's eye with everything in me, letting out a battle cry. I saw myself reflected in it as I drew closer, a young woman in red, shouting in fury.

At the last second before I struck home, the beast turned its head. I jerked my spear up, the tip of my spear scoring the top of the beast's mouth, but one of its fangs grazed me in turn, cutting a thin line across the front of my armor. I heard my braves shout my name as I landed crouched on the ground, one of my hands going up to clasp at the tear.

It was a thin tear, but the edges of it were already blackening. I gritted my teeth, trying to will myself to stop the dissolution. I had some time.

I stood up, holding onto my spear.

My world spun on the edge of a heartbeat, and I fell back down to a knee. I started breathing harder and harder, the world around me fading as the armor on my chest crumbled away. My memories came back to me in reverse order—my battle with the dragon, Lavit and I seated on the plinth together, Lavit coming to join my company. I could feel each memory as if I was holding it in my hands, a thin globe of cut crystal, could feel each memory crack and shatter, vanishing into the mist.

I couldn't breathe. I couldn't think. And in the middle of it all, I could hear Lavit's voice.

"Eshai!"

Lavit leaped in front of me, his spear raised to protect me. It was only then that I noticed the dragon had turned to strike at me. I tried to keep myself together, but the memories were coming together faster and faster, blurring into each other. Every dark thought I had ever had, every happy memory, every shadow. It was all rushing at me, an assault on my senses. I couldn't breathe.

My armor was crumbling faster and faster. The rot was peeling away from my chest, spreading to my arms, my gloves. If my armor crumbled, I would never be a brave again—

—I saw Lanatha, Lavit and I together. I saw braves die in front of me, torn out of the air by a merciless beast, dying, screaming—

"Eshai!" Lavit shouted, gritting his teeth as he fought to hold his spear up, the dragon's mouth bearing down on him from above. "You're stronger than this! Don't give in to it."

I tried not to, but it was so hard, so so hard. The rot spread to the hem of my gloves, the rim of my boots—

—our pilgrimage to Vethaya, Lavit and Atiru, Lavit the day of the feast. Lavit and I hunting monsters together, Lavit and I in Yanasa's house, Lavit, Lavit, Lavit—

"Eshai!" Lavit shouted, leaping out of the way.

I was falling. I couldn't stop myself. I was falling—

—slaying my first beast, waking up to find Yanasa in front of me, Lavit with an outstretched arm, falling, fever, Lavit—

Darkness.

I screamed.

It was a raw animal thing, pulled free from my throat. It hurt so much that it consumed me whole. I didn't know who I was, what I was. All I could feel was the fever hot warmth within me.

Who was I? I wasn't anybody. I wasn't anything. I was—

—Eshai.

The name came to me suddenly, a balm against parched lips. I was Eshai. I was the girl who had survived the fever, the girl who slew beasts. No one could take that from me.

No one. I would not let it.

I pulled strength from those memories, wrapping them tight around me. I was Eshai. And I would not break, no matter what.

My armor rippled across my skin. I pushed back the pain, getting to my feet, and where it was crumbling, it *changed*. Power pulsed outward from the cut, my red silk armor pressing close to me as it took on a new form. It became white, a brilliant white that was almost blinding.

In that instant, all of my memories flooded back into me. I became complete.

The beast was cornering Lavit. It had him pinned down, about to strike.

I didn't think. Instead, I leaped into the air and brought my spear down, stabbing the point of my blade straight through the beast's skull and into the ground.

It was only in the silence afterward, when the beast was dead and still, that I heard my company cheering my name.

They made songs out of that one.

Atiru, Ushi, and the others had always said they would make songs out of me, but I never believed them. Their songs called me Eshai Unbroken, and because of that, those who knew me started calling me that as well. Those who truly knew me, those like Lavit and Ushi and the ones I was close to in my company, knew better than to call me that to my face. Nothing I said would convince anyone that I didn't deserve the name. The story grew, and it grew wilder with each retelling. I tried to stop it, but it wouldn't be stopped, and eventually, at Lavit's urging, I gave up.

Then, about a week after we returned to Vethaya, when I was still recovering from my ordeal, Lavit came to me. He had news. High command had heard about his actions during the monster attack, had heard testimonials from many of my braves that he had defended the wounded and had held off the beast for as long as he could until I recovered. They intended to reward him with his own command.

He was proud but a little sheepish as he stood in front of me and told me he intended to take it. It was everything he had ever dreamed of, and I was happy for him.

He told me he would become a hero to match me someday, so

they would sing his songs along with mine. He asked me to wait for him, to give him the time to do that. And he told me that whatever we had to say to each other could wait—should wait—until we faced each other as equals.

 He embraced me when he said goodbye.

 I agreed. But I also cried.

 He held me until the tears stopped, and then he left me. In that embrace, I felt like he didn't want to let me go.

ESHAI remembers very little from the first nine years of her life, but grew up under the care of Yanasa, the caretaker of the village of Auvai. She slew her first beast at the age of nine, and since then, has dreamed of becoming one of the braves, along with her companion and fellow orphan Lavit. Currently, Eshai serves as a brave commander, working directly underneath the Council of Braves in Vethaya. Receiving her command at the young age of twenty, Eshai is considered one of the youngest commanders in brave history.

ELISA BONNIN was born in the Philippines, where she lived until the age of sixteen. Growing up, she enjoyed reading fantasy, writing, and going to the beach. Now, Elisa is a graduate student at the University of Washington in Seattle, WA, studying oceanography. She still enjoys reading and writing, and can be found working on pieces of creative fiction from time to time.

ART BY **Rhaega Ailani**

RHAEGA AILANI is an illustrator and freelance designer born near the Mediterranean Sea, currently living in London. Visit her online at rhaegaart.wixsite.com.

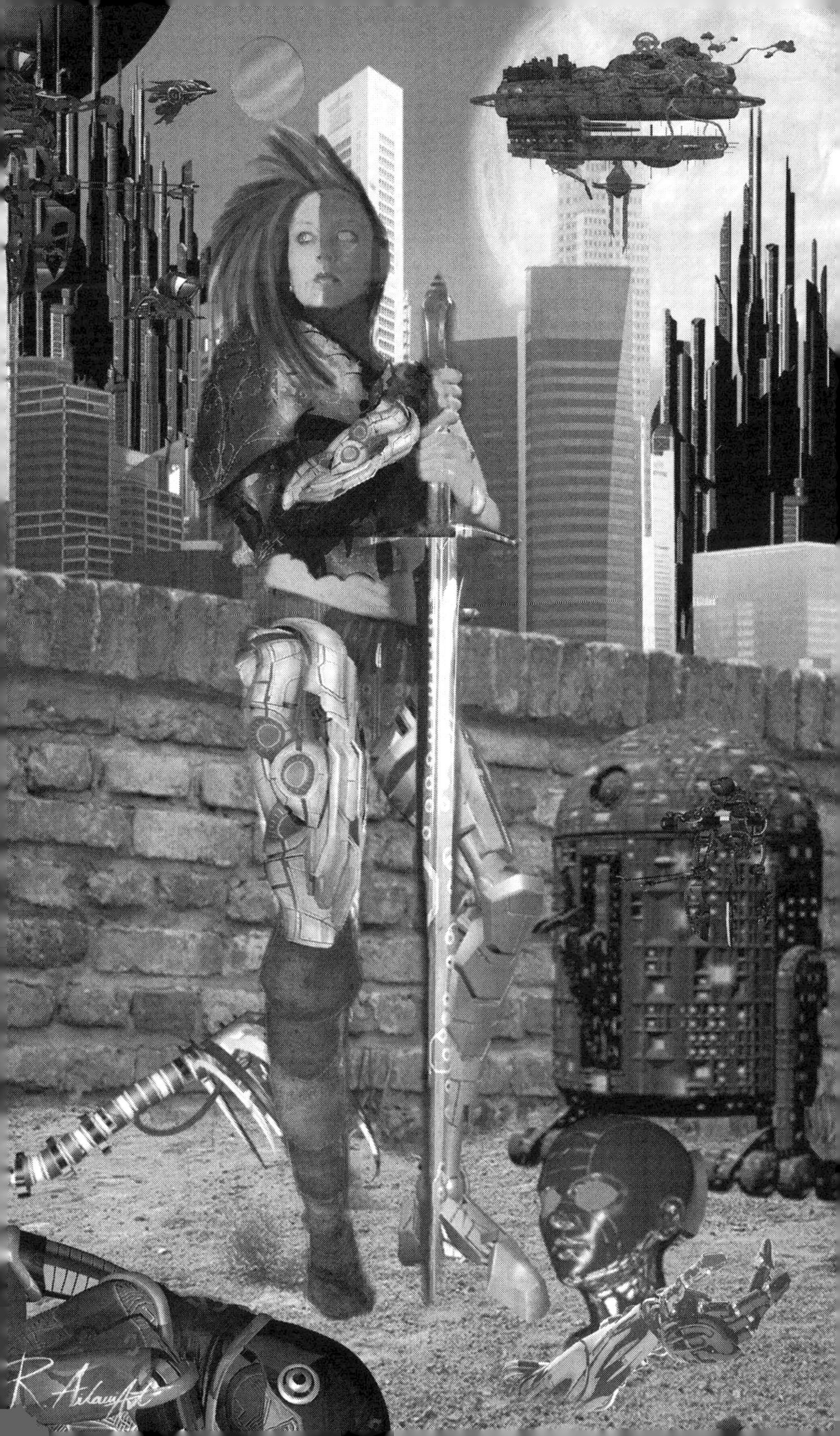

AQUARIUS ASCENDANT

An account by Arethusa,
as provided by Christine Lucas

Yet another tome of the Akashic records proves useless. If the damned thing wasn't made of Aether, I'd throw it against the wall, to meet all the previous tomes. If the collective knowledge of mankind offers no clue as to where the humans have gone, I don't know where else to look. All human cities lay in ruins, the libraries ash and dust, like most of Earth now. And even if I were to stumble upon an overlooked corner of the globe that still has electricity, I have no idea how to access their internet, if that still exists. Computer skills aren't something that Naiads needed ever before.

But it's no longer before. It is now, and we're stranded in a barren world, abandoned and forgotten.

"*Arethousa—*" My well calls to me, and its whisper stings my heart.

I stretch my legs, my toes stiff, my skin cracked. I miss water. I miss my stream. I miss my cousins, the dryads, gossiping overhead about the follies of men. Who could foresee this folly of epic scale? None of the oracles, none of the sacred oaks, and if the Fates knew, they chose not to tell us. Did they tell anyone? Did the humans know that their fiery end would come not from above but from within? Not with a comet or an asteroid or their own bombs, but from a volcano so angry it made Thera seem like a pimple on Earth's chin? I cannot tell for certain if the humans knew. But they seemed awfully ready to fly off their ailing planet toward distant stars, leaving us all behind.

I gather my courage to leave my basin of tepid water and make my way toward the window that opens to vast, barren fields of sand. Once the ever-shifting blue of the Aegean Sea, now a sun-scorched wasteland, littered with the bleached bones of seals, dolphins, and my kin. If I still my heart, I might hear the echoes of long-gone waves and long-dead seagulls. There's an overturned boat over there, its keel dried up, its paint peeling off at spots. And over there, there's the well that brought me here, to this last safe house in the shadow of Poseidon's temple at Cape Sounio. What little grace remains within me keeps it filled with fresh water, so the kraken eggs I've stored inside won't wither and die. And after we've drunk our fill, I can still water the saplings of the sacred oak trees and the dryad infants nesting beneath their barks. And perhaps, one day, when we have tracked down humankind, they'll grow roots beneath different stars.

The loud crash of tumbling furniture in the basement kicks me back to here and now. Then the stench of fire and brimstone follows, and my shoulders slump.

"Children! How many times do I have to say 'No summoning in the house'?"

Or anywhere, really, for humanity may have departed, but have they left their baggage behind—their fear, their guilt, their anger imbued within every possible surface, breeding monsters. Even now, as I stumble out of the water and slip into my coarse dress, the shadows in the room seem to quiver, spurting tendrils to grasp me. I rush downstairs, and the floors creak beneath my steps, my feet shuffle the settled dust of too many yesterdays and erase the markings of too many tiny feet and paws and hooves. As I reach the basement,

I almost trip and fall over the purple lemur with the wine-red lion's mane, who's apparently assigned lookout duties. Again.

"Triton's scaly balls!"

The curse leaves my lips before I can hold my tongue, and the poor thing gawks at me with those huge, teary eyes of his kind. I think that the humans' departure has hurt their imaginary friends most. Most of them dissolved into the Aether to be absorbed by the Akashic records, but not this little fellow. Chirpitiri, we call him now. He sometimes listens, sometimes not. But he lingers in this house, stubbornly clinging in this half-life, clutching a long-faded photograph to his chest. He shows it to anyone who'll listen to his torrent of chirps, gesturing wildly, pointing everywhere and nowhere. But this old photograph shows only a smudge now, and there's no one left who speaks his tongue anymore—if there ever was, apart from the human who left him behind. So we just nod and smile and move on. As I do now, only this time I take a moment to pat his head.

"Sorry, little one. It wasn't meant for you."

It was actually meant for *them*, who once more drew a summoning circle on the dirt: the pixies, the ghosts, the familiars, the shapeshifters. The basement's walls are blackened, the shelves reduced to kindling, the jars and mugs and glassware shattered and stomped on after one too many failed attempts.

But this time they didn't fail. There's a pale form in the middle of the circle. A human? Could it be?

I tiptoe forward, studying the circle as I go. They never used such symbols before; they seem a mix of Japanese kanji and ancient Egyptian hieroglyphs. I can't read either, but apparently *they* can: foxes and cats mix around the circle. So the kitsune teamed up with the familiars? And it worked?

Or have they summoned something they won't be able to get rid of this time? This individual seems too thin and too pale to be an average human, and too many hungry entities roam the empty places between the worlds. I dare another step and, from the shadows between those white-skinned legs, a cat emerges. Not like the familiars, this one; the familiars carry too many shadows, the Aetheral shades of every cat that was or is or could have been. This is just a cat. And its companion bends over to scoop it up in his arms.

So it's a human man, and fireflies swarm my gut. A human. Is the search over? Can he tell us where they've gone? And can we follow?

But then the little details start to sink in: the skin affliction that ails him, the white linen robes of a time long past, the clean-shaved head, and the eyes heavily lined with kohl. Around his neck, an amulet of green jasper shaped in the form of a jackal's head.

Oh, for Poseidon's Trident, the one time the children managed to summon a human, they summoned someone from ancient times. My heart takes a dive for my feet. What could he possibly tell us, except perhaps how to embalm our dead?

"Send him back," I manage a croak, my tongue too dry to form proper words. "He's useless."

None of the children move. They just stare at me with unblinking eyes. Then the summoned man moves. He holds up his free hand, and he's holding a rolled-up papyrus. In his other arm, the cat air-claws to snatch it as if all its nine lives depend on it. He takes a step forward, scanning the floor, bare feet carefully tiptoeing around the symbols. As he reaches the edge of the circle, he extends his arm, offering me the scroll. I reach for it, but then there's sizzling when the papyrus touches the barrier between our realm and the circle, leaving its margins singed. The stench of fire and brimstone waxes again, and my stomach dives to my feet to meet my heart. It's important, I know, but countless yesterdays stand in between.

He sighs and turns to his cat. He speaks a word I cannot hear; perhaps this circle keeps the sound caged as well. But the cat stops its frantic attempts to shred and leaps off his arm. When he leans over to give it the scroll, I roll my eyes. But to my surprise, the cat, scroll in fangs, trots over with light paws that don't disturb one speck of the circle's chalk. It crosses the barrier as if it's out for a stroll in the garden, drops it at my feet with one forlorn stare for the prey that got away, and measures the feline familiars in turn. And then it tries to mount the nearest one.

A cacophony of hisses and growls reverberates in the basement, and the cat darts back into the circle, and man and cat vanish with a whoosh in a swirl of sand and dried palm leaves. The kitsune and the familiars start rolling on the floor to erase the symbols, and I unroll the papyrus.

Of course it's in hieroglyphics. And I can't read it. Perhaps one of Egypt's creatures has sought refuge with us and can decipher this. But I don't recall seeing one—at least not of the kind that walks in the light, and I'm not that desperate yet to seek out those who lurk in the shadows. So until I can track down the Rosetta Stone in the Akashic records, I might as well study the pictures.

By the time I'm up to the ground floor, it's clear that this papyrus is a part of the Egyptian Book of the Dead. I know enough of their lore to doubt its use to us. But by the time I reach the upper floor to continue my studies, my eyes are glued on the last drawing: Ra's Solar Barge, the ship that sails upon the waters of the Eternal Nile that stretches farther than all the rivers of Earth and crosses the Aether to uncharted territories.

I gaze outside. There's a boat out there. But it's not a barge. It's too small for all of us, and too damaged, and what do I know about boats anyway?

Shame curls my toes, and anger slithers up my legs through my spine to whip my heart to a gallop. If a day dawns that a Naiad, a kinswoman of Oceanus and Tethys, frets at the thought of sailing a boat, then the End of Days is really upon us. I study the scroll again, closer to the light this time, and the writing around the barge's image shimmers and swirls as if alive. The ink is not fully dry. My fingertips tingle. I may not know this writing, but I know magic. This is a spell. No, it's more than a spell.

Instructions.

My head spins. I need air. The sun nears the horizon now. I step outside and settle on the front steps. The shadow of the temple's marble columns stretches long on the ground before me. Others have ventured out, now that the heat of this never-ending August has waned a little. Young centaurs race, a satyr tries to carve a flute from a bone, and many others gather at corners, by the boat, by the well. I don't know their tongues, I can't remember everyone's name and species, but I know they're family and kin. They've left their desolate lands behind and crossed endless wastelands, refugees on an Earth abandoned by humans, seeking water—seeking shelter.

And although many of them cannot speak my tongue—or any tongue at all—they've named me the same in their own words or grunts or squeaks or neighs.

Neromana. Mother of Water.

How long will my grace last? How long until my well dries up too, and we've still to find the humans?

The little lemur scurries beside me, chirping and purring and curls up on my lap. I stroke his wild, matted mane.

"What should I do, Chirpitiri?" I dare a whisper, not really waiting for an answer.

He coos and shoves the old photo to my face again. I don't need to know his tongue to understand that. *Find them*, he asks. I sigh, and gently push it from my face and scratch his head, and he shoves it up again. His chirps turn pleading, almost to sobs, and his lower lip quivers. *We'll never find the one who left you behind,* I want to tell him, but I bite my tongue. Perhaps we can still try. I set him down beside me and pull myself up.

"Children! We need to fix the boat." My request is met with stunned silence, gazes darting from the dried sea to my face and then to the old boat. I think I hear one of them chuckle, while others murmur. I seek the words to convince them, even though I'm not convinced myself. I lick my cracked lips. "Oh, come on. What do we have to lose?"

Not one foot, not one paw or hoof move forward. I dry my sweaty palms on the sackcloth over my hips. Will I have to do this on my own? Then Chirpitiri darts forward, all limbs and tail and bright purple fur. He rushes to the boat and starts scraping dirt off. Heartbeat by heartbeat, others join in, and they start to clean the boat.

It becomes a truly joint effort: unicorns and pegasi offer their manes so the Jorōgumo and the arachnae can weave them into sails and riggings. A lone kraken hatchling offers its ink, although it knows it might not survive long enough for the journey—not away from the open sea. But it does so anyway, so its unhatched siblings will find a home in the seas of distant stars. Others offer feathers of iron and steel, and carry sturdy wooden beams for the mast. And I'm left to mix the paint, with drops of blood and pixie dust and my own tears. I shed too many tears these days, moisture I cannot spare, so into the ink they go. The boat is too small. Which of them will be left behind? How many of them will be abandoned a second time?

And who will make that choice?

You know who, whispers every shadow in the house, every crack and crevice, every corner that morphs to a gaping mouth in the small hours before dawn. *You shall become the Dark Mother devouring her young, the gardener weeding out the weaklings so some of the rest might survive the quest upon this ship of fools you're building. Smother them in their sleep, slit their throats when no one's watching, drip poison into the waters that spawned you, before it's too late and the choice becomes unbearable.*

I shut my ears, I shut my eyes, and whisper the few lines I recall from the sirens' song to banish the dark thoughts. My singing is out of tune, my heart is heavy. And still I try to push the weight of this decision one day forward each dawn, and each dusk it returns to haunt me. Guilt feeds the shadows and breeds shapes I'd hoped I'd never see again: the creatures of the dark, as much abandoned as the rest of us who were borne from folk tales and lullabies and everything nice and fun of the human spirit. But not these: spun from fear and guilt and rage, these spurt tentacles and grow claws. Yellow teeth flash in the starlight, and forked tongues lash through venomous jaws, and hiss and growl curses against their eternal enemies. One of them grows bolder and detaches itself from the dark corners of the room, where angles spawn impossible angles and gateways to dark realms crack open.

It loosely resembles a human—a short human of floating dust and ash, its eyes the bleached skulls of little birds, its claws hardened thorns and sharp splinters. It nears me night after night, its jaws stretched too wide, locked in a voiceless scream. With each step, it slouches closer to the pitiful basin of tepid water where I try to sleep. Is it a demon? Or a wraith? Such creatures dread running water and always kept their distance from my stream and my well.

Before.

I miss before.

But now the water that shelters me is filthy and stagnant, and my grace is all but spent. Where now the trills of Pan's pipes? Where now the arrows of the Huntress to shoot evil down? All ash and shards and memories of a dream forgotten at dawn. So I huddle, trembling in this wet crib that's no better than a mud puddle, and pray to all the gods I know that it won't reach me. If the gods hear me, I cannot tell. Perhaps they too have left with the humans. Perhaps they perished. Or perhaps they do listen, for the wraith does not reach me until the boat is fully restored.

Then the day dawns when I have to inscribe the symbols of the spell alongside the tiller and the prow. The ink feels more diluted than it should. Too many tears, I suppose. And my fingers don't want to move. My heart doesn't want this to be finished, for it means the time of reckoning is at hand. And still I grit my teeth and force my fingers to dip into the old jar with the enchanted ink, until the shadows lengthen. Here it tingles, there it stings, on the prow it burns, and on the stern, it makes my skin burst with goosebumps. I feel the weight of too many stares—too many hearts—on my back, until I'm finally done, breathless and bereft. This spell absorbed most of my grace and, by all the gods of waters high and low, I hope it works.

Nothing.

I take a step back, and then I notice the faint glimmer of the hieroglyphs. It worked! Now their light waxes stronger, until it forms a sphere of soft, milky glow. Then I feel the wind in my face, and a burst of light knocks me off my feet. I land on my butt and just sit there, gawking at the brilliance above: the *benu*-bird, its fiery tail the essence of Ra, flaps its wings of lightning and flame over our boat. Another flap, and a great river stretches now before us over the barren sands: a river of languid, dark waters made from Aether and Night.

The *benu*-bird returns to whence it came with another burst of light. Our boat awaits, and it's still too small. No words form in my head, but before I can even start to think, one of the fauns sprints forward and climbs onboard. And the boat tilts sideways and spits him out.

I sit up. What was that? Why?

"You thought you'd leave without us?" A voice that carries a chilling quiver, like the storm during a starless night.

My gut knots up. It's them. The jiangshi, the ghouls, the aswang, the efreet, countless creatures of darkness. They flow out of the shadows, their breath the stench of desecrated tombs, their presence an offense to all born of light. One of them strides forth: tall, dark, gnarled, and crooked, with eyes of vengeance. A Fury, and her mane of writhing serpents reveals to me her name: Alecto.

"Why not? Mankind does not need you," I blurt before my thirsty brain can focus.

"Is this so?" She laughs, her laughter like claws dragged slowly across a granite slab. "But they did leave your lot too, didn't they?"

I pull myself up. "We built this boat. It's ours."

"Oh?" She cocks a prickly eyebrow. "And who do you think summoned the sorcerer with the instructions to do it?"

A demon steps forward from the gathering of darkness. I know this one; I saw her likeness drawn upon the papyrus we were given. Her head that of a crocodile, her body that of a hippo, her paws those of a lion, and her name Ammut, the heart-hound of the Egyptian God of the Dead. Between those massive legs and in the shadow of the monstrous body, other shadows curl, noiseless and sly: feline familiars, one paw stepping in light, one in darkness, denizens of the twilight between the worlds. They arch their backs against Ammut, greeting her as a lost member of their pride. At the edge of my consciousness, a piece of some great cosmic puzzle clicks in place. It makes perfect sense.

And my head turns so hard my neck hurts. The rest of the kitsune and the familiars are suddenly too busy studying their paws and grooming their fur. *Really*, I want to yell, but I manage to compose myself. I should have guessed. I should have recalled that the Art of Summons was born in darkness before it settled in the twilight and oozed into the light. But what does it matter now? What's done is done. So I shrug.

"I don't care. We bled for this. We mutilated our bodies and sacrificed too much to just hand it over."

"Unless you want to bleed more, I suggest that you all step aside," she hisses, and her serpentine mane hisses along.

I chuckle. "You know what? Perhaps we should." Gasps behind me, but I raise my hand and they stop. "Perhaps humankind does deserve this: a ship full of all the horrors that your lot is, so that humans can spend the next few millennia concocting new ways to eliminate you."

Now I hear chuckles behind me, and murmurs that perhaps we should, and then a little tug at the hem of my sackcloth dress, and a low whine. *No, Chirpitiri,* I want to whisper, *we* are *leaving,* I want to say. *Just in a little while.* I stroke his head, but he still whines.

"Who knows what new kinds of magic the humans might have encountered out there?" My parched throat gives my voice a harsh echo that makes my heart tremble. Is that who I am, deep inside? But I cannot stop now, and my voice darkens more. "What kind of starfire to burn you? What kind of waters to drown you? Even if you do depart, your filthy lot shall never *ascend.*"

Alecto's face is the visage of rage. "Shut. Your. Filthy. Hole."

"At least mine doesn't stink of corpses."

"No, it stinks of dead fish," she hisses, and her snakes rise and hiss in unison. A call to arms. "Move or fall!"

So the pleasantries are over. Now it's war.

Fear tingles the nape of my neck. And relief cools the fringes of my thoughts. I won't have to choose. This unforeseen turn of events made the choice for me. One final battle to weed out the weak, so the worthy can claim passage to the future.

And now shame burns my face, for this pitiful creature I have become. Each new moment, each new thought and word reel me closer to twilight. And then darkness isn't that far off.

At the edge of my hearing, I think I hear gods laugh. Was this their plan all along? With humankind gone, are we but their playthings to fill their empty eons with?

So be it.

Behind me, nostrils snort, hooves pound the dirt, muzzles snarl to expose ivory fangs. I steel my back and ball my fists. Even without much grace left, I can manage a punch or two.

"Bring it."

I expected a torrent of darkness to answer my challenge. I expected a wild stampede of hooves and the clashing of mighty horns. I expected guts on the ground, and a river of blood to dye the sands a grotesque mockery of rainbows: black and blue and silver and red and green. But I never expected a purple blur of limbs and tail and chirps to cross the no-creature's-land between the armies of Light and Darkness.

No! I want to scream as he darts forward from my side, and I'm left with strands of wine-red mane in my grip. All words choke on a sob. *Chirpitiri, no! Silly little lemur, where are you going? They'll tear you apart, they'll feast on your entrails, and wear your purple fur like a mantle. And you'll never find your human.*

But then there's silence and purple limbs entangled with ash and smoke. From amidst the host of darkness, he singled out the wraith of ash and smoke, the one that haunted my nights for so long now. Are they wrestling? Does Chirpitiri have powers I never knew of? Even if he does, I can't leave him on his own to fight this one battle he was supposed to sit out. So I take one step forward. Alecto takes a step sideways. A centaur behind me pounds the dirt. A minotaur behind Alecto snorts and lowers his head.

Then all movement stops. I blink. Is my weary mind playing tricks on me again? They're not fighting. They're *hugging*. And that's not a wraith anymore; was it ever? Now it shifts to the shimmering form and essence of a human girl of about ten. They sit huddled, weeping and touching and crying and chirping in their own tongue. Chirpitiri holds up his photo proudly for everyone to see. Aether weaves the image back with threads of pink and azure and gold light, from the pitiful smudge to the likeness of a girl sitting on the front porch of this very house. At the back, the barge straightens. Has its glimmer waxed stronger now?

If the gods are indeed watching all this, I hope they'll choke on their laughter.

I fix my gaze on Alecto. "Well."

"Well." She licks her purple lips. "Out-smarted and out-couraged by an imaginary critter, of all things." She raises her hand to brush her snakes back to order, for they've been staring agape at the reunion.

"No, neither out-smarted nor out-couraged. It's not our smarts or courage that failed us." It's our hearts, I want to add, but I dare not, for I fear the Aether will snatch my words and weave them true. We'll need our smarts and hearts and courage if we're going to survive this. I twist the hem of my sackcloth. "I suppose we can share."

"Yes, I suppose we can," she nods. "But my snakes will need nourishment for the journey."

I cock an eyebrow. "What do they eat?"

"Purple lemurs," she snarls.

A few paces away, the spirit of the girl darkens and howls, her jaws too stretched, her fangs too white, her message too clear.

Alecto raises her hands. "My apologies. A bad joke. Let us share, and I promise we'll behave. No more bad jokes."

I swear that even her own snakes laugh at her lie, but I nod. "Very well. Let us share."

The words have barely left my throat when another kind of racket drowns all sound: the boat creaks and cracks and stretches. The mast spawns more masts. The Aether weaves additional sails from moonbeams. And when it's over, a glorious solar barge—no, a solar *ark*— awaits its passengers and crew.

If we ever reach the humans, I might one day tell them that we boarded in peaceful order, having reached an understanding, and that no hissing or growling or snarling or tripping or elbowing occurred. I might even tell them that it was the end of bad jokes and pranks borne in twilight. But my new friend Alecto insists that I cannot lie with a straight face, and why do we even need the humans anymore?

With a Fury on the prow and a Naiad on the tiller, the Solar Barge now sails toward distant stars.

ARETHUSA is the last of the Naiads, at least as far as she knows. Humans and their ways fascinate her, until they decided to abandon Earth in post-apocalyptic chaos. Now she aims to track them down, mostly to kick some human posterior, alongside her friend and—eventually—life-partner Alecto, the last of the Furies. When she's not searching for those pesky humans, she holds meetings of a support group for survivors of the gods' sexual abuse.

CHRISTINE LUCAS lives in Greece with her husband and a horde of spoiled animals. A retired Air Force officer and mostly self-taught in English, she has had her work appear in several print and online magazines, including *Daily Science Fiction*, *Cast of Wonders*, *Pseudopod/Artemis Rising 4*, and *Nature: Futures*. She was a finalist for the 2017 WSFA award and is currently working on her first novel. Visit her at: http://werecat99.wordpress.com/.

THERE IS ONLY
THE WAR

An account by Ri,
as provided by A. J. Fitzwater

Sixty-two years. The time between your war-made death and your return home.

Your skull bobs and sways between Eya's Feathers, invisible body pushing aside the ripe flax. Coolness grips my guts; this is by no means the first un-dead to return from the war. But one with intimate knowledge of the Purple Blossom's paths? It can only be you.

Splinters sting as I dash out the watch gate. Thankfully no cousins have erupted from the caves below. The cliff top path unravels with none of the snappish delight the cousins reserved for my most recent exit. The dragon Eya is in her prime. The morning air hints at the sweet, oily pop of seeds, the heavy rot of flax, and the dampness from the river far below.

"Your return is a blessing upon the House of the Purple Blossom, grandmother Eztena." A barely serviceable formal greeting.

"Greetings, little cousin." Your jaw bone moves with a fluid grotesquery. "It is a pleasure to be greeted by one of Eya's brood even this early in our morning."

The dam of my hope crumbles. Not only an informal greeting, but do I look so unlike you in life or your only daughter?

Switching the knot of my hands across my belly to show I hold no instrument, I fumble out more meaningless words. "There will be many feasts in your honour. The House of the Purple Blossom stands strong on Eya's back, and we have much to teach each other about the last sixty years."

This is the first lie I tell you. Warriors have no use for tradition, so Donai tells it.

"Has it been that long?" This is the first lie you tell me. "Hmh. I died, little cousin. Dead warriors and welcomes are not a good mix."

Your skull bobs toward the old watch gate, but I gesture toward the freshly gilded welcome gate instead. How obscene it would be to walk you through the neglected watch gate, the warrior's gate! The idea sits sweet on my tongue, but sweeter still is my latest taste of freedom. I am not yet in a mood to antagonize Donai.

"Do you have a name, little cousin? I can't traverse the cliff steps without one, or Eya's Feathers might mistake me for fertilizer." None of your infamous knife-tongue has deserted you, though… yes, it is just as soft and pink as any other.

I choke on a giggle too unlike my years.

"My name is Ri, grandmother," I say. Your jaw sets hard at the formal appellation. "I am your daughter's daughter."

Your bobbing ceases on the lintel of the uppermost terrace as if the unseen parts of you are held taut. "Eya curdle my blood. So Ainama managed to squeeze out a girl." A slurp, and your eyeballs flesh in for you to re-evaluate all those things Donai notices: my wide shoulders, soft belly, thick knuckle scars, red hair. "Where is the rest of your name?"

Footsteps titter below.

Your seaworm-scoured skull should terrify me, but suddenly I want you close, to tell me of real warrior ways, not just the use of mortality instruments.

You are waiting. Do warriors have patience? Another so-say from Donai flits through my mind like an angry bird: confused un-dead make angry un-dead.

"I had it taken from me the first time they sent me away." A simple thrust of an explanation.

Footsteps closer.

"Away? Away where?" You roll this dialect-shifted word between your sharpened eye teeth. "Were you given a new house? But you're here. Stopped? That doesn't make sense. Why would the Blossom stop such an obviously warriorish woman as you?"

A fist of air seizes my throat. Eya roars wetly in my head, her river more blood than water, and I can't take my eyes off your un-face.

"Jail," a practised soft voice replies for me. "Ri makes her amends aplenty in jail, the poor wee thing."

First comes the gilt of the layered yellow dress, runes stitched in ugly gold, then the black tumble of hair that shows nothing of the years you almost share.

A delicious liquid pop of newly formed eyelids. "Donai."

My chance for your spoken favour is gone. I drop my head, but cut looks between you and your sister.

"Oldest sister of the Purple Blossom," Donai says, far too formal for her sibling. "Welcome back to the land of the living. I am so pleased to discover you have something to teach our house yet."

✊

A hasty feast appears on the breakfast tables, better than anything offered upon my many returns. Mirrors are re-angled and the third terrace shivers with gold light from above and silver from the river below. Yellow streamers unfurl, curling and ugly from the balcony. A child dashes through, spreading purple blossoms across a floor I want you to notice as un-swept.

You glance once at the yellow banners that must seem so strange to you—yellow is not the colour of death anymore—and then you only have eyes for food. You gulp and slurp at your first meal in sixty-two years with such delight it hurts my empty belly. No one dares stare. Only the youngest cousins follow where your victuals go once it gets past your teeth, and are disappointed it is disappeared as the rest of you.

You now have neck bones, and a scalp, but no nose or lips, your teeth stripped a beautiful white by time, mud, and sea. Your single thick war loc stands out amongst the tight merchants' braids, slick academic half-overs, and feminine undercuts.

A lot happens at once: Donai ties the purple and gold sash to her oldest son, and he takes the seat by you that should be mine; your comment about my having the seeming of a warriorish woman fades to a dream as Donai's oldest daughter snatches the kaff tray from my hands and serves you in my stead; word comes from your only husband, grandfather Hwajil, that he prefers to cloister in his terrace, as is his right, and none of his spouses make an appearance. You glance once to the corner where your mother and house matriarch Herensughe-mai sits in her wheeled chair, slobbering blindly over her corn porridge.

Only after you've sampled a little of everything do you ask for Ainama.

Silence, lingering longest upon Donai. I want to shout and throw apples, but I dig blunt nails into my thigh instead. No use my wasting your first day scrubbing the dining terrace floor.

"Come on now, make haste," you demand, clapping with your invisible hands. All the cousins jump at the unexpected sound. "I know she must be a little slower in her old age, but where is my daughter?"

Donai shuffles forward on her knees, hands spread in her idea of supplication.

"Your beloved daughter is unfortunately no longer with the House of the Purple Blossom," Donai says.

You snort. "Beloved may be too strong a word." I imagine a throwaway gesture in the way your exposed muscles clench around jaw and mouth. "Did she marry that useless book eater? What was his name? Geram?"

I carve a chunk of strong cheese and grind it between my molars. Use. Hmh.

"His name was Regaim." Donai's voice is just low enough that the whole terrace can hear. "And no, he is gone away too. No other house has them."

"Speak plainly, little cousin!" The insult again. "What is this 'gone away' you're mumbling about?"

Donai smooths an invisible wrinkle in her sun-touched skirt. Other cousins pretend to huddle over their food; this is a story they've heard more often than I.

"On the day word came from Eya's mouth that you had unfortunately been taken by the Tails of the Long Serpent to rest against her muddy bosom," Donai intoned in her weary inflection, words directed toward the floor. "The sweet and gentle Ainama received a double blow. Within moments of one rider from the council handing over your red warrior sash, another rider appeared with the green sash of the librarian's guild. Regaim, offering his services as a witness to the war effort, also enjoyed the Long Serpent's embrace.

"Stricken by such news, Ainama sought solace from Eya's breath rising from the river. Unfortunately, the breath that morning through the canyon was too strong, and Ainama—" Donai knows the perfect place to pause in any story. "—*fell* from the topmost terrace to the dragon's feet. A mighty and swift river cleansed Eya that spring, and Ainama's bones have never found the peace within glass they deserve." She pauses again, selecting the perfect words to use as instruments. "I had hoped you may have encountered her in your… travels."

Your gaze pierces all those seated within the terrace with the strength of your infamous great-sword Midnight, and pins the fabric of Donai's dress to her body. "My daughter does not enjoy the call of Alukat," you say, speaking the name of the silver beaches of the Forbidden Marshes. "Only those who die by violence from another hand become un-dead."

And just like that, the myth of the un-dead homelands is confirmed as truth.

The pestle of your eyes grind in the mortar of their sockets as you look across the silent room to me. Their stony regard should make anyone less than a warrior tremble. I am dizzy from the attention.

You tear off a hunk of the pungent cheese, and we chew in unison.

The reunion between you and the Kizzian was a grand affair.

I return too late from my assigned chores to enjoy the festivities. Scraping the thick salt-sweet unguent of ground flax seeds from my hands, choosing an outfit over-washed to brown, and shaving my head clean had taken too much time. I somehow know under your nakedness you still wear the war colour of red, but I am careful not to show it even when it grows from my skin.

Filth covers the woven flax mats of the dining terrace as if a wedding has ensued, not a demure welcome feast. Cats lap at spills while dogs chase discarded bones. Cousins stand and stare in despair at the delightful travesty, muttering amongst themselves about how you used the pottery as throwing instruments, how they didn't realize the treaty with the Kizzians still stood this sixty years on from the routing they took upon the southern beaches, how the Kizzian—Tibok—was your war-maker and just like you. Un-dead.

I am not quick enough to escape with salvaged dregs. A cousin blocks my way, fists on hips, just as Donai would have taught them.

"Take Herensughe-mai out for some sun," he orders, gesturing to the sack of wrinkles and drool in her wheeled chair.

He stalks away before I have the chance to accuse him of abandoning his station. I imagine his head beneath my mortar, and the singing twang of a blunt knife into a chopping board. It wouldn't be the first time one of the kitchen cousins have lost a finger.

Slipping great-grandmother caramels from the kitchens pleases us both; me for silence, her for the forbidden treat. As the ostensible head of the Purple Blossom, Herensughe-mai says what she needs to me within the law and little more. Her gummy grin, creased sightless eyes, and black-nailed scratch to the back of my hand say much more. It's not much of anything, but we amuse ourselves throwing stones into Eya's cleft from time to time.

Preparing my breath to enter the wide and long expanse of flax is interrupted by a strange sound. A clack-clack-clack fertilizes the upside paddock with suspicion.

Two skulls dash and weave between flax bushes, disturbing pollen and irritated insects from late blossoms. Long stems of dry flowers crackle beneath invisible feet. Hoarse shouts I only recognize as ceremonial from their cadence play harmony against the strange rhythm.

I park Herensughe-mai beneath a tree, and she sucks on a caramel like this is no thing.

A thread of thrill pulls me toward you. You dance into view, flax parting like Eya's flesh around you. Without skin, you do not perspire. Your muscles ripple and flex, sure speed feeding them to an aching red. Staccato cries pierce the air. You brandish a stripped willow branch half as long as your body. Your opponent, the Kizzian, wields the same. You push back their advance with ease.

These are no mere instruments. Childish, disposable, and blunt, but you have *weapons*.

And you are making *war*.

The cotton between my thighs dampens.

The Kizzian is stupid enough to stop and stare at me staring at him. With a wet thwack that makes me wince, you land a satisfying brand on the Kizzian's almost-there shoulder. You have purpling knots on your own exposed muscles.

"Aha!" booms a voice that shouldn't come from such a long, narrow skull. "So this is the granddaughter you've been telling me about!"

You've been talking about me. To him, your war-maker. Who is now joyfully trying to enact some type of revenge.

The size of the upside flax field pushes in around me. A glance back toward the welcome gate proves the tunnels are still empty.

Breath disappears deep through the cavern of your nose to fulfil a strange blue pulse. Eya's arse, is that your lungs?

"Tibok, this is the fruit of the loins of the fruit of my loins," you say. "Ri, this is the man who ended my war, Tibok."

His stick smacks his forehead in salute.

My name sounds so odd spoken out loud by another's mouth.

"What are you *doing*?" I hiss low beneath the scratch of insects.

"We are—" You salute and flourish with your stick. "Partaking of the pleasant afternoon as I show my good fellow here the gardens that make the Purple Blossom famous."

"You are *fighting*."

Tibok's teeth show few and broken. "If that's what you want to call your grandmother's disgusting sham."

Stick clatters against stick. "Is that how it is? Un-death has made your reflexes slow, old man!"

And you are off again, long flax leaves whipping a bow at your passing.

"Stop," I whisper. "You mustn't. It's against the law."

This is no battle, nor desire, nor revenge. Sword play is unknown to me, yet I recognize Tibok's movements are too grand. Peeking through the green folds, I eventually ascertain the rhythm, nipping my shoulders, elbows, and hips in time to the beat. A dance; a terrible brutal courtship that strangles a low moan from my throat. The insects' throb synchronizes to the stomp of your feet and the wet smack of wood on flesh.

Kizzians now kiss their cousins, and the people of Eya struggle with eels and blossoms, forgetting their hands were meant for other things. What you are in this moment is but a promise, but this is consummation, this carnivorous knowledge.

A soft brush against my ear. A breath.

Within the moment between delight and denial, I see terrible things mirrored in Donai's face. Hunched in her black and gold afternoon drape, her hands are turned into an attitude of prayer. Sweat moistens her upper lip and armpits, and her mouth and tongue make motions I have only seen her perform when kissing her wives and husbands when she thinks no one is looking. Even Donai knows something of love in the depths of war.

And then she sees me seeing her.

"What are you doing?" she hisses, breath wine-sour in my face, placing her body between me and the battle.

"What am I…? They're *fighting*!"

"Eya curdle my blood. You wicked child!" Donai leans in, forcing me to take a step back.

"But aunty!" Donai flinches at my use of the new dialect word, a Kizzian word. "They're fighting! With… instruments! And stop calling me a child!"

This last statement is one too far. Donai grips my upper arm tight, but not tight enough to leave a bruise. A laugh batters at my throat. We must look ridiculous, this yellow stick-insect of a woman grappling at me with bare restraint so as not to convene the law of physical contact.

"Why are you watching?" Donai's hiss outbids the insects for repugnancy.

Clack clack clack. In your devotion, you are impervious to all but what is before you.

"Hue hue hue."

A new guttural noise joins the discordant tune gripping the flax paddock.

Donai opens her mouth for another rebuke.

"Hue hue hue hue!"

Louder now, filled with the sounds reminiscent of Eya drowning far below.

The snap of stick-on-flesh ceases.

"Hue hue. You… you. Hue hue!"

Herensughe-mai rocks in her wheeled chair, threatening to send the thing careening toward the cliff edge. Her brown nut hands throttle the air, empty eyes wide revealing congealed white orbs, mouth black as the day Eya ate her way to the sea.

Donai hisses again, but before the words reach her mother, I yank my arm so the full force of her rebuke lands on me.

Two skulls join us.

"Still some life left in the old girl yet." You grin.

"What's she laughing at?" Tibok demands, twirling his stick up to a whirr.

"I can't rightly say," Donai demures. Her grip tightens just so on my bicep.

"Hue hue hue."

Herensughe-mai points from Donai to me to you, beats a twisted fist into her other palm. *War war* goes the cadence.

I can't move, dare not breathe.

Donai teeters. She removes her hand from my arm and stomps over to her mother and turns the chair with such vehemence I don't know how Herensughe-mai doesn't fall out.

A weight on my shoulder. Will I ever see the hand that wields weapons with such delicacy?

"Sister, please refrain from *spectacle* in front of our mother," Donai says. "Her heart cannot take it and we'd rather not have a funeral feast so close to a welcoming one. Please respect the differences of sixty years." Donai flicks her head at me. "My chambers. *Now*."

The squeak of wheels and Herensughe-mai's laughter fade away into the nails-on-stone insect song.

"Ri." You're still holding me in place with your gentle touch. "You don't have to go."

"It's the law," I reply.

"What law?" Tibok asks.

"Red is the colour of war now," I say, glancing at the welts on my arm which will fade quick enough. "It signifies the blood that falls no more."

"Where am I?" Tibok says, vicious as the crack of his stick against the ground. "I don't recognize this place."

Suddenly, my grandmother's war-maker is much more and much less than I had been led to imagine.

"This was my home," you say softly before I can.

✊

Donai thinks leaving me alone on the Remembrance terrace with its algae slick rocks, thick ferns, jewel-yellow flowers, and untended shrine is punishment. Silence holds me closer than walls ever could.

"Ri."

Is this Eya deigning to speak to me with her watery sibilance? No, my name is accompanied by compassion.

"Ri."

I set aside my flax weaving and approach the locked downward tunnel door ear first. Their approach was as invisible as their feet. Assassin or ghost?

"There you are."

"Tibok? How did you get in here? Donai has the only key."

He snorts, and I swear I see mucus move within his nasal cavity. "I have certain skills which make me a very good warrior. *Made* me very good. And who puts locks on doors in a house anyway?"

His voice is so gentle, so absent of war. Eya's fingers trickle up my spine.

"It's only for the very worst of us I'm afraid. Changed after war was made illegal."

Tibok sighs and glances around. "This is a sorry excuse for a Remembrance terrace."

"At least we agree on something."

He laughs long and low, a sweet, grandfatherly sound from someone so full of bones.

Then your skull joins his. You've filled out since the spectacle—the *fight*—yesterday. The tops of your hip bones and your intestines are showing. I am a slug in comparison.

"Oh well. Here we all are. Old fashioned, but an assassination it is. Better get on with it." I hold out my upturned forearms, wrist bones set together. "Or would you prefer I turned my back?"

Tibok laughs again. "We're not here to war-make you, woman!"

My heart slows and sags back into my chest, the mist from the river cooling my too hot face. "A war tribunal then? There hasn't been one of those in, oh, thirty years. Don't bother. We do things different now. Donai sent everyone to stare through the grill in the Shaming Ceremony last night."

Your eyes drink up the wet rocks and sagging banners. "They're so afraid to step in here."

"And the interment caves too," I say, too bold. "Putting bones to glass cradle is too swift for my liking these days. But my liking never comes into it."

Why do I say these things? They will be the death of me.

The whiteness of you fades back, and there is a squeak. You

re-enter, pushing Herensughe-mai before you, placing her in the last remaining ill light from the tarnished mirror.

Eya's pull sags Herensughe-mai's jowls even more, if that's at all possible, as she regards the Shrine to the Grateful Dead. A shrine her hands assisted in repurposing from the Warrior's Terrace, creating this cushion between the dead and the proper living.

A perfunctory bow is all I can offer; I don't know her traditions.

"I don't understand," I say, fear pulling words out of me fast. "If you're not going to punish me, why are you all here? Does Donai know you're here? She never lets me out early. I've only spent one night."

"Ri." The sound of my name spoken by you in that way aches against my chest. "It's been eight days."

"No. That can't be right."

Herensughe-mai grunts and waves a twisted fist.

"She says this has to stop," you say, shaking your head very slowly. I scratch my bare arm and my skin prickles. A skull is still just a skull. One day is eight. Your heart shows against your ribs.

"How do you know what she's saying?" I demand. I'm not sure if I want to know what "this" is.

Tibok stands ill at ease, the light now catching his huge orbs of eyes squelching between combatants.

"You only have to listen and watch her hands," you say. "She says you have to go. And we agree."

"Go? Go where?" I breathe in your old woman musk, the sweet funk of flax oil in your warrior's loc. "Back to the prison cell in the town? Isn't this good enough for you? Are you on Donai's side? But you were the ones who were *fighting*!"

"Hue hue hue," comes the gummy gurgle. Does the old woman *enjoy* my anger?

You and Tibok share a look I swear could be shared by lovers.

"We're on nobody's side but the un-dead's," you say. Your shoulders shift. I imagine your hands held out like someone corralling a frightened animal. "This is not the life death led us to believe was waiting. Herensughe-mai told us the best she could about how yellow is now red, how things changed quickly when the un-dead began coming back to tell the true horror of war." A short bitter laugh. "No one wants to see into the mind of a killer, literally and figuratively. I see now that this house is not my home anymore. Nor has it really been yours. There is no place for a warrior in this life. We cannot complete ourselves here."

"But there is a place for warriors in un-death," Tibok says. That look again, something beyond love, beyond the war-making you shared. "We were foolish to make a detour."

"Alukat," I say.

"It calls us," you say, eyes empty as you look beyond the stone walls. "My family is there. I feel its silver upon my tongue, the quiet between my fingers."

And then *it* is *there*. Midnight. The handle of your great sword makes its presence known between your bony shoulder blades. Instruments—*weapons*—may be illegal but no one would dare take it from you now.

An obscene thirst for metal fills my mouth with saliva.

It's been eight days?

You continue, using that tone of voice you only use on the youngest cousin frightened by your grotesquery: "Flesh I can fight, but not fear that grips too many hearts. This is not my battle."

Eight nights?

"Warriors are not war." Tibok's voice now, still confusing me with his gentleness. "We were justice."

"And what do you know about justice?" The words keep coming, I can't stop them. "You who languished with the sea worms and weeds? We are better at it now. The punishment for war-making is death, and no one has been that stupid since the end of the war!"

"Can't you see the irony? There is always a better way than death." You move closer, that ugly red muscle pushing against your sternum.

My eyes ache; I can see the blood it shoves through the veins.

"There is no other way than death," I whisper, so confused by all the arguing. Even Donai wouldn't go on this long. "It's where we all end up."

A wet rattle and spit. A glance over your shoulder at your mother. She may be blind, but Herensughe-mai can hear everything over Eya's roar.

"She said un-death is better than living." You sigh, and your too-large, too-lidless eyes drop to stare at invisible scars on invisible hands. "Not better, mumma, just different. A different all of Eya's words can't describe. It's only best experienced."

"Is that a threat, or a curse?" I spit over the edge of the terrace.

"We don't have time for this, Eztena. Your family pull too close. They'll decide soon enough, and it won't be in our favour."

Herensughe-mai gestures, and I think I recognize an imperative. Tibok turns to leave, but shivers to a stop in what I guess is your grip.

"She is almost ready," you say.

"For what?" I demand.

Your stance shifts. A light weight on my shoulder. Your hand. All of it. The white bone and pus red of you. The muscles, veins, fibres, flesh, and skin. You've made it whole, for me. "To become a proper warrior. To let your red hair grow free. You deserve to know. To make the choice for yourself. To have a full name, warrior or no."

"Deserve to know what?" My voice threatens to fall apart like my bones.

You reach behind your neck. There is a light shimmer-hum and you examine all of Midnight, visible and not, with your terrible eyes. "Donai lies. It is her nature. She doesn't wear yellow as a sign of new life, she wears it out of defiance against death. Yellow still holds the old meaning of lies. She is a coward who desires immortality. You deserve to know that shame is not law, and that war still happens. Even in this house. There are *always* new un-dead."

These ideas drop into the pool of my mind, hard, smooth pebbles striking each other, the sound hard in the crystal-clear water.

I don't even wait for the last idea to settle before I speak: "Then take me with you."

I've never thought of leaving before, but now it's all I've ever wanted. The great wide openness can't scare me now.

Your breath is sweet on my face, not at all the carrion I expect. "We can't. The House of War and Bone cannot abide the pre-dead. Even outside the law there are laws."

Then you kiss me on the cheek, and lay something in my hands. The kiss is warm, the object in my hands hard and cold.

Midnight stings.

※

Darkness is an instrument.

So are lies.

And cowardice.

They are also all choices.

Nine nights now. The door is still locked.

Allow myself to admit: I have always been at war.

This house, these terraces and caves; this is not peace. No one can hide. You must always be of use, an *instrument*.

Say it out loud.

Weapon.

Eya's eyes glare down, both moons full portent. I will find what I need in the Night Garden, alone, prostrated to Eya who does not talk back to liars and cowards. I can mock: she's always spoken to me, with her tears, her feathers hiding me, her backbone not allowing me to break. *She* caught me when so many others slipped through her grasp, like Ainama.

Will she let me go this time?

The door is still locked.

My hands shake as I stroke Midnight to warmth. Your sword is lighter than I expected, but heavier in other ways. Do I go fast or slow? Watch the face, or look away? Will she fight back? Is one enough to gain entrance to the right kind of un-death?

Will it hurt?

Because I want it to hurt. I'll only do it if I'm allowed to know what real pain is, just once.

I wish you'd tell me if it hurts.

Clouds close Eya's eyes in forbearance.

The lock snicks.

The door is open.

RI is a good girl. Though she is much older and less a woman than Aunty Donai remembers. She is a quiet girl. Especially when she is sent Away. She does not touch instruments of mortality. That is forbidden. But they are so shiny, and have such an edge… just like grandmother.

A. J. FITZWATER is a meat-suit wearing dragon living between the cracks of Christchurch, New Zealand. Their work has appeared in venues of repute such as *Clarkesworld, Beneath Ceaseless Skies, Shimmer Magazine, Glittership*, and many more. They sit on their pointy golden horde of two Sir Julius Vogel Awards. And they emerged triumphant from the trial by word-fire of Clarion 2014.

ADELITA

An account by Adelita Guevera, *as provided by Frances Sharp*

I rode the horse as hard as I could. Looping the reins over one arm, I plucked a cartridge from my bandolier and loaded it into my shotgun. I fired a round behind me, not even bothering to look, much less aim. Then I took the reins in my hands again, giving them a sharp flick, and leaned low over the horse's neck. I prayed to the Virgin I would be fast enough.

Before long, the sound of hoofs behind me faded. And when I finally worked up the courage to turn and look, the vast Mexican plateau was empty. I let my grip on the horse's reins slacken, and the horse went from a gallop to a trot to a walk. I slumped on the horse, feeling its heaving flanks beneath me. Before long, the motion of the ride and the exhaustion of the adrenaline leaving my system made me close my eyes.

I didn't sleep. I passed out. I didn't even feel it when I slipped off the horse and hit the ground.

When I woke, it was someone else who woke me. I was surrounded, in fact. A circle of women hovered over me. A woman in a Mayan style, woven *rebozo* squatted at my side, shaking my shoulders lightly.

"At least I know you're not *Federales*," I croaked. "They don't have *soldaderas*."

The woman at my head cracked a smile, which slowly traveled around the circle. She wore a loose embroidered bodice and flowing green skirt. Around the neckline perched more than a dozen hummingbirds, their iridescent colors shining like a fur collar from a fantasy beast. I nodded at the girl kneeling next to me who extended a hand and helped pull me up.

Once I was standing, the circle closed in on me. The woman necklaced in birds handed me a canteen. "I'm Miranda."

I gulped the cool water down. I drank a little too fast and started to cough. "I-I'm Adelita. I've been loo-ooking for you," I managed to choke out.

"Well you found me. Or, your horse did. It was Dante who led us back to you." Miranda gestured to a group of horses nearby. A black hawk perched on the horn of a saddle cocked its head in acknowledgment of Miranda's words. "And he chased off some vultures that were beginning to get impatient."

"Th-thank you." I turned from Miranda to the bird, not sure who deserved my gratitude. The hawk cawed loudly.

"He likes you." Miranda smiled broadly. "And he's a good judge of character. You can come back with us. Tell us what you want after you've had some food and beer to revive you."

I was ready to beg my case then and there, but there was something in Miranda's words that told me to hold my tongue. In fact, when I tried to voice my assent to the older woman's suggestion, I couldn't find the words. I fought off my alarm. This was why I'd come here, after all. I only nodded and followed the women back to the horses. They'd brought a fresh one for me, the painted mare the hawk was perched on. I swung into the saddle and followed my saviors at a brisk trot across the dirt and scrub.

The *pueblo* we came to was small. A dozen houses, a few wells, kitchen gardens full of herbs, and a handful of livestock. The women dismounted, and I followed suit.

"*Bienvenidos a la Tierra de Mujeres*," one of the riders told me. It was the girl in the *rebozo*.

"The land of women," I echoed her words. I looked around and saw it was true. Every face I saw was soft and round. They all wore skirts and long braids. I'd never seen a place with no men. And after serving in Pancho Villa's army for two years, I had to admit it was refreshing to be without their stink for a while.

"My name is Carolina," my new friend introduced herself, taking my horse's reins and leading it toward the stables. "I'll see you at dinner. You should follow Miranda for now."

I looked around and saw my target walking into the biggest house in town. I followed in her wake. Dante launched himself from the saddle and soared in lazy circles over my head. "Just don't poop on me, ok?" I called up to the bird. He cawed in reply and deposited a glob of waste just a hair in front of my shoe, barely missing my toes. "Thanks," I muttered.

I entered the house behind Miranda and half expected the bird to follow me inside. Instead, I heard a skittering scrabble outside on the roof and then stillness. He must have perched outside.

I opened my mouth to plead with Miranda, but before I could say a word, my host handed me a huge earthenware bowl of fragrant beans. My mouth began to water in spite of myself. How long had it been since I'd had a real meal? Three? Four days?

"Take that to the table, won't you?" Miranda's request sounded more like a command.

I looked around the hot kitchen. Every surface was covered with food and cookware. The only open spot was the one Miranda had just removed the beans from. "Table?" I asked.

"It's outside, behind the house. Come on, follow me." Miranda grabbed a platter of tortillas and spun, her skirts twirling around her, as she led me back outside.

Behind the house was a long table set up for a meal. Swarming around it were a few dozen women of every age and disposition. There were elderly women old enough to be *abuelas* and infant girls barely able to toddle around the table. But most of the women were my age, in their late teens and early twenties. I watched as they arranged the table, working in perfect harmony and discipline like an army of ants. "*Soldaderas*," I whispered under my breath.

But then I saw the real reason I'd ridden so hard and fast. A flower was drooping in a green glass bottle. With a whisper and a wish, a young woman was able to straighten it again. Another sliced her hand on a knife she was placing on the table. A companion rushed over and grabbed it, making motions like she was sewing it up while she murmured words of comfort to her friend. When she released the finger, the blood was gone and the injured woman was smiling.

I felt Miranda watching me as I observed the scene with wonder, but she asked nothing of me. The women were congregating for dinner. They would all hear what I had to say.

Carolina motioned for me to sit next to her at the table. I joined her. The black hawk launched himself off the roof and perched on the back of my chair. "Don't worry," Carolina told me. "You'll get what you want. I've seen it. She'll make you work for it, but you'll get it."

Food was passed around, and jars of beer were distributed down the table. I did feel revived, better than I'd felt in a year. When the beer had loosened my muscles and the food had filled my belly, Miranda finally let me talk. I introduced myself to everyone.

"My name is Adelita. I am *una soldadera* with Pancho Villa's army. We've been winning. We hadn't lost a single battle until Agua Prieta. And then—"

"Defeat?" Carolina offered.

"Crushing. Half our force has deserted. The other half is on the run. They're headed north, to the border. I ran here."

"But why?" Miranda pushed me for more information.

"The revolution is important. The *Federales*… they don't respect people like you, like us. Women aren't important to the conservatives. Villa and Zapata, they care about the people. They want to give control back to us. But it's all falling apart. That's why I came here."

"You think *brujeria* is the key to winning the revolution?" Miranda cocked one eyebrow and hid a sardonic smile in a swig of beer.

"It's our only hope."

"Did General Villa send you?"

"No. This is my plan. I want you to lead, Señora Miranda. You could save the revolution."

Miranda sighed. "No, I couldn't. My place is here. I cannot leave *Tierra de Mujeres*."

"Then we are lost." I crumpled, feeling the hope drain out of my body.

"I didn't say that," Miranda countered, her face breaking into a sly smile. "I cannot leave this place, but you can. And I believe you would make a fine *generala*."

"But I don't know *brujeria*!" I protested.

"*Brujeria* can be taught, *mija*."

"I don't have time for that!" I stood and stamped my foot in protest, then found myself sitting down heavily once more. The beer hadn't tasted that strong, but suddenly my head was spinning.

Carolina reached out to steady me, but the young *bruja's* touch felt far away.

The last thing I remembered before my eyes rolled back in my head was Dante cawing and the sound of Miranda's husky voice. "Time is relative, *cariño*."

I'm getting tired of passing out, I thought as I fought to open my eyes. My head was pounding, my eyes felt scratchy, and my throat was on fire. But when I finally managed to regain consciousness and discern my surroundings, I decided I'd done much more than pass out.

The plateau was gone. I was in a jungle, surrounded by stone monuments. I'd heard of the jungles of southern Mexico, but I'd never seen them. It was said there were hidden cities in those jungles, places hidden from the Spaniards, then forgotten by the people who had protected them. How could I have traveled so far so fast?

I struggled to my feet, using a tree trunk for support. It was harder than it should have been, until I felt a pair of strong arms holding me under my arms, pulling me up. When I was at my full height, I turned to see who had helped me.

It was Miranda. But she looked different to me now. Both younger and… when I turned my head just right, or squinted from a glare, I could swear that Miranda's face and flesh had disappeared, that all I saw was a woman of bones, grinning at me. It should have chilled me, but it didn't. I found Miranda's presence comforting, and I leaned on the older woman for support.

"Where am I?" I fought my parched mouth to speak.

"We're in Mictlan."

"The land of the dead?" I shivered at the implication.

"Don't worry, *mija*, you're not dead yet. It's also the realm of magic. You're here to learn *brujeria*."

"But I told you, I don't have time for that."

"Time doesn't exist here. I'll show you."

Miranda half led, half carried me to a quiet pond. We looked into the still, clear water, and I was shocked at what I saw. While Miranda was younger, I was noticeably older. I reached up to my face to feel the wrinkles. But as I did, my reflection parted down the middle and my younger face appeared beneath. I gawked and again reached to feel my face, not believing my eyes any longer. This time my face transformed into one I recognized but had not seen in many years—my own, childhood visage stared back at me, betraying all the wonder and confusion that I felt. "How?"

"*Brujeria*," Miranda answered.

At that, I heard the shriek of a hawk, and a shadow detached itself from a tree, landing at the pond to have a drink. It was Dante.

"The bird really does like you," Miranda chuckled.

I felt my knees give out, and Miranda helped lower my body to the spongy jungle floor. "Why am I so weak?"

"You're still alive. And you have no magic. This land is not for people like you. But we'll soon fix that."

As if on cue, two more animals appeared from the jungle. A jaguar padded to the pool and drank alongside Dante, but her golden eyes never left me and Miranda. The third was a flying serpent, crowned in a spray of multicolored feathers. It was Quetzalcoatl.

"They are here to guide you. You must pick one. Which will it be?"

I considered the three animals. The jaguar was a powerful hunter, and its guidance would be an asset in a fight. But the Quetzalcoatl was steeped in magic, its mythology known even in modern Mexico. Between them hunched Dante, the black hawk. He was neither strong like the jaguar nor ostentatious like the feathered serpent. But he also didn't frighten me. And he had followed me to Mictlan. He was loyal. And he had already saved my life once. I felt I could trust him to do it again.

"Dante," I declared. "I pick the hawk."

"A good choice." Miranda smiled.

The hawk flew across the pond to us, landing in front of me. He bobbed his head, as though acknowledging my choice. Then he sprang toward me, and in a flurry of feathers and beak, he plucked out my eye.

I screamed. I rolled on the ground, clutching my face in shock and agony. I couldn't see, even out of my remaining eye, and before I knew what was happening, I'd rolled into the pool.

Defying all logic, the pond sunk straight into the ground. Where a shallow and gradual gradient had appeared from the bank, I felt myself sinking into the cold clear water with no sign of solid ground beneath me. But when Miranda spoke, I could hear the *bruja* as though she was right next to me in the water.

"You can learn *hechizos* at any time. But this is what you need to be a true *bruja* and leader: you need a connection to the land and its magic. A part of you is dead now. A part of you will stay here until you return for good to claim it."

I continued to sink, too weak to rise up against the water. When the darkness closed around me, I did not fight it.

When I woke, Carolina was at my side again. But this time she wasn't shaking me. She was waiting patiently, swirling liquid around in an earthenware cup. I didn't move. I watched as Carolina drained the cup, then inverted it over a saucer. Only after she had looked at the leaves intently did she raise her eyes to me. "You're awake! The leaves said you would be successful."

"At what?" I asked, blinking the sleep from my eyes. No matter how I tried, my left eye remained blurry, unable to focus on Carolina's face.

Carolina checked the leaves once more. "At everything."

I sat up in bed. "Can you teach me that *hechizo*?"

"It's not really a spell," Carolina explained. "It's a talent. I see what's to come. This is just one way to focus it. But there are other things, *hechizos*, I can teach you."

"Good." I swung my legs over the edge of my cot. "Let's get started."

I met every woman in the village. I made it my mission to learn something from everyone. When I'd met my goal a week later, I confronted Miranda at dinner in front of everyone.

"I still have much to learn," I admitted. "But I can't stay here any longer. The war is still going on. I have to go back."

"You're right," Miranda nodded. "You still have much to learn. Which is why I'm sending *brujas* with you, to teach you and help you fight. Who wants to go?"

Every woman who could ride a horse hard and hold a shotgun steady rose from their seats.

I looked around in shock. "The-they can't all come. Who will stay here?"

"Oh, there are a few of us who will stay. And don't worry, you'll all come back eventually."

In the morning, three dozen young women mounted horses. Dante perched on a thick leather glove that covered my forearm as he looked around in stern appraisal of the preparations. Carolina's horse stood next to mine as Miranda approached to bid us farewell. The old *bruja* grabbed my horse's halter and whispered something in the beast's ear. Then she turned to me.

"Take care, eh?"

"Of course." I nodded.

"You have a lot riding on your shoulders. Don't let it get you down. Don't let it overwhelm you. You have the power to win this fight. You, and no one else."

I blinked at my mentor, my left eye still fuzzy and unfocused. "I wish you would come with us."

"Me too," Miranda sighed.

"I'll miss you," Carolina offered from her saddle.

"Don't worry, we'll meet again," Miranda promised. "*Ya*. Go." She released the horse's halter and smacked its rear end.

As the horse began to canter away from the village, I tossed the hawk up into the air. Dante rode the air currents up in slow circles then followed us on our trek north, to rejoin the fight.

I woke from a dream of the war. I reached for my shotgun, but found only down pillows. Home. I was home in Mexico City, in my luxurious townhouse, where I had retired after a lifetime of service to the Mexican people. I heard a faint tapping on the window, the noise that had woken me up. I blinked myself awake, my left eye still blurry after all these years. I shuffled over to the window and opened it, allowing Dante to fly in. But today he was accompanied by a guest. A tiny hummingbird flitted in after him. The two birds looked at me, expectation on their faces.

"Very well then," I conceded. "I'll leave after breakfast."

This seemed to satisfy the hummingbird, who rose up into the air, circled me three times, then flew out the window again.

After a morning meal and packing a small bag, I surprised my chauffeur in the garage. "I didn't know you had plans to go out today, *Generala*."

I smiled at the honorific. I was still referred to as a general, a sign of the respect and prestige I'd earned in the revolution. What had seemed so precarious when I'd rode to find Miranda, I'd been able to save. When Carolina had foreseen the assassinations of Villa and Zapata, the *brujas* had been able to stop them. And before long, women and even men had flocked to my *Bruja* Brigade. We had become the third army of the people, and along with Villa and Zapata, had been able to deliver the country back to the common folk. I'd helped to rewrite the constitution and had served in various ministerial positions before being elected president. But despite having risen much higher than a mere soldier, that was always how I was fondly remembered by the people.

"I didn't have plans, Stefano, but I do now. Do you remember where you took Señora Carolina all those years ago when she left us?"

"Of course. You begged her not to go, but she said it was time."

"Well it is my time now. Take me back to *Tierra de Mujeres*."

The car ride was faster and more comfortable than the horses had been. As we drove through the city, I admired how modern it had become. There were still women in long dresses and *rebozos*, but I also saw miniskirts and bellbottoms. My country had grown, and would continue to grow after I'd gone. It filled me with a sense of satisfaction and closure. I was ready, just as Carolina had been.

We continued to drive after the road ended. When I glanced out the window, I saw Dante keeping pace with the car high above. Before long, I saw what I was looking for.

"Stop the car, Stefano."

The young man turned off the engine and ran around to open my door. I stepped out, bringing my bag with me. In the distance, I could make out two horses, only one with a rider.

"Should I wait, *Generala*?" Stefano asked.

"No." I smiled. I handed him a few papers and a pen. "Sign here please."

Stefano did as he was told. "Good. Now the car is yours. When you get back to the city, call my lawyer. She has my will and knows what to do. Say goodbye to the girls at home. You've all done a good job of taking care of me."

"You're not coming back? Ever?"

"I don't expect so, no." Without another word, I started walking across the plateau to the welcome that was waiting for me. When I made it to the horses, I saw Dante perched on the horn of my saddle, just as he'd done during the war. On the horse next to mine, I saw Miranda. But it was only a feeling that let me recognize the old woman. There was no flesh left on the old *bruja*. Instead, there was only a grinning skeleton under a *rebozo*.

"Hello, Adelita. I missed you."

"And I missed you. Though you look quite different."

Miranda's toothy grin could get no bigger, but I could hear the smile in her voice. "I always looked like this. But you were so far from death when you were young that you couldn't see it. Now your eyes are opened to my true nature."

"One eye. My other eye never recovered."

"Don't worry. It will soon."

We turned our horses back to *Tierra de Mujeres* and walked slowly, for the sake of our old bones.

ADELITA GUEVERA (1891-1972) was a Mexican general and politician. Rising to prominence as the head of the *Bruja* Brigade during the Mexican Revolution, Adelita fought for her fellow commoners and women after the war as well, helping to write a populist constitution and enforce it as the country's first female president. She and her partner, Carolina Salvador, adopted two children, Soledad and Tenoch Guevera-Salvador, who continue to be involved in Mexican politics, art, and *brujeria* today.

FRANCES SHARP is a biracial writer from Houston, Texas, who is extremely proud of her Mexican heritage, diverse upbringing, and the Astros. She lives in Northern Virginia with her husband and daughters, who she is also very proud of.

POP MAGIC

An account by Amina Grace, *as provided by Patrick Hurley*

When I saw the troll and the wendigo standing over my wrecked messenger bike, I got so angry I started trembling. But I also felt flattered. These two were the magical equivalent of endangered species; whoever summoned them had flexed some major muscle—all for little ol' me.

"I had one more delivery tonight!" Which they'd obviously waited for, leading me to wonder just what the hell Merlin had strapped across my back.

"Hand it over, messenger boy," snarled the troll.

I pulled off my bike helmet.

"Fool, it's a she-girl," hissed the wendigo.

"Normally, I'd be happy to oblige y'all," I said, "but that bike cost two month's pay."

"Give us the package," the troll growled, yellow drool dribbling from the corner of its mouth. "Or die."

I glanced around. It was late and the streets were empty; folks in Brooklyn Heights were either in bed or in bars.

"You wanna play rough? Okay," I said, drawing my blasting rod.

"*Say 'allo to my little friend!*"

The wendigo and the troll flew backward in a giant ball of fire. I started running. It'd be another full day before I could use that quote again, and I needed to get out of here, fast. Since my bike was trashed, I needed a ride.

"Hey, messenger girl," the wendigo growled. I spun around. He looked down at his burning feet and grinned. "Fire don't hurt me none."

Before I could cast another spell, the wendigo lunged forward and grabbed me by the throat. Struggling for air, I punched his chest.

"Hah!" he hissed. "That all you got?"

Keeping one fist firmly pressed against him, I grasped the dog tags around my neck and whispered, "*Snikt.*"

The wendigo shuddered as three adamantium claws burst from my knuckles and through his heart. As the creature gurgled and died, I let my claws fade.

I should probably explain. My name is Amina Grace. I cast spells by quoting my favorite lines from movies, TV shows, and comics. Being punted around foster homes most of my life, my college was pop culture, my professors dollar movie rentals and primetime TV. The closest I ever came to something classic was Coca-Cola. I'm the youngest magician in America, and my teachers despair of me.

Warm blood trickled down my forearm. Quoting Wolverine's comic book onomatopoeia always came with a cost. If I didn't do something soon, I'd pass out. Quick as I could, I stuffed chewing tobacco in my mouth and muttered, "*I ain't got time to bleed.*"

The wounds on my knuckles scabbed over as I spat the disgusting chaw on the ground. The healing spell, courtesy of Jesse Ventura in *The Predator*, would only last a few hours. I'd need to finish this delivery before then.

I scanned the street and noticed a payphone on the corner. Jackpot. I ran over to it while taking some Reese's Pieces from my satchel. Once I had the receiver in hand, I popped the candy in my mouth, pointed my index finger, and murmured, "*ET phone home.*"

"Hey, Amina," a groggy voice said on the other end.

"How'd you know it was me?"

"Because I shut off my phone before I went to bed," answered Carlos. "Only you can get around that."

"Oh, right," I said. "Sorry."

"What's up?" he asked, yawning.

"I need a ride. Bring your baseball bat."

Fifteen minutes later, Carlos rolled up in his piece-of-crap Corolla. I jumped in shotgun and gave him a quick hug. I felt him flinch and realized calling him had been a bad idea. Though tired, Carlos still looked good, a fine piece of wiry muscle with intense eyes and calloused hands. It had been just two months since our breakup.

"Where we headed?" Carlos asked. I gave him the address, a warehouse in Flatbush, and we started driving.

I glanced around the car and asked, "Where's your bat?"

"Check the glove compartment," said Carlos.

I did and found a Glock. "What the hell?"

"You sayin' we won't need it?"

I couldn't say that, because I didn't know what was going on. Instead, I asked, "Where'd you get a gun?"

"Don't worry about it," he said, keeping his eyes on the road. "What are you dropping off, anyway?"

"You know Merlin never tells me," I said quietly.

"Don't get why you work for him," Carlos muttered. "Most talented *bruja* in the country and he treats you like a goddamn gopher."

Before I could answer, the road exploded. Carlos slammed on the brakes, stopping right at the edge of the crater. I stuck my head out the window. At the bottom of the crater lay a smoking meteorite.

"Turn now!" I shouted at Carlos. The Corolla careened down a narrow alley, knocking over trashcans and crates.

"Amina?"

"Yeah?"

"'bout to run out of road," said Carlos. "Better be make quick with the voodoo that you do."

The alley was narrow, crowded on either side by Dumpsters, so we couldn't turn even if we wanted to.

"Roads?" I said, smiling. I flipped my Ray-Ban sunglasses down over my eyes. "*Where we're going we don't need… roads.*"

I could almost hear the theme music from *Back to the Future* play as the Corolla soared upward into the New York night sky. We climbed higher and higher, only stopping once we entered the clouds, where I let the car rest for a minute out of sight.

"Doc Brown, huh?" said Carlos. "Never knew you could do that."

"Been working on it," I said, unable to keep the pride out of my voice. Far below, New York glittered like a mountain of light. When no other meteors were flung at us, we left the clouds and slowly descended, landing in a deserted Flatbush parking lot.

Ms. Grace, you're late. Merlin's voice echoed like a spike through my head, making me wince.

"What is it?" Carlos asked.

"Merlin," I whispered through gritted teeth. Yes. *The* Merlin. He's the oldest of us, the most powerful, and a whole lot meaner than *The Sword in the Stone* would have you believe.

Why hasn't the package been delivered?

"Someone knew I was coming," I said.

Show me.

I recalled my encounter with the troll, wendigo, and our meteor-wielding mystery attacker, allowing Merlin to view my memories secondhand.

Return to headquarters at once.

"What?" I said. "I'm almost to the warehouse."

The mission's been compromised. We can't risk that package falling into the wrong hands.

I punched the dashboard.

"What's going on?" Carlos asked.

Ms. Grace, do you hear me? I'm ordering you turn back.

I stared out the window. "No."

What?

"You heard me. This is my last delivery for the night, and I'm gonna make it."

If you proceed further, I'll withdraw my protection. You will suffer the consequences on your own.

"Fine by me," I said, cutting off Merlin's telepathic link.

"Amina, tell me what's happening," said Carlos, gripping the steering wheel tightly.

"It's nothing," I said. "Just drive."

Carlos glared for a few seconds. "You know why I quit school?"

He'd been my only friend growing up. He was the first boy I ever dated, the first I ever told about the magic. Not only was Carlos damn fine, he was damn smart. Made it halfway through college before losing his scholarship. I tried to get him to talk about that, but he always refused. Which is why we broke up.

"You wouldn't say."

Some of Carlos's anger seemed to leave him. "You don't know what it's like, knowing all this *bruja* shit and being on the sidelines. I'd sit in my physics class listening to the theory of energy conservation, and it was all I could do not to scream about how I know things that would make my professors piss their pants!"

"You can't say anything," I said, shocked. "You don't wanna know what would happen."

Carlos gritted his teeth. "Can't say anything. Can't do anything. All I am to you is a car and some muscle."

I winced. "You know that's not true."

"Amina, I know you better than anyone else in the whole world. If that white-bearded bastard told you to never speak to me again, you'd be gone. Because next to the magic, I'm nothing."

"That what you think?" I shouted, feeling my face heat up. "Guess you don't know me as well as you say. Else you'd know Merlin told me to ghost you! That's why I do all these delivery jobs. That was his price for staying with you!"

Carlos didn't say anything for a few seconds. "Amina, I—"

"Just drive. I gotta deliver this."

"Listen—"

"Forget it," I said.

We drove the rest of the way to the warehouse in silence. I got out of the car and slammed the door shut. Flatbush looked cold and dark; only a few of the streetlights still worked. I hustled to the warehouse's front gate, the package once more strapped across my back. It felt heavy and long. Maybe a wizard's staff that Merlin didn't want to fall in the wrong hands? Whatever. In about ten minutes it wouldn't be my problem.

My heart sank as I recognized the man waiting for me.

"Why, if it isn't my favorite pop culture deviant," said the magician.

I forced myself to sound nonchalant. "Hey there, Ambrose."

Ambrosius deNimue Merlinius, Merlin's son by Nimue, has never liked me. Before my powers manifested, he was the youngest magician in the world. Ambrose didn't need to quote lines to perform magic. With his Oxford education, he could cast spells in six different languages, silently if he chose.

"Didn't know anyone was doing pickup," I said. "I'm supposed to drop the package off in the vault."

Ambrose yawned. "Obviously the situation has changed. You were attacked along the way and my father felt the package needed more... substantial protection."

"Where the hell were you earlier? Got jumped by a wendigo and a troll, then some spellslinger tried to crush me with a meteor. Could have used you then."

"I had trouble finding you. I didn't think to look for a flying car."

How'd he know about the car? Something was off. Ambrose was a smug bastard, but a traitor to his own father? Even he couldn't be so stupid.

"You know what's in the package?" I asked.

"Do you?"

"Just know it's attracting a lot of heat," I said. "Sorry, man. I gotta place it in the vault myself. You can tag along if you like."

Ambrose sighed. He's the only dude I know who sighs. "I suppose it was bound to come out anyway." He opened his hands and two men in black coats appeared on either side of him. Their faces were stone; they had pupil-less eyes, smooth and white, like teeth.

"Who the hell are they?" I asked.

"Constructs of my own devising," said Ambrose, pride evident in his voice. "Completely immune to enchantment, completely under my control."

"Most impressive," I said in my best Darth Vader.

"Please give me the package and we can avoid any unpleasantness," said Ambrose.

"Look at you, saying please," I said, taking a step back.

"I can ask more rudely, if you like," said Ambrose. His constructs stepped toward me. "Get the package from her."

I took a fighting stance and sang, "*Hands can't hit what the eyes can't see.*"

I ducked under one construct and spun away from the second.

"*Float like a butterfly*"—I flew toward Ambrose—"*Sting like a bee.*"

All the force of Muhammad Ali was behind that punch. Ambrose doubled over, gasping, and I ran. A few minutes later, just as I reached the vault, a hole sliced through reality. Ambrose strode out as calmly as if walking along the beach. But instead of his construct henchmen, Carlos floated behind him, bound in black chains of shadow.

"Surrender."

"You mean you wish to surrender to me?" I said. "Very well, I accept."

My *Princess Bride* quote bounced off Merlin's son like a paper airplane thrown at a tank. Ambrose narrowed his eyes. "I admit you're more trouble than I thought you'd be, Ms. Grace. But the game is over. Give me the package, or I kill your boyfriend."

The shadowy chains tightened, and Carlos cried out.

I threw the package on the ground and put both hands up behind my head in surrender. Ambrose walked forward, keeping an eye on me. Just as he crouched to open the package, I shouted, "*Yippee-kai-yay-motherfucker!*"

Ambrose had time to glance up as I shot him three times with Carlos's Glock, which my *Die Hard* quote had summoned from the Corolla.

The shadowy chains binding Carlos disappeared. My ex shakily got to his feet.

"Sorry I got you involved with this," I said.

Carlos took back his gun, clicked the safety on, and tucked it in his belt. "Don't worry about it. What now?"

"The vault in this warehouse is warded," I said. "All I have to do is drop this off in there and we're done."

"Sweet," Carlos said, then gestured at Ambrose's body. "What about him?"

"I'll worry about telling Merlin I killed his kid after I finish this delivery."

It was only when I felt Ambrose's hand clutch my ankle that I realized my mistake. Yeah, I'd unloaded a couple bullets into the prick, but I never checked to make sure he was dead.

Before I could react, Ambrose chucked me across the warehouse. I landed hard, bruising a couple ribs. With another handwave, he slammed Carlos against a far wall. I rolled to my stomach and saw Merlin's son rise, his flesh knitting itself together. Once he was whole, he started for the package.

Shuddering, I got to my feet and shouted in a slurred Rocky Balboa, "Yo, Ambrose, where you going? I didn't hear no bell."

Ambrose looked up, eyes incredulous. "Are you actually challenging me to a duel?"

A magician's duel, a duel of songs, was deadly serious. And Ambrose was almost as far out of my league as Merlin.

"I'm your huckleberry," I drawled.

Whether it was pride or Doc Holliday, Ambrose stopped in his tracks. He studied my bruised face. Suddenly, the same shadowy chains that had captured Carlos wrapped around my body.

"I call this the *Shadow Wind*, Ms. Grace," said Ambrose. "You should be flattered; I crafted it with you in mind." Merlin's son began to weave his hands in intricate patterns. The shadows around him deepened, and his eyes became pitch black. He chanted in a deep, melodic voice:

"A stygian wind comes swooping in
to wipe away your mind.
A chilling wind growls low and grim,
your memory goes blind.
A lamenting wind smothers and rends.
Leaving no stories behind."

The spell finished, and I could move again. I flexed my fingers. I could hear, I could see, I could think. Far as I could tell, the curse hadn't done shit. Now it was my turn. I tried to think of a quote that would bring Ambrose to his knees—

—and my head filled with roaring darkness.

I tried again—

—and felt icy shadows so horrible I screamed.

I couldn't remember of a single goddamn quote. Whenever I tried to think of a line, all I could see were shadows, all I could hear was the wind howling.

The room began to spin. I fell to my knees and vomited. Tears and snot trickled down my face. I heard Ambrose laugh.

"You see, little hedge witch?" he said. "How could you have ever be one of us?"

He was right. He was so right.

"Man, you better leave her alone," said Carlos. The package I'd been sent to deliver lay open at his feet. He held a glittering sword in both hands. That sword…

Merlin had made me the courier for *the* sword. Forged from a fallen meteor, held in trust by a water nymph. Arthur's blade. The Kingmaker, Stonecleaver, and Star-sword.

Carlos held *Excalibur*. I could see runes and symbols dancing along a blade so keen it could cleave through molecules. No man could draw Excalibur from its sheath unless he was meant to be a king. It was also one of the most powerful artifacts in existence; maybe we'd get through this after all.

Ambrose hurled fire at Carlos and shrieked as it rebounded off the sword and nearly singed his arm. Before Carlos could take a swing, Merlin's son faded into shadows and rematerialized next to me, his hand gripping the back of my neck.

"Drop the sword," Ambrose said, "or she dies."

Carlos held Excalibur in front of him, indecision on his face. He looked into my eyes and placed the sword on the ground.

Ambrose moved. One minute he stood behind me, the next, he touched Carlos's head and my boy collapsed to the ground. Ambrose scooped up Excalibur with a triumphant smile.

I felt sick to my stomach. I had failed—failed Carlos and failed myself. Better to just close my eyes and die. Yet as my eyes closed I heard something inside, something I'd never heard before. It was small but growing. It felt warm. Fierce. A nice steady beat. I reached out with my mind's eye, realizing I knew what it was.

Magic.

My magic.

Ambrose hadn't stolen it. He hadn't touched it at all, just blocked one of the ways I could access it. And maybe, just maybe, I didn't need other people's words to create magic. Maybe I could use my own. I opened my eyes, ready to kick ass. The beat inside me thrummed steady and deep.

"Oh, Ambrosius," I called out. "You just made a big mistake."

Merlin's son looked at me with contempt. "Don't make me kill you, Ms. Grace."

I heaved myself into a crouch. The beat grew louder, became more insistent, and it was time to let loose. I hit the floor to keep time and chanted:

"Do you think, Ambrose, Merlin's son
our contest of wills even close to done?
Drowning in arrogance, wrapped in pride,
but so scared to leave Big Daddy's side."

Ambrose's face twisted. He opened his mouth, but I shouted over him.

"You tried to take my words from me!
Blinded by pride, you cannot see,
I don't need no quotes to make my stand
when wind itself is mine to command.
You tried to use it to wipe my mind,

without its permission—that's very unkind!
Now all that fury, all that bite,
will help ME now, win THIS fight!"

I ended that verse by hammering the ground. The warehouse roof exploded and a storm howled in. My hands pounded the air, using the magic as a beatbox. The wind bellowed gladly and drowned out Ambrose's counterspell.

Wielding Excalibur, Merlin's son was too well warded to attack directly. But there were other things I could do.

"Cloud, thunder, lightning, rain,
banish the shadows inside my brain."

Rain poured; thunder boomed; lightning flashed in the warehouse, blinding us, but also shattering the shadows encasing my memory.

"Spirits of the Earth, spirits of Wild,
turn away from Merlin's child.
Let him rely on his skill alone,
rather than a sword pulled from a stone.
Now you see Ambrose, this is my hour,
I have won; I HAVE THE POWER!"

The warehouse windows shattered; the very ground shook at the sound of my voice. I floated in the air, wind swirling through my dreads, lightning dancing at my fingertips.

"Impossible," Merlin's son whispered as I let the wind die down. He clutched Excalibur like a child holding a doll. "You've never been able to craft original spells. You're bluffing."

That was when I knew it had worked.

"It's possible, Pig; I might be bluffing." I spat on the ground. "It's conceivable, you miserable, vomitous mass, that I'm only lying here because I lack the strength to stand. But, then again... perhaps I have the strength after all."

I pointed at him. "*DROP... YOUR... SWORD!*"

I don't know if it was my rhymes, *The Princess Bride*, straight-up fear, or all three, but Ambrose's hand spasmed, and Excalibur landed on the ground with a clang.

"Carlos!" I shouted. With a groan, my boy got to his feet. "Pick the sword up, now."

As Carlos took up Excalibur once more, a deep voice called out, "I expected better from you, son."

There stood Merlin, impeccably dressed in a silver suit and tie.

"My apologies for disappointing you, Father," Ambrose growled.

"It's one thing to betray me. Such is in your blood. But to lose a duel of songs to someone so much younger than you?" Merlin studied his progeny, his gaze unreadable. Finally, he waved a hand and said, "Take him away."

The invisible servants Merlin had brought with him obeyed the old mage's command, and Ambrose vanished in a swirl of wind and fire. Merlin turned to me. I braced myself for some old-school lecturing.

"Well done, Ms. Grace."

I blinked. "What do you mean, 'well done'? I disobeyed your orders. I nearly lost Excalibur—which, by the way, you should have told me I was delivering."

For a brief instant, the corners of Merlin's mouth lifted in a smile. "I've known for some time there was a traitor in our midst. Tonight's delivery was a trap, and the bait had to be powerful enough to draw the traitor out from the shadows. My apologies for not telling you this, but I couldn't be sure who to trust."

I'd never heard Merlin apologize before.

"I would have acted sooner, but I'm powerless before Excalibur," said Merlin with a grimace. "Which leads me to wonder: what are we to do with you, Carlos Mendoza?"

I stepped in front of Carlos. "You want him, you gotta come through me first."

Merlin smiled. "I'd never dream of it, Ms. Grace. Anyone would think twice before crossing the youngest-ever chanter of original magic."

I had to stop and rearrange my brain, which was primed to defend Carlos. "What the hell are you talking about?"

"The song duel in which you bested my son. A bit crude, but the passion—extraordinary! You reminded me of the bards of old commanding wind and lightning."

"Sounded like a slam poet to me," said Carlos. "*Eight Mile* or something."

"As for you, Mr. Mendoza," Merlin said. "The arcane laws are absolutely clear"—I started to protest, but Merlin cut me off—"and they decree that only the worthiest can wield Excalibur, the Sword of Kings."

What happened next nearly gave me a heart attack. Merlin bowed to Carlos. "I don't know where you will make your kingdom, Highness, but should you ever need help, I pledge myself to your service. Also, since you're now part of the arcane world, this ends Ms. Grace's obligation to me."

"What are you saying?" I asked.

"You're no longer bound to my service and can practice magic however you please," answered Merlin. "Though I would encourage you to keep working on original compositions."

With a nod to us both, Merlin was gone, leaving Carlos and I standing in the middle of a blasted-out warehouse. Carlos stared at Excalibur with wonder. Then he winked at me. "Don't kings need magical advisors?"

"Go to hell," I said and began walking out.

"I don't want to be king of anything," called Carlos, running to catch up with me.

"You don't have to," I said. "We're not in the Dark Ages anymore."

"C'mon, Amina, help me out!" asked Carlos. "I'm begging, here."

"You were the one who wanted to be part of my world."

"Yeah," said Carlos. "Careful what you wish for, right?"

I thought about it for a moment. "I'll help if you can pass one test."

We got to the Corolla. I put on my sunglasses and opened the shotgun door. "It's 106 miles to Chicago, we got a full tank of gas, half a pack of cigarettes, it's dark… and we're wearing sunglasses."

Carlos laughed. *The Blues Brothers* was our favorite movie. He put on his own Ray Bans, got into the Corolla, and put his key in the ignition.

"Hit it," he said, and turned the key.

AMINA GRACE casts spells by quoting her favorite lines from movies, TV shows, and comics. Being punted around foster homes most of her life, her college was pop culture, her professors dollar-movie rentals and primetime TV. She's the youngest magician in America and her old-ass teachers despair of her.

PATRICK HURLEY lives, writes, and edits in Seattle. He's had fiction published in *Galaxy's Edge*, *Cosmic Roots & Eldritch Shores*, Flame Tree Publishing's *Murder Mayhem* anthology, Hy Bender's forthcoming anthology *Ghosts on Drugs*, Myriad Paradigm's *Mindy Candy* anthology, *Abyss & Apex*, *Penumbra*, *Big Pulp*, and *The Drabblecast*. In 2017, he attended the Taos Toolbox Writer's Workshop taught by Nancy Kress and Walter Jon Williams. He is a member of SFWA and Codex.

ART BY Leigh

LEIGH's professional title is "illustrator," but that's just a nice word for "monster-maker," in this case. More information about them can be found at https://leighlegler.carbonmade.com/.

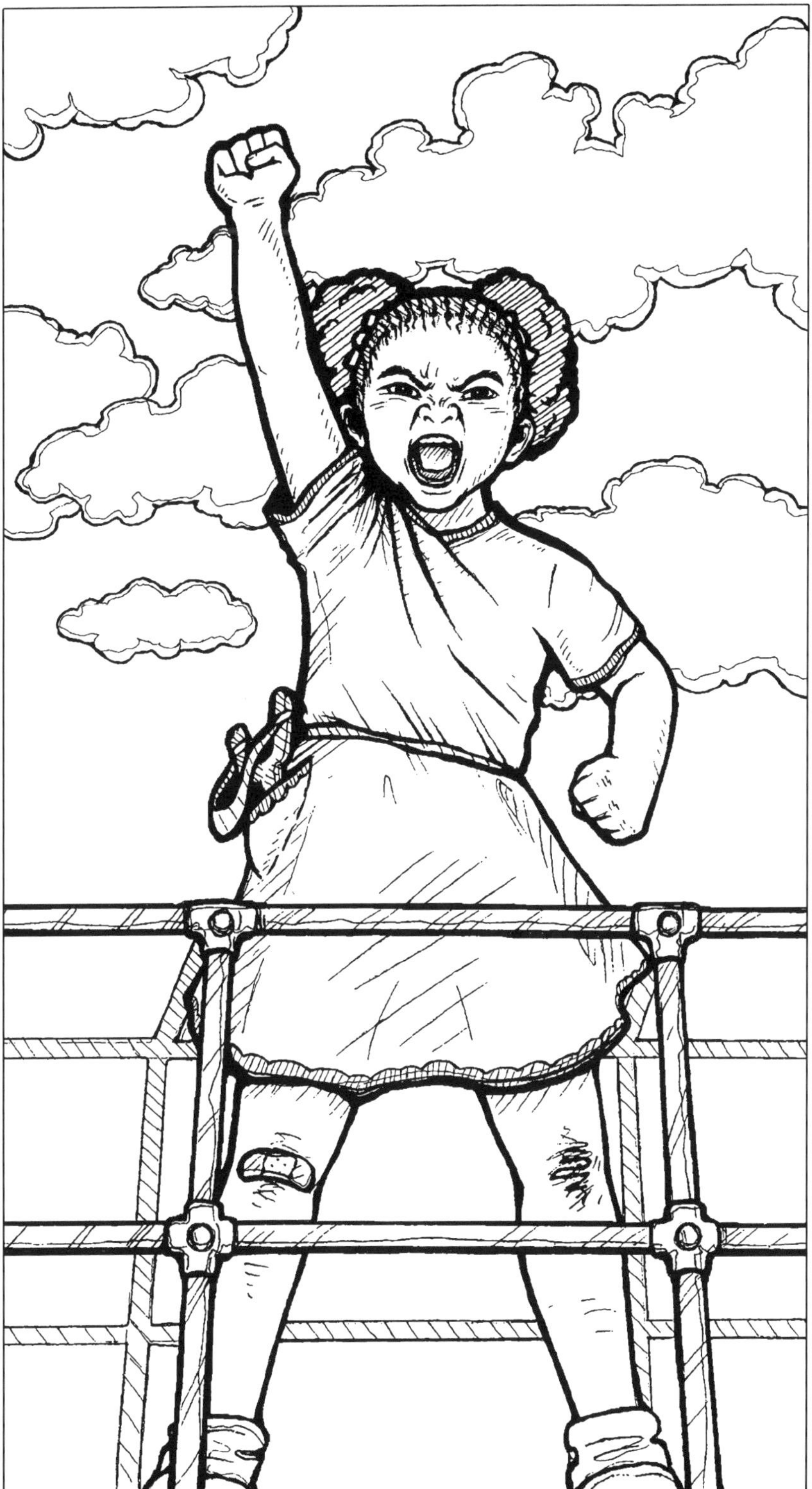

BREATH AND ROSES

An account by Star Friedmann, *as provided by Leora Spitzer*

No one else woulda thought to start a book club with the kids working on Level G, kids who'd always had work instead of school and could scarcely tell the alphabet from mag shoe scratches on the metal floors. It was a fluke that Mo was even able to read. Like the rest of us, she was in debt to the company from that first gasping infant breath, and so she started working at age six just a couple years before I did. But her mom had been a tutor to the Inner Ring kids before she died, and Mo, all of three cycles old, had insisted on coming along and sitting in the back of the classroom, soaking up every word. I heard that those Innies whined like a faulty generator at having to focus, but Mo learned to read. With a skill like that, she coulda got promoted early, maybe got a management position or something, but not Mo. Mo went ahead and started a book club.

I met Mo when I was twelve. I'd already been working for the company half my life and could hardly imagine anything different. Sometimes my dad would tell stories of what it was like back on Old Earth, but my pa would snort and ask how he knew all that, since Dad was so young when they left. Pa says Dad has a tendency to romanticize life on Old Earth, but just because air was free doesn't mean it was good to breathe, and with the worldwide collapse of governments and the environment, my grandparents were lucky to have gotten space on a ship to Jerusalem Station. I can't know if life woulda been better if they'd stayed, but even as a kid, I was pretty sure this wasn't exactly the Promised Land my grandparents were hoping for. By the time I met Mo, there was hardly any time for my parents to talk about the past, with all of us working on different shifts just to afford our own air. I know they regretted not being able to help me out more, but that was the law—you couldn't pay for anyone else's air bills until your own debt was gone, and I didn't know anyone without some debt to the company.

Anyway, there I was, a gangly twelve, just moved up to the o-tank returns room and the adolescent-sized o-mask, when this short kid with deep brown eyes slid into my booth across from me in the cafeteria and said, "Hey, it's Star, right? You should join my book club."

I'd like to say that I said something clever and snarky, but I just blinked at her in confusion. "Don't worry," she added cheerfully. "I can teach you how to read. It'll be fun."

That was not the word I woulda chosen at the prospect of spending my scarce free time doing more work, but I didn't want to get into a lengthy conversation over dinner. I couldn't afford the extra fee to linger in the cafeteria. Unlike most of the Station where we needed o-masks to breathe, the cafeteria was specially sealed and filled with air so we could eat properly and breathe like they used to on Old Earth. Since they couldn't charge us for exactly the air we used in the cafeteria like they did with our o-tanks regularly, they charged for the time we spent there, and the cost per minute started doubling after the twenty-minute mark. They claimed it was to make sure no one used more than their fair share of the air, since everyone's gotta eat, but Mo told me later she thought it was to prevent exactly what she was doing that first day, to keep us from lingering and socializing and sharing information. At the time, I thought she was being paranoid, blaming every inconvenience on some great conspiracy, but after everything, I think Mo was right. The company did have reason to fear workers talking to each other.

That day, though, the policy worked against them. I didn't want to admit to this charismatic kid with the eloquent eyes that I was just lazy, and I didn't have time to come up with a better excuse, especially when I knew that reading would be an incredibly useful skill, and this kid was offering to teach me for free. So I just nodded and agreed to meet Mo in the library that night before heading back to work.

As I carefully fitted my o-mask back over my face in the airlock room, watching the cafeteria door seal itself behind me, I saw Mo still at the booth, eyes closed, tapping her fingers absently against her idle o-tank, breathing deeply.

To my surprise, book club was awesome. Sure, learning how to read was frustrating and stressful, but at least it was a frustration I'd chosen for myself. Plus, I was sharing it with a bunch of other kids Mo had recruited. There was Esther, who was always angry but rarely unkind, and Nile, who was usually tinkering with something, and Tiger, who rarely spoke but had extremely eloquent facial expressions even through her o-mask.

Once we got the hang of the reading thing, we branched off and read whatever we wanted, and then shared our favorite bits with the group. My favorites were the adventure stories, the ones with dragons and lions and daring quests to save the world, even when everything seemed hopeless. Tiger liked poetry. Nile read a weird combination of science books and horror. Esther and Mo read history. And we all learned deeper and wider than we coulda imagined before.

Like everyone on Jerusalem Station, we all knew the basic story of the Great Exodus: expecting Earth to be overpopulated, scientists designed and built the Stations, self-contained systems capable of producing their own necessities. As society on Earth began to collapse after devastating disasters, both natural and manmade, people fled in great numbers to the Stations.

It was Esther who told us that even the "natural" disasters—the hurricanes, the forest fires, the droughts—had been caused by human carelessness and greed, destroying delicate ecosystems all across the planet. Esther explained that ecosystems worked like the factory, each bit dependent on the others to keep working properly. "Like if no one returned their o-tanks," she said, gesturing at me. Everyone knew I worked with o-tank returns. "I'm sure they have surplus tanks but at some point, they'd run out and then everything would fall apart. That's what they did on Old Earth—they just kept taking resources until everything fell apart."

Of course, that was long before any of us knew the word "strike" as anything other than a blow to be avoided. Esther was simply using a metaphor then, and none of us had any idea how closely accurate the metaphor was. As far as we knew, we were utterly replaceable, completely dependent on the company for every breath, and there would always be another worker ready to take our spots, each desperate to pay off their own debt. The company had worked hard to make sure none of the regular residents had any idea how vital we were to the ecosystem of Jerusalem Station, and it was only through a blessed combination of observations both careful and casual, extensive research, experimentation, luck, and a whole lot of determination that we ever came to realize the truth.

Sometimes, reflecting on those days, it seems inevitable that Mo, with her interest in political theory and history, would learn about *socialism* and *unions* and *labor organizing*. After all, she didn't need any books to give her a bone-deep belief in economic justice and an unwavering conviction that we could make things better. She laughs if I say it, but on some level, I think if she hadn't found those books, she woulda written them herself eventually. Other times, it all seems so fragile, that if someone had been more careful in censoring the library and erasing history and science, we never would have found the tools to fight. Maybe they didn't bother because so few of us Outer Ring kids could read, and why would we bother with dry old textbooks when there were free screenings of Old Earth films every week. Maybe the books were left there by some original settler already worried about the company's power. I don't suppose we'll ever know.

The problem with a traditional strike, of course, was that the law of Jerusalem Station permitted the company to cut off the air of anyone who did not make "a good faith effort" to pay off their debt. If you missed a week in a row, or more than ten days in a month, or got fired too many times, or returned too many damaged o-tanks, or a half-dozen other offenses, the company could simply refuse to issue you a new o-tank. Everybody knew somebody who knew somebody who had died that way, quietly suffocating trying to get the last traces of air from an emptied o-tank, and everyone knew someone who'd taken a job in the late shift or the worst departments because they'd been fired and were desperate for employment before their o-tanks ran out. Refusing to work entirely woulda been a death sentence, and we weren't sure they'd be unwilling to let us all die. What we needed was leverage.

And we found it.

It was Nile who gave us the first clue, by accident. I was telling Mo and Tiger about my latest adventure novel while Tiger's eyebrows conveyed how unimpressed she was with the hero's antics, and her flippant hand gesture suggested that perhaps drama could've been avoided if he'd just swallowed his pride and asked for help. Before I could retort that there was nobody he had any reason to trust to ask for help, Nile lurched toward our corner and collapsed into a chair, dropping his cane to the ground in front of him.

"Is it just me," he began resentfully, "or are these stupid o-tanks even heavier at the end of the week than the beginning?"

We all shrugged. "I think it's just that there's less air so you're more tired and it just feels heavier?" Mo suggested doubtfully. Tiger nodded in agreement.

"I dunno," I said, thinking. "I kinda assumed that the o-tanks I deal with in returns felt heavy because I lift them with all different muscles than the regular one, but maybe it's something else. You'd think they'd be lighter, right? Since they'd be empty?"

"Well, I'm not sure they're really heavier, but they sure aren't lighter," Nile responded, slumping exaggeratedly under the weight of his o-tank. Tiger swung her o-tank off her back and lifted it thoughtfully up and down.

Esther walked over, raising her eyebrows at the scene. "Since when is this an exercise club?" she asked. We explained the conversation to her. She furrowed her eyebrows. "The question is," she said slowly, "if the o-tanks aren't empty at the end of the week, what's in them?"

✊

From there, it was like a treasure hunt—one clue led to the next, a jigsaw puzzle, giving us a slowly emerging picture of what sustained life on Jerusalem Station. Even missing pieces, it was far more than comprehensive than any explanations any of us had ever gotten.

First, we looked up basic human physiology and discovered that o-tanks derived their name, not from the shape of the tubes as was commonly assumed, but from the element they provided: oxygen. It was only a short step from there to answer Esther's question—humans breathe in oxygen and out carbon dioxide, so that must be what was in our depleted o-tanks. Nile, in particular, was satisfied to learn that carbon dioxide is heavier than oxygen, so he hadn't been imagining things at all.

I began analyzing the work I did every day, preparing used o-tanks to be refilled and reissued. There was a step I'd never thought much about, between recording serial numbers and passing the tanks on to be filled with oxygen, where a giant vacuum sucked everything out of the o-tank. I'd vaguely assumed it was to get any last oxygen left inside, but now the explanation seemed clear: they wanted the carbon dioxide.

So we all began researching uses for carbon dioxide. Esther described fizzy drinks she'd read about, like we'd seen in the films, but even she agreed it was unlikely that the company would go to all this effort so the Inner Ring folks could have a soda. Mo suggested possible uses for refrigeration, and that had some potential—we all knew how important temperature control was on the Station. But when Nile began explaining photosynthesis and Tiger's eyes widened, we all knew we were on to something.

"I work with greens," Tiger said. "For food, they said. It's all, y'know—" She shaped a large sphere with her hands.

"Enclosed?" Mo suggested.

Tiger nodded. "Thought it was to keep us from stealing. But maybe it has to be enclosed so they can feed the greens the carbon dioxide—"

"And capture the oxygen they release!" Nile finished.

"So they take the stuff we breathe out and use it to produce the air they charge us our lives for," Esther summarized. "We're in debt from birth and they take and take and take, and never admit that without all of us, our breath and our labor, they'd never have oxygen to breathe themselves, let alone sell to us. Those lying, thieving, exploitative assholes."

I felt nauseous thinking of that, and I could see that Nile and Tiger, though excited by the discovery, were also disturbed by the idea. Mo, though, Mo was beaming. Her eyes sparkled.

"This is it," she breathed, tapping her o-tank. "That's our leverage."

Mo assigned me and Nile to figure out a way to release the carbon dioxide from the o-tanks without permanently damaging them. There were steep penalties for returning a damaged o-tank, but there was no rule that said it had to have the carbon dioxide in it, because that woulda meant admitting they needed our breath. Esther and Tiger spread word of our discovery while polling folks in the Outer Ring about their greatest needs to develop a clear list of demands. Mo dove back into the history books, reading about successful organizers of the past and what strategies they had used. She read about garment workers and mill workers, teachers and miners and trash collectors and doctors. And when Nile and I went to her with the technological solution, she was ready. We gathered in the library, the five of us, and listened as Mo spoke.

"People in power lie and hide the truth when they are afraid. They hid the truth about the o-tanks because they were afraid we would realize how much power we have, how much we matter. But now we know, and it's time to show them just how important we really are. We must leave the shadows of deception and bring this information to light. They need us. They need our breath. We can't deny them our labor, not yet, but we can deny them the other production of our bodies, and show the whole station how much we matter. We go on strike. We release the carbon dioxide from the o-tanks. We fight, and we don't stop telling the truth till we run out of air to speak with. It's risky. They'll come after us. They may arrest us. They may even cut off our oxygen. But if we stand together, if enough of us tell them that *enough is enough*, the company will have to listen. This cycle, we are slaves. Next cycle, if we stand together with the voice of truth and the wrath of heaven, we may be free."

There was a long silence when Mo finished talking. I felt a burn behind my eyes, like tears were gathering and hadn't decided whether to fall yet. "Do we have the right, though," I said hoarsely, my throat scratchy behind the o-mask. Everyone looked at me, curled on the floor against the bookshelf.

"What do you mean, Star?" Mo asked. Her gentleness almost hurt. The idea of disappointing her terrified me, but I thought of my pa's stories, the descriptions of famine and hurricanes and violence, and found the strength to continue.

"If we're right about this, about the photosynthesis and the oxygen and everything, withholding the carbon dioxide will upset the Station's ecosystem," I began.

"That is the idea, yeah," Nile said dryly. Mo shot him a look and gestured for me to continue.

"Right, but what if we *permanently* damage the ecosystem, like on Old Earth? What if the greens all die from lack of carbon dioxide and we end up causing a total lack of oxygen? We could kill the station like this. We might kill… *everyone*."

Nile, Tiger, and Mo looked stricken. Esther was already shaking her head. "Did you know, on the Inner Rings, they have whole *bedrooms* airlocked like our cafeteria, where you can just breathe? They can sleep and dream and—and kiss, like the films, without o-masks tripping them up." She spoke with a bitter longing. "Trust me, Star, they've got surplus. This is enough to make them feel it, maybe cut back on their extravagance enough to be willing to negotiate, but we're not going to kill anybody any more than they already do."

There was another brief pause as we all imagined sleeping without tubes, cuddling with a partner without worrying about getting tangled and losing your o-mask in the middle of the night, hanging out without the constant weight of the o-tank on our backs. Mo ran her fingers through her frizzy curls and sat down next to me.

"How do you do that?" she asked me, a self-deprecatory chuckle caught in her throat. "I got so caught up in the idea of a way to beat the company that I nearly lost sight of what winning actually looks like, but you, you never forgot what the oxygen production really means for everyone." She smiled at me and said softly, "Thank you for reminding me what really matters, Star."

Mo turned back to the group and flipped open her notebook. Her fingers tapped the pages absently as she stared at its handwritten calculations and ciphered plans, and I wasn't sure if she was reading or thinking or both. "It's a risk," she admitted finally. "It's a real risk and I'm scared of that possibility, too. But we can't keep living like this, either. Being able to breathe is the most basic human right. Without that you can't have anything else, and it's the company that violates that every day. If the company can't provide air for everyone because they refuse to pay us fairly for our labor and the production of our bodies, that's on them, not on us. Which, you know, I recognize is cold comfort if we all run out of air, but I genuinely don't think they'll let it get that far. They'll compromise well before the point of no return. And also, we can do the math and come up with a guess of when that point is and discuss ending the strike if we are approaching it." She sighed heavily, fogging up her o-mask, and reached to take my hand. "But Star, we all deserve better than this. We deserve better than being in debt from birth, and never having a real childhood, and spending our whole lives just trying to keep existing without any time or ability to feed our souls. Everyone on this station has a right to breathe, but don't we also have a right to freedom?" She glanced around at each of us as she spoke. I felt her palm, warm against mine, and curled our fingers together. She smiled at me, her eyes crinkling, and turned to Esther. "We deserve those kisses, too," she finished.

Tiger chuckled and muttered something. We all turned to her, surprised. "Breath and roses," she repeated, fidgeting with her beaded bracelet.

"Roses?" Nile asked. I knew what roses were the same as kissing, from the Old Earth films, but had no idea what the relevance was here. Mo clearly understood, though, grinning so wide it jostled her o-mask.

"It's a pun on a phrase from a poem," Mo explained. "Well, a poem inspired by a speech, I think, about women workers who went on strike way back on Old Earth. Bread and roses, that they needed the bread to live but also the roses to have something to live for."

Tiger recited:

"Our lives shall not be sweated from birth until life closes;
Hearts starve as well as bodies; give us bread, but give us roses.
As we go marching, marching, unnumbered women dead
Go crying through our singing their ancient call for bread.
Small art and love and beauty their drudging spirits knew.
Yes, it is bread we fight for, but we fight for roses too."

"We fight for roses, too," Mo repeated, squeezing my hand. "We fight."

"We fight!" Esther echoed fiercely, and I wasn't sure if she was grinning or snarling behind her o-mask.

"We fight." Nile's knuckles paled as he clutched his cane, but he spoke with confidence.

"We fight," Tiger whispered, and it flew from her lips like a prayer. Like a blessing.

"We fight," I agreed, hardly conscious of the tears that had flooded silently out of my eyes during Tiger's poem, but extremely conscious of Mo's heartbeat pounding through our tangled fingertips.

"For breath and roses," Mo affirmed, and I saw she was crying too.

⊛

Listen. I'm a sucker for a happy ending, good triumphing over evil against overwhelming odds, the battle's over, the war is won, the heroes go home together, the end. So I want you to know, this one doesn't have a happy ending. Not that it's necessarily a tragedy, though some parts of it were more than tragic. But Mo and me, we've been fighting this war for nearly forty cycles now, and Mo is the first to say that while things are definitely *better*, we're still a long way from *good*, and we're gonna keep fighting as long as there's air in our lungs. Happy, well, that's complicated enough, but an ending? Jerusalem Station keeps cycling. The story isn't over.

⊛

We ended that first strike when the company agreed to accept the carbon dioxide as payment for oxygen for kids under six. No more accruing debt at birth. It was a start, and it showed the whole Station what kind of power we had. For a while, we were floating like gravity had been turned off. But then folks on the Inner Rings started talking about how reckless we'd been, how we could've killed everyone with our spoiled demands (lord, Esther ranted about that one). The company cracked down on any kind of socializing while in the factory, even locking us in to make sure we didn't sneak off or whatever. Nile said it just went to show how much we'd scared them, and Mo started organizing for a strike again.

Now I'm not saying the company deliberately caused the malfunction in the Delta Sector, but they coulda done a whole lot to prevent it—and if it hadn't been for those locks, Nile and the others mighta made it out and be alive today. Mo went door to door like the goddamn angel of death, trailing righteous anger and carrying grief so heavy some part of me was surprised she could even stand. By the time she paused for a breath, nearly everyone in the Outer Rings was refusing to return their o-tanks. We held a rally at the film screening that week, one of those few times and places people could actually gather in large numbers. Mo's voice was hoarse after all that talking, but she held her o-tank in her arms like a baby and spoke through her tears. "I am exhausted," she began, and the crowd quieted.

"I am exhausted and I am furious and I am *sad*," Mo continued. "I would like nothing more than to lie down and sleep and cry and tell stories about my friends, but there's no time for that. There is no time for grief and no time for rest. Even the survivors of Delta Sector had no time to rest and mourn their comrades, because the company might say this was *regrettable* and *they're mourning the loss of their valued employees* but their surviving employees had to get up the next day and apply for jobs because they still have debt to pay and the company isn't about to stop charging them just because they nearly died."

She paused while the crowd booed their anger. "*Valued* employees," she repeated, incredulous. "Do y'all feel *valued* by the company?"

"Hell no," I screamed back, along with the rest of the rally.

"That's because the company doesn't value us," Mo said flatly, and all around me I heard people shushing each other to hear her. "The company only values what they can get from us. Our labor. Our money. Even the breath from our bodies! But they don't care about us. They don't care about our lives, or our loves, and they sure as hell don't care about our deaths." She rubbed at her eyes and tugged at her curls. "The only way to make them care about us is to take back what is ours. No more labor. No more money. And no more letting them steal our sighs, our moans, our every exhale to turn back into profit for them.

"We're not asking for much. All we want is to be able to breathe, to have some chance at making a better life for our families. We want to be safe in our workplace. We want to be treated with dignity. And we want those things because that is the bare minimum of what is right and just."

The room was silent by then, just the ever-present hum of the station and the magnified breathing through hundreds of o-masks.

"They can stifle the air in my lungs but they cannot stifle the words of my heart," Mo declared. "They can smother the air in our lungs but they cannot smother justice!"

And that was when security guards materialized and carried her away to the rising sound of an almost-mob hungering for change.

They charged Mo with vandalism, incitement to rioting, and disruption of public property, since they couldn't prove anyone else was involved in shutting down that day's film, but it almost didn't matter. By the time they let Mo out of jail nearly two weeks later, everyone on the Outer Rings and even a fair number of Inner Ring folks were on strike, the descendants of the engineers and investors who'd made the Stations possible, no longer willing to be complicit in the exploitation that made their lives more comfortable. Factories, from food production to oxygen production to clothing and water production, stuttered to a halt and stood silent. The high-ups were desperate for a solution, especially the Station Senate members who had an election coming up. When it had been fewer of us, we couldn't risk quitting work, or they'd be legally allowed to cut off our air entirely, but with more than half the residents of the Station committed, it would be mass murder to cut us off. They'd already proven not to care about human life, but that scope of death would permanently reduce the available workforce and likely keep Jerusalem Station from running at all. I still worried about our moral culpability with the life-sustaining technology dead in our absence, but I just had to think of Nile's twisted smile and I knew Mo was right—if we didn't take a stand now, there would be repeats of Delta Sector, chipping away at us like replaceable machine parts when we were human beings, and we mattered.

I'll never forget the look on Mo's face as I told her everything that had happened while she'd been isolated. She laughed in sheer amazement as I told her about my conversations with the Inner Ring kids, how horrified they'd been when I told them about everything the factory did, how they'd agreed to release their carbon dioxide, how a few of them had even taken up a collection to pay Mo's bills so she could keep devoting her time to organizing. "Star," she began, and gripped my hand tightly. "Star," she repeated.

"I'm here."

"I just... I don't know what to say. Oh, Star."

"There's some people from the Senate who want to talk to you," I offered, and she laughed again, incredulous.

"Well. Guess my vacation's over. Time to get back to work." Mo tucked a strand of my hair behind my ear, and the sparkling tears in her eyes said everything she hadn't been able to. We walked away from the jail together.

Mo led the negotiations with the factory and the government representatives, bolstered by the statistics Tiger and Esther had gathered about the greatest needs in the Outer Rings. It took a while, back and forth, and a few smaller repeat strikes to remind them how serious we were, but within two years, the Senate passed new safety regulations for every part of the Station, and oxygen prices were dramatically lowered with the exchange of a used o-tank now full of carbon dioxide.

Five years after that, Mo ran for Station Senate, even though, like everybody else with any kind of criminal record, she couldn't vote. She lost, sure, but that campaign sparked a station-wide argument over suffrage. It took another several cycles, but eventually they restored the right to vote to all adults, and her campaign slogan, *let my people breathe*, became synonymous with the growing Air for All movement.

It's only in the last few cycles that I've begun to look outside, to think about the other Stations out there, and wonder about the other people living in them, if they are having the same problems we have or others we can't even imagine. The shuttle completes its circuit between Stations every seven years, bringing basic news and sharing technological advances, like that new water filtration system they developed on Mumbai Station. I knew it would be coming back soon, so I began writing this to send out to those workers, on all the other Stations, so you can read our story and know your own power. You deserve breath and roses, too.

I won't mislead you: we don't know if there will ever be universal access to oxygen, funded by our taxes and not our slavery, but Mo's never given up hope. The pair of us are still campaigning for that dream of freedom, and the company still controls far too much of people's lives on the Station. Like I said, I don't know when or if this struggle will ever truly end.

But like I said, I can't resist a happy ending, so here's as close as we get.

While Mo focused on politics, Esther founded a committee for improvement of human life. Among other innovations, they designed sleeping pods, enabling us to sleep without tubes. Unsurprisingly, they were wildly successful, and shortly after that, they released a larger model, big enough to stretch out a bit—or to share.

It was a bit of tight fit, but eventually Mo and I got our kisses, too.

STAR FRIEDMANN is an activist and factory worker living on Jerusalem Station. She was instrumental in organizing the famous Strike for Delta, following the tragic collapse in Delta Sector that caused the deaths of thirty-seven people. She and her partner, Mo Leibowicz, live on Level F with their two children, Nile and Rose.

LEORA SPITZER is a queer Jewish bibliophile living in St. Louis, Missouri. She graduated from Washington University in St. Louis with a major in Urban Studies and a minor in Drama. Leora is passionate about intersectional feminism, economic justice, and badass women leaders both real and fictional.

AUTHOR'S NOTE

"Bread and Roses" was a slogan coined by Jewish labor activist Rose Schneiderman that resonated immediately with working-class women in their struggle for economic justice. The poem quoted above, inspired by Schneiderman's words and the actions of thousands of women strikers, was written by James Oppenheim and published in *The American Magazine* in December 1911.

THE LEXIMANCER'S
REBELLION

An account by Hope,
as provided by Jennifer Lee Rossman

The first time I breathe life into a word, it is an unintelligible scribble drawn in chalk on the concrete wall of our bunker.

No one thought to watch me, even knowing I have leximancer blood. The chalk kept me busy and quiet, kept me from crying out in terror at every quaking blast from the invasion above our heads, and what harm can a child do? I can barely write my own name, let alone the alphabet.

True, I can neither identify nor trace the letters that my mother's family used to write their magic, but I don't know any better. To me, the scribble is a word, a spell, and the dragon springs from the wall all the same.

It flaps its wings and hovers in the air above my palm, for it is just a tiny thing like its creator, its outlines ragged and its form transparent, wavy green like stained glass. Another blast from the street overhead shakes the bunker, and the little dragon flies off in search of a hiding place.

Shouts of panic go up as the dragon flits past the adults, and the bunker spirals down toward chaos. I cower behind a crate of nutrition bars, hiding from the shouts that ring out louder than the explosions. People take up guns and blasters, thinking the dragon is a spy drone sent by the invaders. They are preparing for a fight that they will not win.

Even as a tiny child, even idolizing my father as immortal and infallible, I know the things on the surface will kill us all. They've killed so many already, destroyed so much of the world.

In all the commotion, my father freezes, still as a statue as the others scramble around him. He looks at the dragon, trying to wedge itself underneath a door, and he realizes something. His head swivels, his gaze locking onto me. He is across the room in an instant, his hand wrapped tight around my wrist as he pries the chalk out of my fingers.

"No, Hope," he growls.

I am too young to have a name for the ache of yearning to write but knowing my father will never allow it, for knowing that I will not craft the word magic of my ancestors, but someday I will call it mourning.

I still don't know my alphabet. My father kept me from practicing because he believes the only thing more dangerous than a leximancer is an enlightened leximancer.

I can only write my name. Hope. Not that I haven't tried to learn, but so much of the language was lost in the war that there is little left to study. Signs turned into shields, books burned for warmth. Of all the landmarks now reduced to rubble in the war against the invaders from the stars, the written word was the most precious.

Every so often, when the planets align and the fates smile on me, I find a scrap of paper in the debris that lines the streets. Stained and creased glimpses of the past. Are they grocery lists or holy texts? I can only trace the meaningless shapes, but the magic they conjure is fleeting and immaterial.

So I keep my spells in my mind, luscious descriptions of the things I would cast into the world the way my ancestors did. Food and supplies of course, but weapons, too, ones that could hurt the invaders. I would write a revolution, win back the Earth and then rebuild it.

New buildings, rising from the soot and ash, catching the last amber rays of the day in their carved marble edifices and turning the color of a sunset. Ivy tracing up their walls, concealing the nooks—no, not nooks. *Alcoves.* The hidden little alcoves where we would install the surveillance tech. The machines that would patrol the skies and keep humanity safe.

The correct choice of words is crucial. That's the last thing I remember my mother telling me before the street split from a missile and the sinkhole separated us: that you must evoke the precise image you want to cast. The difference between azure and cerulean, between a nook and an alcove, can destabilize the spell.

"How do you know which word to use?" I asked her as the ships buzzed over the rooftops, a steel wing sending the spire of the church toppling into the street. Asphalt and bits of stone sprayed up like water.

My mother smiled even as the lasers and missiles fell people and buildings around us. "The right words make your heart sing."

⊛

The invaders stand outside the door of the refugee bunker, their unnaturally tall forms motionless, impassive. I almost wonder if they've been turned to stone by some other leximancer who knows how to spell the word "petrify," until one of them turns its red, scanning eye on me and my scavenged supplies.

"No weapons," I say, though I've never heard them speak and don't know if they understand English. "Just food. Scraps of cloth to use as bandages."

I've made sure to rip the cloth into short-enough strips that no one could use them as a noose. The invaders nearly lost the war when we humans banded together and fought back; they will not allow another revolution. They took someone away just last week for using too pointed a stick as a cane, even though the invaders are effectively impervious in their suits and helmets.

When they deem me safely unarmed, the great steel door ratchets open, a gaping jaw leading to the depths of the expansive bunker. I imagine covert tunnels snaking underground, a backdoor for smuggling things in and people out, a way to bring all these good, hungry people somewhere safe.

I drop off the meager rations I've scrounged—a few cans, a basket of corn grown from seeds stolen by the wind from a farm the invaders have taken over—and go to visit my father in the dusty room we call a hospital.

Father says there used to be something called medicine. Chemicals that you put in the body to help fight the sickness. Even if I could wrap my mind around the concept, even if I could write the words to bring such a miracle into existence, I wouldn't. I remember the fear in his eyes when he saw the dragon, and know his hatred of my magic runs deep. He justifies it by saying the invaders would see it as an attempt to undermine them, but people have feared leximancers long before the ships came. He's no different than all the other men who oppressed my kind throughout history, giving excuses when really my magic just makes him feel less powerful. He would not accept a cure from me.

So I just sit with him, and painstakingly trace letters while he sleeps.

Most are nonsense to me, but I recognize a word on one of the scraps. A woman who remembers how to read, who has no fear of my magic, taught me it means "rose."

As I make the last, uncertain mark on the paper, a red rose flickers in the air before me, there and gone in a blink.

A rose is more than a single word. It is the velvet of its petals unfurling in the first warmth of morning, the unexpected prick of a thorn. A rose is every love poem and funeral dirge, delicately folded into an object of immeasurable, fleeting beauty.

The rose conjured by those words would be *real*. Something that could be touched, smelled, pressed into a book and saved for future generations.

I look up from my paper to see my father watching me. I thrust the paper in my pocket, but it's too late. He's seen it.

"I'm sorry," I whisper, dropping my gaze in shame. "I thought you were sleeping, I didn't—"

"You can still do that?"

His weak voice carries none of the disgust I have come to expect. Rather, he sounds wondrous, curious. Even a little hopeful. I don't know how to respond, and watch as he draws himself up to a sitting position.

"You must be stronger than your mother," he murmurs. "She wrote entire pages to get a flicker like that, but you—" He snatches the crumpled paper from my pocket, smooths it out in his lap. "You did it with a single word."

I feel the urge to apologize again, but suppress it. "You aren't mad?"

He lifts my chin, forces me to meet his gleaming eyes. "Mad? My dear, we may have finally found a weapon to win the war."

My heart sinks. The fever is affecting his memory. "The war is over, Father. We lost."

He doesn't miss a beat. "Then we must start another."

I tell my father the words I need, and he writes them in his tidy handwriting. Then, by the light of a candle that casts dancing shadows on the walls, I copy the words letter by letter.

First is my message, a note written on a small slip of paper or scrawled in multicolored graffiti on slabs of rubble. Written anywhere and everywhere all across the world, existing just long enough to tell those who can read that change is coming, that they have no reason to fear, then fizzling out before the invaders see.

Then come the weapons. I see the invaders' weakness: Earth's atmosphere. They wear airtight suits; something in the air is toxic to them. So I create a weapon, writing the impossible into existence one careful word at a time, describing a projectile that can tear an irreparable hole in their suits.

It is shot from a sleek gun, made of gentle metallic curves that catch the light, and with a rubber grip. The technology within is the peak of human engineering, and I don't know how it works, but I trust that it will, because the technical aspects are only a small part of its story, the same way photosynthesis is part of a rose's. It will work because the future of the human race depends on it.

I put one in every hand across the planet, and around every neck I loop an amulet. Every facet of its purple gemstone is another magic spell, enchanting the gem to protect its wearer against harm.

I'm not sure they will work, but I believe they will. Perhaps more importantly, the rest of the refugees—my father included—believe.

They call me their general, look to me for guidance as the streets become war zones for the last time.

And it *will* be the last. Whether humanity reigns victorious or is finally snuffed out by the invaders, there will be no more rebellions. We win back our planet or we are extinguished, today.

It is a beautiful chaos. Running, shouting, firing weapons. The sound rises to such a high, constant rumble that it all but fades into the background. The fallen, mostly invaders but some humans as well, lay draped across rubble.

The invaders never saw it coming. Early in the morning, my army and I charged out with our weapons drawn, and the stony guards succumbed to the effects of the atmosphere before they could fire a single shot.

But as the battle rages on, the invaders have called in reinforcements. Their numbers grow stronger while my army dwindles. Spirits fall sharply; I feel them giving up.

I hide behind a piece of concrete, scramble for something to write with. I need a spell, something to make my people believe again.

I see it in my mind, every soldier simultaneously struck with the spirit of battle. They feel the rush of renewed energy, the will to win no matter the cost. They rise, courageous and trusting that we will be victorious. The enemy invaders don't stand a chance against human perseverance.

But I can't write all of that on my own, and the nearest person who can help is out of hearing range. I am alone, feeling the rebellion being snatched from me like the chalk when I was a child.

I hadn't known how to write the word "dragon" back then, nor all the words to describe the way it flitted and twirled through the air. I simply made a scribble that looked enough like a word, trusting that it would mean what I needed it to mean.

Maybe it still works that way, maybe my intention is all that matters, and a single word can convey the meaning strongly enough. But which word? I don't know many.

But I can write my name.

Hope.

HOPE is an illiterate leximancer, currently leading the efforts to rebuild Earth. One day, she will know enough words to read the accounts the other inspiring women she shares these pages with.

JENNIFER LEE ROSSMAN is a disabled science fiction geek who knows the right words can do magic. She hopes she used the right words in *Anachronism*, her debut novella available from Kristell Ink, an imprint of Grimbold Books. She blogs at jenniferleerossman.blogspot.com and tweets @JenLRossman.

ABOUT THE EDITORS

DAWN VOGEL writes and edits both fiction and non-fiction. Her academic background is in history, so it's not surprising that much of her fiction is set in earlier times. By day, she edits reports for historians and archaeologists. In her alleged spare time, she runs a craft business, co-edits *Mad Scientist Journal*, and tries to find time for writing. She is a member of Broad Universe, SFWA, and Codex Writers. Her steampunk series, *Brass and Glass*, is being published by Razorgirl Press. She lives in Seattle with her awesome husband (and fellow author), Jeremy Zimmerman, and their herd of cats. Visit her at historythatneverwas.com.

In addition to co-editing *Mad Scientist Journal*, **JEREMY ZIMMERMAN** is a teller of tales who dislikes cute euphemisms for writing like "teller of tales." He is the author of the young adult superhero book, *Kensei*. Its sequel, *The Love of Danger*, is now available. He lives in Seattle with a herd of cats and his lovely wife (and fellow author) Dawn Vogel. You can learn more about him at bolthy.com.

ABOUT THE COVER ARTIST

ERROW is a comic artist and illustrator with a predilection towards mashing the surreal with the familiar. They pay their time to developing worlds not quite like our own with their fiancee and pushing the queer agenda. They probably left a candle burning somewhere. More of their work can be found at errowcollins.wix.com/portfolio.

Made in the USA
Columbia, SC
08 October 2018